THE
DRAGON'S
PROMISE

ELIZABETH LIM

HODDERSCAPE

First published in Great Britain in 2022 by Hodderscape
An imprint of Hodder & Stoughton
An Hachette UK company

This paperback edition published in 2023

1

A CIP catalogue record for this title is available from the British Library

Paperback ISBN 978 1 529 35681 6
eBook ISBN 978 1 529 35680 9

Printed and bound in Great Britain by Clays Ltd, Elcograf S.p.A.

Hodder & Stoughton policy is to use papers that are natural, renewable
and recyclable products and made from wood grown in sustainable
forests. The logging and manufacturing processes are expected to
conform to the environmental regulations of the country of origin.

Hodder & Stoughton Ltd
Carmelite House
50 Victoria Embankment
London EC4Y 0DZ

www.hodderscape.co.uk

To my po po, for the love, the stories, and the fish soup

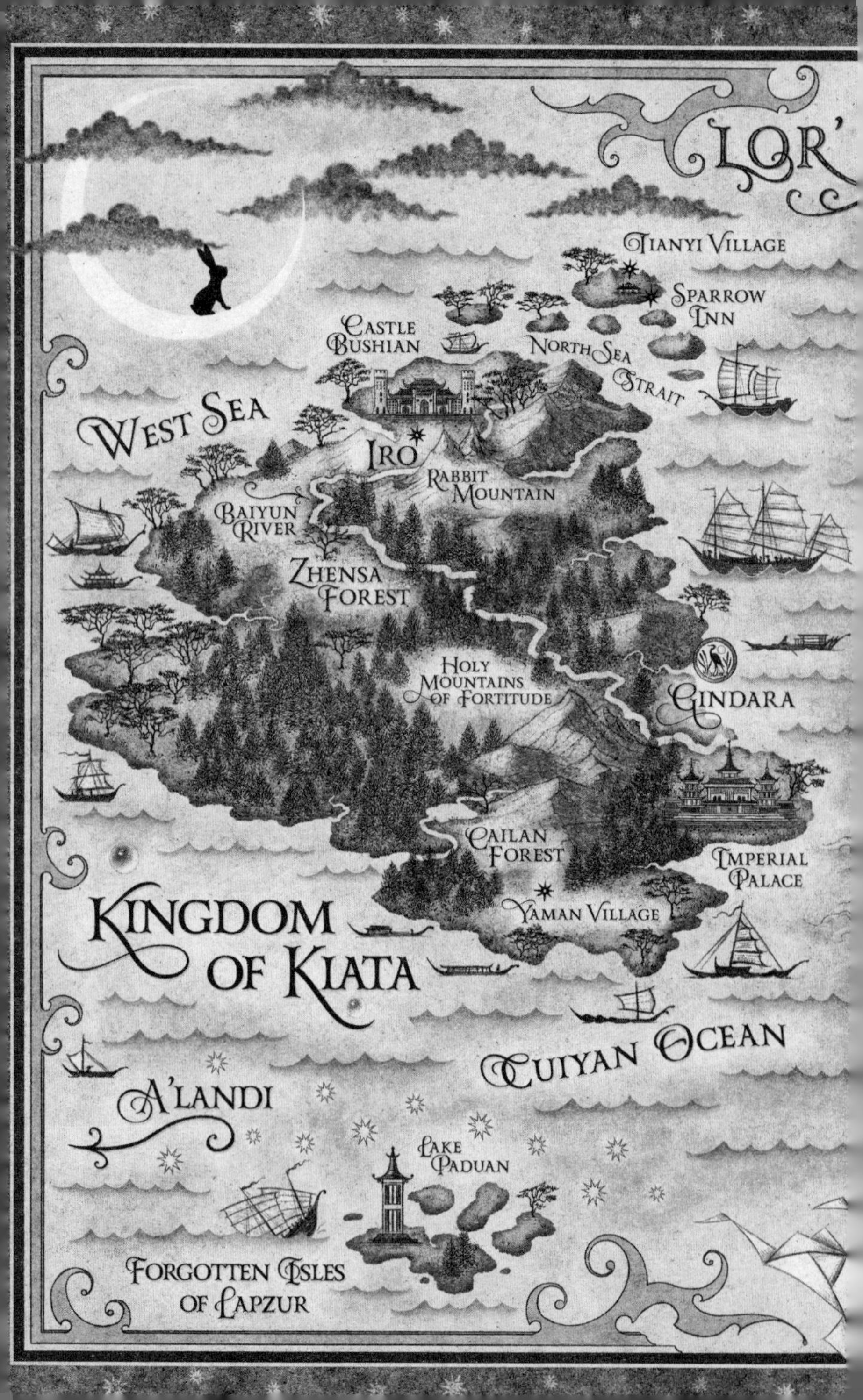

LOR'
TIANYI VILLAGE
SPARROW INN
CASTLE BUSHIAN
NORTH SEA STRAIT
WEST SEA
IRO
RABBIT MOUNTAIN
BAIYUN RIVER
ZHENSA FOREST
HOLY MOUNTAINS OF FORTITUDE
GINDARA
CAILAN FOREST
IMPERIAL PALACE
YAMAN VILLAGE
KINGDOM OF KIATA
CUIYAN OCEAN
A'LANDI
LAKE PADUAN
FORGOTTEN ISLES OF LAPZUR

YAN

TAIJIN SEA

MOUNT
RAYUNA

AI'LONG

REALM OF
DRAGONS

DRAGON KING'S
PALACE

TAMBU ISLES

SUNDAU

I've always loathed writing letters. My tutors used to say they showcase one's intellect and thoughtfulness—and calligraphy, too. But my handwriting has always looked more like a goose's than a princess's. No one cherishes receiving a letter from a goose. Even a royal one.

I know that's no excuse for why I never wrote you, Takkan. If I could change the past, I'd have replied to every one of your letters. I've finally read them, and I can't tell you what a comfort it's been to laugh over your stories, and imagine that we grew up together. I wish I'd asked you your name that day we first met—when we were children at the Summer Festival and I lost your kite.

I've been thinking about that kite lately, and how it must be flying and flying with nowhere to go, nowhere to land. Sometimes I dream that it's me. That I have no end to my string. That I don't belong anywhere anymore.

I wonder if that's how my stepmother felt. It hurts that I'll never get to ask her.

By the time you find this, I'll be in the dragon realm. I don't know how long I'll be gone. It could be days, it could be weeks or months. I hope it won't be years.

If I miss winter, think of me when the snow falls, and whenever you eat radishes.

Your favorite soup cook,
Shiori

CHAPTER ONE

The bottom of the Taijin Sea tasted of salt, slime, and disappointment. But for a few faint beams of mysterious light, it was darker than the deepest chasm. Hardly the magnificent watery realm dragons were said to call home.

I sat up on Seryu's back as he slowed, his long whiskers vibrating toward one beam in particular. Maybe I'd imagined it, but the beam shone brighter than the rest—almost violet.

"You ready?" Seryu asked.

Ready for what? I thought, but I nodded.

With a flip of his tail, he dove through the violet beam—and everything changed.

The water turned azure, and puffs of coppery mist hissed from beds of sand and crystal. And light! There was light everywhere, radiating from an unseen sun.

My heart began to race with anticipation, and I clung to Seryu's horns as he accelerated down, swimming so fast that I almost let go of my breath.

We're almost there, Kiki, I thought excitedly in our shared, unspoken language, but she didn't respond. A peek into my sleeve told me why: my poor paper bird had fainted.

I didn't blame her. We were moving at dizzying speeds, and my head pounded like a storm when I tried to see straight. But I couldn't afford to faint. I didn't even dare close my eyes.

I wanted to see everything.

At last we arrived at a labyrinth of bright coral reefs, fathoms below the mortal sea. Seagrass swayed in an unseen current, dunes of white sand and gold-veined rocks dotted the grounds, and canopies of braided seaflowers formed the roofs of underwater villas.

So this was Ai'long, home of the dragons.

It was a world few mortals would ever glimpse. At a glance, it didn't seem so different from land. In place of trees were pillars of coral, some slender and some thick, most with spiraling branches adorned with bracelets of moss. Even the way the fish glided, their tapered fins spread out like wings, reminded me of birds soaring across the sky.

And yet . . . it was like nothing I'd ever seen. The movement of the water, constantly tossing and turning, was revealed by flashes of color and flurries of fish. The way the seagrass tickled the fish that swept by, as if they could speak to one another.

Seryu smirked as I drank in the view. "I told you you'd be dazzled."

He was right, of course. I *was* dazzled. Then again, Ai'long was meant to astound mortal eyes such as mine. That was its danger, after all. Its trap.

A place so beautiful that even time held its breath.

Every hour you spend here is a day lost at home—if not more, I reminded myself sharply. That time would add up quickly, and I'd been away from my father and brothers so long I didn't want to waste a single minute.

Let's go. I signaled with a kick to the dragon's long serpentine side.

"I'm not a horse, you know." Seryu's green eyebrows arched as he twisted to view me. "Why so quiet, Shiori? You're not holding your breath, are you?"

When I didn't reply, he tossed me off his back, and his claw shot out and pinched my nose.

Out escaped a jet of bubbles—the air I'd been preciously hoarding. But great gods, I could breathe! Or at least it felt like I was breathing. The water tasted sweet instead of salty—intoxicating, like a heady plum wine when I inhaled too deeply, but maybe that was because my head was still spinning.

"So long as you're wearing a piece of my pearl, you can breathe underwater," Seryu explained, reminding me of the glowing fragment I wore around my neck. "It might not be inside your heart anymore, so we can't share thoughts . . . but you do know you can talk, right?"

"Of course I know," I lied.

Covering up my relief, I touched the tiny pearl. Even this deep in the sea, it shone like a bead of moonlight.

"You might want to keep it hidden," said Seryu. "People could get the wrong idea."

"I thought it was just to help me breathe. Why would they—"

"It's too complicated to explain," the dragon mumbled with a grunt. "I forgot how many questions you ask. Maybe I *should* have let you keep holding your breath."

My brows knit into a frown. "You're in a sour mood."

"Humans aren't exactly welcome in Ai'long," said Seryu thinly. "I'm thinking of the infinite ways your visit can go wrong."

I didn't believe him. He had been in a mood all day, starting with when he'd come for me onshore. He'd barely greeted my brothers, had ignored Takkan entirely. . . .

I tried to coax him out of it by teasing, "Will I have no fun stories to share when I go home? Here I was, telling everyone that the prince of dragons himself was going to give me a grand tour of his kingdom."

"The shorter your visit is, the better." Seryu's red eyes flicked to my satchel, which hung off my shoulder. "You're here to deliver something to my grandfather, not frolic about."

So much for cheering him up. Now *I* was in a sour mood too.

I pried my satchel open—just a pinch. That *something* I was supposed to deliver was a dark and broken dragon pearl. Raikama had left it to me before she died, and its power was so strong I could feel it fighting against my satchel's enchantment, which kept it safely confined and concealed. No surprise that Seryu's grandfather wanted it.

It wasn't the only thing inside the bag, though. I'd also

4

brought my starstroke net—for some protection against the Dragon King—and the sketchbook Takkan had given me when we said goodbye.

"More letters?" I'd asked, taking the book in both hands.

"Better," Takkan promised. "So you don't forget me."

What could be better than his letters? I stared wistfully at the sketchbook, wishing I could brush my knuckles against its soft spine and flip through its charcoal-stained pages. But I supposed it would be rude to read while I was in Seryu's company.

Seryu certainly thought so. He narrowed his eyes at me. "I've never seen you blush while looking at the pearl."

"Its light gets bright," I said quickly. "Makes my face warm."

He scoffed at the lie. "At least your human lordling didn't jump into the sea after us. The way he was making fish eyes at you for leaving, I half thought he might. He wouldn't have made it past the reefs before the sharks got to him."

I closed the satchel. "Really, sharks?"

"Grandfather employs a platoon of them." Seryu smirked. "They're always hungry. We'll encounter some shortly."

My heart thumped in my chest. Were we that close to Nazayun's palace?

Seryu misread my apprehension, and his tone lightened a little. "Worry not—the sharks don't have an appetite for a stringy human like you."

They might change their mind, I thought. Once the Dragon King learned why I was *really* in Ai'long, I'd be lucky if he granted me such a swift death.

Nervously, I glided back to Seryu, kicking harder than I needed to. Swimming in Ai'long was nothing like swimming in regular water. The water here was as light as air, and tiny currents tracked under my feet, propelling me where I needed to go. Almost like flying.

I overshot the dragon, jetting a hair too high. Out of nowhere, a bloom of jellyfish descended upon me.

There were at least a dozen of them. Their bodies were shaped like luminous umbrellas, tentacles swirling in a sinuous dance. They approached boldly, brushing against my arms and legs and even weaving through my long hair. I giggled at how it tickled—until Seryu let out a growl.

"Leave her alone." His red eyes flashed at the intruders. "She's with me."

The jellyfish recoiled, but they didn't disperse. Quite the opposite. As Seryu tried to tow me away by grabbing my hair, they followed and drew even closer.

Then, like the Taijin Sea, they changed.

The gold light radiating in their bodies went out in a flash, and their tentacles, soft as silk ribbons, turned hard and pointed. Two slid between Seryu and me, forcing us apart. The rest surrounded us.

I reached for the knife I kept hidden inside my sash. I barely got a chance to brandish it. Cold, slick tentacles suctioned onto my back and encircled my arms.

Tiny barbs grew out of my attacker's tentacles, grazing my skin: a lethal warning not to resist. One sting, and I'd be paralyzed for life.

Defeated, I went still and dropped my knife, letting it float beyond my grasp. In return, the jellyfish relaxed its grip, but only slightly. Its tentacles began to search me for other hidden weapons, and as they rifled through my satchel and robes, Kiki darted out of my sleeve.

She was groggy, her wings in a dramatic midstretch as she yawned to announce she was awake. But when her inky eyes popped open and she saw the jellyfish, she shrieked.

Bubbling, blazing demons of Tambu!

"It's not a demon," I assured her, hugging my satchel as tentacles attempted to pry it open. "It's a jellyfish."

A what?

The jellyfish loomed over Kiki, scrutinizing her intently.

My bird covered her head with a wing. *Oh gods,* she moaned. *Let me faint again.*

To Kiki's relief, the jellyfish deemed her unworthy of its attention and returned to my satchel. Its tentacles tugged hard at the straps, but I held on as tight as I could.

"Sting me all you like," I said. "You are not taking this."

The jellyfish hissed and bared its poisonous barbs.

"Away!" Seryu barked. His tail lashed back and forth, creating innumerable ripples, like tiny tempests. With a swipe of his claw, there came a fierce rip in the water.

While the jellyfish struggled against the sudden current, Seryu slung me onto his back and dove into a jungle of coral, swimming for the crystal spires ahead. He tossed my knife onto my lap. "Really, Shiori? This is what you bring to Ai'long?"

I gave a careless shrug. "Did you think I'd come unarmed?"

"You've met my grandfather before. This little dagger of yours would hardly be a splinter."

"Splinters can still hurt" was all I said, tucking the blade back into my sash. "What were those jellyfish?"

"Patrols."

"For what?"

"Trespassers and assassins."

He didn't elaborate, a signal to let it go. But I was too curious. "There was magic about them."

"Most of Grandfather's subjects have . . . a certain ability. It helps fend off those who try to enter Ai'long without an invitation."

"But why search me? I have an invitation."

"They were looking for your stepmother's pearl, obviously," said Seryu testily. "The jellyfish have a taste for dark magic. They also specialize in sensing deception."

A wave of unease fell over me. "Deception?"

"Yes, like that steel needle you didn't deign to tell me you brought." Seryu's voice hardened. "Worry not. Your time in Ai'long will be short; you won't have to experience our court."

That wasn't what worried me, but I kept silent and glanced at Kiki.

She'd swooned on my palm, and her wings were wilted into a dejected lump. Thankfully, she hadn't been paying attention to my conversation with Seryu. I loved her dearly, but keeping secrets wasn't one of her gifts.

Are we nearly there? she moaned. *I should have stayed on land. I feel seasick.*

"No one gets seasick underwater."

Kiki wrinkled her beak, letting out a theatrical sigh. *Can't you tell the dragon to swim with more care? Even whales move more daintily than he does.*

"You tell him. He's been surly all day."

Why? Her brow crinkled. *Is he upset with you?*

"Of course not."

Is it the jellyfish? Gods, Shiori—do you think they know? Maybe you should tell him you plan on keeping Raikama's p—

My eyes went wide, and I stuffed her into my sleeve before Seryu heard.

Raikama's pearl, Kiki had almost blurted.

No, I hadn't told him. I didn't plan to.

Guilt nibbled at my conscience, but I shoved it away. There was nothing to feel guilty about. I wasn't reneging on my word. I *had* promised Seryu I would bring Raikama's pearl to his grandfather. . . . I just never said I'd let him keep it.

"Only give it to the dragon with the strength to make it whole once more," Raikama had made me swear before she died.

As if it could read my thoughts, the pearl inside my satchel began to pulse. I could practically see it in my mind—spinning and scheming, trying to find a way out. It was only the size of a peach, barely larger than my palm, but at its peak brilliance, it glowed like a bead of sunlight. But now that Raikama was gone, its light was muted, the fracture in its center seeming to widen more every time I looked at it.

That crack would not heal until the pearl was reunited with its true owner. I had a feeling the grief I buried inside me was the same, deepening the hollow in my heart until my promise to Raikama was kept.

"A promise is not a kiss in the wind, to be thrown about without care," I murmured to myself. "It is a piece of yourself that is given away and will not return until your pledge is fulfilled."

They were my stepmother's words from long ago. Words I used to hate because they needled me with guilt, even as I ignored them. Never would I have guessed that I would draw upon them for comfort.

The pearl trembled, responding to my unease, and I lifted the satchel onto my lap so Seryu wouldn't notice. Too many times I had broken my word—to Raikama more than anyone. Not this time.

I will see you made whole again, I vowed to the pearl silently. *I will take you home.*

No matter the cost.

CHAPTER TWO

The walls enclosing King Nazayun's palace were impossibly high. They stretched taller than I could see, all the way to the violet lights marking the fringes of the realm, their sharp finials like needles prodding at the ocean's veins.

An audience of sea creatures had gathered outside the palace. Whales larger than my father's warships, mottled sea turtles that blended into the sand and rocks, dolphins, squid, and, when I looked closer, even crabs and seahorses. Scattered among them were dragons, a few with humans mounted on their backs. All lowered their heads in deference as Seryu passed, but their gazes were fixed on me.

"Don't hold my horns here," growled Seryu. "They're a measure of status in Ai'long, and I'm a dragon prince, not a bull."

I let go as if I'd touched fire. "Sorry."

It quickly became clear what he meant. Other dragons' horns curved downward, like a ram's, often with ridges or fluted edges, and in colors varying from gray to ivory to

11

black. Seryu's were silver and smooth, but most notably they were branched—like a stag's antlers. A natural crown.

"Is there usually a crowd like this to greet you?"

"No." Seryu's voice became tight. "They're here for you."

That made me sit up sharply. "For me?"

"They're wagering on whether Grandfather will throw you to the sharks or turn you to stone."

I couldn't tell whether he was being serious or sarcastic. Maybe both.

"Aren't there any other alternatives?" I asked.

"None that you'd find more pleasant. I told you, humans aren't welcome here."

"But I see so many."

Seryu's long back stiffened, and his scales turned dull. "Look again."

I furrowed my brow, but curious now, I turned again.

At first, I saw nothing out of the ordinary. Yes, the humans riding the dragons were bedecked in the riches of the sea, in jackets and gowns that gleamed like an abalone shell beaded with the petals of ocean lilies. But other than that, they looked the same as me.

At least until my eyes sharpened, and I looked beyond their faces. Saw the gills sparkling on their necks, the fish scales dappling their arms. Some even had wings tucked neatly against their shoulder blades and fins adorning their wrists and ankles. When they caught me staring, they puckered their lips and offered me twisted smiles.

"So," I said nervously, "I really am like a pig."

"What?"

"That's what you said when we first met—that inviting me to Ai'long would be like bringing a pig to meet your family. I thought you were joking."

"I never expected to bring you here, Shiori," he said, his voice so low I almost didn't hear. We were nearly at the gates. "I want you to know that."

It sounded like an apology, but for what, I didn't understand. I never got a chance to ask. A deafening chorus of conch shells blared—then, out of nowhere, an invisible current wrenched me off Seryu's back and swept me into the palace.

It happened with the swiftness of a sword stroke. I didn't realize I'd been torn away until it was too late.

"Shiori!" Seryu was barreling toward the gates, trying to force his way inside before they closed. "Grandfather, no!"

That was the last I saw of him before I was washed away, speeding down a chute of water so fast it made our previous journey feel sluggish. By the time the chute spat me out at my destination, I was sure I had fainted—at least for a few seconds.

I landed in the largest room I'd ever beheld. It was vast and wide, its pillars going on as far as my eyes could see, and except for one window of what looked like cascading black crystal, everything, from the walls to the ceilings, was the color of bone. Or snow, if one was a cheerier-minded sort of person.

I kicked my feet against the ocean floor and propelled myself up.

Did we get eaten by a whale? Kiki whispered from inside my sleeve.

If we weren't in such a dire situation, I might have laughed. The chamber did resemble a whale's rib cage. Marble pillars lined the walls, evenly spaced and rising three times the height of the ceremony hall in my father's palace. Their ends arced impossibly into an open roof, like a cage of bones.

Out of precaution, I drew my knife. The spaces between the pillars were wide enough to slip through, and the palace gates gleamed in the near distance. Was Seryu still there, looking for me?

I held my knife tight. I wasn't about to wait here and find out.

I dove between two of the pillars and had made it as far as one breath out of the chamber when long, wriggling tendrils of kelp sprouted from the pillars and wrapped around my limbs.

Kiki bolted out of my sleeve. *Shiori!*

I hacked at the kelp. The stalks were thinner than the seaweed I boiled in my soups. But looks could be deceiving. This kelp was strong as iron—and alive, sprouting three new fronds for every one that was cut. They lashed Kiki away and spiraled around my wrists, jerking the knife from my grip and pinning me against a pillar.

Next came the sharks.

I hadn't believed Seryu when he mentioned them earlier, but here they were. Each was ten times my size, with rows of briar-sharp teeth and blue-black eyes that expressed no compunction in turning me into a snack.

"Seryu!" I shouted. "Seryu!"

"He will be joining us shortly."

The Dragon King's tail curved around the pillars, and gooseflesh rose on my skin.

"My grandson has told me much about you since we last met, Shiori'anma," he said. "Your gods have given you an unusual amount of attention: the adopted daughter of the Nameless Queen, the bloodsake of Kiata . . . and now the bearer of the Wraith's pearl."

The Wraith? My ears perked. It was the first time I had heard that name.

Long, crooked bolts of silver pierced the shadows—Nazayun's horns. "Show it to me."

The kelp loosened its grip around my wrists just enough for me to open my satchel. I reached inside, my fingers brushing over the broken pearl and then the starstroke net.

My fingers itched to dispatch the net over the Dragon King. Starstroke, after all, was a dragon's only weakness. The only thing powerful enough to separate one from its heart. And demons take me, I'd sacrificed enough to make the net.

The sharks would have torn me to ribbons had I dared, but luckily the pearl didn't give me a chance. Once I opened the satchel, it made a low and chiding hum and breezed out into the open.

I was beginning to suspect that it was alive in some strange way. Back home in my father's palace, whenever I left it in my room, I would find it later floating in the air beside me—as if watching. Waiting.

"The pearl takes fate and twists it to its own purpose," Raikama had said.

After what it had done to my brothers, I wouldn't be fool enough to assume that its purpose included keeping me alive. Which was why I watched, holding my breath, as the pearl rose level with Nazayun's pallid gaze.

Displeasure showed in the bend of the dragon's brow. "It has tethered itself to you."

"For now," I replied. "I made a vow to my stepmother that I would return the pearl to its rightful owner."

He snarled, "You made a vow to Seryu that you would give it to me."

"That I would *bring* it to you," I corrected. "Not *give*. The pearl isn't yours."

"A dragon pearl belongs to Ai'long." Nazayun towered over me, gouging his claws into the ground. "I *am* Ai'long."

"Why do you want it?" I asked. "I've seen what a true dragon pearl looks like. It's pure and awe-inspiring, nothing like this one. This one is—"

"An abomination."

"As you say," I replied. "So why do you want it?"

"Unenlightened human, you truly know nothing!" the Dragon King bellowed. "The Wraith's pearl is a broken thing. It craves destruction as much as it abhors it. On its own, it cannot find balance, so it relied on someone like your stepmother to moderate its power. But the Nameless Queen is dead, and the pearl is too broken to take a new host. Soon it will cleave completely. When that happens, it will release a force greater than anything you can imagine. Great enough to devastate your beloved Kiata."

For once I believed him. "Unless it's returned to the Wraith."

"That is not an option," Nazayun said. "It must be destroyed, and when it is, so too will the Wraith perish. Denounce your bond and give the pearl to me."

I hesitated. The pearl floated above my palm, its broken halves parting ever so slightly along one edge. It looked deceptively fragile, like the petals of a lotus blossom. Yet I could feel what terrible power lay within.

Could Raikama have made a mistake in asking me to return it to the Wraith? Or was this one of Nazayun's tricks?

Only for a moment, my conscience twisted with indecision. Then I closed my fists, and the pearl flew to my side. *I trust Raikama.*

"The pearl belongs to the dragon with the strength to make it whole once more," I said. "That dragon is not you."

Fury ignited the Dragon King's white eyes. "So be it."

Behind him, the sharks sped in my direction, jaws snapping. Visions of a gruesome end flashed in their glassy eyes. Me, filleted into a hundred bloody chunks that turned the water red. Kiki screamed in my ear, *No, Shiori!*

Kelp tightened around my waist and ankles, holding me immobile. Luckily, I'd been anticipating such a moment.

Never go to battle without knowing your opponent, my brother Benkai liked to say. Before I left for Ai'long, he'd imparted as much military wisdom as he could: *He who can surprise his enemy is always at an advantage.*

Here came my surprise: I slammed my hip against the

pearl, striking it into the closest pillar. Its halves split from its base, opening like a clamshell, and a dazzling light poured forth.

The kelp recoiled. It loosened its grip on my limbs just long enough for me to whip out the starstroke net.

I threw it high and shouted, "Kiki!"

My paper bird darted out from her hiding place and caught the other side of the net. Together, we flung it over the Dragon King's enormous chest, pulling it taut against his scales.

I'd used the net only once before, to free Raikama of the burden she carried. I'd never actually used it against a real dragon.

Its magic worked instantaneously, latching on to Nazayun's scales and dulling their brilliant sapphire luster. He howled, and his head snapped back as the net dug into his chest, outlining the shape of his precious heart.

It was at least three times the size of the Wraith's, silvery white and perfectly round, like a swollen moon. All I had to do was take it, and I would have complete power over him.

"Let go of me," I commanded the kelp, and it loosened its grip on my ankles. The sharks too withheld their charge.

I retrieved my knife and stabbed it into Nazayun's scales to hold the net down. The Dragon King roared in pain, but I felt no contrition. Splinters could hurt, after all.

"Where will I find the Wraith?" I demanded.

A laugh bubbled from Nazayun's throat.

"Answer, or—"

"Or what?" Nazayun eyed the Wraith's pearl, which

18

hovered over him like a harbinger of doom. "Or what, Shiori'anma?"

Something was off. The Dragon King's heart throbbed in his chest, a sign the starstroke had to be hurting him. So why was he smiling? Why was he *laughing*?

"You should have given me the pearl when I offered you the chance," said the Dragon King as he twitched in discomfort under the net. "Your crime of weaving such a net cannot go unpunished. Three hundred years you would have slept, long enough for all you know and love to turn to dust. Then I would have returned you to Kiata, as promised. Unfortunately, you chose poorly. For that you shall never see your homeland again."

The knife I'd jabbed between Nazayun's scales suddenly dissolved into the water, and he ripped the starstroke off his chest. It crackled between his claws, singeing his skin before he flung it into a web of kelp, far out of my reach.

"Did you think it would be so easy to take out my heart?" He laughed as his wounds healed before my eyes. "I am a god of dragons. Not even starstroke can harm me."

I staggered, and cupped my palms around the Wraith's pearl. "Then what about this—"

I never got to finish my threat. The walls behind me began to sing, and a surge of water whipped across the black crystal window I'd noticed earlier, creating a whirlpool.

Out of it swooped a second dragon. All I caught was flashes of red scales and a pair of round gilded eyes. Then there came a hard yank at my neck, and I jerked forward.

"If you won't give us the pearl we want, we'll take this

one for now." The scarlet dragon held up the necklace Seryu had warned me to keep on at all times—the chip of his heart that would allow me to breathe in Ai'long.

My hands flew to my throat as my lungs convulsed. Water was everywhere and rushed into my mouth, filled my lungs. My heart whisked in my ears, beating in alarm as the weight of the seas came roaring. There was so much, I couldn't even choke. I was drowning.

"This is my daughter, the Lady of the Easterly Seas," Nazayun said, as if *now* were the time for introductions. "Since you will not give me the pearl, I leave her in charge of its retrieval."

Nazayun's daughter observed me drowning. "I've a theory," she purred, "that the human soul is made up of countless little strings that tether it to life." She pinched her nails at my heart, and I gasped in pain as she extracted a long silver-gold thread I'd never seen before: a strand of my soul.

"Beautiful, isn't it? So fragile, yet so vital." She twisted the strand around her nail. "If I cut enough, and leave, say, one last string dangling, the pearl will break its bond with you in search of someone who isn't on the brink of death." She tried to snip the strand with her nail, but it glowed bright and recoiled back inside me.

Displeasure tautened her whiskers. "A tricky state to achieve, especially with such a stubborn soul as yours—but we have time to experiment."

I had no time. My world was fast constricting, and I called out to the Wraith's pearl.

Save me, I pleaded. *Save me, or you'll never find where you belong. You'll never go home.*

The pearl began to beat. Once. Twice. Then faster, a racing counterpoint to my dying pulse, and a burst of light poured out of the broken halves.

"A fighter," murmured the scarlet dragon as she swam forward, obstructing my view of the pearl. She touched my forehead with a cold palm.

"Never play games with a dragon," she whispered. "You cannot win."

And before the last of my breath left me, the world washed away to nothing.

CHAPTER THREE

"Your Highness," cried my tutor. "Wake up, Shiori'anma! Please, wake up."

I didn't budge. Every day my tutor faced the same task, and I almost felt sorry for her. But what did I care for her waxing on and on about Kiata's poetry, art, and lore? It wasn't as if my brothers would invite me to their meetings if I could recite verses from the Songs of Sorrow or charm the court with my knowledge about vermilion paint versus ocher.

"Asleep like the numb moon," moaned my tutor. "Again."

I hated the saying. I'd been forced to learn the story behind it. Something about Imurinya, the lady of the moon, and her husband, the hunter, and a kiss needed to wake her.

I wasn't a romantic, and no kiss would wake me—unless it was from a tarantula, not a boy. The *only things that worked were the smell of freshly griddled sweet rice cakes and a well-calculated throw of my brother Reiji's wooden dice.*

The funny thing was, Reiji hadn't thrown dice at me in years. Yet something small and hard pelted the back of my head. Repeatedly.

My eyes burst open, and I yelled, "Will you stop that?"

Well, that was what I'd meant to say. The words came out garbled, and my chest ached as if someone had squeezed all the life out of me and then reluctantly funneled it back in.

An unwelcome reminder that I was still in the dragon realm—and a captive in Nazayun's palace, at that. It was too dark to see my surroundings clearly, but it wasn't the rib cage room anymore.

Kelp shackles clinched my body from the neck down, restraining me to a slab of black crystal like I'd seen earlier. With all my strength, I jerked, trying to set myself free. The shackles tightened, and punishing jabs of pain raced up my muscles. I bit down hard on my lip until they passed.

When I could breathe again—and I didn't know how I was breathing without Seryu's necklace—I deflated.

Demons of Tambu, how was I going to get out of this? I leaned my head back, banging the wall in despair.

Watch where you hit your head! Paper wings rustled in my hair, and Kiki crawled down to my ear. *There are other ways to tell me you're awake, Shiori.*

"Kiki!" I was thrilled to see her. "What happened? Where am—"

23

You've been sleeping, she reported. *You're lucky, you know. The Dragon King's daughter has come back several times to hack at your soul, but she couldn't even snip a strand. Nazayun's furious about it. He told her to wake you up.* A gulp. *He said he'd do it.*

"When was this?"

Who can tell time in this place? Kiki shrugged. *I was spying. I couldn't ask what day it was. She thinks the pearl protected you.* Her inky eyes bulged. *Did it?*

"Maybe. That must be why I still have it. Why I'm still alive."

That was some comfort, but not much.

Kiki peered at the pearl as it wobbled to life. *It was asleep, you know, same as you—until now. It's almost like it has a mind, like it's living.*

"It's a dragon's heart," I said. "It *is* alive, in a way."

For a dragon's heart, it isn't very clever, said Kiki. *It should find its own way home instead of making us do all the work.*

Silently, I agreed. The Wraith's pearl floated above my head, hovering near. I couldn't decide whether I was angry or relieved to see it. What *was* becoming clear was that I couldn't always count on it to come to my aid.

Look what you did, Kiki scolded the pearl. She sat on it, lounging in the crack between its edges with her wings spanned out. *I could be back in Kiata, lolling on silk pillows and chasing fireflies. But look where we are! Shiori's stuck in this horrible dragon dungeon—and you, you're no closer to finding your owner.*

The pearl let out a flare, illuminating our surroundings: a narrow cell that seemed to go on forever. But that was only an illusion. In reality, there were thousands of mirror shards bobbing along the walls, and their reflections made the room seem endless.

I shivered. "What is this place?"

Kiki shrugged again. *I've searched a hundred times for a way out, but the mirrors—Shiori, they're alive! They kept watching me. And there's this eerie ghost—*

"A ghost?"

Over there. Kiki pointed with a shaky wing. *It tried to speak to me.*

Darkness bathed the other end of the room, where the pearl's light hadn't reached.

"Show me," I commanded the pearl.

With a hiss, the light bloomed brighter, illuminating a lone statue. And given the gurgling and mumbling sounds coming from its direction, a *living* statue.

A boy, it turned out.

He was stone from the neck down, but his head was still flesh. Uncommonly blue eyes, tan skin, and a shock of unruly black hair. It was hard to place where he was from, but he couldn't have been older than twelve or thirteen. He looked like he'd been cursed in the middle of a grand throw. His right arm was extended in a dramatic flourish, his chin raised and left leg slightly lifted. His clothes were stone, along with the rest of him, but there was a bright splash of red silk over his mouth.

My stomach curdled at the sight. What was a human

25

child doing in the dragon realm, let alone practically turned to stone?

"Kiki, help him. His mouth is gagged."

But he could be a ghost! Or worse, a sea demon.

"Help him, all right?"

Obediently, my bird flew to the statue and untied the gag over the boy's mouth.

He coughed and spluttered, then blew his hair out of his eyes with exaggerated gusto.

"Firstly," he said in crisp, accented Kiatan, "I'm not a ghost. Ghosts—but for a few exceptions—can't touch objects in the physical world and would hardly be encased in stone, as I am." His nose twitched. "Secondly, it took you long enough to wake up. I was starting to think all that throwing would be for nothing."

"You're the one who woke me?" I said.

"I had nothing else to do."

"How?"

With a smug grin, the boy leaned his head back. "See these floating mirror shards? Their edges are sharper than they look, and they'll cut you if you try to escape." He turned his face so I could see the little gashes on his nose and cheeks. "Took me all week, but I managed to get their attention. When they came at me, I grabbed a couple and pitched them at you."

"You threw glass shards at my head?"

"How else was I supposed to wake you?" he said. "Don't worry, I sanded off the edges on my arm. Helps to be made of stone, I guess. Your cut's already healed."

Cut? Well, that explained the pain in my temple.

"It should have taken only a couple of tries," continued the boy. "Usually I have excellent aim, but my right arm turned to stone in the middle of a throw. Luckily for you, my left arm had a little more time. I'm less precise with my left, though."

Lucky indeed, Kiki said, gaping at the boy. Both of his arms were solid granite, though the veins in his left hand were still pulsing.

"Thank you," I said gravely. "Is your face—"

"Don't worry about me. Either the cuts will heal or I'll make a less attractive statue."

He sounds unnervingly cheerful about his predicament, Kiki muttered. *Do we trust him or not? I vote not.*

I frowned, ignoring Kiki. "Did you say I've been here for a week?"

"That's what I counted." The boy twisted his lips. "Time is so lugubriously slow when there's nothing to read. Please tell me you have a book in that bag of yours."

I'd stopped listening. A whole week, lost! My chest went so tight I could hardly breathe. That was five months back home.

I pursed my lips, trying to rein in my anger. *It could be worse,* I told myself. Five months—not five years. Not five centuries.

"No books?" the boy was saying, misreading my horror. "That's too bad. Well, at least I can practice my Kiatan. It's ironic, you know. Kiata's the last place I ever plan to visit. Never thought the language would be of any use."

27

My attention snapped back to him. "Careful. That's my country you're insulting."

"I don't mean offense, only that Kiata's a magic desert. A country without magic is hardly the place to make one's reputation as a brilliant young sorcerer."

"Aren't you a bit young for sorcery?"

"They start us young," explained the boy. "How else do you think I ended up in Ai'long?"

"Maybe a dragon abducted you. It's been known to happen."

"Abducted?" A sniff. "I'm an enchanter-in-training, not the sailor of some shrimping dinghy. You think it's so easy to abduct someone who's mastered the Four Forms of defensive magic?"

He has the ego of an enchanter, Kiki remarked, curling her wing around the pearl.

The boy eyed Kiki shrewdly, as if he understood. Then he flexed his fingers and winced—through the mirrors I saw that his knuckles had gone gray. "I guess I might never get a chance to live up to my potential."

"You can't give up. There has to be a way out of this place." I struggled against my shackles, but it was no use.

"Don't bother. I've spent weeks trying, and I have magic."

"I have magic *too,* you know."

"I've heard. You're the bloodsake of Kiata. Impressive, how you made that paper bird come to life." The boy cranked his head to the side. "But as the bloodsake, your main well of power comes from your homeland, and you're quite a ways away."

28

I frowned. "How did you know that—the part about me drawing magic from Kiata?"

He shrugged. "I read a lot," he said quickly. But before I could interrogate him further, he added, "Didn't help me here, though. Even if I could undo this curse, I'd drown once I made it past Ai'long's borders."

"Why?"

"Well, for one—my sangi would run out."

"Sangi?"

"The tea that the dragons poured down your throat so you can breathe underwater." The young sorcerer wrinkled his nose. "Awfully bitter brew, worse than Nandun's Tears. Back to my point, the waters past the borders aren't enchanted like they are here. I can't just glide around like I'm dancing on a cloud. I'd have to actually swim to keep from sinking. And I never learned to swim."

Kiki slapped her head in disbelief. *He can't swim and he came into the dragon realm by choice?*

"Don't give up," I said. "My friend is a prince of Ai'long. He can help."

"Doubtful. He's as much the Dragon King's pawn as Lady Solzaya is."

At the name, the mirrors suspended in the water around us pivoted to regard the boy.

"Lady Solzaya," I repeated. "Who's that?"

"The High Lady of the Easterly Seas. I'm sure you've met her, since you're here. This room is where she tortures King Nazayun's most troublesome guests. She turned the last prisoner in your spot into sea foam after he gave up his secrets.

It really was quite gruesome. Stone is preferable to sea foam, as far as curses go."

I swallowed. "The scarlet dragon."

"There are plenty of scarlet dragons around here. I distinguish her by the mirror shards around her neck. You must have seen them."

"I didn't notice. I was too busy trying not to die."

"You'll notice them the next time. Now that you're awake, you'll need more sangi to keep breathing. Someone will be here soon to fetch you—very soon, I'd say. Nazayun's been lusting after that broken pearl of yours for ages."

"Lusting? He said he wanted to destroy it."

"And you believed him?" The young sorcerer scoffed. "Dragons are bound to promises, not the truth."

His eyes flickered yellow as he observed the floating pearl. "I can see why he'd covet it. It's different from the others. . . . It reeks of power. Chaotic, uncontrollable power."

"But it's on the verge of breaking."

"Reason has never stopped a dragon from coveting something it can't have." He tried to scratch his nose but couldn't reach. "I used to want a dragon pearl myself. It's what got me obsessed with Ai'long."

"Is that why you're here?" I said. "Were you trying to steal one?"

"Do you take me for an idiot? I wouldn't try to steal a pearl . . . not as an apprentice, anyway. I'd wait until I was a full-fledged enchanter."

I twisted my lips at the boy, both amused and mystified by his gall. "So why are you here?"

30

"A dragon came to me on land. He'd heard of my potential." The boy grinned. "Gave me sangi and said he'd teach me the recipe if I *borrowed* something for him in Ai'long."

I raised an eyebrow. "Borrowed—without permission?"

"Precisely. We enchanters aren't meant to be common thieves, but knowledge is my weakness. Always has been. And no one's been to Ai'long in centuries. I couldn't resist—"

"You got caught," I finished for him. "What happened to the dragon?"

"I don't know," he lamented. "I was a dolt and never got his name."

He *was* a dolt, but he was young, and now that I'd heard his story, I couldn't help feeling sorry for him. "Do you have a name, young thief?"

"I do, but I don't like it." He half closed his eyes. "It's Gen."

"Gen," I said firmly. "I promise I'll get you out."

An eye blinked open. "Don't make promises you can't keep, especially not in Ai'long."

It was an odd thing to say, but I didn't get to ask what he meant. My breath became short, water rushing into my mouth the way it had before I'd gone unconscious.

In response, the mirrors tinkled, clanging against one another in an unnerving percussion.

"Your sangi's running out," Gen whispered. "They'll be here any minute."

But no one came.

Instead, my shackles dissolved, and a whirlpool suddenly roared behind me. Catching me midbreath, it devoured Kiki, the Wraith's pearl, and me into its gushing void.

Down into a watery abyss I plunged, Kiki's scream echoing the one I let out in my head. I held two things tight: my breath and the pearl. My life depended on both.

I came to a halt, and a current tossed me upright before the Dragon King.

Only he was not a dragon anymore. From the waist up, he had taken on a human form. Pale blue hair sprang from his scalp, and sapphire sea silk swathed his body, the color the exact vibrant shade as his scales. The cloth trailed far behind him like a river, blending into his long, winding tail.

My starstroke net was draped over his shoulders like a cloak. Its shimmering threads made his heart glow and bulge; for him to don it so boldly was a show of might.

Still, it must hurt him. I wondered if he liked the pain.

The last of my breath was leaving me, and the lack of air made a searing heat tremble up from my lungs to my throat, nose, and temples. By the great gods, it was agony, and I lifted my chin, struggling for calm. The Wraith's pearl did nothing to help. It knew, as I did, that Nazayun wouldn't kill me.

He'd simply make me suffer . . . as long as possible.

The Dragon King's eyes turned hard, and another excruciating second passed. The agony fractured my calm, and the very moment I thought I might die after all, a riptide of water thrashed me into a kneeling bow, and air suddenly rushed into my lungs.

"I almost admire your brazenness, human, unenlightened

as it is," Nazayun growled. "But that is not what saves you today."

Still on my knees, I gasped, choking on my breath. Over my chest dangled the necklace with Seryu's pearl—as if I had never lost it.

I inhaled and exhaled, over and over until my lungs stopped burning and I no longer felt the crushing weight of the seas against my head.

"Why?" I rasped.

"My grandson has informed me that he gave you that piece of his heart." The Dragon King stroked his glacier-blue beard. "Fortune smiles upon you, Princess. In accordance with dragon law, you are under his protection."

I had a feeling the Dragon King and I had very different definitions of the word *fortune*, and I didn't like where mine was heading.

"The binding ceremony shall take place immediately," said Nazayun. "Be grateful for this chance. Another one will not come."

"Binding ceremony?" I croaked, finding my voice. "What is—"

"Quiet, Shiori." Seryu unfolded from the shadows, his claw swiftly covering my mouth. He forced me into another bow. "You will show His Eternal Majesty respect."

Seryu's attitude bewildered me even more than his sudden appearance. I craned my neck toward him and searched his red eyes. I didn't know what I was looking for: remorse, guilt, a hint of a plan? Whatever it was, I didn't find it.

And that left me with a sinking, undeniable truth: Seryu had betrayed me.

I lashed out, but Seryu caught my arms easily.

His talons grazed my skin. Like his grandfather, he had discarded his dragon form, mostly. Gone were the scales, the serpentine tail, the leonine nose and sharp, pointed teeth—replaced by a human face and body. But his hair and skin still glowed a faint mossy green, and he'd kept his crown of horns, naturally—as well as the claws.

Claws he lifted from my mouth when he finally released me. "Don't fight," he whispered into my ear. I couldn't tell whether it sounded like a plea or a command. Maybe both.

King Nazayun observed us. "In case the *human* does not understand, then I remind you, Seryu: this will be her final opportunity to present the pearl to me. You know the consequences should she waste it."

"I do, Grandfather," Seryu said staunchly. "I thank you for your mercy."

"Bring her to your mother. She will initiate the girl for the ceremony."

Seryu stiffened. "There isn't any need. I can prepare Shiori myself—"

"You cannot be trusted with the girl," interjected the king. "Take her to your mother. Solzaya has a love of spectacle, and a spectacle this will be: the first Kiatan companion in nearly a thousand years."

Companion . . . binding ceremony. The pieces were coming together, but I couldn't make sense of them. The possibilities were too preposterous to consider. I pulled away from Seryu, but he held fast to my wrist.

Even as Seryu fought me, his ears turned red, and the shine in his horns dulled. Which was all the answer I needed.

Gods spare me, I thought. I would've kicked him in the ribs if I could, but my legs hadn't adjusted to the stupid, shifting currents, and I feared I'd miss him entirely.

Seryu made a low bow to his grandfather, forcing me once more to do the same.

"As you wish, Your Eternal Majesty," he murmured. The train of his long robe struck me from behind and held me down by the neck.

Amusement glinted in Nazayun's hard eyes. "I promised you death for reneging on your word, Shiori'anma, and death shall come. Only not the sort you were expecting.

"Prepare your final farewells. After the binding rites, you will be reborn as the companion of a dragon prince. All that you knew in your past life will cease to exist, and you will never again return to Kiata."

He paused dramatically. "Ai'long will be your home from now on."

CHAPTER FOUR

It was lucky for Seryu that his grip was strong. Otherwise, I would have shoved him into one of the rushing cascades of black crystal we kept passing. After my earlier experience with the whirlpool, I figured they were portals of some sort, and I fantasized about shipping Seryu to the bottom of a volcano.

I settled for digging my nails into his arm as we made our way through the palace, paying no mind to the sharks that circled the crystal walls or the crabs that scurried up and down, their bulbous little eyes watching from every direction.

"Companion?" I hissed. "That had better not mean what I think it does. I'm no concubine, Seryu. Especially not yours."

Seryu hardly flinched as my nails sank into his thick skin. "Better a concubine than sea foam."

You spiteful reptile! Buzzing out of my sleeve, Kiki slapped the dragon's cheek with her wing. *To think I liked you. Take us home right away!*

Seryu batted her away, his fuming red eyes darting toward the watchful crabs as if they were eavesdropping. "Do you not have any sense of propriety?" he snarled. "I am a prince of this realm."

As the crabs skittered away, his claw fell on my shoulder, and we were whisked into a private chamber shuttered by bubbling panes of ice.

"You might as well put me back in your mother's dungeon," I said. "I'm not giving up the pearl."

Seryu growled at me. "Sons of the wind, can you be quiet for once? Can't you just be thankful that I saved your life?"

"Be thankful? You lied to me."

"Let's be clear. You lied to *me*. You promised to give Grandfather the pearl."

"*Bring* him the pearl, not *give* him the pearl. It doesn't belong to him."

"Do you think he cares?" Anger made Seryu's whiskers taut and straight. "My grandfather is not someone who can be reasoned with. Why else do you think I proposed the binding ceremony? You have a piece of *my* pearl, Shiori. Do you even know what that means in Ai'long?" He raked a claw through his green hair. "Of course you don't."

"What does it mean?"

"That Grandfather is sworn by dragon law to honor the bond between us."

"There is no bond between us." My hands went up to the necklace he'd given me. I wished I could hurl it at him to prove my point, but I'd drown. "I'm already betrothed."

"To that pathetic lordling?" Seryu snorted.

"Will you stop calling him that? He's my—"

"Fiancé? You ran away from the betrothal ceremony. You're hardly engaged."

"I wasn't running away from him," I half fibbed. "Kiki flew out of my sleeve."

Seryu's expression darkened. "What is so wonderful about him, anyway? He'll live seventy or eighty years, at best; he has no magic, hardly any power to his name. His castle doesn't even have a proper pond or a proper river. I had to visit you in a horse trough when you were there." Seryu gritted his sharp teeth. "Yet you act as though *he*'s the one who gave you a piece of his heart. As if *he* saved you from drowning in the Sacred Lake."

It was the last thing I'd expected him to say. My heart pinched with an ache I'd never felt before. "Seryu . . ."

His ears went flat, their tips turning redder than summer poppies. He seemed to be wishing the ground could swallow him whole. "Look, it was the only idea I could come up with. If I'd known you would be so vehemently opposed to it—"

"I'm not vehemently opposed," I interrupted. "Just . . . opposed." I couldn't look him in the eye. "I can't stay here forever."

"What if you have to?" Seryu pressed. There was a new edge to his words that I didn't like. "What if it's best for your country?"

My ribs went tight. "What do you mean?"

"Staying here is your best recourse," he replied slowly, as if reading the words aloud. "It always has been. A new bloodsake is born only after the previous one dies. If you live an eternity in Ai'long, another will never be born."

I said nothing. I couldn't. My mind was reeling, everything coming harshly into focus. Nine blazing Hells, Seryu had a point.

The demons trapped in Kiata's Holy Mountains needed my blood in order to be free. But if I stayed in Ai'long, they'd never get out.

Seryu spoke my mind: "Your father, your brothers . . . your lordling would be safe. Everyone in Kiata would be safe."

It was a beautiful solution, and I hated Seryu for it. Any arguments I had clotted in my throat. All reason pointed to me staying here.

"So," Seryu spoke, more quietly than I'd ever heard him before. "Do you think you could try . . . to carve a place in your heart for me?"

I was glad we were alone. My ire at him had vanished completely, leaving a hollow feeling. How was I supposed to respond? *Yes*, he was waiting for me to say. Such a simple word, a word I'd uttered so many times in my life. Yet it sat leaden on my tongue, and all I could think of was Takkan on the beach, promising he'd wait for me. Asking me not to forget him.

It hurt to speak: "If I stay with you, I'll never see my family again."

Seryu's whiskers wilted, and his demeanor went cold. "You'll have one final chance. My mother has an enchanted mirror—its glass will give you a last look at your family. Before you forget them."

In an instant, I was on my guard again. "What do you mean, forget them?"

"It's a part of the binding ceremony." He forged on, as if knowing and not caring that I would react badly. "In exchange for immortality, you'll consume an elixir when you take your oath to Ai'long. You won't remember anything about your past, not even your name."

I jerked back, stunned by what he'd said. "Is that the only way you dragons can find mates? By making us forget who we are?"

"Immortality comes at a price. You'll be reborn stronger. Better."

"Better?" I repeated. "I'd rather have the demons rip me apart than forget who I am."

Was this what the Dragon King had meant when he warned me that death was inevitable? I couldn't believe I'd almost felt bad for Seryu. "That's why Nazayun's so confident I'll give him the pearl," I realized angrily. "Because I won't even remember what it is."

Seryu started to speak, probably to spout some nonsense about his grandfather needing to destroy the pearl for the safety of both our worlds. I wouldn't hear it.

"You dragons are no better than demons." I tore away before he could touch me. "If you won't get me out of here, I'll find my own way. I made a promise to Raikama. The pearl needs to be returned to the Wraith."

Seryu huffed at me in disbelief. "You would risk your family, your country—your own life for that? What does a promise to your stepmother matter? She's dead."

I couldn't control myself. My anger had reached its peak, and my hand lashed out. Before I knew it, I had struck Seryu on the cheek. Hard.

If he'd been human, his head would have jerked back, maybe even hit the wall.

But Seryu simply recoiled, looking stung. I was too furious to care. I thought he would say something—a rebuke, an apology—anything. Instead, his emerald scales turned cloudy, and his head dipped.

He wasn't bowing at me, but at someone behind me. "Don't say anything," he hissed as he pushed me into a bow as well. "Be angry with me all you want, but hold it in until my mother goes away."

At the word *mother*, my curiosity overwhelmed my anger, and I looked up.

A shell-beaded curtain parted, and two women entered our company. Neither looked entirely human, but my attention turned immediately to the lady with the golden eyes. They were eyes I'd seen before, liquid and viscous—like amber meant to ensnare its prey.

Lady Solzaya: the dragon who'd tried to cut out my soul. *She* was Seryu's mother?

"Am I interrupting?" she purred.

Seryu plastered on his most charming smile, erasing any trace of our quarrel.

"Aunt Nahma," he exclaimed, greeting the lady at his mother's side. Genuine surprise lifted his thick green eyebrows. "I didn't expect to see you before the rites."

"I asked her to come," Solzaya replied before the lady

could speak for herself. "But really, Seryu, where are your manners? Shouldn't you greet your mother first? Or are you so relieved to see Nahma that you've forgotten the one who bore you?"

"I would never." Seryu straightened. "Mother. As always, even in your human form, you dazzle the stars."

Solzaya harrumphed. "It's far from my favorite form." She inclined her head in my direction. "But humans find us less intimidating this way."

She was wrong. Solzaya was the color of fire, blushing cinnabar and orange, like the brightest autumn trees. She was almost too brilliant to look at, and my eyes stung as they searched for the necklace gleaming against her collarbones.

Just like Gen had said, it was made of mirror shards. Seven, I counted. They looked like ordinary pieces of glass at first, but their shapes kept changing, from smooth teardrops to jagged knives so sharp they should have pierced Solzaya's delicate skin. A crisp reminder that she wasn't human at all.

"Welcome at last, Shiori'anma," Solzaya said. "I regret that our previous encounter was under such . . . unfortunate circumstances. Misunderstandings happen, even in a realm as enlightened as Ai'long. It gladdens me to have this second chance to receive you, and to ensure you have a proper introduction to Seryu's home."

"Oh, dungeons make for wondrous introductions," I said, not bothering to bury my sarcasm. "The boy turned to stone was a particularly welcoming touch."

Seryu shot me a glare to stay silent. "Shiori only recently

learned about our binding rites," he said. "She is still . . . acclimating to the news. But she is honored to be chosen."

"Undoubtedly you are, mortal child." Solzaya petted the top of my head. "You have been bequeathed the gift of immortality. I hope it will suit you as it suits Lady Nahma."

I'd forgotten about the woman at Solzaya's side. She was small and pale, with a thin, oval mouth and waist-long black hair that fell flat against her cheeks and back, gathering the shadows about her. Her arms hung woodenly at her sides, and her eyes had no spark of life to them.

If *that* was how immortality suited Lady Nahma, I wanted no part of it.

Solzaya was already circling me, the shards around her neck glinting as she assessed the bits of moss stuck in my hair, the scars on my hands, the circles under my eyes, and my plain, unadorned white robes.

Only when her gaze fell upon the Wraith's pearl, floating at my side, did a muscle in her cheek twitch. Desire for it made her skin flicker gold—for just the briefest of moments.

"Rather unremarkable, isn't she?" Solzaya said to Lady Nahma. "I would have thought the bloodsake of Kiata would have more presence, more beauty. Then again, what human is pleasing to the eye? There is much work to be done."

"What I lack in beauty, I make up for in strength of soul," I said, making a direct jab at Solzaya's earlier failure to cut my strands. I scooped the pearl into my satchel, not caring how petty the gesture was.

"Such pride," mused Solzaya. "I forget you are a princess

in your world. Human titles mean nothing to us—Lady Nahma was a peasant when she first came. But yes, I'll grant you that your soul is unusually strong." She paused. "It shall make a fine addition to Ai'long."

Annoyance mounted in my chest, and Kiki pinched my arm, warning me to stay calm.

While I gritted my teeth, Solzaya regarded her son. "Never once have you mentioned a desire to find a companion. I find it odd that you saw fit to bestow on this girl a piece of your pearl—"

"A very small piece," Seryu muttered.

"—especially before you've even reached your full form." Lady Solzaya touched her necklace, and the shards tinkled a soft, chiming song. "But His Eternal Majesty has approved your choice. It will be honored. Today."

"Today?" I repeated, my eyes widening.

"No need for such agitation. It will be a private affair, only for family."

That wasn't the reason I was agitated, and I was certain that Solzaya knew it.

"All of Seryu's cousins have already arrived," she went on, "and they have pledged not to try and kill you—or each other."

"All of them?" Seryu said with a frown. "I doubt Elang is making an appearance."

"The High Lord of the Westerly Seas knows better than to show his face at court," said Solzaya airily. "But maybe he'll come to see the pearl."

I glanced at Lady Nahma. She had been silent ever since

her arrival, her composure unruffled by Lady Solzaya's antagonism toward me. But at the mention of Seryu's cousin, Nahma's lips pursed ever so slightly.

I was the only one who noticed, and Nahma looked up from the ground, catching my stare.

Her eyes didn't glitter or gleam, as did the dragons'. Her eyes were moored to the earth and were brown, like mine. Easily overlooked. Easily capable of hiding a trove of secrets.

"You will be in good hands," Solzaya was saying. "Lady Nahma is my brother's wife, the honorable Lady of the Southerly Seas, and it isn't every day that she personally offers to prepare someone for the binding rites."

Nahma made a graceful bow. "I was one of the first companions ever selected in Ai'long," she said quietly. "I know better than most how difficult the change can be."

"Now, now, don't scare her off," Solzaya chided. "Have a care, Nahma. I don't want to live with a despondent son for the next millennium."

"Just kidnap him another princess, then," I said acidly. "We humans are all the same anyway. I doubt he'd notice."

The barb was meant for Seryu, but if he flinched, I didn't catch it. Solzaya's laughter was too distracting.

"Seryu, Seryu . . . ," she said, tilting her head back with amusement. "You've made an interesting choice. I look forward to seeing what Shiori'anma becomes."

The way she said it unsettled me. What she *becomes*.

"Now, you both have lingered enough," Solzaya said. "Say your goodbyes. You'll not see each other again until the ceremony."

Seryu caught my sleeve before I turned away. "Remember what I told you."

"That you're saving my life?" I dipped my head into a mock bow. I was still furious with him. "Thank you, Prince Seryu. I look forward to finding out what I *become*."

"You'll find Aunt Nahma's company pleasant, I'm sure," he said, ignoring my tart remarks. *More pleasant than my mother's,* he left unsaid. "She'll take good care of you."

"The way you did?" I replied. My words were low, though I was sure Solzaya and Nahma could hear. "I thought you were my friend, Seryu. I trusted you."

Seryu's laugh had little humor to it.

"I know," he said, and as he let go of me, a wave of water swept me off my feet and carried me deep into the Dragon King's palace.

CHAPTER FIVE

An aggressive current jostled me forward, forcing me to trail Lady Solzaya and Lady Nahma down a wing of green marble pillars. I fought back as best as I could, and at some point I must have successfully annoyed Solzaya, for the mirror shards on her neck popped off and flew to my side, each bearing the dragon's irritated reflection.

She spoke through the shards. "The longer you detain us, the less time you'll have for your farewells."

Even if I had known what she was talking about, I wouldn't have cared.

My every thought was dedicated to devising a means of escape. My options were bleak. The walls emitted a siren when I edged too close, alerting everyone to my movements. And sharks, jellyfish, and octopuses patrolled every corner. The palace was far too well secured.

You should smile, whispered Kiki from inside my sleeve. *Tell a few jokes. Sing a song. Maybe then Seryu's mother will let down her guard.*

I gritted my teeth. "It's a little too late to ingratiate myself, don't you think?"

Solzaya's mirror shards glinted in agreement. They nipped at my heels, pushing me insistently forward.

Soon my surroundings transformed. The singing walls vanished, and the marble columns stretched into long walls that closed off my view of the open seas.

One of Solzaya's shards scraped my cheek, and the water gathered in strength, scooping me up and delivering me to the dragon's side.

Seryu's mother clucked her tongue. "You're wasting your time looking for an escape. The halls change at my whim, and the palace is impossible for humans to navigate. Nowhere in Ai'long can you hide a pearl as dark and abominable as the one you carry."

"I wasn't looking for an escape," I lied.

The dragon's golden eyes danced with mirth. "It's funny. Most mortals would beg to be in your position. During Nahma's time, humans threw themselves into the ocean for a chance to become our companions." Solzaya paused deliberately. "I suppose you and Nahma have your resistance in common. Both of you did start out with a death sentence."

I sent a curious glance at Nahma, but she was silent as ever.

"That isn't how the story is told on land," I said. "People didn't willingly throw themselves into the sea. They were kidnapped. Or sacrificed to appease your kind."

"Humans have a terrible memory," replied Solzaya. "To

48

be expected, given your short lives. Consider yourself blessed, Shiori'anma. Other bloodsakes perished before reaching the age of eighteen, but you . . . you will live forever. Here, with us."

"You dragons have a deluded sense of what it means to be fortunate," I muttered.

"Would you prefer to endure a selection rite, as Lady Nahma did? Because that can be arranged."

"The entire affair is barbaric."

"Is it so different in your realm? You had an arrangement to be married, did you not? To a young lord in the North, I saw."

At the mention of Takkan, my heart skipped. "You saw?"

"The mirror of truth showed me plenty about the life you left." Lady Solzaya leaned close. "Poor Bushi'an Takkan. He misses you so. You can ask to see him yourself—one last time."

All at once I deflated.

Solzaya chuckled smugly. "I'm curious to see how immortality suits you. Many have gone mad, but I have faith you'll keep your wits, bloodsake. You have more spirit than most."

"I don't plan on being here long enough to satisfy your curiosity," I retorted, but my words lacked conviction, and Solzaya knew it.

She petted my head again, then she surged forward, her long gossamer sleeves brushing against my arms as if motioning for me to follow. I recoiled from their touch.

Hopelessness rose like a stone in my throat. How was I going to get out of here? Even if my magic *was* at full strength, it wasn't enough to put up a fight against the Dragon King. All I had was the pearl. . . .

You can't use the pearl, Kiki said, invading my thoughts. *It might break.*

"If it does, at least it'd take all of Ai'long down with me."

And me! cried my paper bird. *Think of me, at least. Scattered in tiny pieces in the ocean forever. I'll be devoured by shrimp! Or . . . or become sea foam! I'm not meant to become sea foam.*

"No, you're not," I agreed, and then grimaced. In a kingdom where time was eternal, how ironic was it that mine was running out?

Someone touched my arm. "Look," said Lady Nahma, pointing at one of the gemmed mirrors engraved into the wall. "The glass here reflects the sky above. Imurinya smiles upon the seas."

All I saw was an endless abyss of dark water.

"Her mortal eyes are too weak to perceive it," said Solzaya snidely.

Nahma wasn't deterred. "Look closer." She pointed at a flutter in the waves. "The bend of silver in the waters. That is a reflection of Imurinya."

"I see it," I said softly.

"We too revere the lady of the moon in Ai'long," Nahma replied. "When her light is at its most powerful, so are the dragons' pearls. It's a good omen that she is bright on your binding day. I hope that will be of comfort to you."

It was not, but unlike Solzaya, Nahma meant well. I couldn't help warming to her.

"You'll learn to take such sights for granted soon enough," said Seryu's mother dismissively. "Once you're a companion, there will be far more important things on your mind."

"Such as?" The words came out before I could stop them. Much as I dreaded the binding ceremony, I was curious about how the dragons lived.

Solzaya smiled. "Securing an heir for my son, naturally."

I balked, wishing I hadn't asked. "An heir?"

"Ours is a dwindling race, Shiori'anma. You didn't think sacred beings such as dragons would welcome humans into our realm simply for company?"

Honestly, I hadn't given it any thought. "Is that . . . even possible?"

"It will be." She laughed at my horror. "Once you become a companion, you won't exactly be human anymore."

She'd alluded to my changing before, but never in any detail. Lady Nahma's appearance offered no hints, either: with her long black hair and her modest gown, she looked like a priestess at a shrine.

So why was the dread in my heart mounting?

An arched bronze mirror appeared, marking the end of what had seemed a perpetual hallway. Its craftsmanship was exquisite, with five dragons each holding its own pearl.

We stopped in front of it, and my reflection gave me a leery stare. Back home, my eyes were famous for their mischief, my lips for their sly and impish curve. But the reflection I saw was of a girl who was lost. A girl who *had* lost.

That couldn't be me.

"This is where you will prepare for the ceremony," said

Solzaya, the pitch of her voice rising as she dramatically gestured at the bronze mirror. "Where you will take your last breaths as a mortal of land."

Too late I started to back away.

The mirror glass turned liquid, melting into two silvery arms that slid around my ankles. Before I could run, they gave a wrench.

And into the mirror I flew, spiraling deeper into the Dragon King's lair—to my doom.

CHAPTER SIX

I landed on soft carpet, facing a shell-encrusted ceiling with floating lanterns. Chests and trunks lined the walls, each flowing with the most extravagant, impossible raiment I had ever seen. Dresses woven out of abalone and moonlight, skirts that were cascading waterfalls, shawls painted with butterfly wings and flamefish fins, and jackets embroidered with peonies whose petals moved to an imaginary breeze.

As I pulled myself upright, Lady Nahma glided into view. "Solzaya is gone. She'll not return until you are ready for the ceremony."

Was that an explanation or a warning?

"There is food, should you require nourishment," Nahma continued. "The rites will not be long, but some find comfort partaking in delicacies from their homeland."

She gestured at a table that I swore had not been there a moment ago. On it was a spread of Kiatan sweets: rice cakes with toasted sesame seeds, phoenix-wing candies, and steamed buns bursting with pumpkin custard. A porcelain bowl was filled to the brim with fresh, plump peaches.

I inhaled, hating how insolently familiar the aromas were. I couldn't ignore them even if I wanted to.

"Eat," she urged, helping herself to tea. "You'll need your strength."

As she poured, the steam curled around the rim of the cup. But I didn't budge.

"It isn't poisoned, Shiori'anma."

I didn't trust her, and she knew she couldn't convince me.

"Very well. Then we shall begin." Lady Nahma set down her cup, and it floated in the water. "How you attire yourself for the ceremony is of utmost importance. This will be the court's first impression of you, and dragons are quick to judge."

She clapped, and the chests exhibited their wares. "Take anything that speaks to you," she instructed. "Jewels, combs, gowns, jackets."

Nothing called out to me. There were no swords, daggers, or poisoned darts. No vines of starstroke or torches of demonfire.

Everything was just so pretty. And useless.

There were bone hairpins that made one's tresses grow longer, sand silk robes with embroidered fish that danced when I touched them. There were lace ribbons scalloped with threads of dawn, and jewels that made the wearer ravishingly beautiful. Out of curiosity, I held an agate brooch to my chest—and watched, aghast, as my eyes turned bluer than a kitebird, my cheeks bloomed with a pleasing flush, and my lips became full.

I threw the brooch back into its chest. My situation was on the narrow edge of hysterical and hopeless.

"If the dressing rites do not interest you, I shall help you choose." Nahma motioned for one of the chests to approach. "What about this one?"

She held up a silk gown in a muted shade of pink that reminded me of the begonia trees at home. Seafoam lace embellished the long fluted sleeves, which were as gossamer-thin as spiderwebs, and countless tiny pearls beaded the skirt. It was the humblest choice by far, but still far richer than anything I'd ever owned.

I gave a reluctant nod, and Lady Nahma reached for my satchel, which had no place among such fine things.

I refused to hand it over. "The Wraith's pearl is inside. I'm to present it to the king."

Nahma gave me a wary stare, which I returned.

It wasn't a lie. I *was* to present it to the king; I just had no intention of doing so.

"Very well," she said finally. "You may keep it."

She didn't speak to me again until I was dressed, painted and powdered, and properly adorned. A refreshingly speedy process, after which she made a low whistle. It wasn't a comment of approval on my appearance, as I thought at first, but a summons—

Hundreds of tiny fish swam through the walls. Each carried a glass shard in its mouth, which they pieced together within a wooden frame. When they were finished, the shards fluxed and fused, creating a mirror.

It was taller than me by a head, its glass thick and clean, the frame veined with gold. A strangely familiar magic hummed from within its glass, but the mirror itself didn't look particularly special, and neither did my reflection.

Nahma had woven an emperor's ransom of pearls and opals into my hair, and adorned my ears, neck, and wrists with more wealth than all the pirates of Lor'yan might amass in their lifetimes. Still, all the glittering treasures in the sea could not mask the hard defiance in my eyes, or change me from Shiori into a nameless dragon concubine.

I took heart in that. At least for now.

"This is the mirror of truth," I said.

It wasn't a question, but Nahma gifted me with a nod. "It is Lady Solzaya's most prized treasure, won in a wager with one of the first enchanters. Since then, it has been a part of the ceremony's tradition."

Dragons do love to gamble, I thought.

"There were only a handful of shards on Lady Solzaya's necklace," I remarked. "Why did hundreds appear just now?"

"There are seven shards to Lady Solzaya's mirror of truth, each of equal sight and power. During the rare occasion that they are not in her possession—for example, a rite such as this—she conceals them among ordinary mirror pieces so that they may not be stolen."

"Stolen," I said slowly. "By companions such as yourself?"

"I have no desire to possess the mirror of truth."

"But weren't your memories taken away when you made

the oath to Ai'long?" I couldn't help the acidity of my words. "Wouldn't you want to remember your past?"

The barest flicker crossed Nahma's features. "The changing is different for all. I happen to remember more than most." She focused on putting away a pair of hairpins. "It has been a curse as well as a blessing. Some things are best forgotten."

"What do you remember?" I probed.

For a long time, Nahma said nothing. I had given up hope that she'd respond when finally she replied:

"In my time, things were different. Dragons weren't legends, and if a nation did not make proper sacrifices to the seas, the dragons would steal its sons and daughters from the shores. Among those given to Ai'long, a few were chosen to become companions through rites of selection."

I remembered. "Solzaya said that was how you ended up here."

"Yes. My year, there were twelve."

Her flat response made me frown. "What happened to the other eleven?"

"I visit them from time to time, whenever I visit this palace." Nahma's expression was inscrutable. "They stand in King Nazayun's weeping garden."

My throat shriveled as I grasped her meaning. The eleven had been turned to stone.

"Why?" I whispered.

"Because of the Oath of Ai'long. All under the Dragon King's domain are bound to it. Immortals are not invincible, Shiori'anma, not even dragons. The oath ensures that no dragon shall harm another without the gravest of consequences. Visitors to Ai'long are unbound by such a promise, which makes them dangerous."

My jaw locked. "Like Gen."

Through our reflections in the mirror, Nahma's gaze met mine. "Like Gen," she repeated.

"So Nazayun will condemn a child just for trespassing?"

"Gen isn't as innocent as he looks."

"Because he tried to steal something?" I said. "A dragon asked him to do it—he's not a thief."

"He tried to steal the *mirror of truth*," Nahma said pointedly. "No mortal would be aware of such an ancient treasure anymore. And no mortal would be able to infiltrate Ai'long unless aided by someone very powerful, and very dangerous. Lady Solzaya has interrogated the boy for months about which dragon that might be, but he hasn't said anything."

"Because he doesn't know!" I cried.

"That is of no consequence. He won't have long."

"He's just a boy. Don't you care? Can't you do anything?"

"It is not my place," said Nahma.

"Then you really aren't human anymore."

I meant for my words to sting, but Nahma was unmoved. "Some would say I never was."

Her words were so soft I wasn't sure whether I had heard correctly. I frowned. "What did you just s—"

"You will find," Nahma interrupted, steering the topic elsewhere, "that dragons feel little empathy, and even less love. It is to your fortune that you will be bound to Seryu'ginan. He is better than most."

Better than most. "What an inspiring endorsement."

"It is the truth," Nahma said. "I will not lie to you, Shiori'anma. But if you will not listen, then I will send for someone else to attire you. This task is one I rarely undertake, but I thought to make an exception for you. For who you are."

"The bloodsake of Kiata?"

"No. The daughter of the Nameless Queen."

My eyes flew up, the thoughts spinning in my head coming to an abrupt halt. "You knew my stepmother?"

"She was married through a ritual not so different from ours." A small, hard smile played on Nahma's lips. "A contest, if you will. Every king and prince sought her hand, and every enchanter and demon sought the pearl in her heart."

"Dragons too," I said darkly.

As I said it, Nahma pinned a last strand of opals into my hair. "Many from Ai'long styled themselves as human suitors to enter the contest. Even our king himself considered it. Back then, we did not know she possessed the Wraith's pearl."

"What happened?" I asked. Raikama's life before coming to Kiata was a mystery to me, and I was desperate to hear more.

"I am not a well of the past, put here to slake your thirst," she said, not unkindly. "I tell you of your stepmother's history because she was different from the others—as you are. And as I was." A pause. "I give you the warning I wish I'd had."

"Warning?" I echoed.

Lady Nahma drew back her hair, revealing the gills along her neck and cheekbones. She rolled up her sleeves, showing

59

me the fins glistening on the underside of her arms, and as she splayed her fingers, I could see their iridescent webbing. Lastly, she lifted her skirt. In place of human legs was a fish-tail, violet like summer bellflowers.

I couldn't hide my awe—and horror. "You're a . . . a . . ."

"A sea maid," she said, as if it were the most natural thing. "Our realm is not far from Ai'long. You likely saw a few on your way into the palace."

I was still staring. With her fins and tail, she could never go back to land, even if she wanted to. "Is that what will happen to me?"

"Every companion's experience is different," she replied dispassionately. "Many become sea maids, while others retain a more human physique. It's hard to predict. But the changes will be permanent—a small price to pay for eternal life."

I wasn't convinced she believed her own words.

Letting her hair fall back in place, Nahma rolled down her sleeves and summoned forth the mirror. I'd forgotten about it. "Now for the last part of the preparations: the final farewells."

The mirror started to sing again, vibrating like a moon lute being strummed. I ventured a step closer, and the glass rippled.

"This mirror . . . ," I began, staring. The glass was looking more and more like a pool of water. "It feels . . . Kiatan."

"I'm not surprised it speaks to you," allowed Nahma. "The mirror of truth was forged from the Seven Tears of Emuri'en."

I drew back, letting Nahma's words sink in.

Emuri'en was Kiata's goddess of love and fate, who oversaw the destinies of mortals, using strands of her hair. Each strand she cut and dyed red—the color of strength and blood—and upon her instruction, her thousand cranes flew to earth to tie mortals' fates together. But her fondness for humans was so great that she overspent her power and lost her godhood. Cast away from heaven, she wept, and her tears scattered across Kiata, leaving seven magical ponds that offered a glimpse at the threads of destiny.

The Seven Tears of Emuri'en.

When I was younger, I'd always dismissed it as a legend. But thanks to Raikama, I learned that the Tears of Emuri'en were real.

Consulting its waters was how she'd known early on that I was Kiata's bloodsake, and that I was in danger.

I spoke through the lump forming in my throat. "Will I . . . will I be able to speak with my family?"

Nahma gave me a pitying look. "No, even with the aid of magic as ancient as the mirror's, the dragon and human realms cannot overlap."

"But you said it was a farewell—"

"The final farewell is a time to reflect on the life you leave behind." She spoke over me and gestured at the mirror. "Inquire of the past or present, and it will show you what you are meant to see. No more, no less."

Inquire of the past or present? The lump in my throat dissolved. If the mirror held such power, I could ask it about the Wraith's pearl! Perhaps I could even find a way out of the Dragon King's tortuous palace.

I smothered my excitement, drawing a sour line with my lips so Nahma couldn't possibly know what I was thinking. Yet her face suddenly darkened, and she saw fit to warn me, very quietly: "Be careful what you seek. Lady Solzaya observes from the other side, and any questions about the Wraith will be a waste of your time. The mirror cannot touch the realm in which he lives."

I frowned. "How did you know—"

"Your time begins now," Nahma said, and she stepped through the wall, disappearing without another word.

Kiki flitted out of my sleeve. *This isn't really the last time we see home, is it?*

Nahma's tea floated by, and I cupped it in my hands.

"I won't let it be," I replied. "Maybe I can enchant away the elixir during the ceremony."

It's worth a try.

With all my might, I focused on the tea, commanding its contents to steam out of the cup in little misty tendrils.

But the tea only spurted, narrowly avoiding my face and splattering against the mirror.

"Strands of Emuri'en!" I cursed, hurrying to wipe it.

At my touch, the glass flickered and warbled, its low hum turning into a birdsong I had heard every spring and summer of my life.

Kitebirds.

They crooned, too clearly for me to have imagined it. I blinked, inching closer to the mirror. The glass had stopped flickering. Now it panned across a hazy expanse, as if searching for what it wanted to show me.

Chrysanthemums. Little buds and blossoms on the cherry and plum trees. The petals hailed down over a round latticed window whose elaborate geometric designs I had seen plenty of times but could not remember where—

The mirror pushed through the window. And there were my six brothers.

They were so close, so vivid, I could see the threads on their silk hats, the tea stains on Wandei's collar, and the wax shining in Yotan's hair—cut to the latest fashion, as suited him. I wanted to reach out and touch them, to call their names. But my brothers were gathered around a bed, and once I saw whom they were watching, all I could do was hold my breath.

Father.

Spring had come, and as Raikama had promised, the spell of slumber she had cast over Gindara had lifted. The city was awakening, and my father with it.

"Look!" Yotan whispered, pointing. "He's waking."

Dawn slipped through the latticed window, imbuing the emperor with splendid patterns of light. He blinked, his eyes slowly fluttering open.

Joy and homesickness tugged at my heart, pulling my emotions in opposite directions. How I wished I could be there to see Father. To be there with my brothers when he awoke.

I bit my cheek, trying to hold myself strong. Trying not to fixate on the months I'd lost while in Ai'long. At least my family was well. My father, my brothers . . .

"What of Takkan?" I whispered to the mirror.

63

At the question, the glass flickered again. The vision of the emperor and princes vanished, and the mirror turned its focus from the palace on the Sacred Lake to deep in the woods. Fire ravaged the forests, racing through the trees and leaving the nearby villages smoldering.

Then came the Holy Mountains. I recognized them straightaway, but there was something different about the mountain in the center.

Its face bore a jagged scar that hadn't been there before. As the mirror brought me closer, a wisp of smoke stole out of the scarlet rock. And my heart went still.

In one breath, the wisp unfurled into a creature I had prayed I'd never see again.

The Wolf.

He sprang forth, his misty gray coat more shadow than fur, his blood-red eyes as fiery as the scarred rock that had borne him. The Holy Mountains trembled.

Bandur, rasped the demons within, in a fearsome chorus. *King of Demons.*

The name latched on to my thoughts like a ghost. I'd never heard it before, yet it chilled me. *Bandur.*

"No!" I whispered. That was impossible. Bandur couldn't be free. My stepmother and I had sealed the mountains!

The mirror would show me no more. It cracked and cleaved into shards again, but the tiny fish did not return to take them away. Instead, the shards drifted aimlessly around the chamber.

I was so shaken by what I'd seen, I barely noticed that

Nahma had returned. *Kiki, I can't go through with this. I have to go home. I—*

I stopped, my thoughts cut off by an invisible string.

If you wish to ever see your home again, Nahma's voice pushed into my mind, *then you must go to the ceremony.*

I gasped, shocked by her words as well as by what she'd done. "You . . . you—"

I was born able to sense thoughts. Nahma let go of my arm. Under the veil of her long black bangs, her eyes turned white, dark pupils disappearing. *It helped me win the selection rites, and gain the trust of even Lady Solzaya. She sees much through the mirror of hers, but it cannot read the mind or heart. She will assume I am telling you of my experiences as a companion.*

I met her gaze. *So this is what you meant when you said you weren't really human.*

Nahma's eyes were cold. *I was unwanted, like your stepmother. When my parents learned of my magic, they threw me into the sea, to the dragons. On land, magic is feared. Here, it is revered.*

I swallowed hard, wondering what my father would think once he learned of my own talents. *How will going to the ceremony help me find my way home?*

I've heard you are a resourceful girl, Nahma replied. *You'll find a way.* She tossed me a peach. *Eat. Your power is weakened here, but even a bite will replenish some strength.*

I rolled the peach in my hand, still skeptical that it might be poisoned. In Kiatan legend, peaches were the fruit of the gods, and one particular tree in their gardens bestowed immortality.

I can try first, if you want, Kiki offered. *I don't mind living forever.*

Very funny. What makes you think they'd poison it with immortality?

Kiki shrugged. *I'm an optimist.*

No, you're not.

When I finally ate, Nahma eyed my paper bird warily. *You'd do well to keep that bird hidden too, unless she wants to become a pebble.*

Kiki slid behind my collar, and I set down the peach. *Why are you helping me?*

Because King Nazayun should not have the Wraith's pearl. She paused. *Because there is another in Ai'long who can help you. I have seen the Wraith in his mind.*

It was hard for me to hold in my curiosity. *Who?*

I cannot say. She spun me to face the mirror. *But he will desire the pearl even more than Nazayun. Present it at the ceremony, and he will come.*

Easy for her to say. If I drank the elixir, I wouldn't even remember my name, let alone be able to interrogate the dragon she spoke of. But she was right: I *was* resourceful.

"Now," she said, speaking aloud once more so Solzaya could hear, "are you ready?"

What choice did I have? I gave a small, uncertain nod.

There was no turning back.

CHAPTER SEVEN

Solzaya had lied about the ceremony being an intimate affair.

Over a hundred dragons had come. They sat on giant plates of coral—clouds, Nahma called them, since they floated in the water. Most dragons wore some kind of an unconvincingly human form; they didn't bother to hide their horns and whiskers and claws—some even had tails curling out from under their jackets. From their snickers and giggles, I could tell it was a game to make the mortal feel uncomfortable.

I shouldn't have given them the satisfaction. But as I glided into the ritual dome, surrounded by a room full of rapt dragons, I really did feel like a pig. Especially thanks to the cursed pink dress I was wearing.

"You're the first sorceress to become a companion," said Nahma, though I hadn't asked. "Not to mention, a dragon prince's companion. Of course they will stare."

While she escorted me to the highest tier of clouds, a gray-spotted whale announced my arrival. A trio of octopuses blew into conch shells once she had brought me to Seryu's side.

I hardly recognized him in his princely finery. In place of his usual emerald robes, he wore a silver jacket studded with blue pearls, and his green hair, which I'd never seen untamed, had been braided and tucked under a tasseled cap. He was taller than I remembered, his shoulders broader too. He'd grown since the first time I'd met him. He looked more regal, more handsome—but also more like a stranger. Aside from the slightest twitch of his nose, he didn't acknowledge me when I landed on his cloud.

"Thank you for your part in the rites, Aunt Nahma," he said, still ignoring me. "You have honored me greatly."

Nahma murmured a few perfunctory blessings, then ascended to the highest cloud, where Lady Solzaya sat with the lords and ladies of the South, North, and East. The Lord of the Westerly Seas' seat was empty, just as Seryu had predicted it would be.

I leaned back against a spine of coral, aiming to sit sullenly still, but my mind was spinning. Could Elang be the dragon Nahma had promised I'd meet?

I'd meant to keep the silence between Seryu and me, mostly out of petulance, but my tongue had other ideas. "Why does Elang never come to the palace?"

Seryu glared at me sidelong. "Is that really what you want to ask me right now?"

"Would you rather I slap you again for getting me into this mess?"

The dragon's glare darkened. He growled, "Elang is different."

"How?"

Seryu wouldn't say any more. His gaze roamed over the glossy pink gown Nahma had attired me in, fixing on the weatherworn satchel at my hip. "Whatever tricks you have in mind, don't. Every dragon of importance is here right now. They're watching as we speak."

"Then let them hear this," I said acidly. "I hope you rot in the Nine Hells, Seryu."

Seryu's red eyes flashed. "I'm doing my best to help you. The least you could do is pretend to like me. Or is not humiliating me in front of my entire family too much to ask?"

"Is not killing me in front of your entire family too much to ask? Or does it not count, since I'll be reborn *stronger* and *better*?"

Seryu hung back as if stung, and I almost regretted my harsh words. Almost.

"I never should have said that," he said, his red eyes downcast. "I'm sorry."

The plaintive chord in his voice struck me, and though I wanted to stay angry, the fire in my temper went out. "I know you didn't mean for things to go this way."

For a short eternity, he leaned over the ridged edge of our cloud, his arms folded. When he spoke again, his voice was low. "You wouldn't be a concubine, you know. You'd be my bride. My equal." He went on quickly, before I could reply. "I know that doesn't make it much better, but I thought you should know."

I leaned forward too and glanced down at the hundred dragons. They *were* watching. "Seems annoying gossipy relatives aren't unique to the mortal realm."

"Indeed not," said Seryu, still pensive. "A dragon's binding ceremony is one of our oldest rites. It's supposed to be founded on love and trust, but more often than not, it serves as a mere transaction."

I had some experience with that.

"I didn't want mine to be that way," he confessed. "I was hoping, if it turned out to be you, that you would want to be here. Because you cared for me."

"I do care for you."

It was the truth, and I thought of our summer together, idling by the Sacred Lake and exchanging quips about magic and sorcery. I cared for him then, and I still cared for him now.

"Would it be so bad, staying with me?" he said quietly. "I'd make sure you were safe. I could do that for you. I've always done that for you. I deserve a fair chance, don't I?"

He did, and I'd be lying if I said I had given him one.

At my silence, Seryu reached for my hand. I let him rest his palm on mine. His skin was cold, but not in an unpleasant way, and I felt the tiniest spark as his green nails curled gently around my fingers.

I gazed at our hands. What if I did stay in Ai'long? Would it be so tragic, marrying Seryu? He was handsome and fun . . . and fond of me. Maybe even in love with me.

I'd be a princess of dragons with sparkling gills on my neck and arms. I'd chase turtles and whales with Seryu, get on Solzaya's nerves as often as I could, try on magical dresses with Lady Nahma, and uncover all of Ai'long's secrets. I'd live forever.

No one here would think twice about me being the blood-sake. Like Seryu said, Kiata might even be safer if I didn't return. Father could find a sorcerer who'd seal Bandur back into the mountains, and that would be the end of it. The demons would be trapped forever, and no more bloodsakes would die. Magic would stay buried in Kiata, just like everyone wanted. Instead of being blamed, I'd become a legend.

"Kiss me," I murmured to Seryu.

Seryu stared at me, thunderstruck. But he nodded, and the dragons cheered, drumming their claws on their coral balconies as he bent forward.

His hand was still on mine, and his lips were just a breath away. My heart hammered in my chest. I'd kissed plenty of boys before. What difference did it make to kiss Seryu?

The difference came stampeding into my thoughts.

Takkan.

I breathed out, my heart suddenly light and heavy all at once.

More than anything, I wanted to throw my arms around Takkan. I wanted to see his shoulders square with embarrassment when I quoted passages from letters he wrote me as a boy, to rest my chin on his shoulder and fall asleep to the lilt of his songs. To catch him staring when I wasn't looking, and tease him until the corners of his warm eyes crinkled.

To finally tell him I loved him.

But if I ever returned to Kiata, I'd be branded a sorceress— and blamed for Bandur escaping the mountains. Was a future with Takkan even possible?

All I knew was that I'd risk everything to find out.

I turned my cheek. "Wait—" I started to say, but I didn't need to. Seryu had seen the emotions warring on my face. He was already retreating. Before I could explain, he sank back in his seat and crossed one leg over the other.

"You know, I prefer not to kiss princesses in pink," he demurred, waving off the disappointed crowds below with a semi-believable smirk. "Something about the color just isn't . . . alluring."

He was trying to save his pride, and I knew I should let it go. But I couldn't.

"It's not you." I faltered, my words all twisted and knotted. "You know it isn't."

"Part of me hoped you wouldn't say that." He touched my cheek, then let his hand fall back to his lap. "It was worth a try. Hold on to that lordling of yours when they make you drink. They say your last thought is the only memory you keep."

The elixir! I had almost forgotten about it. "Seryu, how do I . . ."

Instead of answering, Seryu plucked Kiki off the railing and set her on my collar. His response was so low I almost didn't hear him. "Stay hidden."

I didn't know whether that was meant for me or for Kiki, and I never got a chance to ask.

A distant chime pealed, the sound reverberating around the dome. The ceremony was beginning.

Out of a cloud of shimmering sand, the Dragon King burst into the hall. He still wore the starstroke net, styled into a sash around his waist. It radiated with demonfire, the strands of fate, and the blood of stars—the three magics I had labored for months to interweave.

Under Nazayun's feet emerged a dais—constructed of whale and shark skulls. Kiki shuddered at the sight.

Why would anyone want to work for him? she whispered to me, glancing at the swarms of sharks and squid patrolling the chamber.

Because they didn't have a choice, I thought as the Dragon King took his throne.

Lady Nahma had warned me that the rites would be quick, but I was still expecting some sort of pompous introduction. None came, and my cloud rattled, rising until it was level with the Dragon King's throne.

Beside the king, Lady Solzaya and Lady Nahma waited, poised like mistress and handmaiden. Seryu's mother held a bowl carved of abalone shell in her long palm, and Nahma held a thin silken cord. The latter was a nod to Kiatan wedding traditions, where the bride and groom were knotted together.

Takkan and I would have been married like this, I thought with a pang. *If only I hadn't run away from our betrothal ceremony, how different life might have been.*

"Come forward, Shiori'anma," Lady Solzaya said, shattering my reverie. Her iron grip claimed my arms, and I floated with her to the Dragon King's dais. Seryu started to follow, but Solzaya motioned for him to remain.

I could read the anxiety in his expression.

Don't do anything too reckless, it said.

I wished I could summon a smile. *I'll try.*

"His Eternal Majesty has deemed Princess Shiori worthy of taking the Oath of Ai'long," said Solzaya. "In this hour, she shall leave behind her mortal life and reawaken as the companion to my son, First Prince of the Easterly Seas, Seryu'ginan."

"Hold out your hands," Lady Nahma said, "so Lady Solzaya might bestow upon you the elixir of immortality."

I glanced at her, apprehension roiling in my gut. How far into the ceremony would I have to play along?

She provided no answers. She'd closed her mind to me.

Woodenly, I held my hands out.

Solzaya placed the abalone bowl between my outstretched palms, murmuring words in a tongue I could not understand.

Inside was the elixir. A tiny cerulean bead, small enough to balance on my thumb.

I almost sighed with relief. I'd expected a soup or even a tea, but the elixir was no more substantial than a pill one took for a stomach ailment. It looked like jelly, wobbling as my hands shook.

While Solzaya spoke, I lifted the bowl, pretending to press it to my lips.

Invisible fumes tickled my nostrils, sweet and bitter at the same time. One sniff, and all the doubts and fears I'd buried bubbled high, but I kept my mind focused on seeing Takkan again. On going home.

How are we going to do this? Kiki said, leaping into the bowl and using her wing to block me from accidentally drinking.

Roll it down my collar quick, I said. *Can you manage?*

Using her wing, Kiki tried to scoop the elixir toward my neck, but the potion was too slippery. *It isn't as easy as it looks!*

"Is something the matter, Shiori'anma?" Lady Solzaya asked, floating into my periphery. "Do you need help drinking?"

I was never given the chance to respond. Solzaya's hand shot out and tipped the bowl against my mouth.

Panic surged in my blood as Kiki fell back in the bowl. All too quickly, the bead of liquid slid down to my lips, and Kiki bolted out of my collar into the bowl.

With one gulp, she devoured the elixir.

Kiki, no!

It was too late. The potion had lodged itself into her paper throat, making her long neck gleam blue. The silvery-gold flourishes on her wings faded, like blotted ink, as she teetered on the edge of the bowl and fell back into my sleeve. Against the crook of my elbow, I felt her go still.

Heat swelled in my throat. *Kiki!*

No answer.

My heart thundered in my ears. I wanted nothing more than to scoop her up and hold her close, but King Nazayun and Lady Solzaya were watching me intently.

Lady Nahma took the bowl. "Shiori'anma has drunk," she announced before anyone else could speak.

Through our minds, she warned, *Blank your face. Try to look tired.*

I relaxed my muscles. It was easy to make myself go cold,

to make my body deflate. I could barely move, let alone think straight. All I could think about was Kiki, crumpled against my elbow.

"Bow and present the pearl," instructed Nahma.

"I am ready to proceed with the ceremony," I said, bowing deeply. My voice sounded flat, any sign of rebellion vanquished. But inside my chest, anger stirred. "Allow me to present the Wraith's pearl."

I opened my satchel. Elang was nowhere in sight, and I couldn't count on his arrival to save me from the rest of the rites. Kiki had sacrificed too much for me to fail.

My fingers closed around the broken pearl. *I won't be any good to you if I'm bound to Ai'long forever,* I told it, praying it would hear me. *If you want me to bring you back to the Wraith, help me get out of here. Help me defeat the Dragon King.*

I rose from my bow. The pearl tingled in my grasp, a promising sign.

"Wait!" Nazayun barked.

Wait? I struggled to keep my face blank, to keep playing along. The jewels hanging from my headdress tinkled, but I didn't dare look up from my feet.

"Search her."

To my relief, it was Lady Nahma—not Seryu's mother—who stepped forward. *Help me, Nahma.* I reached out to her as she searched me. *Kiki's unconscious. She drank the elixir. Help me. Please.*

Nahma raised my sleeves, looking inside. The edge of

Kiki's wings grazed my elbow, and I held my breath, certain that Nahma would pretend she had seen nothing.

But she gave my sleeve a shake and plucked Kiki by the beak. "What have we here?" Nahma murmured. "A paper bird."

I went numb with betrayal. What was she doing?

"An *enchanted* paper bird." Nahma held Kiki high for all to see. Kiki's beak still glowed blue from the elixir, and her neck drooped limply.

"Give her back!" I cried.

Nahma did no such thing. She pinched Kiki by the neck, squeezing the elixir from the bird's throat. Then she crumpled Kiki in her fist.

"No!" I screamed.

I launched myself at Lady Nahma, but the dais gave a tumultuous shudder. It tilted, and I slid uncontrollably toward the Dragon King.

His eyes clouded with fury. "If you will not complete the ritual of forgetting, then we must find a punishment you will remember for the rest of your days." He flung me onto Seryu's cloud and barked, "Bring the boy."

The boy?

My anger at Lady Nahma vanished, replaced by fear.

In the center of the chamber, surrounded by sharks, my fellow prisoner Gen arose on a stream of bubbles.

In the hours since I'd last seen him, Solzaya's curse had progressed quickly. He was unconscious now, his eyes closed and his bottom lip already turned to stone. His cheeks looked sunken in, as if he'd been trying to gasp before the curse over-came him. The fingers that had hurled glass to wake me were completely gray, still outstretched in a gesture of defiance.

"Let him go," I appealed to Nazayun. "He's only a child."

I might as well have pleaded with the sharks.

"Soon he will be new gravel for the bedrocks," Nazayun responded, the fair hairs of his beard crackling with light-ning. "If you will not forget your past, then you will remem-ber the pain you inflicted on this boy. It will be a scar you bear forever."

Splotches of grisly gray appeared on Gen's face, spread-ing fast, like spilt ink. As the lightning in Nazayun's beard rippled, the boy's eyes bulged and his temples convulsed with pain. He was seconds from turning entirely into stone. Sec-onds from being blasted into a pile of rubble.

"Stop!" I cried.

Seryu held me back, but I threw up my satchel to release the pearl.

"Help Gen!" I shouted to it. "Help him!"

The Wraith's pearl didn't even float out of my bag. It was a deadweight in the satchel.

The dragons jeered, and I cursed. Stupid, treacherous pearl. Without its help, Gen would surely die.

King Nazayun was laughing along with his guests. "Sit back down, Shiori'anma," he said. "You'll have your moment soon enough."

I wouldn't sit. With a hard thrust of my shoulder, I twisted out of Seryu's grip and dove toward Gen. The jeers and laughs only multiplied. The sharks were nearly upon me.

"Help," I pleaded with the pearl, shaking it. "Help!"

A low growl resonated from outside the hall. At first I thought it was the pearl, at last responding to my pleas, but as the sound drew nearer and louder and nearer and louder—

In one calamitous boom, the ceiling crashed open. Boulder-sized shards rained upon the dome, and a battalion of sea turtles barreled inside, led by a dragon in white.

I didn't need to see him to know who he was. From everyone else's astonished reactions, the answer was clear enough.

Elang, the High Lord of the Westerly Seas, had arrived.

CHAPTER EIGHT

Amid the din of dragon outrage over Lord Elang's appearance, Gen and I were speedily forgotten. I didn't think twice and dove after the boy, but Gen was heavy, and when his body hit the ocean floor, it sank into the sand and muck. I pried and lifted and dragged, but I could hardly move him.

"Didn't I tell you not to do anything reckless?" Seryu said from behind me.

I swiveled, never more glad to see the dragon. "Can you help him?"

Seryu's nostrils were flared. I half expected him to swim away, but instead he swept off the crabs and mollusks that were starting to crawl up Gen's legs. He grabbed the boy, and me by my sash, lifting us both easily and placing us on a ledge set in the wall of the dome.

I pressed my palm against Gen's forehead. His skin was cold, but a lone vein throbbed with the faintest pulse. He was still alive.

"He can't stay here," I said to Seryu. "Can you get him out of here?" I glanced at the shimmering panels of black crystal against the wall. "Use a whirlpool."

"You think it's that easy?" Seryu balked. "Whirlpools connect within the palace. They don't take you *out* of the palace. The only way is—" He let out an aggravated groan, then with his tail he smashed the closest sheet of black crystal he could reach.

His pearl throbbed in his chest as he dug his claw into the crystal. A whirlpool materialized, barely large enough to fit Gen within. Seryu all but shoved the boy through, and the portal vanished before I could follow.

"Not you," rasped Seryu. "You're not done here."

"Where did you send him?"

"As far as I could manage." Seryu's voice had turned hoarse. He was paler than before, and if he weren't a dragon, I'd say he looked seasick. "Somewhere he won't be pulverized into a pile of rocks."

Before I could thank him, he grabbed me by the sash again and started to drag me off the ledge, back up to where we had been sitting earlier.

I yanked my sash away, half surprised when Seryu actually let go. He *was* weaker. "I'm not going back up there. Your grandfather tried to kill me!"

"And he will again if you don't return." Seryu muffled my mouth with his hand. "Just trust me."

"I trusted Nahma. Look where that got me." I grimaced. "And Kiki."

81

His red eyes didn't waver, but they slanted to the chip of pearl around my neck. The fragment of his dragon heart. He sounded tired. "Trust me."

I bit my cheek. Demons take me, I hoped I wasn't making a mistake. "All right," I said, though I wished he had thrown me into the whirlpool too.

Thanks to Elang's arrival, hardly anyone noticed me come back to my cloud with Seryu. The ceiling had fully collapsed, leaving a gaping hole in the dome, but no one seemed to care about that, either. Every dragon's attention was instead riveted on the center of the devastation, where Elang, standing astride two turtles, awaited King Nazayun's welcome.

"This place is more like a theater than a ritual hall," I mumbled, but in spite of my grumbling, I too was curious about the Lord of the Westerly Seas.

At first glance, Elang disappointed. He looked like every other dragon in the dome. A long white cloak sailed from his shoulders, its hood obscuring his face, but he wore a mostly human physique. He had the upper body of a man, with metallic scales spread across his arms, neck, and torso, and a long tail whipped out from under his cloak, its ends fanned like a hungry flame. I hardly looked twice; I'd become accustomed to seeing dragon tails.

The most impressive thing about Elang was his sea turtles. I counted nine of them, each as large as a boar, with glowering eyes and spiked shells. Not quite the peaceful sea creatures I imagined turtles to be.

Solzaya extended her claws in a dramatic welcome.

"Nephew, you must tire of your empty court if you've decided to grace us with your presence. We worried you were dead."

"Alas, Aunt," he said gruffly, "the assassins you sent weren't skilled enough."

His voice startled me. It was thick and rough—but young. Even though I knew he was Solzaya's nephew, I'd pictured the High Lord of the Westerly Seas to be older, or at least Seryu's elder.

But Elang was barely older than Gen. He was just a boy.

With a terse bow, he paid his respects to his grandfather. Then he threw off his hood, revealing a head of ink-black hair, and I saw his face.

The left side was as human as mine. But when he turned, my breath caught. It was as if the gods had drawn a line straight down his face, from the middle of his hairline through his nose to his chin. One side was human; the other, completely covered with tear-shaped scales, was dragon.

He was scowling, which furrowed his thick brow and cast a shadow upon his face, so I didn't see it at first. Then his brow lifted, and I noticed his two infamous eyes: one dark like the gray sky before a monsoon, and one that was as bright and yellow as a pool of sunlight.

"I came to see the pearl," he said.

"Of course you did," replied the Dragon King, leaning back in his jade-and-marble throne. "Your timing is commendable, Elangui. Shiori'anma was just about to present it to court."

As he spoke, a rush of water swept me from my seat and deposited me beside Elang. A beat later, the pearl settled in my shadow, dark and dull as ever.

The water around me thickened, and I could practically feel the tension coiled in Elang's muscles. His gaze bored into the pearl, as if transfixed by the crack down its center. Was he thinking of how it mirrored his own face, split into two halves?

I glared at the pearl too. Its silence was a reminder that I couldn't count on it for anything—not to help Gen, not to rescue Kiki, certainly not to help me. My chest squeezed with anger, the pang especially sharp when I touched my empty sleeve. I'd get Kiki back from Nahma soon enough. Once I had dealt with the Dragon King.

"There it is—the Wraith's pearl." Nazayun's voice was booming. "Not much to look at in this state, but who can blame it? It is broken and corrupt, belonging to no one. But that shall change."

My eyes shot up to Nazayun. *That shall change?* What game was he playing? I thought he meant to keep the pearl for himself.

"Shiori'anma has sworn to return it to its rightful owner," he continued, "the dragon able to make it whole once more. Let any who wish to claim the Wraith's pearl make a case for it now and attempt this trial."

The entire chamber went still. Out of the corner of my eye, I saw Solzaya's claw twitch with temptation. She wasn't the only one. The lords and ladies of the Four Supreme Seas were all on edge, enraptured by the pearl.

Still, not a dragon dared step forward.

Except one.

"I will try," said Elang in his gruff, overly graveled tone.

"I thought you would," Nazayun replied. "Shiori'anma, give him the pearl."

"It doesn't belong to him," I protested. "He isn't the Wraith."

I thought my refusal would anger the Dragon King, but it had the opposite effect. "He is not," conceded Nazayun. "But you see, Shiori'anma, he and the Wraith have something in common no other dragons share. They are missing their pearls. Their hearts. Will you not give my grandson the chance to claim this one as his own?"

I didn't reply. There was an undercurrent of glee in Nazayun's words, as if he found pleasure in Elang's torment.

"A half dragon," I whispered, finally understanding why everyone spoke of Elang with such repulsion and fascination. Taking in his mismatched eyes, and the striking halves of his face, I realized that the other dragons were mocking him as well as me by donning human forms.

"Yes," Nazayun went on, relishing my surprise. "Elangui is half mortal, born to a human mother who had not taken the Oath of Ai'long. His pearl left him at birth, and without it, he cannot assume a full dragon form."

The water around Elang had turned so thick it betrayed every movement he made. I caught the twitch in his brow, and how his breathing had gone shallow. As if all his hopes rested on this very pearl.

"It isn't yours," I told him, trying hard to be both kind and firm. "It might hurt you."

Elang's expression turned to ice. He sniffed, as though I bore a stench, and cast a glare my way that was easy to read: *How dare you pity me.*

"I will try," he repeated.

With a grunt, Elang unhooked his cloak and let it fall. He approached me, reaching for the pearl with a clawed hand.

Even if I hadn't wanted to give it to him, I had no choice. The pearl spun away from my side and catapulted into his waiting hands. There it sat, light spilling as its halves parted, with the showmanship of a bird's wings spreading feather by feather.

Elang held the pearl against his chest, his palms curving around the broken halves, trying to force them closed. The pearl writhed in resistance. It began to spin, and light poured out of the crack, overwhelming the half dragon. Blisters bubbled upon his human side, and his silver scales went deathly pale.

I lurched to intervene, but the Dragon King held me back.

"Let him be," he said as the dais trembled. "He is welding it whole."

As I watched, I knew that wasn't so. If anything, the pearl was breaking more. The crack along its dark surface turned molten and bright, its light coalescing into a single beam aimed at Elang. It was going to kill him.

Enough was enough. I yanked on Nazayun's starstroke net and threw it over his face. It was something no being— mortal or immortal—had dared do to the Dragon King, and every soul in the chamber thought me a fool, but I didn't care.

I dove for the pearl. "He isn't the Wraith!" I shouted as I snatched it from Elang. "Return to me!"

The pearl turned to face me fully, its fractures blinking in annoyance. But a moment later it flew back into my hands and went dark.

Nazayun's reaction was cataclysmic. In one breath, he grew a hundred times in size, swelling from man to dragon. His sapphire robes melded into his flesh, turning into plates of glittering scales. He crumpled the starstroke net in his colossal fist and hurled it across the dome.

Fool that I was, I instantly went after it. Or at least I tried. Nazayun's claw came slashing down to block my path, and the seas roared.

Everywhere I looked, dragons were bolting out of the broken ceiling. There was no time to search for a whirlpool or use magic. Even Elang was making his escape on the back of a turtle. Entire walls shattered, pillars of marble and crystal showered down like raindrops. While the dome collapsed, I hid behind a coral cloud for safety.

I tried to track the net amid the chaos, but Seryu caught my hand. "You really are the most troublesome girl," he griped. "Leave the net. We have to go."

The crystal gate he'd used to send Gen away was still intact. He rushed us toward it, and a whirlpool bubbled under his claw—an oasis of seagrass just visible at the end of the tunnel.

"Wait," I said, twisting away. "Kiki—"

Seryu held me back. Lightning crackled from the Dragon

King's beard, and with his claw, Nazayun drew the bolts into a cyclonic storm.

"That's a search storm," Seryu said. "It'll be looking for you, and if it finds you, it will kill you. You still want to stay?"

Without waiting for my answer, he pushed me inside the whirlpool—an instant before lightning struck him in the back.

CHAPTER NINE

We spiraled down a dizzying chute of water until the whirl-pool spat us out, one by one, in a field of seagrass outside the palace. With a thump, I landed on top of Seryu.

I rolled off his back and shook him. "Seryu?"

His whiskers made the slightest lift. He wasn't dead.

Encouraged, I gave his shoulders a light shove. "Wake up."

Still unconscious, he sank deeper into the seagrass, his nails curving into claws and his skin turning gradually, un-mistakably green.

I backed away.

A dozen times I'd witnessed my brothers transform into cranes. Every dusk and dawn, for the longest, most excru-ciating minute, Raikama's curse shattered their bones and ripped apart their muscles, contorting their limbs into wings and stick-thin legs, their noses into long dark bills, and their hair into crimson crowns.

I'd never forgotten the sound of their screams.

Seryu's transformation was nothing like my brothers'.

It was swift and effortless, as if he were slipping into a suit of armor. Scales ridged over what had been smooth human flesh, and his legs, sprawled over the morass of seagrass, stretched into a long and winding tail. Whiskers sprouted from his cheeks, and lastly, his horns appeared, half covered by a mass of dark green hair.

He blinked awake, his red eyes wide and his face as pale as it'd been earlier. But maybe being unconscious helped him recover more quickly this time, for he grabbed me by the sleeve. "You must have a death wish, Shiori. Didn't Aunt Nahma tell you to play along?" He groaned, rubbing the singed scales on his spine. "Never mind. Get on. The sharks will be on our tails shortly."

"What happened back there with your grandfather?" I asked shakily. "I thought dragons couldn't harm each other, but he . . . he—"

"Grandfather is a god of dragons," Seryu replied. "He created the oath; he is not bound by it. Which is why we need to get someplace safe. Now."

I understood. But first: "We have to rescue Kiki."

"Did you hear a word I said?" Seryu's exasperation manifested in a grumble. "It's bad enough you went back for the stone boy. Forget about Kiki."

"Forget about her? You know what Kiki means to me. She has a piece of my soul."

"*Had,*" Seryu corrected. "And it was a small piece. You won't die without it. You *will* die, however, if you keep arguing."

"But—"

"We can look for her when the search storms recede." He cocked his head at a whirling column of water and air by the palace, twisting and churning as it scanned every rock, creature, and leaf for Seryu and me. "They'll catch you in their current and take you to Grandfather if we don't hurry."

He grabbed my arm, but I struggled, trying to wade through the seagrass. My knees knocked against stone, and I gasped.

"There's Gen!" I cried. "Oh, thank the Strands, I think he's still breathing. We need to bring him too."

"We don't have time for him," Seryu huffed.

"No arguments." I was already trying to heave Gen onto Seryu's enormous back. "He'll die if he stays out here."

"Why should you care?"

"He's a child! Every day he's here is a month his family wonders what's happened to him." I thought of how much misery I must have brought Father when my brothers and I disappeared. "We have to help him."

"This is your only chance to go home. To be with your beloved lordling and your brothers. Isn't that what you've been agonizing over this entire week?"

It was. And I mourned the precious, precious time that I would never get back. But Raikama had sacrificed far more than time for me. I would do right by her.

"I came here to find the Wraith," I replied. "If I leave, the journey will have been for nothing."

"Grandfather isn't going to tell—"

"Elang knows who the Wraith is," I said, cutting him off.

Surprise sprang on Seryu's brow, but he shook his head. "Visiting Elang is out of the question. He despises humans. He'd never welcome you."

"If you won't come, then I'll go on my own."

"On your own?" Seryu laughed. "You can't even swim to the surface on your own."

A beaked whale loomed above us, blanketing the seagrass in shadow. Seryu shoved me down to my stomach. "Quiet," he whispered.

The water rippled, and the shape of a sea maid disembarked from the whale and began swimming toward us. When I saw who it was, I tensed reflexively.

Seryu, on the other hand, shot up. "You were supposed to stay in the palace. What are you doing here?"

Nahma opened her palms, and Kiki burst out, flying into my face. "A little bird showed me the way."

"Kiki!" I cried. I pressed my bird to my cheek and stroked her beak. Tears of relief welled in my eyes.

"She's a clever bird," allowed Nahma. "She swallowed the elixir, but managed to keep it lodged within her throat. She wouldn't wake until I eased it out of her."

It was Seryu's idea, said Kiki. *I'm better at keeping secrets than you think.*

I didn't understand. "Seryu's idea?"

The dragon wouldn't look at me.

I pursed my lips tight, not knowing what to say to him— or to Nahma. I regarded Nahma first. "I thought you'd betrayed me."

"My deception was a necessary one," she replied. "It's

taken me centuries to earn Lady Solzaya's trust. I could not risk her discovering that I was helping you."

"You're sure you weren't followed?" Seryu asked her.

"I've been slipping out of the palace since before you were born, Seryu," chided Nahma. "Don't forget I'm your elder. And as your elder, I suggest you take Shiori to Elang. He can save the boy. More than that, he will know where to find the Wraith."

"He won't help us," Seryu scoffed.

Nahma reached into her cloak for what looked like a pewter plate. No, a dragon scale. "Show him this."

Seryu's eyes flew up in disbelief. "You have his token?"

She merely nodded. "He will not be able to refuse. Use it to help the boy."

After some hesitation, Seryu took the scale, then nicked off one of his own and placed the emerald scale into Nahma's waiting hands.

"Your token is exchanged for mine in thanks," he said, uttering words I assumed were part of a dragon tradition. His lips drew thin and tight. "A favor for a favor."

Nahma pocketed the scale and made a low call for her whale.

"Wait," said Seryu. "You won't make it back to the palace undetected. The search storms will find you, and Grandfather will punish you."

"Come with us," I said. "Come with me back to the surface."

"I can't." Nahma smiled kindly. "I would not leave my children. I have two—both dragons like their father. Besides, I belong here now." She touched my arm, then buttoned the collar of my dress the way a mother would. "The Westerly Seas are cold. Go swiftly and be safe."

She turned then to Seryu. "As for Nazayun, he won't believe I helped you—*if* you make it convincing enough."

Seryu seemed to know exactly what that meant. "Back away, Shiori."

As I obeyed, he wrapped his tail around his aunt's neck and touched her forehead with a claw. Immediately Nahma went limp, falling into the seagrass with a soft thud.

Kiki gasped. *Did you kill her?*

"Of course not!" said Seryu, clearly offended. "It's a simple sleeping spell. An old dragon trick—works best when it's not anticipated." He flashed a wicked grin at me. "You should test it on Kiki when she gets seasick."

Don't you dare, Kiki warned.

"I need you awake, silly." I lifted Kiki by the wing, setting her on my shoulder as I hopped onto Seryu's back. I pressed a kiss on my bird's beak, then tapped Seryu's head to get his attention.

"I'm sorry I didn't trust you," I said.

"A mistake you won't make again," he replied. "I know."

He hooked an arm around Gen's statue. "Hold on to my horns." The color of his scales began to change, blending in with the green and yellow seagrass below. "If we're going to outswim Grandfather's sharks, this isn't going to be an easy ride."

I gripped Seryu's horns, and Kiki dove into my hair, holding on for dear life. With a low roar, the dragon ripped through the sea, making for Elang's castle in the West.

CHAPTER TEN

The Westerly Seas *were* colder. Grayer too, the farther we traveled from Nazayun's palace. Sprawling coral forests dwindled into skeletal sponge beds, and all I could see in any direction was a graveyard of rock and bone. It was hard to believe this was still the dragon realm. Everywhere I looked, a pall clung to the water, leaching it of all vibrancy and life.

Finally, Seryu dove into a chasm between two cliffs. The walls were studded with round stones so unremarkable I didn't give them a second glance.

Until they started to move.

Round marbled eyes peeked out, and what I'd taken for stones turned out to be—

"Turtles," Seryu said as the creatures skittered to life. "Elang's guards."

Guards! Within seconds, the turtles grouped, erecting a high wall to protect the fortress ahead. The battle turtles Elang had brought to the palace had swum with vicious speed, but to see them rapidly stacking upon one another and turning their shells out to face us took my breath away. Not even my father's best regiment could work that quickly and precisely.

My awe was exceeded only by my distress. "I always thought they were gentle and slow."

"Gentle and slow?" Seryu huffed a laugh. "Slow on land, perhaps, but in the seas they're faster than sailfish, and their tempers run hotter than your festival firecrackers. Step on the wrong shell, and you'll be spinning so fast you won't need an elixir to forget who you are."

He lifted his tail high and slammed it down on the rock. Once . . . Twice . . .

In response, a legion of spears flew out from between the turtle shells. Their sharp tips rushed toward Seryu's heart and my throat, halting within a hair's breadth of skewering us.

Irritation bubbled in Seryu's voice. "Let me through, Elang." He held out the pewter scale Lady Nahma had given him. "I'm here to call in a favor."

The spears, tips still angled dangerously close to my throat, crept forward.

"Cousin, I know you're listening." Seryu folded his arms over the spears, as though they were a balcony railing. "Open the gates. It's against your honor to renege on a favor, and I call in Lady Nahma's."

Silence ensued, testing Seryu's patience. Finally, the turtles moved, creating the thinnest crack in their formation. Behind them, chiseled into the flat edges of a cliff, was Elang's castle.

There were no gleaming spires, no grand marble pillars or black crystal gateways. Its roofs were brilliantly camouflaged into the mountain, and its towers were hewn of unassuming gray stone, easily passed over.

I liked it.

Elang was perched on a ledge, his silhouette wreathed in darkness. He'd been watching us this whole time, and he shot down as we approached.

His silver scales blazed, and his mismatched eyes narrowed with displeasure. The strain in his voice hinted that he had not fully recovered from his injuries: "Yonsar Castle does not welcome krill."

"Krill?" I repeated.

"The stuff whales and shrimp eat," Seryu spat. "Also another name that dragons call mortals. Humans, usually."

"Take her away," ordered Elang. "Her stench has already infiltrated my castle. It will be days before we are rid of it."

"Stench?" I said hotly. "You're half human yourself."

"My nose is dragon."

"Looks human to me."

If Elang's demeanor had been cold before, it turned glacial now. "The mollusks have better manners than you. Of all the mortals in Lor'yan, I thought my cousin would have chosen someone with better bearing."

He flicked up his chin, and the sea threw me back to the gate of turtles.

"Wait!" I shouted, kicking Gen off Seryu's back. The statue rolled until it landed just before the dragon lord.

The water stilled. "What is *he* doing here?" Elang demanded.

"You know him?" I asked.

97

From the way the half dragon's expression darkened, he did.

Curious.

"He's been turned to stone," I went on. "Lady Nahma told us you could help. Please. He'll die if you don't do something."

"It's against dragon law to refuse the invocation of a favor," Seryu reminded his cousin. "Even if it's for a human."

"It's also against dragon law to harbor a wanted criminal," countered Elang. "*Especially* if it's a human."

As he spoke, a swirl of gray mist piled high in the far distance, making its presence known with a low droning hum.

"They won't find her if you let her inside," said Seryu. "I know you take pains to live your life in isolation, cousin. But are you so far removed from us that you're afraid of a little search storm?"

Elang grimaced. "Get inside before I change my mind."

The interior of Elang's castle was brighter and warmer than I expected. Rich purple banners hung from the walls, and floating shell sconces illuminated the entrance hall, which was framed by structures of green coral and rich panels of sunken wood. A surprising blend of land and sea.

Elang gave no tour of his home, but a pair of turtles—smaller and daintier than the gigantic guards—appeared, carrying Gen on their backs. We followed as they sped down a maze of hallways, stopping eventually to lay him upon a marble bench in a windowless room. Kiki sat on the boy's forehead, her beak wrinkled with worry. *He isn't breathing.*

I swallowed. "Is he dead?"

"Not yet," Seryu said. "If he were, Elang wouldn't be upholding Aunt Nahma's favor."

Elang didn't deign to reply. He tore off his white cloak, the same one he'd worn as defense against Nazayun. It glowed as he blanketed Gen's body with it.

"The cloak is enchanted, isn't it?" I observed.

"Most things in Ai'long are," responded Seryu. "The cloak's silk is stronger than any armor, and the lining will heal most flesh. It'll keep the boy alive while Elang prepares a healing potion."

"Something I cannot do with an audience gawking over my shoulder," Elang said.

"Sorry."

"If you're sorry, you'll leave."

Seryu glared at his cousin, but he heeded the instruction, and we left for the hall.

"He certainly has your grandfather's temper," I said once we were outside. "It's hard to believe he's younger than you."

"Why is that?"

"He's so . . ." I was going to say *angry,* but another word came out instead. "Bitter."

"What do you expect? He doesn't have a heart."

True. I touched mine, which ached with homesickness, and swallowed. I couldn't imagine what it was like for Elang. "Do you think he'll save Gen?"

"He'll do his best. He has to."

"Because of Lady Nahma's token." I understood.

"Few things are more valuable than a favor in Ai'long," replied Seryu. "I'll never know how she got Elang's, but now she has one of mine."

"Thank you," I said softly.

"It's fine. She was kind to you. For that, I won't mind being in her debt—too much."

I managed a smile at Seryu. We were still friends.

Seryu didn't smile back, but he didn't frown, either. Neither of us had discussed how abruptly the rites had ended, how we'd almost been forced to marry each other. It made for a tense air of awkwardness between us, one Seryu knew just how to break.

"You must be starving," he said. "Come, let's get you something to eat."

The glowing orbs that drifted along the ceilings were starting to remind me of onions, and the gilded triangles etched on the walls began to look like carrots. I kept sniffing for food, the sharp emptiness in my belly sorely dejected, when Seryu ushered me into what looked like Elang's study.

There were books everywhere, stacked high atop an oblong slab of marble that served as a table. Paintings too slathered the walls, each encased in a protective bubble that my mischievous fingers would have itched to try popping were I not so hungry. In the corner, a blue fire blazed over a sandy hearth—but no pot brewed over the flames.

"I thought you were taking me to the kitchen," I said.

"There is no kitchen in a dragon's castle."

"Don't you all have to eat?"

In response, Seryu swept the table clear of its books and scrolls. Then, with a dramatic flourish, he clapped.

A small feast appeared: a steaming clay pot of crisped rice with cabbage and mushrooms, a pot of fish stew with carrots and glass noodles, and a bowl of fruits.

Salivating, I planted myself in front of the stew and started shoveling bites into my mouth, eating so desperately and quickly that stray grains of rice flew at Kiki. The stew was a comfort, reminding me of my own fish soup—a special dish I'd make for my brothers, Takkan, and myself when we weren't feeling our best.

A few courses in, I stopped. "Seryu, you aren't eating."

"I'm spectating for now." A small grin. "The Shiori I knew would consider this only the first round."

I laughed. I'd forgotten how much I missed him, our easy banter, our mutual love for food. I started at my plate again.

"Not so fast, Princess." A teapot had materialized on the table, and Seryu poured its contents into a cup. "Here, drink some tea. It helps with indigestion."

He poured another cup for himself and took a sip.

"Dragons get indigestion?" I asked.

"No, but Elang hoards the best brews in Ai'long. He's the only one who travels back and forth from land to sea often enough to keep up with what you mortals are drinking."

"You travel too."

"Not as often as him." Seryu drank deeply from his cup. "It isn't encouraged to visit the mortal realm. But I was bored—and curious about your world, thanks to him. All Elang did was complain about you humans, but . . . I liked the food he brought back."

That I agreed with heartily. "You're friends."

"We were. Before his father died and he became High Lord of the Westerly Seas." A pause. "Then Elang stopped seeing anyone, even me."

"Because your mother sent assassins after him?"

"That has a little to do with it."

I set down my spoon. "Why does she want him dead?"

Seryu took a long moment to respond, making me think he was condensing a lengthy story into a short one. At last he said, "His title is a coveted one."

"But your mother already has her own title."

"Dragons like my mother and grandfather see Elang's very existence as a threat. All children born to companions are either dragon—or not. There are no half dragons except for Elang and the Wraith. They're . . . aberrations."

"*That's* why they won't accept him," I murmured. "But when he finds his pearl, he can become a full dragon."

"*If* he finds it," countered Seryu. "Until then he's trapped between two worlds. Half human, half dragon. No matter where he goes, he won't fully belong."

"I'll get a taste of that soon," I said, watching the tea leaves in my cup sink. "When I return to Kiata, everyone will know I have magic. It'll be hard for things to go back to the way they were."

"My offer still stands, you know," said Seryu seriously. "You could stay with me."

I shifted uneasily, clutching my teacup. "Seryu . . ."

"If only you could see how uncomfortable you look. I was joking." He let out a breath through his nose, and his seriousness fled. "There's only so much rejection a dragon can take. You're lucky our hearts are stronger than human ones."

He took a long sip, then smirked. "Besides, we'd get bored of each other before long. And eternity would feel even longer with someone as troublesome as you, Shiori."

I laughed. As simple as that, we were friends again.

"Now finish your tea," he said, lifting my cup to my lips. "It's expensive."

While I drank, Seryu cranked his head up, ear perking. It was the only notice he gave before Elang himself appeared.

The half dragon looked tired. Gold-rimmed spectacles sat unevenly on his nose, a touch that made him appear vastly more human. But when he caught me staring, he tore them off and his eyes narrowed.

"I didn't say you were welcome to my tea," he groused.

"It's the finest in Ai'long," Seryu replied, raising his cup in appreciation. "Where else would we find tea fresh off the Spice Road?"

"And my food?"

"Shiori was hungry," Seryu said crisply. "She's intolerable when she's hungry. Besides, you should have offered. You're looking tired, cousin. I keep forgetting you've inherited the inconvenient human need for sleep."

Elang looked like he wanted to strangle Seryu. But he did straighten, fists uncurling at his side. "The sorcerer is awake."

I sprang to my feet as Gen shuffled into the room, wearing

a lopsided grin. His movements were still stiff and jerky, but his skin had a promising tinge of pink.

"Praise the Sages, I'm alive," he announced. "The world nearly suffered the loss of its greatest future enchanter."

"If only your mouth were still stone," muttered Elang, "the world would have been spared yet another enchanter who talks too much." A lidded bowl of herbal tea appeared in the half dragon's hand, and he offered it to Gen. "Drink."

Gen took the steaming bowl but didn't drink. His attention was on the wall of books opposite the table, and he brushed his knuckles over their spines. "Can't I stay, Elang? Your library is most impressive. Some of these volumes I've never even seen before. Let me read—"

Elang plucked a book from Gen, obsessively placing it back in its place. "It's *Lord* Elang to you, and no. You're leaving once you finish this tea."

"Then I'll drink very slowly."

"You'll drink while it's hot," Elang said. "It'll make the sangi last longer. Unless you prefer to drown."

It was odd, watching the two spar. Elang acted like he was years older than Gen, but they were almost the same age.

"Consider my debt repaid," Elang informed Seryu. "As soon as the boy finishes drinking, he's going home. He hasn't enough sangi to last long in the water, and no number of Nahma's favors will persuade me to make more."

"But Grandfather's storm—"

"My turtles will escort him to the surface," Elang spoke over Seryu. "It'll be safe enough. No one's looking for him."

Unlike you two, he left unsaid.

I inserted myself between the cousins. "While you both bicker, I'd like to speak to Gen before he goes."

For privacy, I steered Gen to an antechamber behind the bookshelf, where a blue fire burned between two cushioned chairs.

"I take it Elang is the dragon who lured you to Ai'long."

"Very perceptive, Shiori," replied Gen as we sat. He stretched his long legs near the fire, then let his limbs float. "Ironic, isn't it? Twenty years wasted, only to end right back where I started."

"Twenty years? I thought you were only here a few weeks."

"Solzaya put me to sleep for a whole dragon year: punishment for not giving up Elang's name." Gen grimaced. "Don't give me that pitying look."

I couldn't help it. "I'm sorry," I whispered. "Your family, your home . . ."

"My home ceased to exist long before I came to Ai'long," Gen replied. "It was destroyed during the war. My father and brothers probably died soon after they sold me off." He dismissed my concern with a shrug. "It's fine. I hardly knew them anyway. Stop apologizing like it's your fault."

"Where will you go?"

Gen tilted his head to the side. "I take it Kiata doesn't have any resident sorcerers."

"If you're thinking about visiting, don't. You won't be welcome."

Gen sipped his tea. "It's tragic how much your country despises magic. They ought to revisit that opinion."

"Why do you say that?"

"You asked how I knew about your magic when we were in Solzaya's torture chamber."

"Yes, so I did."

"One of my teachers used to talk about Kiata," Gen explained. "He was horrible, ill tempered, possibly mad. When he drank too much, he would ramble on about going to your country and killing the bloodsake to unleash the demons trapped inside the Holy Mountains." Gen side-eyed me. "Since that was twenty years ago, I'm guessing you weren't born yet?"

A drink of the now-lukewarm tea in my hands did nothing to repel the shivers crawling up my spine. "Why?" I pressed. "Why did he want to free the demons?"

"He said they'd revere him as their king. And a true king he planned to be—by becoming a demon himself."

I flinched, a wave of dread rising in my stomach, but Gen didn't notice. "Demons can live forever, you see," he went on, "whereas enchanters lose their immortality after a thousand years. The only problem was that he would be bound to an amulet as a demon. The way to free himself, he learned, was to acquire a dragon pearl."

My chest went hollow. "Seryu told me once that demons and enchanters covet dragon pearls more than anything."

"Yes, because only a dragon pearl is powerful enough to break our oaths."

That I hadn't known. I stared into the blue flames flickering over the watery hearth, thinking of the wolf I'd seen steal out of the Holy Mountains. The King of Demons, he'd called himself. Bandur.

I said, in my lowest voice, "Your teacher was the Wolf, wasn't he?"

Gen stilled, his cheeks going so taut he almost looked like stone again. "If you know him," he said slowly, "then he must have made it to Kiata."

"He was bound to one of my father's warlords," I replied, thinking of the former Lord Yuji. "He murdered him . . . and became a demon. Bandur."

"By the Sages, he actually broke his oath," Gen whispered. Disbelief colored his words, and he nearly dropped his tea.

"You can't let him know of the Wraith's pearl," he said, grabbing the arm of my chair. "It is different; it's corrupted by demon magic. Should Bandur obtain it, he'll use its power to end his oath. In doing so, he'd break the pearl, and that would—"

"Destroy the pearl," I said. Suddenly it hurt to breathe. Bandur already knew of the pearl.

"I should travel to Kiata instead of—"

"That's not necessary," I interrupted. I needed to snuff out the spark in Gen's eyes, needed to dissuade him from walking to his doom. "Bandur's trapped in the mountains. There's nothing to worry about."

Gen started to reply, but Elang swept in from behind, cutting me off. "What did I say about finishing the tea? The boy's prattled enough. It's time for him to leave."

Tipping his head back, Gen downed the remainder of his tea and hopped to his feet. "Don't worry," he said, donning a carefree smile. "I heard what you said, Princess. If Bandur's locked up in the mountains, like you say, all the better for everyone. Me especially. I have twenty years of studies to catch up on—and as I've said, Kiata's the *last* place in Lor'yan I'd want to visit."

A turtle had appeared in the middle of Elang's study, ready to take Gen to shore.

Gen stepped onto its back and picked up the reins. His smile turned roguish. "Always wanted to ride a giant turtle."

I ventured toward the boy. "May our strands cross again. Go well, Gen."

"May our strands cross again!" he yelled as the turtle bent its legs to spring upward. "Preferably in a place with more air"—he tipped his head at Kiki—"and birds!"

With a mighty whoosh, the turtle leapt out into the sea, taking Gen with it. In a blink, they were gone.

The study went silent once more, and without wasting a beat, Elang turned to Seryu and me. "Now, what's to be done with the two of you?"

CHAPTER ELEVEN

I held up the Wraith's pearl before Elang. "Lady Nahma said you know who this belongs to."

"Get that thing away from me!" Elang recoiled from the pearl. "Nazayun will not tell you who the Wraith is, and neither will I. That's the end of the discussion."

"Lady Nahma said—"

"I don't care what she said. Seryu used up her favor to save the boy. You are testing the bounds of my goodwill, and that goodwill is quickly being depleted."

I sucked in my breath. "Then let *me* propose a favor."

"There's nothing you could offer me."

"Isn't there?" I challenged. I could think of something.

Ever since we'd arrived, I'd been puzzling over how Elang had recognized Gen. Why he had gone through the trouble of sending Gen home, when Nahma's favor had only required him to heal the boy.

"*You're* the dragon who brought Gen into Ai'long," I

cried. "You asked him to steal something for you. Something you've been coveting for years. I'll help you get it."

"You've just outworn your welcome," Elang said thickly.

"What is it? I'll help you get it."

"You've got some nerve, krill. Grandfather's entire army is searching for you, and you want to play thief? You don't stand a chance. The boy failed, and his magic is far stronger than yours."

"My magic is Kiatan, like the mirror's. I can do it."

He clapped. "My turtles will show you to the door—"

"I'll help her," interrupted Seryu.

Elang halted midclap and spun to face his cousin. "I wouldn't be so quick to volunteer. Do you even know what I require?"

"I will once you tell me."

Elang's gaze widened to include both of us. "A shard from the mirror of truth," he said. "I believe you're both acquainted with it. You especially, cousin."

Seryu bristled. "You want me to steal my mother's mirror?"

"Still committed to helping the girl? I thought not." Elang smirked at Seryu's silence and circled me. "Aunt Solzaya's moods are legendary. Last year, a companion dared insinuate that she was old. Crabs and slugs and barnacles fell out of the poor girl's mouth with every word, until she finally choked to death." Elang stopped in front of Seryu. "Imagine what she'll do to Shiori for stealing her mirror, especially after rejecting her precious son in front of the entire court—"

"Shiori didn't reject me," Seryu griped, as if that were the most important point. "And yes, I'll still help her."

Even as he said it, he wouldn't look at me. I swallowed. "It's settled, then," I said, getting back to business. "A mirror shard for the location of the Wraith. Do we have a deal?"

Elang scowled at me. Something was holding him back. "You're a fool to go ahead with this, krill. My grandfather and Aunt Solzaya would happily take the pearl off your hands, even reward you if you played them cleverly enough. Instead, you've chosen to make an enemy of them. Why do you care so much about finding the Wraith?"

"I have a promise to keep," I replied.

"To your stepmother. Yes, I heard." Elang frowned. "I take it she didn't tell you why his pearl is the way it is, dark and broken and . . . extraordinary?"

"Because he's a half dragon, like you?"

"Like me?" Elang laughed. It was a bitter sound, and I didn't think he found my question funny at all. "The Wraith and I are the only ones of our kind—both monsters, both cursed. But we are very different. I'm the embarrassment for being half human, whereas the Wraith is, well, the Wraith"—he leaned in close—"for being half demon."

It was a good thing my tea was mostly gone, for my knees knocked together in surprise, and it would have splattered all over me. "Demon?"

Even Seryu looked stunned. "Are you certain about this, Elang?"

"Haven't you wondered why the Wraith's pearl looks as it does? Dark as an eclipsed night, when a dragon's pearl should be radiant like the moon? It is corrupted because of what he is. It is breaking because of what he is. Dragons and

111

demons are born enemies, and the Wraith's existence is an abomination. That is why Grandfather fears him, and why he will never tell you his true name."

"His true name?" I repeated.

"Certain names have power. Not as much as a starstroke net, but enough to unsettle a dragon—at the hands of an experienced sorcerer, anyway." Elang frowned. "It's also useful in breaking curses, such as the one Solzaya placed on Gen."

"The lords and ladies of the Four Supreme Seas know each other's true names," explained Seryu. "Elang knows my mother's, and my mother knows his."

"And an unfortunate consequence is that I can't steal the mirror myself," Elang muttered.

I was quiet because I understood. To break Raikama's curse over my brothers, I'd needed to learn her true name. Not Vanna, as the rest of the world believed. But Channari.

"You know the Wraith's true name?" I asked.

"I do, and I know where to find him. Both I will tell you—*if* you return with the mirror."

I didn't appreciate how he emphasized *if*. "It's a deal, then."

"An arrangement," Seryu corrected. "On the Oath of Ai'long, Elang, your word is given and cannot be undone. Same as the oath."

"My word is given and cannot be undone," Elang repeated. "Same as the oath."

As the water rippled with the power of the promise, Elang shook his head at Seryu. "You must really be fond of this mortal. I hope she's worth your mother's wrath."

"It's not so much fondness as a desire to get her to go home," said Seryu, still avoiding my eyes. "She brings trouble wherever she goes."

"I'm beginning to believe that." Elang summoned his turtles with a clap. "They'll see you to your rooms for the night."

"Wait," I called. This was not the time to ask for a favor, but I didn't care.

I waved up and down at the ceremonial dress I was still wearing, but Elang and Seryu both gave me blank stares. *Dolts.* So I made a show of kicking up my skirt, embellished with so many pearls it looked like I'd robbed a school of oysters. The entire garment tinkled.

"I need new attire," I said. "I can't go in this to steal from Lady Solzaya. I can't even sleep in this without waking myself up."

"I've no magic to waste on conjuring clothing." Elang clearly regretted not locking me up. "You'll make do. A concealment potion will arrive for you at first light, along with your net."

My breath caught. "You have the starstroke net?"

Elang confirmed this by ignoring the question. "You and Seryu will leave in the morning, when the tides turn east. Should fortune be on your side, I will meet you both on the surface before the moon falls."

"And if fortune isn't on our side?"

"Then you'll be dead, Shiori'anma. And there will be nothing I can do."

CHAPTER TWELVE

A half demon.

Why hadn't Raikama told me?

I tossed in my bed. I couldn't sleep. Every time I closed my eyes, my mind conjured the Wraith. A dragon borne of shadow and nightmares, his red demon eye haunted me even in the quiet stillness of the Westerly Seas.

At least Kiki slept. Her paper wings didn't even twitch as I twisted anxiously in my bed.

Hours passed, and when the first glimmers of light touched the water, I blinked an eye open. In the corner of the room, the Wraith's pearl was suspended, bathed in shadow. As I rose, it glided to my arm and rested in the crook of my elbow.

I cradled it, brushing my knuckles against the deep crack in its center.

"Is that why you haven't led me to the Wraith sooner?" I asked the pearl. "You're lost, like him. Trapped between two worlds, and unable to find your way out."

The pearl was still.

"I know that Raikama was more powerful, and more capable, and you miss her," I told it. "But let us come to an understanding: I need you just as much as you need me. If you want to find the Wraith again, you have to help me when I ask. No more games, no more ignoring me. Or else I won't trust you."

No answer. Of course.

With a sigh, I rolled the pearl off to a corner of the room. Why should I put my trust in a dragon pearl that was half demon, anyway? I doubted even Raikama had been that foolish.

There was a tray floating beside my door, and I fetched it, hoping Elang had sent new clothes.

He hadn't.

Nor had he sent the starstroke net, but my promised potion had arrived, bubbling from the open lips of a spiky shell. Underneath was a note, sprawled in basic Kiatan: *Drink this.*

Curious that I hadn't heard a messenger come and go, and I'd been awake most of the night.

I raised the shell cautiously to my lips. The potion smelled of sulfur, and it prickled my nostrils.

It smells disgusting, Kiki remarked, flittering over my shoulder.

Her voice startled me. "Well, good morning," I said. "I thought you were asleep."

Sleeping is an indulgence, not a necessity, she replied with a yawn. Her nose pinched. *Are you really going to drink a concealment potion without asking what it'll conceal you as?*

"Elang told me to."

What if you turn into a goblin shark or, worse yet, a blobfish? Caution is the creed of the wise, Shiori. Even the pearl agrees with me.

The pearl *was* pulsing, but I doubted it had anything to do with the potion.

"Something's not right." With a frown, I set down the shell, but the pearl continued to pulse.

Then again, maybe we shouldn't trust you, Kiki was musing to the pearl. *Bad enough you're a dragon heart, but turns out there's demon in you, too. Wouldn't surprise me if you killed us in our sleep.*

The pearl was silent and unreadable, its lustrous black surface reflecting my bird's scowl.

"That's enough, Kiki." I beckoned her onto my shoulder. "Let's look for Seryu."

The problem was, Seryu was nowhere to be found. In fact, the entire castle seemed empty. The turtles guarding the halls had vanished, and the floating bauble lights were dim, casting a leaden sense of gloom over the cavernous halls.

I knocked on Seryu's doors a third time. "Seryu!"

"He isn't here," Elang said, stepping out from behind the shadows. "He left last night."

I nearly jumped, startled by the half dragon's unexpected appearance. As usual, he was scowling.

"Seryu wouldn't leave without telling me."

Elang ignored my words. "You aren't very good at follow-

116

ing instructions." His mismatched eyes bored into me. "I told you to drink the potion."

"Where did Seryu go?"

Instead of replying, Elang glided down the hall, motioning for me to follow. "Plans have changed," he was saying. "I have good news for you. It turns out you won't have to go back to the palace after all. We have a guest."

"A guest?"

Out of nowhere, a rope of seaweed tugged at my ankles, dragging me into a gate of black crystal behind a pillar. With a rush, a whirlpool sucked me in and brought me to the entrance hall, where, waiting before the gates, was Lady Solzaya.

I lurched, immediately recognizing the betrayal. But I wasn't fast enough. An octopus wrapped its slick tentacles around my limbs and my neck. As I struggled, Kiki dove for Elang's eyes with her beak.

You treacherous lizard! she shrilled.

Elang snatched her up. "A dragon only looks after his best interest."

"But you swore!" I had a slew of curses for Elang, but not one of them made it past my lips. Solzaya's octopus was strangling me.

"This will hurt less if you hold your tongue," said Solzaya silkily. Her jagged nails grazed against my cheek. "It's a good thing Elangui came to his senses. He saved us the trouble of sending assassins. For both of you."

"I welcome a reprieve from your assassins, Aunt," said Elang coolly. "You've sent so many that I've run out of room to properly bury them all. Perhaps you should wait until Seryu reaches his full form before you try to seat him on my throne. A half-grown dragon does not command much more respect than a half-blooded one."

Solzaya's scales purpled with irritation. "Where *is* my son?"

"I'm not his keeper. Nor am I the girl's." The half dragon started to turn. "Our business is done. You asked for the girl, and I've given her to you. Now take her away."

The octopus dragged me toward the gate, and Solzaya drew her claw in front of her chest, brewing a cage of coral and stone—into which she dropped Kiki.

"Let her go!" I shouted. "Kiki!"

Twice now Kiki had been taken from me. Angrily, I thrust out my hand, and silver-gold beams of magic rushed from my fingertips. The floating shells that illuminated Elang's ceiling trembled to life.

"Attack!" I shouted, and the shells rocketed for Solzaya.

The dragon didn't even flinch. A mere look was all it took for her to dispel the onslaught and freeze the shells in place.

Seryu's mother lifted Kiki's cage. One of the shells had come dangerously close to crushing its bars.

"Such recklessness, Shiori'anma," Solzaya said, clucking her tongue. "Didn't my son teach you to watch your temper while using magic?"

The tiny hairs on the back of my neck rose.

"Yes, the mirror has shown me *all* about your friendship with my son," said Solzaya. "Just as it's shown me that you are not worthy of bearing the Wraith's pearl."

She clapped twice, and thick locks of kelp sprang up from the ground, wrapping around my limbs until I couldn't move. The entire time, the pearl hovered over me like a curious spectator, and my resentment at it grew.

Solzaya's octopus threw me over its shoulder and clamped a cold tentacle over my mouth. A shroud of ink fell over my eyes, and my world turned to fog. The last thing I heard was a rush of water—and the thunderous sound of Elang's gates closing.

CHAPTER THIRTEEN

Must they be in such a rush to kill you? Kiki grumbled as Solzaya and her octopus sped us back to the Dragon King's palace. My paper bird wrapped her wings around her cage's coral bars, looking seasick. *Couldn't we slow down just a little? I swear, I'll never complain about Seryu's swimming again.*

I threw Kiki a sympathetic look, but my mind was churning. Ever since we'd left Elang's castle, I couldn't stop wondering why he'd betrayed us. If he wanted Solzaya's mirror, he wouldn't get it by handing me over without a fight.

A dragon only looks after his best interest, he'd said. But what interested Elang?

Kiki whimpered. *Come on, Shiori. Use your wits. Use the pearl.*

My mind still churning, I glanced at Solzaya. The mirror shards shimmered against her scales, reflecting the sea rushing by. Seven shards, each about as large as the span of my hand.

All I needed was one.

"You know, I had a feeling we wouldn't be welcoming you into the family," Solzaya said, as if sensing my stare. "Since the Wraith's pearl protects you from my magic, perhaps the old ways are best. A simple spear to your chest should do the trick."

"Or perhaps you should just let me go," I replied. "Save everyone the trouble of dissolving into sand. I understand that's what will happen if you kill me."

"Did I say I'd kill you?" The dragon's molten eyes were unblinking. "No, I said I'd stab you in the chest."

And leave me on the brink of death, I understood, so the pearl would desert me.

"The Wraith's pearl doesn't belong with one such as you," said Solzaya. "A half-fledged sorceress." She scoffed. "A shadow of your stepmother."

Beneath the mockery, Solzaya's tone was sour. Which struck me. At the ceremony, she had wanted to claim the Wraith's pearl for herself.

A dragon only looks after his best interest.

"Who should have it, then?" I said slowly. "King Naza-yun? Your father is the Dragon King. He doesn't need the pearl." I drew out my next words. "Don't *you* want it for yourself?"

Solzaya's laugh cut short, and the kelp knots tightened, squeezing into my joints. It took all my willpower not to let out a cry of pain.

"Don't presume to tempt me, girl."

"I could give it to you," I pressed, trying hard not to

121

wince. "The pearl is bound to me, but I . . . I could transfer it to you."

Kiki flew uneasily in her cage. *Shiori, what are you doing?*

"Or I could simply spear you in the chest." Solzaya's whiskers twitched ever so slightly, belying her sneer. "And let you bleed until the pearl decides to come to me."

"If it were that easy, your father would have done so already," I replied. My life depended on how I sold my next words: "Besides, there's no guarantee the pearl would choose *you*."

Ever so slightly, Solzaya's whiskers curled.

"But if I offered the pearl to you voluntarily—as the result of a wager—then . . ."

"A wager?"

This was it. I had her attention.

"Yes." I pounced. "A shard from your mirror if I win, and the Wraith's pearl if I lose."

Solzaya's pupils constricted. "A shard for the broken pearl? Do you know the power of what you carry?"

"I have some idea."

"Why the change of heart? You wouldn't give it to my father during the ceremony."

"He has power enough without it." I licked my lips. "And he won't help me find the Wraith. The mirror would."

"Would it, now?" Solzaya's sneer deepened. "Name your terms."

I spoke quickly, before I lost my nerve. "You hide the mirror of truth's shards among a thousand others. If I can find one, then you will allow me to keep it and you will release us. If I fail, I will give you the Wraith's pearl."

I rolled the pearl into Solzaya's view. Even in its most subdued state, its power was impossible to ignore. Solzaya's shoulders grew taut, and a sheen of desire imbued her fiery scales.

She said, "If you give me the Wraith's pearl, your protections in Ai'long will come to an end. You do realize what will become of you when that happens?"

I didn't waver. "You'll have to win for me to give you the pearl."

"Didn't I warn you never to play games with dragons? We always win."

"I've never been a good listener."

She let out a throaty laugh. "I accept your wager. *But* on the condition that you find all *seven* shards—before the sands run south." A thin hourglass appeared on her palm. "Do so, and I will set you free."

All seven shards? If I'd thought I was clever for coming up with this contest, I certainly didn't think so anymore. "I agree, but only if you set Kiki free before the trial. And promise to the conditions. A dragon's word is nothing without a promise."

"The promise is made," Solzaya swore. She blew into the hourglass, and grains of fine white sand funneled through a narrow neck. "We begin."

No sooner had the words left her lips than the kelp bindings released me.

True to her promise, Solzaya freed Kiki from the cage. Then she stretched her mouth wide and blew.

From her lips spilled thousands upon thousands of mirror shards, showering over me and hanging in the water like a storm of suspended raindrops. Each shard glittered like a diamond, and as I wove my way through, I confronted my own reflection at every turn, multiplied a thousandfold. In every one, I could see my rising panic.

Blazing Eternal Courts, what have you gotten yourself into? Kiki cried. *They all look the same.*

They did indeed, but I buried my panic. I wouldn't have bet the Wraith's pearl without some forethought. But I had assumed I would only have to find *one* shard, not all seven.

Wits, Shiori, I told myself. *Fear is just a game; you win by playing. Think this through.*

I knew the mirror of truth had been created with Kiatan magic, same as mine. I was counting on that fact—and my unique ability as the bloodsake—to help me pick out the seven shards. All I had to do was impart a piece of my soul into each of the shards and find the ones that resonated with Kiatan magic.

But there were *thousands* of mirror pieces. I couldn't split my soul into enough bits to inspect them all. That would kill me. And to tackle the task in smaller batches would take more time than I had.

Just start looking! Kiki shrieked. *Hurry! The sands are spilling fast!*

Flickers of magic wisped from my hands, threading around the floating shards, searching for traces of Kiatan magic in the mirror pieces. As I tried and failed, and failed again, my stomach dipped with disappointment. The wisps dissolved, and I had to start over.

Think of happy things, urged Kiki. *Your magic's always stronger when you're happy. Focus! Silk pillows with soft tassels, tree branches with springy worms—*

"You're not helping, Kiki," I muttered. "If anything, you're making me more anxious." The paper bird's beak parted, but I pushed her voice out of my head and closed my eyes, trying to concentrate.

Summoning my magic was like trying to light a fire, and in Ai'long all I'd been able to ignite was sparks. I needed more tinder. If only I had sufficient threads to fashion a net that could sweep over all the shards at once.

The pearl began to hum, pulsing wildly in counterpoint to my own racing heart. For once, I wished it silent, and as I tossed it into my satchel, my fingers brushed against the spine of a book inside.

Takkan's sketchbook.

He had given it to me on the shores of Kiata, right before I'd left for Ai'long. So I wouldn't forget him.

I opened it absently, as if it might contain answers.

How are Takkan's paintings going to help you? Kiki asked.

Good question. A few days in Ai'long, and I had come perilously close to losing all my memories of home. I needed a reminder of what I was fighting for. *Who* I was fighting for.

The first page: a drawing of Takkan's sister, Megari, and me throwing snow at each other on Rabbit Mountain. Next:

125

me, with that cursed wooden bowl over my head, gazing at plum blossoms.

I kept flipping pages, past sketches of my brothers as cranes, of me folding paper birds or stirring a pot of fish soup. Then I stopped on the last page—

The drawing wasn't finished, but I recognized the river, the gently sloped hill, the two silhouettes bent over the water with lanterns in hand. It was of Takkan and me, our wrists connected by a red thread that traced all the way to the moon.

My heart squeezed. There was so much left unsaid between us, so much we still had to work out. But whatever chance we had would disappear if I failed to find the shards.

I closed the book. They were waiting for me: my brothers, my father, Takkan. I couldn't let them down.

Clasping my hands together, I held tight to the memory of Takkan, my family, everything about home that I loved and cherished. I gathered every bit of strength I had and held my breath until I was ready—until the pressure inside me was about to burst. Then I let it go.

Like fire, silver-gold threads emanated from every point in my body.

They were strands of my soul, I understood—thanks to Lady Solzaya—but I'd never seen them before when I had used my magic. Then again, maybe I'd never known what to look for.

As they streamed forth, I whispered my intent, *Find the seven.*

With a wave of my arm, I cast the strands across the field

of mirror shards. I could feel the enchantment, like a breeze tickling the pores of my skin. It swept through the sea, making the shards tinkle a soft percussive song.

Seven shards began to glow, their edges luminous, as if touched by the moon. One by one I tracked them, clasping them in my hand, until I was down to the final piece. . . .

It was farther than the rest. Nearly at the edge of the field. As I swam for it, sharp ripples cut my path, holding me at bay.

The sand is nearly out! Kiki yelled. *Hurry, Shiori!*

I glimpsed over my shoulder at the hourglass. Kiki was right: only a thin layer of grains remained.

I needed to hurry. The seventh mirror piece was still glowing, but I knew my concentration would break any second now. I kicked furiously, stretching my arms and scrabbling for my quarry.

My nails scraped its corner, and as I was about to fold my fingers around the last piece, all the shards shuddered and began to tilt.

In one swift, foul swoop, the current changed direction. I flew back, grabbing Kiki by the wing and shoving her into my sleeve.

Too late, I spun to save Takkan's sketchbook. But the shards ripped through it, tearing its precious pages to shreds.

I couldn't even salvage the scraps. The last grain of sand slipped through the hourglass, and Solzaya's test vanished, everything within its bounds disintegrating into the sea. The dragon reappeared with a smirk, and my heart sank.

"Six out of the seven," she said. "A better effort than I

expected from such a meager sorceress. Unfortunately, you've failed."

I couldn't speak. I'd lost everything.

Everything.

My hands shaking, I had started to reach inside my satchel for the pearl when Kiki crawled out of my sleeve.

Stop! she cried. There was something between her wings, and she tossed it onto my palm.

The seventh shard.

I held it up, a grin spreading across my face as Solzaya's smirk disappeared.

"Well done, bloodsake of Kiata," she said, though her voice trembled with barely contained wrath. "A promise is a promise. You may keep the last shard."

I hugged my bird. "I could kiss you."

I'd rather you get us out of here, Kiki said. *As soon as possible, ideally.*

She was right, and I turned to Solzaya. "How do I leave Ai'long?"

"See there?" Solzaya pointed toward the surface, at the shimmering whorls of soft pink and yellow glancing off the waves. "Where the beams cut through the sea marks the western border of Ai'long. Past it is the mortal realm. I would recommend you reach it before my father arrives."

Fear chipped away my excitement. "But I thought—"

"That I would let you go?" Solzaya spoke over me. "I have." A new smirk twisted her lips. "But I never promised to protect you against my father. And it appears he is here."

I glanced behind me, where an army of sharks and jelly-fish had assembled, led by the Dragon King.

Stupid, stupid, stupid, I cursed. I should have known better than to trust a dragon.

Adrenaline rushing to my head, I grabbed Kiki and swam for the surface. I could nearly touch the streaks of violet refracting downward, could make out the changing folds of the surface, where the edges of Ai'long dissolved into the mortal realm. The promise of salt tickled my lips.

I was close.

Then the water thickened. Twisted and churned. Its temperature plummeted, and cold shot through my muscles, turning my legs to lead. For every kick, I rose one pace and dropped ten.

Kiki bit my hair, trying to pull me up. *Come on, Shiori. Fight!*

I was trying, but I may as well have been swimming through tar. No amount of paddling and kicking did any good. The water fought against me, pulling me down, back into Ai'long.

Nazayun plucked me up between two claws. Lightning crackled from his eyes and hair. "Sever your ties with the pearl, Shiori'anma, or I shall do it for you."

I clenched my jaw. "The. Pearl. Isn't. Yours."

"Very well." The Dragon King sighed. His eyes and hair raged with lightning. "Then, like the pearl you bear, you shall break."

CHAPTER FOURTEEN

Everything happened so fast I scarcely knew I'd been hit.

But then I was flying back, a wave of heat scalding my skin. I assumed I'd turn to dust, to stone, or to sea foam, but everything was awash in green. And I was still breathing. My heart, still pumping. I pressed my cheek against prickly seagrass, and I spat out the sand that coated my teeth.

It appeared an eel had come blasting to my rescue.

At least, it looked like an eel. I couldn't be sure. My vision was watery, and my heart was still roaring in my ears. All I saw was that long green blob with two red eyes.

Seryu!

Seryu had returned with a battalion of turtles—and my starstroke net!

He charged from the left, and the turtles came from the right. Together, at the same time, they rammed into the Dragon King, the turtles' tough shells absorbing the impact of Nazayun's strikes.

I crawled onto my forearms, pressing my forehead to the seagrass as my breath steadied. A turtle the size of a donkey had landed at my side, and it scooped me onto its back. With great haste, we spiraled up, and I craned my neck to see why the creature was in such a rush.

Seryu was fighting his grandfather. And losing.

Nazayun had his claws wrapped around Seryu's throat, and my friend floundered, like a fish on a hook. His tail had gone slack, his claws making one last swipe at his grandfather's iron-hard scales before falling to his sides. The starstroke net flagged in his grasp.

I couldn't simply watch and do nothing. I leaned forward, urging my turtle to swim faster. "We have to help."

"You shall not intervene," came a voice from behind. A tentacle hooked around my ankles, dragging me off my turtle and bringing me face to face with Solzaya.

"What are you doing?" I yelled at her. "Nazayun's killing him!"

"Nazayun will not harm Seryu," said Solzaya.

"Look at his eyes," I cried. "Look at *both* their eyes."

The Dragon King's eyes flashed white, wild and pupilless. As Seryu squirmed in his grandfather's grip, his scales dulled. The spark in his red eyes was fast fading. . . .

"He's killing him!"

"Enough!" Solzaya barked. Her octopus covered my mouth with an arm, stifling my cries. Still, I could sense the indecision plaguing her. A muscle twitched in her jaw, and her gold-tipped horns darkened with tension.

But if she meant to act, she had missed her chance.

Seryu's tail went deathly still, and his whiskers drooped as his head lolled back. In triumph, Nazayun flung him away.

I bit into one of the octopus's tentacles and screamed, "Seryu!"

With a resounding thump, he landed on the bedrock.

His tail curled up involuntarily, but otherwise he didn't move. The starstroke net was crumpled in his claw, its ends peeking out through his closed fist. Nazayun's lackeys descended upon him, trying to pry it away, but they couldn't open his fingers.

I clenched my fists too, not daring to even move.

The net was sizzling, and Seryu's brow made a fearsome crease before it went slack.

"Seryu!" I cried out again, my voice echoed by Lady Solzaya this time.

A growl boomed from where he'd landed. Then there came a flash of light, so bright that even Solzaya teetered back. From Seryu emanated an aura of the deepest green.

And suddenly he began to grow.

His eyes swelled like full moons, and his horns tripled in length, branching out into a crown over his hair. The scales on his back bulked out into plates of emerald armor. In a rush of green, he grew and grew until his grandfather could no longer strangle him with one hand. Until he rivaled the Dragon King himself in size and magnificence.

Seryu opened his fist, brandishing the starstroke net.

Nazayun laughed. "You cannot harm me. It is against your oath."

"I know I cannot harm you. But Shiori can."

With a roar, Seryu lashed out his great tail, seizing his grandfather by the neck. His strength took the Dragon King by surprise, and both dragons turned to Lady Solzaya.

"Mother!" cried Seryu. "Let Shiori go."

"Contain your son!" Nazayun bellowed at the same time.

Solzaya hesitated, and her golden eyes turned wintry. "My son has arrived at his full form, Father. He is no longer mine to contain." The remaining mirror shards flew from her necklace and lodged themselves into the Dragon King's tail, pinning him still. "Just as I am not yours."

Spurts of ink clouded the water as Solzaya's octopus released me, and I raced to Seryu's side. Kiki took one end of the starstroke net, and I the other. Together, while Seryu pinned the Dragon King down, we threw it over Nazayun's chest.

"Now, Grandfather, let's try this once again," said Seryu through his teeth. "A dragon's word is his honor. His honor is his pearl. You will promise that no dragon—including yourself—shall harm Shiori and her kin, so long as they live."

"How dare you," Nazayun rasped as the starstroke net's magic gripped the contours of his heart. "I am a god of dragons. I will not bow down to any mortal."

Out of his eyes shot forth a bolt of magic, and the water turned cataclysmic.

A monstrous wave folded forward, and Seryu grabbed me by the ankle and pulled me onto his back as he bore its brunt. Fierce currents wheeled our way, uprooting the seagrass, the coral forests—everything in their path.

Seryu and I were next.

As Seryu shielded me with his body, the Wraith's pearl flew out from under my arm. It rose like a dark moon, its halves cracking apart and spreading wider than ever before.

Dazzling light burst from its center. Nazayun's waves crashed against an invisible wall. They could not touch us.

The pearl's light met Nazayun's defensive shield head on and pushed forward, advancing for the Dragon King.

I reached for it, offering what strength I could. It was like embracing a broken star about to explode. I wasn't sure whether it could control itself.

"Don't break," I told the pearl. "Use as much force as you need to, but don't break. Please."

The pearl shuddered. It was straining against Nazayun, and new fractures had appeared upon its dark, gleaming surface. Its halves cracked wider, fanning light in all directions.

Don't break, I repeated before letting it go once more.

While the Dragon King was distracted by the pearl, I gathered the ends of the starstroke net and pulled with all my strength.

Nazayun's heart emerged, brilliantly gold. I cupped my palms around its curved surface, cradling it. It was hot and cold at the same time, and blazed like glass that was newly forged. With a heave of my arms, I yanked it free.

I had his pearl. The Dragon King's pearl!

The two pearls were as different as could be. One dark and broken, the other whole and bright and shining. Well, Nazayun's pearl was not so bright anymore. Its light became subdued, and the mountainous currents that he had summoned rolled away and vanished.

Once the sea had stilled, Seryu closed his fist around his grandfather's heart. "You will swear now," he said icily.

Nazayun snarled, writhing with anger. His tail lashed this way and that, dislodging the mirror shards and crushing the rocks below into dust. But he had no choice.

"I will honor the promise," he said with vehemence. "Neither I nor any dragon of my realm shall harm you, Shiori'anma—or your kin. You will be safe from us, in sky, in sea, and on earth. This I vow, as King of Ai'long and Ruler of the Four Supreme Seas."

The power of his oath made the seas tremble, and a cold tingle rushed along my skin.

"Thank you," I said, not knowing how else to respond.

Seryu said nothing. He merely held out his grandfather's heart.

Nazayun snatched it. He tried to snatch the starstroke net too, but Seryu cast his own spell, and it fizzled into foam.

"A weapon against one dragon is a weapon against all of us," said my friend. "It shall not be used again."

Before the Dragon King could show his displeasure, Seryu lengthened his body, a subtle reminder that his new might rivaled Nazayun's own.

"Tell the girl to close the damned pearl," Nazayun growled. "Before it destroys us all."

Light spilled from the pearl's broken center, and no amount of my strength could push the halves shut. "Enough," I told it again. "You've won."

135

Close up! Kiki trilled, flicking her wings at the pearl. *Come on, you fussy little bead. Close up, or you'll never go home.*

Kiki flicked again, and the pearl finally obeyed. With a snap and a hiss, the halves shut, and it went dark.

The chaos that had descended upon Ai'long finally calmed, leaving the waters serene and silent. Fish and crabs poked charily out of the shattered reefs, Solzaya's octopus detangled itself from a clot of seaweed, and a crew of turtles paddled for the surface.

Exhausted, I grabbed the pearl and rolled it into my satchel. When I looked up again, the Dragon King was gone.

Only Seryu and Lady Solzaya remained.

No smirk twisted Solzaya's lips, no malice gleamed in her eyes. Rather, she looked almost pleased.

"Mother—" Seryu began.

"You have reached your full form," said Solzaya, cutting him off. "You have come of age, at last. Seize your victory and take the girl home. Quickly."

We didn't need to be told twice. As Solzaya retreated, her six remaining mirror shards rearranged themselves into a necklace at her throat, and I grabbed onto Seryu's horns.

For the last time, we rode the waters of Ai'long and ascended to the surface. For home.

CHAPTER FIFTEEN

Glorious gods, it felt good to breathe! Had air always been so fresh and sweet? I inhaled greedily, embracing the brackish spray that stung my nose and the wind that lashed my face.

Best of all was the sun. I arched my neck back to bask in its warmth. It felt like I was already home, sitting too close to the fire until my cheeks were as toasty as griddle cakes. My stomach growled, dreaming of cakes. Sugared rice cakes, monkeycakes, red bean and strawberry cakes. I'd eat them until I collapsed.

But I was getting ahead of myself. It wasn't time to leave the water just yet.

I followed Seryu toward a distant figure on a rock island shrouded in fog. It was Elang, watching the sunrise, long human fingers skimming the water. When we approached, he whirled to face us, his mismatched eyes narrowing at the sight of Seryu.

"I see you've finally reached your full form, cousin.

Congratulations." Elang's tone was colorless. There was nothing congratulatory about it. "You have the shard?"

I'd tucked the precious mirror shard into my sash for safe-keeping. As I took it out, Seryu snatched it from my fingers and waved it angrily at his cousin.

"You think we're going to hand the mirror of truth over after you tried to drug and lock me in that pitiful cellar you call a dungeon? Shiori was nearly killed, thanks to you."

"You're being overly dramatic," Elang replied dispassionately. "I equipped you with my turtles, did I not? And the starstroke net? I hardly broke my promise."

"I think differently." Before I could stop him, Seryu raised the mirror high over his head and snapped it in half. He hurled half the shard at his cousin. "This half is for you, the other for Shiori."

Elang caught the mirror piece in one hand. A pause. "Half a shard is acceptable. The deal is honored."

I held my half of the shard. The glass reflected the glistening waves. "I don't know what to do with this."

"Keep it," said Seryu. "It'll help you find the Wraith."

Elang disagreed. "No, it won't. The shard will tell you many things about the past and present, but it will not reveal the Wraith. Not while he dwells on Lapzur."

"Lapzur?" I asked. "I've never heard of the place."

"Most haven't. It is a realm steeped in darkness and over-run by ghosts and demons. Not even the mirror can see what unfolds there."

"Then how will I find it?"

"That I cannot help you with." Elang picked up his turtle's reins, preparing to descend into the sea.

"Wait," I called. "You promised his name."

Elang's back was to me, but he halted. After a long pause, he replied, "His name is Khramelan."

Khramelan. My satchel shuddered against my hip, the pearl inside growing suddenly warm.

"Do not discount the mirror's value," said Elang, his back still to me. "It will not bring you to the Wraith, but it still holds great power."

"Thank you."

For once, he didn't dismiss my gratitude. He stepped onto his turtle, flicking Kiki off its shell. He was about to dive into the sea when I blurted one last question:

"Why turtles?"

To my surprise, Elang actually replied. "They are solitary creatures, though they live in large groups. I find I have more in common with them than with humans—or dragons."

"Their shells are hard," I mused, "and their hearts are soft."

That earned me a glower. "I have no heart."

"You aren't without heart. You wouldn't have helped me if that were the case."

"I helped you to get my mirror," Elang said gruffly. His mismatched eyes narrowed. "Only by the miracle of the gods did you manage to succeed."

"So I did," I said. "I hope it shows you what you need to see. Have faith, Lord Elang. Your pearl is out there somewhere. You'll find it."

"I will," he assured me, "and I will celebrate the day I never have to set foot in your waste-ridden land again in search of it."

I stifled the urge to roll my eyes. Coming from the half dragon, this was as good a farewell as I would get. "That waste-ridden land is my home."

Elang pulled his turtle's reins. "You'd do well to remember this: your *heart* is your home. Until you understand that, you belong nowhere."

And before I could say another word, he launched into the sea.

I watched until the ripples of Elang's departure had vanished and the water went as still as before. *Your heart is your home.* I let the words sink into my memory. *Until you understand that, you belong nowhere.*

I turned to Seryu. "Your cousin isn't so bad, for not having a heart. It makes me hopeful about the Wraith."

"Then you're deluded, Shiori'anma. The Wraith's half demon. He's a—"

"An abomination?" My shoulders fell. "They used to say that about Raikama too. All her life, she was a monster. First to the human world, which thought her a snake, then to herself, when she was cursed to wear her sister's face."

I swallowed, certain that there were plenty of people back home who thought me a monster now.

A cloud drifted over the sun, casting a long shadow upon the sea. I said, "Whatever the Wraith is—dragon or demon or monster—he deserves his pearl back. Same as Elang." I swallowed again. "Will you help me find him, Seryu?"

Seryu said nothing. His face was completely inscrutable, which was unusual for my ever-expressive friend. When he caught me staring, he turned away abruptly.

"Get on my back," he said curtly. "Let's get you to shore before the fishermen see us. All this sun is starting to hurt my eyes."

Seryu dove, but not before I glanced at the sky, just to confirm.

A sea of clouds still buried the dawn. There was no sun.

It wasn't until I was wading ashore, bunching up the folds of my dress as I trampled toward the beach, that I noticed the sand in my hair.

Kiki landed on my head. *We just got home. How is your hair so dirty already?*

I dropped my skirt and crouched by the water to stare at my reflection.

"It's not sand," I realized. It was a streak of silvery white hair at my temple, no different from Raikama's.

With a deep exhale, I blew it out of my face and patted my cheeks. Better a few locks of white hair than a fishtail or horns. Father would still recognize his only daughter. I just hoped the rest of Kiata would too.

When I'd left home, my country was on the cusp of spring. Now heat clung to the air, and my skin was sticky with humidity—a sign that we were well into summer.

I'd been gone for half a year.

My knees buckled at the realization. Six months, lost.

It could have easily been six years, or sixty, I reminded myself. When I looked at it that way, a laugh bubbled up in my throat. I was home. I'd won.

The wind threw Kiki up, and she squealed, flailing her wings. It felt like magic. It brimmed in the air, faint but stronger than before. As my cheeks tingled, Kiki and I dissolved into a fit of giggles.

Seryu shook his head. He'd shifted into his human form, but his hair was still green, darker in the sun than it had been underwater. "I'm starting to think I should've let you drown in the Sacred Lake."

Still laughing, I sat up, digging my heels into the sand. "Then you would have missed out on a grand adventure, Seryu. And a wonderful friendship."

"Your friendship has caused me nothing but trouble." Seryu kicked at the sand. "Who knows what Grandfather will do to me when I return? He might cut off my horns. Or exile me from Ai'long."

"Your mother wouldn't allow that," I replied. "She might take joy in tormenting *me,* but she cares for you. When you reached your full form, I swear she preened." I offered him a slanted grin. "It must be an important rite of passage for dragons."

"It is," said Seryu. "Were you impressed?"

"Very. You don't look like an eel anymore."

His chest puffed out, just a little, with pride. "Then I guess it was all worth it."

I stopped smiling. "You could stay here, you know. On land, with my brothers and me. We'd make you welcome."

"I'd rather Grandfather turn me into a squid than live among your kind for the rest of my immortal life," Seryu huffed. "And I'd rather choke on seaweed than watch you and that horse-trough boy make fish eyes at each other."

"We don't make fish—"

Seryu covered my mouth with a sleeve, silencing me. His snide expression had fled, and he lowered his arm. "I have to know," he said quietly. "If not for him, did I ever have a chance?"

A lump swelled in my throat. I didn't want to hurt him. "Takkan and I are connected by the strands of fate."

I expected him to be jealous, but the corners of his mouth lifted. "Then I'll have to find you when you're reborn—before your strands have time to knot with his again." His red eyes twinkled. "I only pray you won't be a human again in the next life. Now that I've reached my full form, I'm far too majestic to stomach your world again."

I didn't know whether to punch him or laugh. Or cry. My shoulders softened, and I spoke. "So this is goodbye?"

The twinkle left his eyes. "I doubt I'll be permitted to visit your realm for many years. Maybe not until you're an old woman. All pruny and wrinkled, with seventeen great-grandchildren." He snorted in distaste. "See, your hair is already starting to gray."

I let out a laugh. "White," I corrected, combing through the snow-touched locks with my fingers. "It turned white from using the Wraith's pearl, not from age."

"Same difference." Seryu waved a dismissive hand. His sleeves and robes were already dry, unlike mine. A useful enchantment.

He was in a mercurial mood, his true thoughts impossible to decipher. But when he spoke again, he sounded strangely gentle. "If you do end up marrying that lordling, I hope they take after you, not him."

"Who?"

"Those great-grandchildren," he replied, tartly now. "Gods forbid they be dull and stiff-necked."

I couldn't help defending Takkan. "He isn't dull and stiff-necked. You barely spoke to him!"

"Something I regret deeply," Seryu replied. "He should know I won't be saving you again, so he had better be up to the task."

I put my hands on my hips. "You do realize I'm capable of saving myself from time to time."

"Even still. With all the trouble you get into, Shiori . . . all the trouble you're *going* to get into . . . you need whatever help you can get. Make sure he knows that." After a pause, he said, "Make sure he deserves you."

There came a twinge in my heart, and my hands fell to my sides. Not long ago, I could have imagined falling in love with Seryu. If Raikama had never cursed me, if I'd never spent that winter in Iro, it might have been him that I longed for, not Takkan.

But that would have made for a different story. Not this one.

"He does," I said softly, "deserve me."

"I'll take your word for it," grunted Seryu. "I'll be visiting those great-grandchildren, you know, and telling them stories about you. Unflattering stories, to repay all the grief your friendship has given me."

I hid a smile. For all his churlish remarks, Seryu was trying hard to be impassive and dragon-like. But I knew him better than that.

"Tell them some nice things too," I said lightly.

He grunted again. "I suppose I'll have time to think of some."

Seryu arose now and turned for the sea. His horns were growing—the first sign that he was beginning to transform back into a dragon.

"Wait!" I shouted after him. "Don't forget this."

I held out the necklace he had given me what felt like a lifetime ago and pressed it into his palm.

"Don't you dare say it," he muttered, hooking his claws through the necklace.

"Say what?"

"All those idiotic Kiatan farewells: 'May our strands cross again' and, worse yet, 'May the luck of the dragons be with you.' If you say such things, I'll have no choice but to drag you back into the sea."

I wanted to laugh, but I couldn't. "Farewell, my friend," I whispered. *I'll miss you,* I wanted to say, but the words caught in my throat.

Instead, I hugged him.

The dragon was caught off guard and immediately stiffened, but he didn't push me away. Before he could utter anything that might ruin the moment, I pressed my lips to his cheek. A kiss, like the one I'd given him all those months ago by the Sacred Lake the first time we'd said goodbye. "Thank you for everything."

Seryu's breath hitched, and his skin felt far too warm for him, a cold-blooded dragon. He drew back and, mustering a lofty tone, said, "It would never have worked between us, being companions and all. We're both far too proud—and I'm far too magnificent."

I tilted my head but didn't speak. I knew he wasn't finished.

His voice went solemn. "All the same, I'm glad to have known you, Shiori. You're interesting, for a human. When you look into the sea, think of me sometimes."

"I will," I said softly.

As he whirled, a hard gust of wind made me fall back into the sand. By the time I got up again, all I saw was a splash in the water—followed by a sharp flare of sunlight. I shielded my eyes, trying to stare through the light to glimpse the dragon's tail.

But Seryu was gone.

For a long time, I watched the water, half wishing he might bubble up again.

Kiki landed on my shoulder. *I'll miss that dragon, horns and all.* She peered up when I said nothing. *You all right, Shiori?*

No, I wasn't.

Seryu's strand and mine had been knotted once, tied so

146

closely by fate that we had almost been bound forever. Now I wasn't sure whether they would ever cross again.

The taste in my mouth was bittersweet, and I swallowed hard, finally answering: "I will be."

I will be. I pulled myself to my feet and wrung my skirt of seawater. "Come, Kiki, it's time to go home."

CHAPTER SIXTEEN

Sand kneaded between my toes as I hiked across the beach, chasing the rolling hills in the distance, the curved red roofs that peeked out from behind a sprawling wall of pine trees.

Gindara. The palace. Home.

In a few hours, I'd be back. Maybe in time for lunch with my brothers—and Father, whom I hadn't seen in over a year.

Look! Kiki cried, spying ships. *Your father's sent the navy to greet you!*

An entire fleet was assembled behind the sea cliffs, crowding Kiata's coastline with brilliant red sails and banners.

My throat tightened. I replied in a low voice, "Those are A'landan ships."

I clambered up the dunes to higher ground and shielded my eyes from the sun, squinting to figure out why A'landan ships were docked on Kiatan shores. But it was impossible to see from so far away.

Nine Hells, Kiki uttered. *Has Kiata been conquered?*

Six months ago, when I left, relations with A'landi had grown increasingly volatile. Had the situation escalated while I was in the dragon realm?

"It's too early to make assumptions," I replied as calmly as I could, but my fists were clenched at my sides. Answers would come once I reached Gindara.

Or sooner.

In the middle distance, a group of men were calling my name. "Princess Shiori!"

The coast's keen winds distorted their voices, but I recognized their crimson-feathered helmets. I'd grown up surrounded by them.

My father's sentinels.

Relief washed over me. I straightened my back and squared my shoulders, trying to summon an air of royalty. There was little I could do about the sand clinging to my cheeks or the kisses of algae in my hair, but I could at least stand like a princess.

"Princess Shiori'anma?" the captain asked. He and his men kept their distance, and their hands were not far from their swords.

Honestly, I couldn't blame him for questioning who I was. I looked like I'd been spat out from the sea, and I still wore the robes of the dragon court. Though they were stained and wrinkled, their gossamer layers were undeniably from another world, sparkling with pearls. And there was that bolt of white in my hair.

"It's me," I confirmed. "Shiori'anma."

At the familiar sound of my voice, the sentinels bowed as one, and the captain relaxed his stance, slightly.

"Forgive us for asking, Your Highness," he said in a careful tone. "We've been stationed here for months to await your return. We were told to expect you, but we didn't know where or when or . . ."

His voice trailed, but an unspoken *how* lingered in the air.

How had I come back, the sentinels were surely wondering, without ship or mount?

And where had I been? The men were striving hard not to stare at my dress, but I could read their bafflement easily.

I put on a smile. "I didn't have to wait long. Thank you."

The captain cleared his throat. "We should have found you sooner, but with the arrival of the A'landans—"

"Yes, I saw the ships down by the cliffs," I interrupted. "Are we at war?"

"Not if Prince Reiji's wedding proceeds smoothly."

The smile fled my lips. "Wedding?"

"I assumed that's why you'd returned."

I had no idea what wedding he spoke of. I knew I should keep quiet, but I couldn't help myself: "When is it?"

The captain didn't manage to hide his surprise in time, and I wanted to kick myself. Of course he assumed I would know. I was the princess of Kiata—how could I not be aware of my own brother's wedding?

"It is today," he replied as his men exchanged awkward looks they thought I wouldn't see. "Right now, in fact."

150

The sentinels advised me to change my dress before barging into the Temple of the Sacred Crane for Reiji's wedding. Their suggestion was perfectly sensible, and I meant to take it.

But once I returned to the palace, my mind changed like the wind. I'd been away for far too long, and I'd missed far too many important moments. I wouldn't miss Reiji's wedding.

One of the sentinels had given me his cloak, and it flared out over my shoulders as I raced to the temple. This was home: the white sand courtyards, the pavilions with sloping eaves and hanging bronze lanterns. Jays and thrushes whistled from the gardens, and I could smell the citrus orchards ahead.

But not everything was the same.

Colorful banners swirled from the palace's vermilion pillars, welcoming our A'landan visitors. Around the temple, hundreds had gathered to observe my brother's alliance with the foreign princess. Naturally, the A'landans stuck out from the crowd, their ostentation rivaling that of the dragons in Ai'long.

Bedecked in the boldest shades of red, blue, and gold, our visitors strutted about, intent on outshining everyone. I wondered if the court officials, with their kingfisher headdresses and elaborately embroidered coats, tripped over each other on the way here, given how long their sleeves trailed.

Do they always dress like that? asked Kiki.

"Like a pride of peacocks?" I scoffed. "Only when they come to Kiata."

The rivalry between A'landi and Kiata was as old as our countries. I could tell from our freshly pruned trees, the way the lacquered benches outside the halls shone, the stiffly ironed uniforms of the servants, that we had played our own part in this petty competition.

What an unwelcome sight I must be, wearing a sentinel's cloak over my shoulders, with sand sprinkling from my slippers and seaweed stuck to my hair.

My return stunned everyone who recognized me: the lords and ladies kneeling outside the temple, the priests milling by the stairs. Even the guards jerked their heads for a second look when I passed.

"Princess Shiori!" one of the priests by the temple doors exclaimed, flustered by my arrival. "We were not told that you had returned."

"I have," I said in my most authoritative voice. "Now open the doors."

"I'm afraid that isn't permitted, not even for you, Shiori'anma," he replied. "The ceremony has already begun, and they are in the middle of their prayers—"

"I'll be quiet," I said. "No one will even notice me come in."

"But, Your Highness—"

I never used to pay attention to the priests before, and I wasn't going to start now. With a lift of my arms and a whisper to the trees, I summoned a calamity of leaves to the temple's grand entrance.

The leaves flew, pasting themselves to the priests' faces like paper masks. As the priests cried for the guards, I traipsed up the temple steps, removed my slippers, and let myself inside.

I *was* quiet, as promised, closing the hefty doors with care. Still, everyone noticed me enter.

The temple held not the crowd of hundreds that I'd expected. The gathering inside was intimate; I could make out the backs of my father, my six brothers and a lady next to Andahai, the high priest and two monks, and a smattering of A'landi officials.

Takkan was nowhere to be found. And I didn't even see Reiji's bride.

Grumbles and sniffs punctuated the ceremonial silence, and I started to regret barging inside—until my brothers turned around.

How strange and wonderful it was to see them all, sitting beside Father and dressed in their court finery, as if nothing had changed. It gave me hope that I might slip back into my old life.

All six beamed at me, surprise and joy unraveling their ceremonial formality. Even Reiji, who knelt in the center of the temple beside a painting of Princess Sina Anan, his future wife, offered a nod.

I risked a glance at Father, daring hope he might acknowledge me too. But the emperor did as the A'landans did. With a clipped motion, he turned back to face the high priest.

Disappointment rose up to my eyes in a scalding wave, and I bit the inside of my cheek, shrinking into a corner to wait until the ceremony was over. Unfortunately, Kiki's gauge of human emotion was sorely lacking, and she didn't sense to leave me alone.

I thought your brother was marrying an A'landan princess, tittered my bird. *All I see is a piece of parchment.*

I shrugged.

Who's that girl beside Andahai? She looked nervous to see you.

Did she? I'd been so happy to see my family that I had barely noticed her. With oval eyes and berry-colored lips, she looked as delicate as the lilacs embroidered on her lavender jacket. Her hands were demurely set on her lap, and if her ornate robes caused her any discomfort, she was a master of hiding it. She possessed the poise my tutors had long since given up trying to instill in me.

"Yihei'an Qinnia," I said. "Andahai's fiancée."

Andahai was supposed to have married her last autumn, mere weeks after Raikama had turned my brothers into cranes and sent us all away. Obviously, that wedding had been postponed.

I watched my brother and his betrothed. Their heads were tilted close, shoulders touching. This tender side of Andahai was new to me. Then again, I had been away for half a year.

Much had changed.

Including Father.

He'd aged during the time I'd been away. There were new lines on his brow, etched with a melancholy that hadn't been there before.

I ached to see him, to speak to him and make him smile, but not once did he glance back at me. With every passing minute, my heart sank a little deeper. I hoped he wasn't furious I had left—or disappointed.

Finally, a gong resonated across the hall, and my brothers scrambled back to join me, barraging me with an unprincely slew of hugs and questions.

Wandei, the concerned: "When did you get back, sister?"

Andahai, the eldest: "You should have told us you were coming back."

Benkai, the thoughtful: "You look well."

Hasho, the sincere: "You look different."

Yotan, already focused on the irrelevant: "But what are you wearing?"

There were other queries in my brothers' eyes too, secret ones concerning magic and Ai'long. But no one spoke them aloud. There'd be time for those questions later.

I peeked back at the A'landans and the ministers in the room. Polite smiles strained their expressions, similar to those of the sentinels at the beach when they'd first seen me.

"Did I sprout horns on my head while in Ai'long?" I murmured to Benkai. "Why is everyone staring?"

Benkai's handsome face stretched to fit a smile. "You did just barge in on a state wedding, you know—after we told the A'landans you were in Gaijha, studying the Songs of Sorrow and the Epics of War and Duty."

I balked. "You should have told them I was studying cookery. At least that would be somewhat believable."

Benkai chuckled, and my other brothers merely smiled. Hasho, who had always been the worst at secrets, shifted his weight from foot to foot, looking uneasy. What weren't they telling me?

"Late as usual, Shiori," Andahai chided, but his stern eyes

were smiling for once. "We expected you back months ago. You missed my wedding, but at least you didn't miss Reiji's."

I should have guessed that Andahai had married while I was away, but still my mouth parted in surprise. "You're married?"

"It was a small ceremony, within the one hundred days of Raikama's death." He pursed his lips. "I wanted to wait, but . . . but we didn't know when you were coming back."

Even without the explanation, I would have understood. I hadn't known when I'd return, either. And from the looks of it, Father needed all the alliances he could get to protect Kiata.

"Allow me to reintroduce you to my wife, Princess Qinnia."

Qinnia came timidly forward. Up close, she was very pale, and shadows clung to her cheeks. She looked like she'd lost weight recently. I bowed quickly before she noticed I was staring, and before making eye contact. It was the proper thing to do: as the crown princess, she now outranked me.

"Please, Shiori'anma, bowing isn't necessary—"

"It's my honor," I said, bowing even more deeply. I rose with a grin. "And call me Shiori, please—I thank the Strands I won't be the only princess of Kiata anymore. I suppose this means you can take my place in the morning prayers?"

"She's joking," Andahai reassured his wife.

I cleared my expression of mischief. "I've always wanted an older sister. Welcome to the family. Can you tell the twins apart yet?"

That made her smile. "As of last week. Yotan has a mole on his chin—and unlike Wandei, he's constantly smiling."

"Wandei also tends to squint when he's looking in the distance," added Reiji, finally joining us. "He spent too much time reading by candlelight when he was young."

I hugged Reiji. When I let him go, I dusted off the sand I'd gotten on his ceremonial robes. "Where is *your* bride?" I asked.

"Still in A'landi. It's a marriage by proxy."

"You mean, she isn't coming?"

Eyeing the A'landans remaining in the temple, Reiji explained in a hushed tone: "I'm to go to Jappor and marry the khagan's daughter so we can establish peace."

"You'll be a hostage there!"

"I want to go," said Reiji. "Andahai and Benkai have always upheld their duties. It's time I did something useful too."

There was no bitterness in my brother's voice. Reiji's tone was light, and I could tell he was being sincere. So why did his words make my heart feel heavy?

"When do you leave?" I asked.

Reiji didn't get a chance to reply.

All six princes immediately stepped back into a line, bowing. Father was right behind me.

It took all my restraint to bow too and not look up. I hadn't seen him since my brothers and I had been cursed. More than anything, I wanted to embrace him as I had my brothers, and answer the hundreds of questions he must have. But it was a good thing I held back.

157

"Months away without any word," the emperor reproved, "then upon your return, you insolently disrupt a sacred ceremony. Shaming Kiata before A'landi's envoys!"

My spirits deflated. "Father . . ."

"You will return to your chambers at once," he said, turning for the shrine exit. "Attire yourself in something befitting an imperial princess, and await my visit. You have much to answer for, daughter."

CHAPTER SEVENTEEN

The sting of Father's rebuke followed me all the way to my room, and I was quiet in Qinnia's company. My new sister-in-law had insisted on walking with me, and she graciously filled the silence with anecdotes about what Andahai and my brothers had been up to while I was away. It was a kind gesture, and I warmed to her for it.

You should make friends with her, urged Kiki from inside my sleeve. *She seems nice.*

Not today. I wasn't in the mood.

"Here we are," Qinnia announced, sliding my doors open.

I stepped inside. In my memory, I'd only been away a week; I remembered precisely how I'd left my room. A mess, with towers of silk pillows beside my bed, and clothes and half-empty plates strewn across the floor. But everything had been tidied up and put away, even the tiny nook of cushions I'd made for Kiki. Ivory mourning sheets hung over my windows, and scrolls and prayer plaques hemmed my bed, wishing me safe passage to the afterlife.

"I'll send for someone to take all this away," Qinnia said, looking more stricken than I was by all the mourning arrangements. "The emperor had them put up again when you left."

"It's all right," I said. "It doesn't bother me."

I headed straight for the washing chamber. I could feel the brine between my toes and the weight of the sand still in my hair. It'd be good to bathe. I bet I smelled horrible.

Qinnia followed. "You'll need help with that."

She was gesturing at the hundreds of buttons on the pink dress gifted me by the dragons. They'd be impossible for me to undo on my own.

"Oh," I said sheepishly. "Thank you."

Carefully, she undid the button loops. "This material is exquisite," she murmured. "The stitching is finer than anything I've ever seen."

Aside from a few tactful remarks, Qinnia asked no questions of where I'd been, of the scars on my fingers or the white streak in my hair. I wondered if she'd hound Andahai for answers later. Or maybe she already knew.

"There," she said when the last button was undone. "Would you like me to send my maids over to have it cleaned and mended?"

"There's no need." I took one last glance at the dress, and the memory of Seryu's farewell brought a twinge to my heart. "Thank you for the offer, but I'll keep it as it is."

I disappeared into the bath alone. When I emerged, dressed in a simple purple robe with embroidered butterflies, the summer sun was flooding my rooms.

Qinnia was taking down the mourning sheets one by one. She was breathing hard.

"Let me help," I offered, but she was already on the last sheet. "You're the crown princess, you shouldn't be—"

"No task is beneath a princess," she said with a smile. "My mother taught me that. It makes you stronger."

I gave a small smile in return. That was something Raikama would have said.

Qinnia was looking tired, and I offered her a seat, but she shook her head.

"I should take my leave. Your father will be here soon." She touched my arm, preempting any response. "Andahai wouldn't want me to tell you this, but you should know— when His Majesty woke from the winter slumber, the first person he asked for was you, Shiori."

I lifted my head. "Me?"

"The emperor grieved for you all the months that you were away." Qinnia folded the mourning sheets over her arms. "He thought you had died along with your stepmother, and nothing your brothers said could convince him that you were still alive."

Heat pricked the corners of my eyes. I didn't know what to say. "I'm glad you told me."

She squeezed my arm. "And I'm glad you're back. I'll see you at the family dinner."

When she left, Kiki flitted out of my sleeve. Ever oblivious to the finer human emotions, she thought nothing of me standing in a corner blinking back tears.

That was close! she exclaimed. *Qinnia almost saw the*

pearl in your bag. You'd better put it away before your father comes.

That got my attention. I'd almost forgotten about the pearl. My shard from the mirror of truth, too.

Father wasn't here yet, so I quickly slipped the shard into the box where I kept Takkan's letters and opened my satchel. Its straw exterior was scratched and waterlogged, but the wooden lining inside was untouched by my adventure in the sea.

I scooped the pearl out, dreading when I'd have to explain to my brothers that it was still in my possession and that I needed to go to the Forgotten Isles of Lapzur.

At my touch, its halves parted slightly. The sight of it unsettled me, for the fracture was longer and deeper than ever before.

"Once all this demon business is taken care of, I'll find my way to Lapzur," I vowed to the pearl. "I'll bring you home."

Deep down, I feared that fulfilling my promise to Raikama was only the first step to *me* returning home. That there really was a piece of myself missing, and that even after I reclaimed it, I'd still feel like the kite I'd once lost, flying without an end to my string.

But at least I had a direction to go. Raikama was counting on me.

As carefully as I could, I wrapped the pearl in an ivory sheet and tucked it into the back of my closet.

"Stay there for now," I said to it. "It won't do you any good to follow me around in the palace. People will ask questions."

I'm guessing I should stay in your room too, Kiki was

saying as she lazed upon a mound of silk pillows. *I for one don't mind. I'm thrilled to be back. Though you'll be next, won't you?*

"Next for what?"

To be married. To Radish Boy.

That was Kiki's nickname for Takkan, harking back to the days when I'd worked as a cook in his fortress.

Hearing the name almost made me smile, but marriage to Takkan was the last thing on my mind. I'd been gone for six months. I didn't dare presume that we could pick up where we had left off.

"He's probably gone back to Iro," I said.

Kiki leaned back on the pillow, burying her head under its silver tassels. *Knowing him like I do, I doubt that.*

"It doesn't matter. I have to go away soon enough. The pearl's almost broken in half."

Your father won't be happy to hear that. He's upset enough that you left.

"I'm not worried about Father," I lied. As soon as I said it, the doors slid open.

I immediately straightened, bowing low as the Emperor of Kiata strode into my room. After everything I'd faced in Ai'long, a meeting alone with Father shouldn't have made me nervous. Yet as he folded back his sleeves, I steeled myself. The worst sort of reprimand was the one I knew I deserved.

"Seventeen years old, and still as brazen as a child," said Father. "What a scene you made in front of the A'landans."

"Forgive me, Father," I said, my voice a meek counter-point to his anger.

"Forgive you? Your actions have brought deep shame to me and to your brothers. Most of all, Reiji! It is a miracle the entire marriage has not been called off."

I knelt at his feet, steeling myself for further rebuke. "I shouldn't have been so impulsive, I know . . . but I didn't want to miss Reiji's wedding. I've already missed so much."

I stared at the ground, anticipation mounting in my chest.

"You dishonor me," Father said. Then, to my surprise, he let out a long breath. "And yet, I wouldn't have expected anything less of my youngest child."

The words were harsh, though when I looked up, Father was smiling. Just a sliver of a smile, but still it warmed me to see it.

"I'm glad you came to see us right away, Shiori."

He opened his arms to me, and I practically flew into his embrace, the way I had when I was a little girl. "I missed you, Father," I whispered.

"And I you, my daughter," he said. "I prayed every day for your return. It appears the gods heard me."

I lifted myself from his arms and shuffled back to my place. "I didn't start a war by barging in on the ceremony, did I? I know the A'landans are mulish about their traditions—"

"You didn't start a war," said Father. "At worst, the ambassadors will spread the word about how the youngest princess of Kiata is disrespectful and brash, but I care little what the A'landans think."

"It's the truth anyway," I admitted slyly.

"Is it now? I find you much changed, daughter. You and your brothers." He touched the prayer plaques that Qinnia had stacked on the corner table, and his countenance turned grave. "A part of my spirit died when you all disappeared. It has only started to return."

I wished I knew how to comfort him. The father I'd grown up with never needed comforting. He'd always had Raikama by his side.

He said, solemnly, "When you were gone, your stepmother said that she often dreamt you were alive. I took more solace in that than you can know."

Raikama had told him we were alive? Ironic, given she'd been the one to curse us.

My chest gave a little twinge. "I was with her when she passed," I said softly. "She told me to tell you she was sorry. She cared for you very much."

Father's face drew long and thin, the ghosts hidden in his eyes coming to the surface.

"Your brothers said you left on a journey at her behest," he said. "One that took you far beyond our realm."

"To Ai'long," I confirmed.

"The dragon kingdom . . . ," he murmured. "I didn't believe them, but you did look as if you'd stepped out of the sea when you arrived. No one would tell me why you had gone, or why her last wishes would send you to such a place."

"They didn't know."

Father gave a slow nod, understanding. "Your stepmother was good at keeping secrets. I swore to never ask hers, even if at times it was difficult."

"A promise kept is worth a thousand secrets," I said, reciting the proverb he used to tell my brothers and me.

"An easy lesson to teach my children. Not so easy to teach myself." He sighed. "I suppose more of your curiosity comes from me than I'd like to admit."

I offered him a wan smile. My brothers and I had sworn never to tell Father about the curse Raikama had cast over us, nor that he had married a sorceress. What he believed was that Lord Yuji had ordered his sons turned into cranes and his daughter cast away, and that Raikama had been killed by demons. I yearned to tell him the truth, but the truth would only bring pain.

"One secret burdened her more than any other," Father went on. "I oft wondered whether it had to do with you, daughter."

He eyed the paper bird sitting on my window. Kiki was artfully still—which had to be torture for her. If Father remembered what she truly was, he didn't mention it.

His next words were said quietly. "I have learned, since you were away, that you have a talent for magic."

He didn't give me a chance to confirm it. "For your safety, I have done what was necessary to prevent the word from spreading."

I stared down at my skirt, picking at a loose thread on one of the embroidered butterflies. "That would explain it. The sentinels who found me . . . They seemed afraid."

Father tensed, as if he were deliberating whether to console me or tell me the truth. "People are frightened that magic is returning," he said. "Gindara was put under a deep sleep for over a month, and to this day we know not how it happened. When we all awoke, your brothers had returned, your stepmother was dead, and you . . . you were missing. Worse yet, they said you were Kiata's bloodsake."

He said *bloodsake* as if it were a curse. "You don't believe that I am," I said.

"It doesn't matter what I believe. The immolation of a bloodsake is a barbaric ritual that ended at the beginning of my reign. My own grandfather permitted the death of the last one to appease the priestesses of the Holy Mountains. I will not let those heretics take my only daughter, no matter what comes to pass."

I fell silent, remembering what I had seen in the mirror of truth. "What about the demon Bandur? He's escaped the mountains and is attacking Kiata."

Father flinched, caught off guard that I knew. "Kiata is safe. You will be too."

"But—"

"There are reports that the farmlands are having an arid season, while heavy rains plague our skies, unusual for this time of year in Gindara. If I am called away to more meetings than usual, that is why. This talk of demons is nonsense, nothing but a child's nightmare."

"It's not—"

"It's a nightmare," Father repeated. "You've only just returned. Do not concern yourself over matters of state."

I fixed my gaze on the ivory sheet strewn across the ground. He was trying to protect me, that much I knew. I had never known him to lie—not to me, and certainly not to himself.

"Yes, Father," I said, only so we could change the subject. "But what about Reiji? Is he really leaving next week?"

"It was his decision to go," replied Father, not without some pride. "Your brothers all vied to save him from such a fate. . . . Benkai even offered to wed the khagan's nephew instead."

"But as the future high commander, Benkai is too important to leave Kiata," I murmured, understanding Reiji's reasoning. And if Father sent any of my younger brothers, the khagan would be insulted beyond measure.

It had to be Reiji, the third in line.

"The country is in a fragile state, Shiori," said Father, "and relations among the warlords are strained at best. Reiji's marriage to the khagan's daughter will cement a much-needed alliance with A'landi, and Andahai's union with Lady Qinnia has brought vast support from the South. Now that you've returned . . . there is also your own betrothal to discuss."

My heart made a nervous jump. "My own betrothal?"

"Yes, your brothers hinted that you may look upon your intended more favorably than before." Father stroked his beard. "If that is true, it would be welcome news indeed."

The way my face flushed was answer enough.

"We'll discuss it further tonight," Father said. "Dinner will be in my quarters—to celebrate your return and Reiji's marriage."

A last family dinner, of sorts—before Reiji had to leave. "Yes, Father."

A smile played on his lips. "I'm surprised you haven't asked about him. He's been waiting to see you, perhaps even more keenly than I."

Takkan? I held my breath. "I thought he would have gone home. I didn't think he'd still be here—"

"Lord Bushian returned to Iro some months ago," said Father.

My spirits sank. "I see."

The emperor's smile widened just a touch. "But . . . his son has remained."

Now my eyes flew up. All at once, my world was floating, and it was a struggle to try and sound calm. "Where is he?"

"He wasn't invited to the ceremony. At this time of the day, I'd imagine he's sitting in on a council meeting. He's taken quite an interest in—"

That was all I needed to know. "Thank you, Father!" I exclaimed. "I will see you soon."

I was already running.

CHAPTER EIGHTEEN

Only for Takkan would I venture into the Hornet's Nest, my unaffectionate nickname for where Father's council met. But I was well rewarded for my trouble.

There he was, sitting in the front row of the assembly, his spine as straight as the stack of books before him. At the sight of him, I let out a chuckle. Of all the places to go on this glorious summer afternoon, Takkan *would* be inside, listening in on a tedious council meeting. Any other young man his age would be out strutting about Gindara or currying favor with other nobles through games of cards.

Not Takkan. By now he had probably read every scroll in the archives. And knew all the ministers by name, and their children too.

Chief Minister Hawar was droning on and on, and Takkan was actually paying attention. He didn't see Kiki and me peeking at him through the latticed window.

My heart gave a nervous flutter. "Looks like he hasn't heard I'm back."

What? said Kiki. *Are you worried he's forgotten you?* If she could've rolled her inky eyes, she would've. *It's been six months, not six decades. Hurry up and go in before you ruin the surprise. I want Radish Boy to fall off his chair when he sees you.*

That made me grin. Before I lost my nerve, I barged past the guards and into the Hornet's Nest.

It ought to have impressed me how spryly the old ministers sprang to their feet, but I couldn't have cared less. I barely heard their cries of "Shiori'anma, you've returned!" and "Shiori'anma, what is the meaning of this intrusion?"

I had eyes only for Takkan. Kiki was right: at the sight of me, he nearly toppled off his rosewood stool. He rushed to stand and join the ministers in a uniform bow.

"Not you," I said, pulling him up by the arm.

I regarded my father's officials, overlooking their furrowed brows and fallen jaws. "I'm borrowing Bushi'an Takkan for the rest of the afternoon," I declared. "Carry on without him."

Only the chief minister dared to show his disapproval. I felt a stab of annoyance as he turned up his mushroom nose and clucked at me.

I grabbed Takkan by the hand, towing him out of the chamber. "Run!" I whispered once we were out the door.

We sprinted through the imperial gardens. Dragonflies buzzed, kitebirds sang, and the overpowering perfume of lilies and chrysanthemums flooded my nostrils. But I didn't slow until we were far from prying eyes.

After we passed the first footbridge, Takkan asked, rightfully, "Why are we running?"

"Because we can," I replied between breaths. "Because I've been a thousand fathoms beneath the sea for the past week. Because my father told me to act as though nothing has happened, and this is the first thing the old Shiori would have done."

"I see," he replied. Then he winked. "Race you!"

Ahead he sped, and I ran too, shouting after him, "You don't even know where we're going!"

"I have an idea."

He didn't stop, and curse him, he was going in the right direction.

Fast as he was, he'd had only six months to explore the palace's vast gardens. I'd had seventeen years. I diverged from the pebbled paths, dashing through the bushes across a plot of flat limestone rocks, and past the reflection gallery. Thanks to my shortcut, I arrived at the Cloud Pavilion— a hidden retreat nestled between two begonia trees—seconds before Takkan.

I twisted my lips, relishing the stunned look on his face when he realized I'd beaten him. He bowed, partly to acknowledge my victory and partly to lean forward and catch his breath.

"All that dallying with the ministers has you out of shape, young Lord Bushi'an," I teased. "What happened to the runs you went on every morning in Iro?"

A smile spread across Takkan's face, and I knew I wasn't imagining the mist that suddenly touched his eyes. "I'm only out of breath from seeing you again, Shiori."

Shiori. The way he said my name hadn't changed, like the first notes to a song he loved to sing. Suddenly I was glad I'd bathed and changed.

A blush crept up my cheeks. "The ministers surely didn't teach you to talk like that," I said hastily. "You sound like you're quoting one of those silly love poems my tutors used to make me read. You should know they always made me laugh. No one's *that* romantic."

Takkan was still smiling. "Then laugh," he said in all seriousness. "I've missed the sound of you."

I've missed the sound of you. Only Takkan could make something so ridiculous seem like a fact. I could barely summon a breath, let alone a laugh, and before I could stop, I threw myself into his arms and said, "I've missed *all* of you."

He held me close, and I let the beat of his heart wash away the noise of summer. Even in this secluded veranda, the cicadas trilled stridently, and Kiki, who had long since flitted off, was exchanging throaty calls with the other birds. There was nowhere in the world I would rather be.

"How'd you even know about this place?"

"Hasho said you used to run off here when you skipped your lessons."

I made a face. "Traitor."

Takkan laughed. "He said it was your favorite pavilion. It's become mine too."

Maybe not so much a traitor, my youngest brother. I liked the thought of Takkan spending his mornings here, reading under the trees or painting or just thinking . . . about me.

"When did you get back?" he asked.

"Dawn. But I've only been in the palace a few hours. Word didn't spread to the Hornet's Nest?"

Takkan raised an eyebrow at the name, but he didn't question it. "We've been in meetings all day."

"Then you ought to thank me for saving you," I said cheekily. "Wouldn't you rather be here with me than with all those stuffy old ministers?"

"I *am* stuffy. *And* older than you."

"Only by a year." I grinned at the face he made. "Still miss the sound of me?"

Takkan traced the dimple that had appeared on my left cheek. "Always."

Just like that, my entire face warmed. I became acutely aware of how close we were—side by side, elbows brushing—and how impulsive it had been of me to lead him alone into the gardens. I hadn't meant for this to be a tryst, but no one else would know that.

The gossip would be lurid if we were found out. Not that I cared.

For an entire winter, I had lived in Takkan's home, Castle Bushian. Thanks to Raikama's curse, my face was hidden under an enchanted wooden bowl and I hadn't been able to speak. Yet even then, Takkan and I had grown to care for each other.

It had taken me far too long to realize I loved him, and I could count on one hand the number of times we'd been so close and alone. We'd never even kissed before.

I wished I had the courage to give him that kiss. Just

reaching out my hand to touch the ends of his hair made my heart thump riotously. Still, I didn't draw back. More than a few black strands were out of place, thanks to our sprint, and as I tucked them behind his ear, I let my fingers linger.

He'd gained some color from Gindara's blazing summers, and in my head, I traced the outline of his features—the straight, sloping nose, the tapered jaw and tiny divot in his chin, the most honest eyes I knew.

Gods, I'd missed him.

"What are you thinking about?" he asked.

Kissing you, I thought with mortifying clarity, but for once my mind was quick to restrain my lips from blurting the words aloud.

"Being at court hasn't changed you," I said instead, playfully. "You haven't given up Iro's linens for Gindara's brocades. It's even that muted shade of blue you wore every day at home."

"You look . . . you look the same too. Mostly."

"Mostly?" I pretended to sound wounded. "My hair hasn't turned green, and my eyes aren't red."

"Your eyes are the same," he agreed. "Full of mischief and laughter. But this"—his fingertips brushed the silver-white streak in my hair—"this is new."

At his touch, my heart skipped and went tight at the same time. It was tempting to give in to the moment, to make some coy remark and plant a kiss on his cheek and ignore the questions in his eyes. But I couldn't lie to Takkan. I didn't want to.

"It's from using the pearl," I confessed. "I . . . I ran into some trouble with the dragons."

"With your friend the dragon prince?" Takkan arched an eyebrow.

"No, not with Seryu." I hesitated, the whole adventure still so fresh in my mind I could taste the seawater on my lips. "It turns out the Dragon King wanted the pearl for himself," I explained. "It was messy, but Seryu helped get me out of Ai'long."

"So you still have the pearl."

Astute as always, Takkan, I thought. "I do," I replied, "and I'll have to leave again soon, to fulfill my promise."

"Then I'm coming with you. I'll not have you dealing with more dragons alone."

"I wasn't alone. I had—"

"Seryu." Takkan flinched. "I know."

I cocked my head. That wasn't a reaction I'd seen from Takkan before. "I had Kiki too." I poked, "Don't tell me you were jealous of Seryu."

Takkan shifted uneasily, and I couldn't help it—the imp in me enjoyed seeing how uncomfortable he looked.

"You *were* jealous!"

"He's a dragon prince," admitted Takkan with an exhale. "A dragon prince who whisked you away to his underwater kingdom. And he was clearly attached to you."

"Attached?" I echoed. "How would you know—you didn't even speak to him."

"I would have, had I the chance." Takkan's tone was steely, which made me hide a smile. "Anyone could see he cared for you. Your brothers certainly did."

Oh, I could just envision it. Reiji and Yotan preying on poor Takkan, giving him ideas that I would stay in Ai'long forever and become a dragon princess. My brothers could be fiends in that sense—like me. It was a struggle smothering my smile as Takkan went on:

"In a way it comforted me, knowing he'd be with you when I couldn't."

"But?"

"But the thought that you might stay in Ai'long kept me up more nights than I'd like to admit," Takkan replied. "They say the waters of Ai'long have a way of muddying the mind—even erasing the past. I worried you might forget me."

I thought of the elixir I had almost drunk. "All legends have a spark of truth, it turns out," I said softly. "But I'm back now. And I didn't forget you." I touched my nose to his and winked. "Though it's mostly because I adore your sister so much."

The tension in Takkan's shoulders fell away, and he chuckled. "I'll have to write Megari that you're back. She keeps hounding me about you in her letters."

"I hope she isn't upset that you're still here. I thought you would've gone home to Iro with your father."

"I wanted to be here when you returned," said Takkan. "I waited on the beach every morning, but today of all days the council wanted to meet to discuss—" He stopped.

"To discuss what?"

The brightness in his face clouded over, and I suspected I knew the answer.

Demons. Magic. Me.

"I should return," he said. "The Hornet's Nest will be buzzing, and I don't want to miss anything important."

"What are they saying about me?" I asked. My father had tried to protect me, but I trusted Takkan to share the truth.

He hesitated. "The ministers have been wary since you disappeared for Ai'long. Your brothers and I tried to make excuses, but when rumor spread that you were a sorceress—and the bloodsake—there was little we could do."

I leaned against the veranda, my face half in the shade and half in the sun. "They hate me. They just won't show it to my face because of Father."

"Shiori . . ."

I didn't give Takkan a chance. "When I was in Ai'long, I was granted a glimpse of home." My throat closed up. "I saw the forests burning. . . . I saw Bandur come out of the mountains." When I said the demon's name, a cold tendril snaked over my heart. "He was free."

"So you know. Your father didn't want you to."

"Tell me everything."

Takkan inhaled. "Gindara slept for weeks even after you were gone," he said at length. "But when spring arrived, and everyone woke, it was clear that magic had returned to Kiata. People panicked, and some of the villagers started reporting that the trees in the forest were dying. They heard wailing and laughter deep in the night from within. Your brothers and I went to investigate, and we found a tear along the face of the central peak."

The same tear Raikama had cleaved to free me from Bandur's clutches. I wouldn't have escaped the mountains without her.

"We call it the breach," said Takkan. "All day and night it glows. But so far as we know, only Bandur has the ability to pass through. The other demons remain within."

The magic I worked upon the mountains will not hold forever, Raikama had warned me.

If only I'd listened. Using the pearl had cost her her life, and for what? Half a year later, Bandur had already found a way out.

I wished she were here. She would have known what to do.

"He's been seen prowling the villages that border the Holy Mountains," said Takkan. "There have been reports of attacks on the townspeople, but he seems weakened, and cannot stay out of the mountains for long. So far there's been no sign of him in Gindara."

"That'll change now that I'm back," I said through clenched teeth. "He's been waiting for me."

I said nothing more, but Takkan could read the warring emotions on my face: *I shouldn't have come back. I should have stayed in Ai'long.*

"Whatever you're thinking, don't," he said quietly. "This is home. This is where you belong."

These were words I'd clung to during the long months I'd been under Raikama's curse, alone without a voice and without a home, and while I'd been in Ai'long, yearning to see my family again. I desperately wanted to believe him, but deep down I knew: until magic had a place in Kiata, I never would.

There was no use moping. What was done was done.

I'd come back, and I needed to face the consequences. *First things first, we'll have to send Bandur back into the mountains,* I thought. *The sooner the better.*

"Will you take me there?" I asked Takkan. "I want to see the breach for myself."

"When?"

"Not today," I said, considering. "It'll be dark soon, and I'm expected at dinner with my father. I'll go tomorrow." I hesitated. "You'll be joining us, won't you? At dinner, I mean."

Takkan blinked. "I've never been invited."

Of course he hadn't. Dinner with the emperor was a high honor, and the last interaction I remembered of Father and Takkan involved me jumping out a window to escape our betrothal.

"You are now," I said. "Come eat with us. Reiji leaves for A'landi at the end of the week, so we'll have little time for family meals."

I blushed, realizing I had inadvertently called him family.

Even if I hadn't, it was an invitation laden with meaning. Everyone would assume that we were resuming our betrothal.

Takkan must have sensed my realization. He started to speak, uttering a jumble of polite nonsense about how I didn't need to invite him, but I cut him off with a gesture.

I spoke over him, firmly. "I'll see you at dinner."

CHAPTER NINETEEN

I had underestimated just how pleased my family would be to see Takkan at dinner. From the moment he was announced at the emperor's door, my brothers started grinning from ear to ear.

It was clear Takkan had gotten to know my family while I'd been in Ai'long. When Father wasn't looking, Reiji welcomed him with a slap on the back, and Yotan set a wooden cup brimming with rice wine in his palm.

"Drink up," said Yotan. "Though not too fast. We wouldn't want you tottering about drunk at your first *family* dinner, would we?"

Takkan choked on his breath, and I raised my sleeve to hide a laugh. I could count on Yotan to lighten any mood.

You'll be fine, I mouthed to Takkan. It took all my restraint not to reach for his hand and squeeze it.

He was wearing blue—his family's color, and the color I loved most on him. A simple linen jacket hugged his broad shoulders, and I didn't know how, but the black-corded belt around his waist made him look rugged and scholarly at the same time. The "rustic ensemble," as Yotan would have described it, confirmed that Takkan had spent no time observing the court fashions. Any other lord would have decked himself in silk and jade and gold for dinner with the emperor, but I doubted that had even occurred to Takkan. He was probably more concerned about the ink stains smudging the pads of his fingers. They were ever present, even when I'd known him in Iro, though fainter than I'd ever seen tonight. I wondered how long he'd scrubbed at them before dinner.

"Welcome, Takkan," Father said, addressing the kneeling young lord.

"Thank you, Your Majesty."

"For the first time I can remember, Shiori is not late. I trust I have you to thank for that."

"You do, Father," I answered for Takkan. I hoped my cheeky response hid how nervous I was. "And you ought to thank the chefs too. I heard they were serving steamed eggs and duck?"

Indeed they were.

After my journey to Ai'long, I would have been content with a simple bowl of rice and soup. But an astounding array of dishes arrived: bean curd that melted on the tongue like liquid silk, steamed eggs as fragrant and yellow as summer lotus blossoms, and roasted duck that was both tender and crispy, with a savory sauce that I drizzled over my rice.

If only I could enjoy the meal without everyone teasing me about Takkan's presence. Even Wandei, who usually minded his own business, waggled his eyebrows in my direction every chance he got.

Reluctantly, I set down my bowl and cleared my throat. "Father asked me this morning whether I would like to have a betrothal ceremony again with Bushi'an Takkan." My voice trembled. "I should, very much . . . before Reiji has to leave for A'landi." I glanced at Takkan. "But I understand if he should wish to wait, given that his family is in Iro."

A smile perched on Takkan lips. "With you, Shiori, I've learned that it's best not to wait."

My brothers hid their laughter behind raised cups, but for once I didn't glare at them. I smiled too.

"It's settled, then," said Father. "I've already asked High Priest Voan to select a date. The ninth of this month appears the most auspicious."

That was only three days away! I settled into my seat, the smile on my face quickly losing luster. I should have been happy. I wanted to be.

But I kept gazing at the empty space beside Father, where Raikama would have sat, and my unfulfilled promise gnawed at me. Takkan knew I still had the pearl, but I hadn't told him—or anyone—that I had to leave for Lapzur.

"To Lord Bushi'an and Shiori," Andahai was saying, raising his cup. "May your strands be knotted from this life to the next. I wish you every happiness."

Reiji seconded the toast. "And what a relief that the attention is off me," he added. "All week we've been celebrating my marriage to a paper princess."

"Yes, and hoping for your sake that she's as pretty as she looks in the painting," Hasho joked.

Reiji snorted, but he downed his cup in one gulp none-theless.

I lifted my cup of wine to my lips and drank slowly. I'd never loved rice wine, and this was particularly bitter, like chewing on a handful of raw tea leaves.

Then it began to burn.

I spat my wine back into the cup, but the poison traveled fast. A vicious pain lanced through my chest, and I began to choke, blood draining from my face. The wine cup slipped from my hand and clattered on the tiled floor.

The next thing I knew, I was on the ground, my cheek pressed against the cold tile.

The world swayed as footsteps rushed toward me. My brothers—all six of them—were at my side, their faces blurred into one.

"Poison!" Hasho was crying.

"Someone get help!"

Their shouts faded into the background, and all I could see was Qinnia, trying to loosen my collar so I could breathe. Black smoke swirled in my eyes, and as the breath fled my lungs, a shadow enshrouded her. Her skin turned ashen, her pupils blood-red.

"Welcome back, Shiori," Bandur spoke through Qinnia's rose-painted lips. "You haven't forgotten me, have you?"

"How . . . how are you here?" I choked. "In . . . in Qinnia?"

"You don't remember?" Qinnia picked up a handful of

red dates. The movement was languid, and my heart gave a lurch when she crushed them in her fist.

Juice ran through her fingers like blood, in thin meandering streams. "Your blood freed me. I am not chained to the mountains, as the others are. I've been here. Watching you."

My eyes rounded in horror.

Qinnia's face warped into a horrible mockery of a smile. "Why so upset? You ought to thank me for my help while you were away. Nine priestesses of the Holy Mountains committed themselves to Lord Sharima'en, thanks to me. Three walked into fire, two into the sea, and the other four . . . well, they felt an urge to taste the end of a dagger." He licked his lips. "Couldn't have them burning you to ashes. Your blood is too precious for that."

"Get out of Qinnia," I whispered. "Leave her alone."

"Her face bothers you?" Bandur pretended to pout. "Who would you prefer I inhabit? I could be anyone you know. One of your servants, your father. Even your beloved Takkan."

Enough was enough. I launched myself at Qinnia, aiming for her eyes.

Thank the great gods, she screamed. Andahai shoved her away from me an instant before I would have stabbed her.

Shadows snuffed the lantern lights, and Bandur's laugh ricocheted off the walls. *Save your energy, Shiori. Do you mean to kill the crown prince's wife? It is she who would die, not me.*

In horror, I staggered back, and my world tilted. I was on the ground. Hasho was trying to force something through my mouth. I bit down on my lip, refusing to drink. I didn't trust anyone anymore, not even him.

Stop fighting, said Bandur. *Your brother is trying to save you.*

His advice only made me bite down harder.

You think I poisoned you? He laughed. *Only an imbecile would kill you while you are bonded to the Wraith's pearl. Though I must tell you, I'm relieved that you kept it from the Dragon King.* Bandur's shadow swept over me, flickering across the streak of white in my hair as he purred, *I was worried I wouldn't get my chance with it.*

"Never," I seethed.

Nazayun failed because he didn't provide you with the right . . . enticements. Bandur's voice found my ear. *I will not make that error. Patience is a demon's virtue, not a dragon's.*

One of my brothers was pinching my nose, and as I struggled, warm liquid dribbled down my throat. Almost instantly, the bitterness in my mouth dissolved.

Yes, that's it. . . . Breathe. Bandur inhaled, mocking my gasping breaths. *There, there.*

The world began to clear, and my brothers and Takkan hovered worriedly over me. Qinnia had retreated to the far wall.

Coils of smoke drifted out of her eyes—smoke, it seemed, that only I could see. As it evaporated into the distance, I could still hear Bandur. *Enjoy your time at home, Shiori. Don't let anyone kill you before I do.*

In a puff, he vanished, and Qinnia let out a violent shudder before collapsing in her chair.

"I'm fine," she said when Andahai rushed to her side. Her eyes were cloudy, and from the glazed way she smiled, I doubted she knew what had happened. "I'm fine," she repeated. "Help Shiori."

Takkan was pressing his fingers to my pulse, and he perched me on my chair. "That's it, Shiori. Breathe. Slowly."

As I inhaled, Hasho placed a small bottle into my grasp. "It's from Raikama," he told me. "Drink more if you're still feeling unwell."

Raikama?

"She left it for us," my brother explained, seeing that it comforted me to hear of her. "It's an antidote for most poisons. She must have expected that we'd need it."

I finally stopped biting my lip. Even in death, my stepmother had saved me.

Pulling myself up, I grabbed Hasho's sleeve. "He was here," I whispered hoarsely. "Bandur . . ."

My brother and Takkan exchanged looks. "Are you certain?" asked Hasho.

"Without a doubt. He . . . he was in Qinnia." I glanced at her. "Is she well?"

The crown princess looked as confused as she was shaken. She dropped the dates from her hands, trembling visibly as she wiped the stains from her fingers on a cloth. She wouldn't look at me, which was understandable. At least her eyes were clear.

Bandur was gone. For now.

"Are you hurt?" Andahai asked his wife. His voice was tight. He hadn't heard what I told Takkan and Hasho, and he had to be fuming.

As Qinnia gave a meek nod, some of the servants frowned. I could imagine what they thought. That I was jealous of the new princess, that during my absence I had gone mad. That I really *was* a dangerous sorceress.

My mouth went dry. I wanted to explain everything, but now wasn't the time.

"I'd like to be excused," I said to Father in my lowest, quietest voice. "May Takkan escort me to my room?"

Usually that was Hasho's role, or even Benkai's, but my father glanced at Takkan, then nodded. "Go. And don't leave your room until I send for you."

Before I left, I exchanged a look with Hasho, knowing I could trust him to lead the investigation. He would explain to my brothers—especially Andahai—what had happened.

"What did you see?" Takkan asked quietly once we were alone in the hall.

"Bandur." I shivered, still haunted. "He spoke to me—through Qinnia."

"What did he say?"

"He was in a chatty mood. He bragged that he could take on anyone's body if he wished. He said he wasn't the one who poisoned me but that he did kill nine priestesses of the Holy Mountains."

Takkan paused in his step. "Perhaps we shouldn't go to the breach tomorrow."

"Shouldn't go?" I exclaimed. "Bandur knows I'm back. There's no point hiding."

"Shiori, he tried to kill you."

"It wasn't him."

"How do you know?"

He told me so, I almost said before realizing how ridiculous that sounded. "There has to be a ritual—to sever my bond with the pearl."

"He wants you at the Holy Mountains. You'd only be playing into his hands."

"I need to see the breach," I insisted. "I can find a way to seal him back inside."

Takkan didn't argue, though I could tell I hadn't convinced him. "Let's discuss this tomorrow. You need rest." He took one step back. "I'll keep watch outside."

"You're not my bodyguard."

"I'm not," he agreed. "I'm your betrothed. Officially again, as of tonight—which means you can't dismiss me." He settled in a corner. "Go to sleep."

I was still standing in my doorway. "You're impossible, Bushi'an Takkan," I muttered, loud enough for him to hear. "I liked you better when I had the bowl on my head and you had no idea who I was."

It was a lie, and we both knew it.

He bowed, completely unruffled. "I'll see you tomorrow, Shiori."

Somehow, in the midst of the danger awaiting us, those were the sweetest words I had heard in months.

CHAPTER TWENTY

It was barely past dawn, and Hasho was still snoring when I slipped into his room. My brothers and I had shared connecting chambers ever since I was born, and it wasn't the first time I was stealing their clothes to slip out of the palace unannounced. Hasho's clothes, usually, since his room was adjacent to mine. Lucky him.

I'd already put on my plainest set of robes, but I needed a hat to hide my hair and face. Hasho had plenty, and I helped myself to a blue one that matched the striped cotton tunic I wore. As an afterthought, I lifted two daggers from his weapons rack and strapped them to my belt.

Takkan was already up and waiting for me. He really *had* spent the night outside my door.

"Where are the guards?" I asked in lieu of a greeting. At least two were posted outside each of my siblings' chambers.

"Dismissed. Your maids, too. Your father isn't trusting anyone to attend you until the assassin is found." Takkan paused, acknowledging my disguise with the slightest lift of an eyebrow. "I take it you haven't changed your mind about the Holy Mountains."

"Do I look like I've changed my mind?" I fidgeted with Hasho's hat, tucking in a flyaway strand of silvery hair. Then I patted my satchel. Inside were the pearl and the mirror of truth. "Let's go."

Takkan stepped to the side, blocking my way. "Your father has forbidden you from leaving your room."

"If he wanted me to listen to him, he shouldn't have lied to me about the demons."

"Your brothers asked me to ensure you stay as well."

"Then they should be the ones guarding my chamber, not you. I don't need their permission to leave—or yours."

I strode past him, and Takkan's jaw tightened, a clear sign he didn't approve of what I was doing. Kiki didn't, either, only she was far more vocal in her displeasure.

Is your head still full of seawater, Shiori? Someone tried to kill you last night. You should be staying home, where it's safe.

"Safe?" I echoed. "Bandur was in the palace. He possessed Qinnia. . . ." I balled my fists. "I didn't come back from Ai'long just to do nothing. I'm going to find him."

But—

"Whoever it is that tried to kill me is in the palace. They're not going to stop trying just because I'm stuck in my room. I'll be safer outside."

My paper bird yanked at Takkan's hair, a plea for his support.

Before he could speak, I warned, "You're not going to change my mind. You can come too, or I can go by myself."

He wouldn't budge. Emuri'en's Strands! I'd forgotten how pigheaded Takkan could be.

"Shiori, please stay in your room."

"Move aside," I commanded haughtily. I raised my hand to his forehead. "Seryu taught me a sleeping spell, and I'm not afraid to use it on you."

A muscle in Takkan's jaw ticked, and he tried again, gently. "Think of what happened last night—"

"I *am* thinking of last night. There's a demon on the loose, and I'm the only one who can stop him." I flicked Kiki into my hat before she protested too. "Now, you can either come with me as my bodyguard, or you can take a nap and greet me when I return."

"The gates will be closed—"

The gates were the least of my concerns. "I know a shortcut."

Though Takkan didn't say a word, I could sense his confusion when, instead of heading for the main gates, I took him deeper into the palace. We avoided the most heavily trafficked corridors and paths, cutting through the citrus orchard and rock gardens to the place I had once loved and dreaded.

"The Moon Gate apartments," I murmured, sliding open the wooden doors.

Raikama's residence had always been quiet, yet it rattled

me not seeing guards stationed at every corner, or servants milling about the rooms. Inside, bouquets of chrysanthemums and stale incense flooded my nostrils—the smells of prayer and mourning.

The doors to her audience chamber were wide open, something that never would've happened when Raikama was alive. She didn't accept many visitors.

I took a tentative step inside. "When I was little, we used to chase each other around this room," I said, gesturing at the gilded walls. "After, when we were dizzy, we'd feast on cakes and peaches and pretend we lived on the moon." I missed that time so fiercely it hurt to breathe. "One day, I sneaked into her garden and broke her trust. The last time I ever came here, I thought Father had summoned me to apologize to her, but instead it was to make an announcement of my betrothal—to you."

To his credit, Takkan didn't flinch. Then again, he knew how much I *hadn't* wanted to marry him.

"I gather you didn't take it well," he said.

"I would have preferred a death sentence," I replied dryly. "I cried so wretchedly that Father nearly annulled our engagement then and there, but Raikama wouldn't have it."

Even after all these years, the memory was sharp.

I had thrown myself to the floor, practically kissing the wood as I bowed. I hoped the display would elicit Father's sympathy, but I was wrong.

"Have you finished making a spectacle?" he asked.

I was only nine years old, but familiar enough with the

emperor's ire to know it was most serious when he didn't sound angry. His voice was even, just the slightest hint of displeasure coloring his words.

Raikama's demeanor only added to my agitation. She hadn't moved at all. Hadn't said anything at all.

"Stepmother," I cried, throwing myself in her direction. "Please don't send me away because I have offended you." I pressed my forehead to the ground, all my pride dissolved. "I'll be good. I promise."

Raikama raised her fan, embroidered with snakes and white orchids. She opened it with a snap that punctuated her next words: "A promise is not a kiss in the wind, to be thrown about without care." A flicker of gold glinted in her eyes. "That lesson must be learned, Shiori, for your own good."

I started to protest, but my head felt suddenly light. The grand speech I'd rehearsed fled my tongue, and my body melted dazedly into a bow. I repeated, "Yes, Stepmother. I will leave Kiata, if that is what you wish. You will not see me again."

Raikama's fan fell limp, and when I glanced up, there was the slightest wetness in her eyes. For an instant, I dared hope she might give in. That she might sweep me into an embrace and declare her forgiveness.

But her eyes went cold once more, and she snapped her fan shut so brutally I thought it would crack in two. Without another word, she stood and left the room.

That was the day I learned to harden my heart. That was the day I lost a mother.

Takkan touched my shoulder. "Shiori?"

I had expected to confront demons today, not my own past. I swallowed the lump in my throat and continued down the hall. "She would have been in her embroidery room this time of day," I said, "stitching a scene of moon orchids or lilies. She was always sewing, though she had no great talent for it. Two ladies would be at her side, but she hardly ever talked to them. They were probably bored out of their minds."

Her embroidery frame was still in the room, but the threads and spindles had been stowed away, the windows shuttered, and the lanterns removed.

I gestured at the corner of the room by the window.

"That's where I sat," I told Takkan, my voice soft. "Curled up in that corner, I worked on an apology tapestry for you and your family. It took nearly a month, and Raikama would come over every other hour to make sure my stitches weren't crooked." A wistful smile touched my lips. "How I hated her then—and you, for making me waste my summer."

Takkan smiled back. "I'm relieved your feelings changed—toward both of us."

"I am too."

I crouched beside her sewing chest, nervous to open it. Last night, I had searched my room for the ball of red thread Raikama had once kept. I could have sworn I'd left it in my closet for safekeeping, but it wasn't there.

By the Eternal Courts, I prayed it had somehow found its way back here, among Raikama's belongings.

With trembling fingers, I opened the chest and rummaged inside. Nestled underneath a trove of yarns and flosses was a clump of red thread so ordinary and plain that no one would ever think it anything special.

I certainly hadn't.

"What's that?" asked Takkan as I lifted the red thread out of the chest, handling it with the care I would have given a crane's egg.

I took his hand, tugging him toward the Moon Garden. "You'll see."

The pond still brimmed with carp, beds of lotus blossoms floating peacefully. The canopies of purple wisteria had grown long, draping over the tall trees that shaded the garden. But one thing was different: there were no snakes.

"This was Raikama's sanctuary," I said at last. "She used to come here every day to sit by the water and talk to her snakes. She'd bring my brothers here, but never me. I never knew why, and it bothered me. We were close then, as close as a mother and daughter.

"I'd wanted to come for ages, so one day I sneaked inside on a dare. I was supposed to steal one of her snakes, but Raikama caught me."

"That was what broke her trust," Takkan said, putting the pieces together.

"She was furious. We were never the same afterward." My voice turned thick. "For years I assumed it was because of what I did, but that wasn't it. Snakes are sensitive to magic. They sensed mine and told Raikama. She did all she could to hide my powers and keep them from manifesting, even if that meant distancing herself from me."

"She knew what would happen if the wrong people discovered you were the bloodsake," said Takkan. "She was protecting you."

"She was." I sank into a bed of silvergrass, kneeling beside the weeping willow that had sheltered my stepmother in the final moments of her life. "She was always protecting me."

Pots of moon orchids had been placed about the garden on flat rocks to honor the imperial consort, but some of the flowers had begun to dry in the summer heat. I touched their fallen petals, releasing the tiniest strand of magic to carry them off into the brightening sky.

For a moment, I could see her in the clouds. Her opalescent eyes, the long sable hair that gleamed even in the dark, the mysterious scar across her cheek. Too soon she faded, alive only in my memory.

I swallowed, slowly finding my voice again. "She wasn't perfect. She made mistakes, selfish mistakes. But she cared for me more than I ever knew." I held out the red thread. "Before she died, she used this thread to help me escape the Holy Mountains."

Takkan touched the loose end of the thread, tucking it back inside the ball. "It's enchanted."

"With Emuri'en's magic," I confirmed. *The power of fate.*

I rolled the ball in my hands. "I'm starting to think that magic never left Kiata. Not completely. The gods buried it deep within the heart of our land, where it lay dormant."

I pictured a garden under a perpetual snowfall, roots and bulbs waiting for the thaw.

Magic was slowly awakening. I could feel it in my stepmother's thread, in Kiki every day as she grew more alive. I could even feel it as I leaned toward the pond, searching its depths for the enchanted passageway that lay beneath.

I held the ball of thread over the pond, and its waters rippled ever so subtly. As if in anticipation.

"Take me to the Holy Mountains."

CHAPTER TWENTY-ONE

We followed the red thread and emerged deep in the forest, not far from the Holy Mountains. A journey, Takkan informed me, that usually took an entire morning on horseback.

The breach was a short trek away, but Takkan wanted to scout the area before going too close. "The demons know you're back," he explained darkly. "We can't be too careful."

He led me down a path that sloped into the mountain pass, and we ascended slowly, quietly. When at last the glow of the breach came into view, I caught my breath. I'd glimpsed it before in the mirror of truth, but up close it looked different.

It's grown, I realized.

The breach now extended halfway up the tallest peak, as tall and wide as a willow tree. Scarlet light poured out of its crooked seam, like a wound that wept blood. Or a river of demon eyes.

I grabbed a low tree branch and hoisted myself up for a

better look. At the breach's base was a camp of sentinels and soldiers, forming a cordon around the mountain.

"Is it wise to have all these men here guarding against Bandur?" I asked Takkan. "If he can possess Qinnia . . ."

"He isn't invincible," said Takkan, "and he can't stay far from the breach for long. After a few hours, he always comes back. The soldiers send word to Benkai whenever there's movement, and whenever he returns. It's harder to see when he leaves, since it's usually at night."

"He's inside now," I stated.

A nod.

That was a relief, but I still frowned. "I understand the patrols, but we don't need this many soldiers to play watchman."

"It turns out demons aren't our only concern." Takkan directed my attention back to the forest. "See those patches of scorched wood?"

I stepped up for a better vantage point, but I already knew what he was talking about. The mirror of truth had shown me, and I'd noticed the groves of charred trees when we first arrived. "That wasn't Bandur?"

"No. It was local Kiatans." Takkan lowered his voice. "Word is spreading that there is a demon in Gindara. Your father and brothers have done their best to contain it, but fear spreads faster than any fire. Since you've been away, many have come to the breach and tried to burn the evil out of the forest."

I swallowed hard. It was only a matter of time before the

whole country knew about Bandur. Deep down, that troubled me more than the Demon King himself.

"The soldiers are necessary reinforcements until we find a way to seal the breach," said Takkan. "Your father's permitted a pair of enchanters to come investigate the mountains. We're hoping they can find a solution."

Now that was a surprise. No enchanters had visited Kiata in centuries. "Are they at the breach?" I asked, leaping off the tree. "I'd like to meet—"

I halted midsentence. The air had changed. Gone was the heat, the sticky veneer of humidity. Cold needled my bare skin.

"Shiori . . . ," whispered the wind. "Shiori."

The ground began to tremble. At first, it was only a vibration, rustling the trees nearby. Then a fierce tremor shook the earth. Birds shrieked, and rocks spilled from the mountainside, forcing the soldiers to scatter from their posts.

I bent my knees to catch my balance, and Kiki slipped back under Hasho's hat. In the distance, the breach flashed red.

"*SHIORI!*" the wind whispered again, this time more urgently. "*SHIORI!*"

That was no wind. It was the demons. They knew I was here!

"The bloodsake has come," they clamored.

"She has come to free us.

"We must wake the king. . . ."

"I haven't come to free you," I hissed. I dared a step forward. "I've come to make sure you never get out."

"We shall see."

The demons' anger pulsed under my feet, and I grabbed Takkan by the hand. Together we stumbled back a step, then another and another until the earth was still again and the cold dissipated.

"What was that?" Takkan asked.

I never got to reply. Because out of the trees there flew the largest, most feral-looking hawk I had ever seen, with tiger stripes on its burnished plumes and ears pointed like a cat's. Kiki let out a gruesome shriek as its talons narrowly missed her, lifting the hat clean off my head instead.

"Heedi!" shouted an unseen voice. "What did I teach you about diving on our friends? Apologize at once."

The hawk dipped its head at Kiki, then swooped down onto the arm of a young boy. A boy with a lopsided grin I would recognize anywhere.

"Gen!" I cried.

The sorcerer swept a bow. "My apologies for Enchantress Heedi. She gets excited when there's demon activity. And thank goodness for it—otherwise, I would've missed you and Kiki! How well you both look, freshly exiled from the dragon realm." He blew a kiss to my bird. *Especially you, Kiki.*

You can *hear me!* the paper bird exclaimed, instantly forgiving Gen for the hawk incident. *I'd been wondering.*

"I've always had an affinity for birds," Gen confessed. "They're often smarter than humans."

Kiki preened, and I sighed at how easily my paper bird was charmed.

You look well, too, she said.

It was true. Gen's cheeks bloomed with health, his curls were neatly combed, and he'd even donned Kiatan robes. But for his blue eyes, he might have passed for one of us.

"Come," said Gen, "let's chat a little farther from the breach. The demons have been testy all day."

"You all know each other?" said Takkan, more aware than ever he couldn't hear Kiki's side of the conversation.

"Know each other?" Gen said. "We shared a dungeon in Ai'long. After all we've been through together, Shiori's practically my aunt."

"Aunt?" I scoffed. "You spent twenty years of your life as a statue. Just because you didn't age doesn't mean you're younger than I am."

"But I look younger. Especially when you're wearing *that*." Gen scrutinized my clothes. "You were far better dressed in Ai'long, even when the dragons were trying to kill you."

"They're my brother's clothes," I replied, snatching my hat back from the hawk. "It isn't easy sneaking out when you're a princess. I thought I looked convincing."

Gen wrinkled his nose. "Maybe to the soldiers. But not to me." He proved his point by gesturing at my satchel, casually hidden beneath my cloak. "You still have the pearl. Are you sure it's wise carrying it around?"

"Wiser than leaving it in my room unattended," I said crustily. My hands went to my hips. "Didn't you say Kiata was the last place you'd ever want to visit?"

"It was, but you lied to me about your demon problem," Gen said. "I came as soon as I could get an invitation."

I had a hard time believing that my father and his ministers would take the counsel of this overconfident man-boy. "My father invited *you* to Kiata?"

"He invited my teacher." Gen stroked the hawk on his shoulder. "Enchantress Heedi."

"That's Enchantress Heedi?"

Gen laughed. "No, the real Enchantress Heedi died about two hundred years ago. But you Kiatans are so out of touch with magic, I picked the most famous name I could think of." He winked. "A little deception never hurt anyone."

"A little deception could land you in the dungeon should the emperor find out," said Takkan sternly. "We invited a great enchantress, not her novice apprentice."

Gen flicked a glance at him. "Yet all this time, you've kept my secret, Lord Takkan. I think that would make you an accomplice."

"How do *you two* know each other?" I asked.

"Your betrothed is the one who persuaded your father to give me a chance." Gen gave a sly smile. "He's a smart boy. I see now why you turned down Seryu's proposal."

"What do you mean, Seryu's proposal?" said Takkan.

I shot Gen a displeased look.

"She didn't tell you?" Gen grinned. "It's quite the story."

Takkan was *not* grinning. "I'd be curious to hear it."

All of a sudden, I wished for one of Ai'long's whirlpools to appear and swallow me up. "It's . . . it's like I told you," I stammered. "The Dragon King was going to kill me because I refused to give over Raikama's pearl. Seryu convinced him to spare me, but there was only one way to do it."

"Marriage?" asked Takkan.

Nothing got past him. I gave a nervous nod. "Dragons have a tradition of taking human companions. I . . . I had to pretend I was going to be his."

"Don't worry," Gen cut in before Takkan could react. "It was playacting on both their parts, though personally I would've taken the dragon up on his offer of immortality." He tapped his chin, as if stroking an imaginary beard. "And now that I think about it, Shiori never once mentioned you."

My displeasure with the young sorcerer increased tenfold. "There was hardly time to mention *anyone,* given that you were a statue," I told him frostily. "If I'd known you were going to be such a gossip, I would have left you in Ai'long."

Gen grinned, curse the boy.

I turned to Takkan, trying to sort out my words before I spoke. He wasn't one to fixate on rank or station, but I knew it was a mystery to all why Father had promised us together. I could imagine the palace gossip during the months he'd awaited my return: Why was the only princess of Kiata betrothed to a lowly lord from the North, when she could've had her pick of all the eligible princes of Lor'yan?

Even a dragon prince.

"I did consider Seryu's offer," I admitted quietly. "But only because I thought Kiata might be safer if I didn't come back. But every moment I was in Ai'long, I missed home. I missed you."

Takkan's hand rose from his side, and he tousled the ends of my silver hair. "I'm glad you changed your mind," he said softly. "More glad than you can know."

My stomach fluttered. So simple was his understanding.

"I'm glad too," Gen piped. "Now that you're back, I'll finally get to visit the palace."

"Will you, now?" I glared at the boy. "All of a sudden, I understand the wisdom of banning sorcerers from Kiata."

Gen's grin turned rueful. "Kiata's the only place in the world where we aren't welcome. Your father's bureaucrats won't let me stay in the nearest town, let alone the palace." He made a show of rubbing his neck. "I've been camping here with the soldiers for weeks. I'm convinced my cot's filled with stones, it's so lumpy."

Kiki bounced on my shoulder. *You can get him a villa in the palace, can't you? The poor boy could use a good night's sleep—after being turned to stone and all.*

"I'll see what I can do," I relented, throwing my hands up. "Don't look so cheered, Gen. It's not a promise. To be honest, I'd rather you stayed out here. Takkan says Father's ministers are stirring up trouble and—"

Gen's hawk cut me off with a screech, the only warning before a large stone flew out of the trees and hit the young sorcerer squarely in the nose.

Eyes bulging, he touched his nose and let out a groan. Then he crumpled to the ground, unconscious.

CHAPTER TWENTY-TWO

"Gen!" I screamed.

Blood streaked down his face, vivid and garish, and his nose was an alarming shade of purple. Almost certainly broken.

I bent to stir him awake, but another rock came flying at my head.

"Sorceress!" Dozens of men and women poured out from behind the trees, wielding knives and fishing spears.

I pulled Gen to his feet, and Takkan threw him over his shoulder. We couldn't stay.

As Takkan and I scrambled for safety, the villagers followed, and the spears they threw landed with startling accuracy.

"Bane of Sharima'en," I muttered. "Here I was, worried about the demons." I pushed Takkan ahead. "Take Gen to the camp."

Stubborn Takkan didn't listen. He grabbed my hand, practically towing me. The villagers were closing in.

Kiki hammered my cheeks with her wings. *Do something!*

"Like what?"

All I could do was run, praying the trees would continue to shield us until we reached the encampment by the breach.

Another spear flew past, piercing a branch over me. I ducked just before it knocked Hasho's hat off my head. My hair tumbled loose.

"Get her!" shouted a woman among the villagers. "It's the demon princess!"

Takkan was at my side in an instant, his sword raised. "His Majesty's sentinels are on their way!" he said to the villagers. It was the first lie I'd ever heard him tell—Father's men were nowhere to be seen, and they weren't coming. "Go home—return to your townships!"

The woman who'd spoken earlier shoved her way to the front. Deep grooves were etched into her cheeks, and her white hair was tied into a simple bun. With her plain cotton robes and walking staff, she looked like a kindly grandmother. Yet there was something about the gray dirt smeared across her face that chilled me. "Step aside, sentinel. You dishonor your vows to Kiata by defending the traitor Shiori'anma."

"I see no quarrel," Takkan replied. "I swore to protect my country, my king, my princess."

"The princess is the bloodsake. For the good of Kiata, she must die. The sorcerer too." She pointed her staff at Gen's unconscious form. "Their magic is why the demons have awoken. It is unnatural. Forbidden by the gods! Only their deaths can seal the mountains once more."

Her fervor roused the villagers, who crowded in closer.

This old woman's no village grandmother, Kiki observed warily. *Do you think she could be a . . . a . . .*

A priestess of the Holy Mountains? I nodded grimly in agreement. *She's not alone,* I replied. From the mob I picked out at least three fellow cultists—all with the same ashen paste on their cheeks.

I fixed my attention on the villagers. "Don't listen to her," I said, extending my palms in a gesture of peace. "You have nothing to fear from me."

"Nothing to fear?" the priestess cried, echoing my words with a sneer. "Evil afflicts these mountains, which were sealed for a thousand years—until she started meddling. Should Shiori'anma release her demon army, they will kill our brothers and sisters, our mothers and fathers—our children! Kiata's men will be condemned to an endless battle, for how can we win against foes that cannot die? Tell me, how can we have nothing to fear?"

The crowd roared in agreement.

"Bring her to me!" the priestess shouted. "Only her death can rid us of this evil!"

It was the command the villagers had been waiting for. They charged forward, rushing Takkan to get to me.

"Run, Shiori!" Takkan shouted as he fended off attacks from every direction. He didn't wish to hurt the villagers, a sentiment that was not mutual. "Run!"

I did the opposite of run. I plucked Hasho's daggers off my belt and slammed the hilts on someone's head. I was lunging for another attack when Kiki yanked my hair, narrowly saving me from an arrow tipped in fire.

I didn't get to thank her. The priestesses were nocking new arrows into their bows, and my heart leapt in alarm as another volley sliced the air.

Stop them, I said, summoning my magic. The daggers in my hands flew up, inspirited, and deflected the incoming arrows.

The priestesses calmly stepped forward and nocked their bows again. Their kind had tried to burn me alive once before, and I knew they wouldn't give up easily. They knew that using my magic would tire me, and that Takkan alone couldn't defend us from so many.

What were we going to do?

The next wave of fiery arrows arched high, and just as I was bracing for the worst, the pearl inside my satchel began to hum and tremble. Louder it grew, the sound amplified by the sudden groan that emanated from the mountains.

"LEAVE SHIORI'ANMA ALONE!" rumbled the wind, carrying the demons' message across the forest. *"SHE IS OURS."*

A tremor began in the mountains and reverberated all the way to where I stood. The trees swayed. One toppled in front of me, and as I staggered back, the villagers shrieked in terror.

The arrows in the sky whined to a halt, spiraling down upon the priestesses. As they scrambled, I grabbed Takkan by the hand. "Are you hurt?"

The swiftness with which he lifted Gen over his shoulder answered my question. He took my arm, linking it with his.

Then we fled.

We ran until we were deep in the forest, far out of sight of the breach. Once we were certain no one had followed, we took refuge in a grove marked by two fallen pine trees. There was a small pool nearby, and Takkan laid Gen beside the water, rinsing the boy's face of blood while I sank onto a tree stump.

Of all the champions to swoop in and save us, it had been demons that had come to our aid!

Only because they want the pleasure of killing me themselves, I thought. I felt like a fish in Ai'long, saved from the sharks only to be slain by dragons.

"Are you all right?" Takkan asked. "You're shaking."

I was. "The priestesses . . . and the villagers. They nearly killed Gen . . . and you."

"And *you*," Takkan said quietly.

I was thankful my betrothed was not the type to gloat that I should've stayed in the palace. I would have.

I dug my heels into the dirt. "They're right, you know," I said at length. "People are dying because of me."

"People are dying because of Bandur."

"I'm the one who freed him," I replied. "It's my responsibility to find a way to seal him back in the mountains."

Or you could leave Kiata forever, Kiki suggested. *Radish Boy would go with you, I'm sure. He'd follow you anywhere in the world.*

My face warmed, even though Takkan couldn't hear the paper bird. *I'd never ask that of Takkan,* I chided her. *And besides, if I'd wanted to hide, I would've stayed in Ai'long.*

211

Well, you can't do that anymore, quipped my bird. *I doubt you'd be welcomed back—maybe not even in ten lifetimes.*

Kiki wasn't being helpful.

"I still have the pearl," I said aloud, opening my satchel. "Its power is what sealed the mountains in the first place. Maybe I could use it to trap Bandur back inside."

"Unlikely," said Gen weakly. He was waking now, groaning as he propped himself up in a sitting position. "Curse the Sages, my nose is broken, isn't it? Hurts like demonfire."

Stop crying like your bones are shattered, Kiki chided as she hopped onto Gen's shoulder. *It's only a fracture. Takkan's already cleaned the worst of it.*

Gen reclined against the log, pinching his nose with a handkerchief to stanch the blood. He let out a loud sigh of relief. "It's just the bridge," he said, waving away Takkan's offer of help. "Nothing a few nights of healing sleep won't fix. Wish I could say the same for that pearl."

The Wraith's pearl had emerged from my satchel, and it hovered shakily over my lap like a broken moon.

"It's near its breaking point. Can't you see?" Gen pointed at the crack in its center. "That was barely a scratch the last time I saw it."

Shiori used it against the Dragon King, said Kiki. *Nearly killed them both.*

"Tragic," said Gen under his breath. "It won't have the strength to seal Bandur in the mountains. Not that you could have pulled it off, anyway. He'd have dragged you inside to feed his demon brethren the moment you got close." He smirked. "Unless your loyal subjects killed you first."

I grimaced. "Not *everyone* hates me."

"Most do," said Gen. The boy didn't mince words. "Enchantress Heedi used to say humans are their own worst enemies. I'm beginning to understand what she meant."

"What *did* she mean?"

"That humans are weak-minded, fickle fools. Take your priestesses of the Holy Mountains. For generations, they've been shunned as zealous heretics. But they're heroes of the people now that you've become the greater enemy."

"Fear unites the most disparate of foes," Takkan murmured in agreement.

I frowned. "Are you saying I should worry more about the villagers than the demons?"

"Depends on the demon," replied Gen. "Most are dangerous but predictable. They're like wild beasts, only with magic. With the proper protections—*magical* protections, which don't exist in your country anymore—most harm can be prevented."

"What about a demon like Bandur?" I asked.

"Bandur belongs to a different class of demon," Gen replied darkly. "The most dangerous, most powerful class— able to steal one's soul with a touch, to slip into your mind and possess your thoughts, to ensorcell other demons into their command. Bandur chose Kiata precisely because he knows your people are unprepared against magic. Now he leads an army of demons who have been lusting after freedom for a thousand years. If he releases them, he will be an unstoppable force."

"Then I'll make sure he doesn't," I said. My mind was

spinning, cobbling together a plan out of the puzzle pieces Gen had presented. "I'll lure Bandur out of Kiata."

"Where would you take him?" Takkan asked.

I hesitated, knowing he wasn't going to like the answer. "The Forgotten Isles of Lapzur," I replied. "I have to go there anyway to find the Wraith. I was thinking that he's Lapzur's guardian . . . and if we can't trap Bandur on Kiata, maybe we can try Lapzur. It's an island hardly anyone knows of, far away from every place else. We can trap him there, with the Wraith's help."

Takkan's voice was tight. "You don't even know this Wraith, Shiori. He could be worse than Bandur."

"Then we'll use his pearl as leverage. We'll make him help us."

Takkan looked only half convinced. "Gen, what do you think?"

The young sorcerer had been quiet, and he poked at the dirt with a long, twisted branch before answering. "I think it's the craziest idea I've ever heard. But . . . if you don't get killed first, it just might work." The branch suddenly snapped. "So long as you get Bandur's amulet."

"His amulet?" I repeated.

"All former enchanters—like Bandur—have one. It's their weakness. You might even call it their heart. You can't lure him out of Kiata without it."

"Why not?" I asked.

"Because the amulet's the source of his power and the anchor for his physical body. Where it goes, so goes he."

I remembered how Bandur had come to me in the palace,

214

writing in shadow and smoke and borrowing Qinnia's body in place of his own. Gen was right. "So you're saying he's trapped."

"His amulet is trapped," Gen corrected. "It's lodged within the Holy Mountains, which in turn binds Bandur."

"What happens if we have it?" Takkan asked. "Would it allow us to control him?"

"It'd help subdue him," said Gen carefully. "To an extent. What you should be asking is how to extract the amulet. Taking it away from the mountains will come at a cost, one that isn't sustainable for long." He didn't elaborate. "Eventually, you'll have to return it."

"Or bind him somewhere else," I said, going back to my original idea. "Like Lapzur."

"It would take enormous power to do that," said Gen. "But perhaps the Wraith can, with his pearl."

"We have our plan, then," I said, letting out a giddy breath. "Or at least a start. Gen, I guess you do deserve a room in the palace."

The boy shrugged. "I know a thing or two about demons." A pause. "It's a good idea, Shiori, but it's not without great risk. You have to know that the Forgotten Isles are rife with ghosts and demons—they thrive there. The ghosts of Lapzur can turn you into one of them with just a touch, and the demons . . . they'll toy with you slowly. They'll prey on your fears and distort your memories until you can't even remember your name. Then they'll kill you."

"Sounds like the perfect place to leave Bandur," I replied. "He'll feel right at home."

Gen frowned, as if my flippant response troubled him.

"I've had enough experience with demons," I reassured him. "I won't fall for their tricks."

"With so much demon power concentrated on the isles, Bandur's strength will be greater there," he warned. "The first thing he'll try to do is get the amulet back. Take care that he doesn't."

"I will."

Takkan nodded too. He'd been quiet, considering the plan from all angles, I presumed. This he confirmed by asking: "Do we know how to get to Lapzur?"

"I have maps that allude to its location," Gen responded, "but Lapzur is a place kept secret by the enchanters." He grimaced. "If only I'd been able to steal that mirror for Elang. I'd—"

"The mirror of truth?" I reached into my satchel and held up the shard I'd won from Lady Solzaya.

"You have a piece of it?" Gen exclaimed, snatching the shard. "Why didn't you tell me? This—*this* is how you'll find Lapzur."

"Lady Nahma said it won't show me the Forgotten Isles."

"Not by itself, it won't," Gen agreed, and before I could stop him, he dropped the shard into the pool behind us. "But it will with some help."

"Gen!"

The boy put his finger to his lips. "Look. The water's enchanted. Can't you tell? Even with a broken nose, I sensed it."

I whirled, finally taking in our surroundings. There was something familiar about this place, this pool. . . . My mind flashed back to the day Raikama had cast my brothers and me out of the palace. I'd followed her here! I didn't know it then, but she'd come to ask the waters if I was in danger.

"It's the Tears of Emuri'en," I said, finally remembering. "The waters reveal fate's possibilities." Something I wished I had known long ago. Maybe then I wouldn't have assumed Raikama was trying to kill me. Maybe she'd still be alive now.

"Emuri'en's magic should heighten the mirror's ability," said Gen. "Go on, try it."

As I drew closer to the pool, my own power manifested itself, pale filaments of silvery gold wisping from my fingertips. "Strands of my soul," I murmured, fascinated. "I saw them for the first time in Ai'long."

"Your magic is your own," replied Gen simply. "It's always been there for you to see, but you probably weren't looking hard enough."

I couldn't unsee it now. I trailed my fingers over the water, and the strands shone, as if beckoning me forward. Slowly, I pulled my trousers up to my knees and approached the Tears of Emuri'en. The Wraith's pearl followed in my shadow. Once I entered the water, the mirror shard bubbled to the surface.

I reached into the pool to retrieve it, but as my fingers gripped its smooth edges, my reflection vanished. In its place was the Wraith's pearl, and the waters darkened to match its black and gleaming surface.

Then, in flashes, I saw.

The Forgotten Isles, shaped like long skeletal fingers scraping against the ocean. A tower where the blood of stars fell. A storm that ravaged the oceans.

This was where I'd find Khramelan. The Wraith.

I started to pull away, but the Tears of Emuri'en hadn't finished. The waters were still as black as the pearl, and roiling. They gathered around me, throwing me forward into the pool—and into the future.

Six cranes flew me over a sea of red, raging demonfire. We were headed for a dark tower silhouetted against a broken moon, and hundreds of paper birds trailed after us—wildly flapping as the flames singed their wings.

There, on the ramparts, besieged by demons, was Takkan. Blood stained his hair and face, and he was hovering in the air, suspended by invisible strings.

"Takkan!" I shouted.

Bandur loomed into view, his rubescent eyes swathed in darkness. His smile curved like a scythe, and he said nothing, gave no warning. In one terrible stroke, he slashed Takkan through the chest.

And, as if my own heart had been struck, I screamed.

CHAPTER TWENTY-THREE

The sound of my own scream jolted me back to the present, where I was still submerged in the pool. Water rushed into my mouth, burning down my throat with a raw, searing heat. I thrashed, in desperate need of air.

"Shiori!" Takkan grabbed me by the arm and pulled me to the surface. "Shiori, open your eyes."

Kiki touched her wing to my cheek. *Shiori?*

My paper bird tried slipping into my mind, but I wouldn't let her in. An invisible fortress walled my thoughts from her prying eyes.

She's shutting me out, Kiki told Gen in distress. *I can't read her thoughts.*

"She's recovering from her vision," replied the sorcerer, plucking the mirror shard from the water. "Give her a minute."

I was still coughing and spitting as I rolled onto my side. Sunlight stung my eyes, the green blur of the forest slowly coming into focus. The pool was crystal clear, and I wondered whether I'd hallucinated its dark waters—and the terrible future they had shown me.

If only.

Gen poked my shoulder. "What did you see?"

My eyes found Takkan and didn't leave him. *I saw you die,* I almost said, but the words withered in my throat.

I couldn't tell him. I knew he'd say something obnoxiously reasonable, like that there was more than one way to divine a turtle shell. Or that the waters were showing only one arrangement of fortune's leaves.

He'd insist on coming. Then he'd die.

"Draw a map," I said, my tone subdued. "I know where Lapzur is."

My own composure surprised me. Inside, my emotions were in turmoil. I didn't want to go to Lapzur anymore. I wanted to abandon my promise and fling Khramelan's heart deep into the sea, never to be seen again.

But the pearl inside my satchel weighed on me heavier than ever before. Its time was running out.

Meanwhile, Takkan had taken out his writing brush and prepared the ink stone. At his side, Gen was ripping pages from Takkan's notebook and laying them across the flat surface of the tree stump. After Takkan sketched a map of Lor'yan, I pointed to a spot in the lower left of the Cuiyan Ocean. "The Forgotten Isles are here."

"Here?" A frown wrinkled Takkan's brow as he marked the location. "It's so close to Tambu. That cannot be a coincidence."

Gen let out a low whistle. "Impressive, Lord Takkan. You

do know your lore. The first demons were indeed born in Tambu."

I suppressed a shiver. *What the waters showed is only a possibility,* I reminded myself. *If Takkan doesn't go to Lapzur, he'll be safe from Bandur.*

Takkan and Gen were so preoccupied with their demon lore that neither noticed me shrink away, pulling my tunic tight around me.

But Kiki noticed.

That was rude, shutting me out, she admonished as she landed on my lap. *Your soul is my soul, Shiori. You can lie to them, but not to me. What are you hiding?*

She dipped into my thoughts again, breaking past the walls I had clumsily constructed. With a gasp, she caught a glimpse of what the waters had shown me: my brothers as cranes once more, flying me through storms and seas to Lapzur.

My walls shot up before she could get any further.

Shiori! she cried.

I ignored her. Aloud, I said, "We'll have to fly to Lapzur."

Takkan's brush drooped. "Fly?"

"Lapzur lies far across the sea, and the island is protected by the enchanted waters of Lake Paduan," I explained. "They'll sink any ship. We have to fly."

"How?" Takkan blew on the ink to dry the map. "How will we fly to Lapzur?"

I flinched at the *we.*

"There are plenty of options," Gen said, his pitch rising. Clearly, this was a topic that excited him. "We could conjure wings to make a flying horse . . . enchant a carpet . . .

summon birds to carry us." He frowned. "But that would require great magic, magic even greater than what's available here in the Tears of Emuri'en."

Kiki poked me. In her driest tone, she said, *You know the answer, Shiori. Aren't you going to say something?*

I didn't respond. Unease stirred in my chest as the image of six flying cranes flashed once more to mind.

"What about a spell the pearl has cast before?" I whispered.

"That could work," Gen allowed. "If the pearl is already familiar with it, and the formerly enchanted objects are still in your possession. . . . Think of it like rereading a book." He chuckled at the metaphor, then raised an eyebrow. "Pray tell, what are you thinking?"

I bit my lower lip. There had to be another way. I couldn't involve my brothers again. Couldn't put them in danger again. But it didn't seem I had any choice.

"Gen," I said, my voice so small I barely recognized it, "you get some rest. Let me speak with my brothers."

I found them congregated in Benkai's chambers. Since Raikama's curse, the princes were together more often than not. That was our stepmother's gift to us. Through our trials and through all we had endured, we were closer than ever. Even Qinnia was here, engaged in a chess game with Yotan.

"Aren't I much more likable than Reiji?" Yotan was asking her. "I think the khagan's daughter would have liked me the best."

Reiji snorted. "Yes, you're so charming you'd spill all of Kiata's secrets after one week in A'landi."

"Better than starting a war with that perpetual grimace."

"Shiori!" Qinnia said, looking distraught that I'd arrived. We hadn't spoken since the incident at dinner.

At the sight of me, my brothers rose and all began speaking at once:

"We heard what happened in the mountains, how you were nearly killed! Are you hurt?"

"How could you leave like that, and after what happened last night! Father is beside himself with worry."

"You should have at least told someone."

"She *did* tell someone," Wandei observed. "Look who's outside the door."

I'd asked Takkan to wait outside, but little escaped Wandei's notice. As he steered my betrothed inside, I spoke up. "I needed to see the breach."

"That was impulsive, sister. You—"

"Don't tell me I should stay in my room," I warned Andahai, "or that there's nothing to worry about. You won't defeat Bandur without my help."

At the mention of Bandur, Qinnia's entire body tensed. She touched Andahai's sleeve, whispering something into his ear.

"Takkan, my wife is feeling ill," said Andahai stiffly. "Would you kindly escort her to our apartments? Last door down the hall."

Takkan acquiesced with a bow and followed the princess

out. Qinnia was clutching her sash even as she left, and I eyed Andahai worriedly.

"Is she—"

"She's fine," he interjected. "Nothing to worry yourself over. Did you learn anything at the breach, or was the visit for naught?"

I glowered at him, but I *did* have news to share. "I think I've found a way to defeat Bandur, and I need your help."

"You have it," said Benkai without hesitation. My other brothers nodded in agreement. "What can we do?"

I swallowed hard. If only it were that simple.

"I need to go to Lapzur," I said. "It's an island west of Tambu, forgotten by all but enchanters and demons. There is a half dragon there imprisoned as guardian of the city. He is the true owner of Raikama's pearl."

Andahai frowned. "What does this have to do with Bandur?"

"I still have the pearl," I finally admitted. "I'm going to return it to the guardian and free him from Lapzur." I paused. "Then trap Bandur into taking his place."

Now I had their attention.

"A clever idea, sister," said Wandei, "but how will you do it?"

Yotan agreed. "Bandur isn't exactly someone you can lure onto a ship."

"Ships won't take me where I need to go," I said evasively. I lowered my lashes, staring at my feet and wishing I'd never looked into the Tears of Emuri'en. "I need to fly."

"Fly?" repeated Reiji.

"Stop uttering nonsense, Shiori," Andahai chided, not understanding. "You said you needed help. Benkai will lend us his swiftest ship."

"She knows exactly what she's saying," said Hasho, his dark eyes fixed on me. We'd always been close, and he could read what was behind my distress. "The answer is yes, Shiori. Do it. Turn us into cranes again."

Curse Hasho. My head jerked up, same as my brothers', and a feeling of dreadful inevitability churned in my gut. I knew it was the only way, and yet I couldn't bear putting my brothers through such a curse again. "No—"

"Wherever it is you need to go, we'll take you," he said firmly. "Won't we, brothers?"

One by one, my brothers nodded. Even Andahai, though he was last.

"But to turn you into cranes again . . ." I inhaled. I looked up at them, voicing what worried me most. "What if I can't turn you all back?"

Hasho smiled wanly. "Life as a crane wouldn't be the worst fate. I've missed being able to talk to the birds."

"I quite enjoyed the flying," added Yotan. "Not the eating of worms and mice, though."

"Raikama wouldn't have given you the pearl if she didn't believe in you," Benkai told me. "We have faith in you too. Now stop chewing on your lip. Let us help you."

I glanced at my eldest brother, who gave a grim nod. "We're taking you," Andahai confirmed, "a week of worms and all. Only answer me this: How do we bring Bandur? You *have* thought that out, haven't you?"

"We'll need his amulet in order to coax him out of Kiata," I replied. "Gen says it's inside the Holy Mountains."

"You're listening to the boy sorcerer now?" said Reiji. "How old is he, twelve?"

"Thirteen," I corrected. "He knows more about demons than any of us. He can help."

A hint of skepticism clouded Andahai's expression, but he nodded. "If you trust him, then so will we," he said. "Tomorrow, Benkai will have his men investigate. Hasho and I will go too. Reiji will deal with the A'landans, and Yotan and Wandei will devise a way to carry Shiori and Takkan to Lapzur."

I suppressed a flinch at the mention of Takkan. I hadn't exactly invited him. "When will you leave for the breach?" I asked. "Gen is still there, and I can—"

"You?" Benkai laughed. "*You're* not coming, sister—or have you forgotten that your betrothal ceremony is in two days? You'll have much to prepare tomorrow. Unless you plan on missing it for a second time."

Nine Hells of Sharima'en, I *had* forgotten about my betrothal ceremony.

I bit down on my lip again. "Maybe I could ask Father to postpone it."

"And break Takkan's heart?" Yotan teased. "He's been waiting months for you. He'd probably have waited for years if he had to."

"He could wait a little longer," I said weakly. "Distract Father and the council, maybe. Until we get back."

Andahai frowned. "Isn't he coming to Lapzur? You aren't having second thoughts about him, are you?"

My cheeks heated. "It isn't that. It's just . . . Takkan can't come. The six of you can't carry us *both* anyway."

"I'm sure the twins will come up with something sturdy enough for two," said Hasho wryly. "We're not putting you on a blanket again, you know."

I shot him a dirty look. Usually I could count on Hasho to be on my side, but during my months away, my brothers and Takkan had formed a lasting friendship. They wouldn't take my side against him.

Kiki wasn't helping either. *I can recruit other birds for assistance,* she offered, *if it's Takkan's weight you're worried about.*

"That isn't it . . . ," I said.

Then? Kiki and my brothers asked at once.

I leapt from my chair in frustration. "He can't come with us," I repeated vehemently. "The Tears of Emuri'en showed me the future. If Takkan comes, Bandur will kill him."

It took a beat before my brothers reacted. Benkai, the second-eldest and gentlest brother—at least toward me—came first to my side. "So that's why you're upset," he said. "It all makes sense now. Let me guess, you haven't told him?"

"Of course not. He's a courageous fool. He'd insist on being a hero."

"That courageous fool can hold his own in battle," said Benkai. "I don't say that about many men."

It was true that Benkai rarely praised another's fighting skill, but I wasn't swayed. "Bandur isn't like the other demons."

"Don't begin your life together with a lie," said Hasho quietly. "Tell him what you saw. Whether or not he comes should be his decision."

"Hasho's right," said Andahai. "Tell him the truth, Shiori."

"You're one to talk," I countered. "You sent him away with Qinnia."

"My wife has no place in this conversation," Andahai said. "She's in a delicate state."

"A delicate state? What's wrong with her?"

"Nothing," said my eldest brother too sharply. "My wife's well-being is a private affair. Takkan's involvement concerns all of us."

I started to argue, but Wandei cut into the conversation. "You love Takkan," he said matter-of-factly, like he'd just informed me that all of us were breathing air. "We can't always protect those we love by shutting them out. That was Raikama's mistake."

His words stung me into silence. I was used to my quietest brother appealing to logic and reason, not to my heart. It took me aback, and my shoulders sank in defeat.

"I'll tell him," I said weakly.

It wasn't a lie. Yet the words lodged in my throat like three sharp thorns, stuck until the truth set them free.

CHAPTER TWENTY-FOUR

As promised, I sent for Gen the next day, braving Father's displeasure at me for sneaking out to make the case that the young sorcerer had saved me from the ambush in the mountains. A half-truth, but it seemed to appease Father slightly, and the joy on Gen's face when he arrived was worth the trouble.

"Finally, the imperial palace!" he exclaimed, his voice high with excitement. "It's just as grand as I imagined. Cleaner too."

I couldn't help smiling. The boy's company was a welcome distraction from the dark thoughts that haunted me. "I would've guessed that with your worldly experiences you'd have been to dozens." I cocked my head. "You make it sound like this is your first."

Gen attempted a grin, but the effort made him wince. "It is, if you don't count the Dragon King's. I hardly saw anything aside from the dungeon . . . and Elang's abode is more like a cave than a palace."

"Such standards," I teased. "Trust me, life in the palace isn't as exciting as it sounds. You'll be wishing you were back in the camp by the end of the week."

"I doubt it. I look forward to court." He dusted his sleeves, then straightened so he was nearly as tall as I. "Are there parties I can attend? Any festivals or banquets?"

"Not really. There won't be a Summer Festival this year."

"Not even a banquet for your brother's wedding?"

"There was only a small, private ceremony. My stepmother passed not long ago. We are still in mourning."

"Ah," Gen conceded. "So why all these weddings in quick succession? Andahai's, Reiji's, then yours—"

"Father has no choice but to marry us off. Kiata is still healing from Lord Yuji's rebellion."

"I see . . . to secure alliances and such. It's the same story in all kingdoms." Gen stifled a yawn, as if the very thought bored him. "I don't envy you royals, but at least you have Takkan—where is he?"

"In a meeting with the ministers." I quickly changed the topic. "How's your nose? You still don't want to see the physician?"

Gen wheezed. "I'll do a better job of healing it than your doctors."

"Suit yourself." I gestured at the cobbled path ahead. "Your villa is in the south court. I've made it known that you're my guest, so no one should bother you. Try to stay out of trouble."

Demons take me, I was starting to sound like Andahai. Usually *I* was on the receiving end of such warnings.

"You're not going to give me a tour?" cajoled Gen. "At least show me where the library is. I'll find materials for you. You could use some magic lessons, you know."

I thought of Seryu and our lessons by the lake. How he'd once made a flock of birds out of water, and taught me to resurrect Kiki after Raikama tore her to pieces.

"I'd like that, but it'll have to wait," I said with an apologetic shake of the head. "I have a full day ahead—my reward for sneaking out yesterday. A morning packed with more ceremonies for Reiji's wedding, then a fitting with the imperial seamstresses for my own betrothal." I tried not to make a face about the fitting. "Then I have to see Qinnia."

"The crown princess?"

I was impressed he knew. "Wandei asked me to give her my sturdiest robes. For what, he won't say. He can be secretive when he's plotting something."

"You're not looking forward to seeing her."

I wasn't. I'd seen Andahai's wife with my brothers and at morning prayers, but since my first night home—when I'd nearly stabbed her with my eating sticks—I'd been avoiding her, and I sensed the effort was mutual.

She's in a delicate state, Andahai had said.

I could read between my brother's words: she must have been traumatized by Bandur, thanks to me. She must hate me. I didn't blame her.

"What's wrong?" said Gen. "You look sick."

"I'm just hoping I won't have to sew," I said. A deflection, but it wasn't *untrue*.

"Understandable," responded Gen. "It's a tedious craft."

With a cheerful wave, he disappeared into the vast courtyard, and I released a sigh. Gods, I prayed he wouldn't attract too much attention. At least he hadn't brought that enormous hawk.

"Keep an eye on him, will you?" I asked Kiki.

By midday, Kiki had reported that the young sorcerer was performing sleights of hand for the children of the court and had finagled several dinner invitations from their parents. He'd even donned an illusion to appear older and approached a handful of ministers, winning them over with well-timed compliments and silvery charm. He was going to dazzle them into appreciating magic, he said.

"Ha!" I said. "He really hasn't spent much time with bureaucrats, has he?"

He's playing a dangerous game, Kiki muttered. *He might be more rash and bold than even you.*

"He'll grow out of it."

As you have?

I glared at my bird and tossed a set of heavy red robes over my shoulder. My neck instinctively tilted to nuzzle the silk lining, soft as cream.

You sure you want to donate those? asked Kiki.

They were the winter robes I'd received for my sixteenth birthday, lined with wool and sturdy sand silk. Garments I sorely wished I'd had during my long months in Iro last year.

"Wandei asked for my sturdiest," I replied. "These are it. They're also red, with a pattern of cranes. All good omens."

Kiki's small shoulders heaved. *I suppose we'll need all the luck we can get.*

Silently, I agreed. Then I shut my closet door and trudged to my last meeting of the afternoon, the one I was dreading most.

⁓

Qinnia herself answered the door, welcoming me into the apartments she shared with Andahai.

"The maids have been dismissed for the afternoon," she said, though I hadn't asked. "I thought it would be best if we met alone."

Her features were schooled into the polite mask that all ladies of the court had mastered. Still, I could tell she was nervous to see me. Her hands were folded stiffly over her dress's purple sash, as if to keep her fingers from fidgeting, and every time her earrings made an audible tinkle, she cleared her throat. She had a kind earnestness about her that wasn't easy to come by in Gindara. No wonder Andahai loved her.

She took the robes I'd brought, setting them beside her sewing basket. There was a neat stack of jackets and robes— one for each of my six brothers.

"I'm guessing Wandei wouldn't tell you what they're for," I said.

"Not even Yotan would give a hint," she replied with a shake of her head. "They expected you to ask, so they didn't tell me anything. Only that all would be unveiled at the Sacred Lake."

"The Sacred Lake?"

Qinnia shrugged, and I twisted my lips, nettled. Takkan

would know what this was about, but I'd snubbed him at every opportunity since the plan had been set in motion. I dreaded seeing him even more than Qinnia.

I turned to go, but Qinnia motioned for me to sit. She'd been expecting me, ready with two plates of peaches, the yellow slices beautifully arranged in the shape of a flower, on her table.

"These arrived from my family's orchard this morning," she said, offering me a plate. "Have some before Andahai returns and eats them all. I won't be humble—they're so sweet the bees think they're honey."

My stomach was easily won over, and at the sight of dessert, I forgot my nerves as well as my manners. Without making the necessary insistence that Qinnia eat first—since she outranked me—I devoured a slice, then another and another. "This is what I'd expect the peaches of immortality to taste like." I smacked my lips. "Now I know why Andahai really married you. For your family's orchards."

"I'll have a box sent to you and Takkan," Qinnia replied. Was it my imagination, or had her smile widened a hair? "An early betrothal present."

"Maybe you ought to wait until *after* the ceremony," I mumbled with my mouth full. "Make sure I show up this time."

Qinnia's smile broke into a laugh, which she hastily hid behind her sleeve. She sat up a little straighter and returned to her formal tone. "I wanted to talk to you about what happened the other night."

I gulped and set down my plate. This was it. It was time.

Being away from home had worn down my pride, and I clasped my peach-smeared hands together and knelt before her. "I beg your forgiveness, Princess Qinnia. I have caused you great distress and offense, and I seek only to—"

"Shiori, what are you doing?" Qinnia pulled me off my knees. "Did Andahai put you up to this? Please, get up. Get up."

I sat back on the divan and leaned into the stiff pillows behind my back, suddenly appreciative of their support. "Didn't you summon me here to apologize?"

"I summoned you here because Wandei needs me to help sew those robes." She gestured at the area around her sewing basket. "And because I . . . I wanted to apologize."

"You?" My brows drew together. "But I . . . I attacked you. I could have hurt you. I'm the one who released Bandur from the mountains. It's because of me he . . ." I wheeled my hands, not knowing how to articulate that he'd possessed her mind.

"It might have been *me* who poisoned you." She bit her lip. "Four priestesses were captured at the Holy Mountains. Andahai thinks they supplied the poison that nearly killed you . . . and someone in the palace administered it. Someone we all trusted."

I hid a grimace. The mirror of truth had confirmed as much but shown me no faces.

"With Bandur's ability to switch bodies, it could have been anyone," said Qinnia. "I worry it . . . it might have been me. I pray it wasn't me."

"It wasn't," I said with certainty. "Bandur has his own plans for me."

Qinnia bunched the pink fabric of her robes in her fist. "Are you sure? I could feel his wrath at you."

"What else do you remember?"

"I was so cold." She shuddered. "And . . . numb. It was like being trapped in a nightmare."

"I felt the cold too," I said softly. It was how I had known that Bandur was near.

Qinnia lifted her sleeve, showing me a bracelet of wooden beads. "I've worn this ever since I was a girl. My mother had it blessed by High Priest Voan to protect me from evil. Many in the palace have been wearing such trinkets to ward against demons. But they don't help, do they?"

"Not against Bandur."

"I thought not." Qinnia unclasped the bracelet, beads rattling as she did so. "I grew up so superstitious I would count my steps to make sure I never took four at a time. I wouldn't even eat four slices of peaches or wear white flowers in my hair—lest I invite misfortune to my family's door. Yet I never believed in magic—not in dragons or sorcery, certainly not in demons."

She rolled her sleeve back down. "But then you and the princes disappeared for months. Andahai told me he was turned into a crane, and you had to break his curse. I didn't believe him at first, but sometimes at night his crane spirit still haunts him." She bit her lip. "In the old legends, they say that once you've been touched by magic, it never fully leaves you."

I fell quiet. Seryu had told me nearly the same about Kiata—that the gods couldn't erase every trace of magic from the land. That my very existence proved it. Did that mean I needed to be stamped out and dug up like a weed? Or was I a seed—a sign that it was time for magic to return? I twisted my hands. Magic or no magic? Which was better for Kiata?

It was a problem I didn't know how to solve, so I pushed it aside for the moment. "Andahai told you about the curse?"

"He told me everything," she replied. "About the bowl on your head, the pearl Raikama left you, your journey to Ai'long. But ever since that awful dinner, he's been withdrawn. I know he's trying to protect me, especially since . . ." Her voice drifted, her hands touching her belly.

Suddenly I understood, and I clapped my hand over my mouth. "Emuri'en's Strands! That's wonderful news."

"It's still early," Qinnia said shyly. "I told Andahai the day before you returned. But I almost wish I'd waited. I mentioned to him once that I was feeling weary, and ever since then he's had the physician visit every day. He's become . . ."

"Overbearing?" I suggested. "Overprotective and impossible?"

We shared a laugh.

"Yes. Exactly."

"That's the Andahai I've tolerated all my life," I said. "It's only around you that he's tender and sweet."

"I'm lucky," admitted Qinnia. "But so are you. We've all grown fond of Takkan."

I blushed, and a rush of warmth stole over my heart. He'd truly won my family over, as I knew he would. Another reason I had to keep him safe.

"Are you feeling better now?" I asked Qinnia.

"Food helps with the nausea. The tiredness comes in waves."

"Food has a magical way of making me feel better too," I replied. "I swear anything sweet has magic powers." As we both bit into our peach slices at the same time, we exchanged shy grins. There was no way to explain why, but it felt as if we'd been friends for years. Friends who made weekly jaunts into Gindara to window-shop and gossiped over breakfasts of fried crullers and congee.

"If Andahai ever gets boorish about answering your questions, ask me," I offered. "I'll tell you what I can."

Qinnia scooted to the edge of her chair, accepting the invitation into my inner circle with a grateful nod. I leaned forward too. I knew what she wanted to ask.

"I think we've come up with a way to defeat Bandur," I divulged. I couldn't share too much in case it compromised her, but I wanted her permission. "I will need Andahai's help. The seven of us will have to go away again. Soon."

Qinnia looked thoughtful. "All I ask is that you bring Andahai back alive," she said. "That's a command, sister."

She'd never called me *sister* before, and I smiled, warmed by our new friendship. "I will."

I was in good spirits when I exited her chambers, but that mood quickly vanished.

There, at the end of the hallway, stood Takkan.

CHAPTER TWENTY-FIVE

I fled, putting as much distance as I could between myself and Takkan, until I was nearly at the Sacred Temple. Ironically, this was where Takkan and I were supposed to have our ceremony tomorrow.

He wouldn't think to look for me in this part of the palace.

I slipped off my jacket, a brightly embroidered eyesore that was sure to draw attention, and stuffed it under a begonia bush. Then I veered away from the temple toward the nearest kitchen.

It was the smallest of the palace's three cooking houses, and the sight of me stealing inside made the servants freeze, stricken in their spots, until they remembered to bow. At the first chance, they scattered out of the building. I pretended not to hear them muttering *witch*.

Since it was farthest from the royal banquet halls, this kitchen was scarcely used, and the produce in the pantry was ancient. Honestly, some of the vegetables looked like they'd been around since before I left for Ai'long. The potatoes had knobbed sprouts, the cabbage was wilted, and the carrots flopped when I held them up.

A perfect opportunity for me to practice my magic.

"Revive yourselves," I told the carrots.

They grew fatter, and their color—leached white by age—brightened into purple and orange. Silver-gold strings of magic wove my spell in place, and I turned next to the radishes and potatoes and cabbage to inspirit them too. By the time I finished, the water was boiling.

I'd made fish soup so many times I could do all the steps without thinking. I'd made it for my brothers when they were sick, for Takkan when he'd been injured, for the fishermen at Sparrow Inn when I'd been forced to work there. Not once had I made it for myself.

I was mindful of every carrot I peeled, every bean curd I sliced, every radish I boiled—and in my pot, I conjured a taste of happier times, when I was just a girl standing on her tiptoes to watch her mother cook. The smell brought a fierce ache to my heart, and for a moment, I was the old Shiori again. Running across the gardens with stolen kites, jumping into puddles, and arriving at my lessons late, charming and aggravating everyone I knew. I was a girl without secrets, without shadows invading her dreams. A girl who didn't have to wonder whether home would ever feel like home again.

How I missed that girl.

I was so engrossed in my work that I didn't hear the door groan open.

"You're a hard one to track, Shiori. If I didn't know better, I would think you're avoiding me."

My breath hitched.

As Takkan let himself into the kitchen, I let go of my ladle.

Had he seen me dart out of Qinnia's apartments earlier? Or had my brothers sent him? Had they told him of my vision?

Unaware of the tempest he'd ignited in my thoughts, Takkan spoke: "The messengers said you didn't read my invitations to lunch. Or tea—or dinner."

Those snitches. They used to be on *my* side.

"I've been busy. I've hardly had a moment to myself until now."

"Oh . . ." Takkan blinked away his confusion and raked a hand through his dark hair. "Should I leave?"

Yes, my mind said. "No," my treacherous lips uttered instead. I wanted to smack my face with the ladle.

But Takkan's eyes softened, and relief eased the deep crease of his brow. "I looked for you. I had a feeling I might find you in a kitchen." He leaned over my pot and brightened at the smell. "Making fish soup again?"

I almost laughed at how hopeful he looked. "It's not for drinking," I said, fishing out my ladle. "See?"

With a breath, I broke my concentration and released the strings of magic I'd been holding. The carrots turned gray, the potatoes sprouted again, and the fish head floated to the top.

Takkan stared.

"I was practicing magic," I explained, wrinkling my nose at the spoiled soup. "My skills are rusty. Making radishes fresh again isn't much, but it's a start. . . ."

My voice trailed. I needed more than a start to go up against Bandur. The vision of Takkan bleeding to death bubbled to my memory, and my throat closed.

"I should go to my chambers," I said, exaggerating a yawn. "Magic always makes me sleepy."

"It's only sundown. You're not having dinner?"

"I'm not hungry," I lied, three words I had never said before in my life.

Takkan cocked his head with suspicion, and it didn't help that my stomach gave an incriminating growl.

"What's going on, Shiori? Will you look at me?"

"I need to get back," I mumbled. "Wandei's been in his workshop all day, and I should check on him—"

"Wandei's the one who told me to find you," Takkan replied. "He and Yotan said you might be like this."

"Like . . . like what?" I stammered.

"Avoiding me. They wouldn't say why."

First the messengers, now the twins. Was there no one I could trust?

Takkan passed me a towel when I spilled some soup on the table, but still I didn't look up at him. He touched my arm. "Shiori, don't be like this."

His voice was tight. He had a right to be angry at me for avoiding him without explanation after so much time apart. Patient as he was, I could tell he was frustrated.

"Do you remember what I told you," he said, more gently, "many months ago when you were still trapped under that wooden bowl? If anything should trouble you, don't hide from me."

"Nothing's troubling me," I lied, immediately regretting it. "I've just been busy."

"Don't lie to me. Please." He looked worried. "Will you at least let me guess?"

"There's nothing to g—"

"Is it what happened with the villagers?"

I said nothing. With my free hand, I doused the fire under the pot with a splash of water.

"Is it the betrothal ceremony?" His tone danced the narrow line between caution and humor. "If you and Kiki are planning on taking another summer swim tomorrow afternoon . . ."

Curse Takkan. I looked up, and seeing the concern etched on his brow, the mirth twinkling in his eyes, I couldn't help but soften.

"No swim." That was all I would say. I poured out my soup and dusted my hands.

"What a waste of soup." He stared dolefully after the empty pot.

He looked so genuinely disappointed I couldn't smother my laugh in time, and as he smiled, like magic, the last of my resolve to avoid him melted away.

"I'll make you another batch," I promised. "Out of fresh, unenchanted vegetables." Still laughing at him, I linked my arm with his. "Come, walk me home."

The palace was beautiful at night. Lanterns bobbed from the eaves, and fireflies flickered over the garden ponds. Takkan and

I walked side by side, our steps falling into a natural rhythm. It would have been a perfect evening if not for the secrets I held. I sensed Takkan was holding something back as well.

He wasn't naturally chatty, but usually our silence was comfortable, easy. Not tonight.

"Takkan . . ." I knelt. "What's on your mind?"

"The meeting with the ministers this morning," Takkan confessed. "It didn't go so well. I think we should leave for Lapzur sooner than we planned. You're not safe here."

I almost laughed. Hawar and his nest of bureaucrats were the least of my troubles. "Don't tell me you're concerned about the hornets," I said with a dismissive chuckle. "What a worry-wart you are. Father would have them flayed for scowling at me."

"That might be, but I wouldn't discount their influence, Shiori. Hawar's especially. After what happened in the mountains, your father's promised that you won't leave the palace again."

That *was* news, and I rolled my eyes. "Did he, now? What did that rat Hawar say to him?" I rummaged in my bag for the mirror of truth. "No, don't tell me, I'll look for myself. It's about time I learned to use this, anyway."

I rubbed the glass clean and held it high. "Mirror, show me what the ministers said."

The mirror misted, then it dove inside the Hornet's Nest, showing the ministers sitting along the paneled walls and Father standing in the center, with a mourning sash over his kingly robes.

"You cannot ignore it, Your Majesty!" cried Minister Pahan in vociferous protest. "Just yesterday, Shiori'anma visited the Holy Mountains. While she was there, the earth quaked—"

"The earth quakes often, regardless of my daughter's presence," Father said sharply.

"The demons reacted to her influence," Minister Caina insisted. "She is a peril—her magic plagues our land! We must send her away."

"Send the sorcerer away too!" the ministers clamored.

"What if sending her away isn't enough? There are thousands of demons in the Holy Mountains, sire. If one can escape, surely it's only a matter of time before the others do too. Perhaps we should listen to the priestesses. There have been bloodsakes for centuries. Each one has been sacrificed to keep Kiata safe, and Kiata has been safe—until Shiori'anma!"

Takkan, sitting in the front row, had had enough. He shot to his feet. "The princess's death will only continue the foolhardy cycle of bloodsakes dying every generation. She has the power to fight the demons. I've seen it myself. We have to give her that chance."

The ministers disagreed. "One death every generation is a small price to pay for the safety of our great nation."

"Is it?" Takkan argued. "Other nations deal with demons and magic daily—"

"And chaos is their ruler. Kiata is the leading light of Lor'yan precisely because we take charge of our own destiny. But what would you know, Lord Takkan? You've hardly spent any time in Kiata's heartland."

"You are quick to call others barbarians," said Takkan coldly. "But look at yourselves. Ready to spill innocent blood without considering other options."

Huffs and sniffs ensued. Takkan was ignored as the ministers turned their attention back to the emperor. "Your Majesty, listen to reason. Give your daughter to the priestesses before it's too—"

"That is enough." Father strove to sound calm, but an undercurrent of anger pulsed through his words. "I will not collaborate with those cultists. The next person who suggests it shall wake to-morrow in Lord Sharima'en's realm."

The ministers went silent.

"Nor will Shiori'anma become a weapon against the demons," said the emperor, rounding on Takkan. "Even if she wants to."

Chief Minister Hawar had kept his silence until now. When the room went still, he spoke: "Then we should keep the princess confined to the palace, Your Majesty. At least until we have a chance to fully question the captured priestesses—and *execute them for their betrayal. I am happy to join the imperial commander in the interrogation— once Her Highness's betrothal ceremony is completed, of course. This would be for her safety."*

"Your Majesty," Takkan protested. "I don't think—"

"Yes," the emperor interrupted. "That is a fine idea, Minister Hawar. Lord Takkan, I bid you ensure that my daughter does not leave the palace."

I threw down the mirror. I'd seen enough. "I can't believe Father would listen to Hawar. He's a two-faced liar." I blew a long sigh, deflating as my air left me. The same could be said of me, only Takkan didn't know it.

"I don't think your father trusts Hawar," said Takkan, ever loyal. "But he does want you safe. That's why he appointed me as your—"

"Bodyguard? You must be delighted now that your role is official." I sank and dug my nails into the dirt. "Thanks for voting not to have me killed at least."

"I have selfish reasons for wanting to keep you alive."

That made me smile in spite of myself.

"I believe in your magic, Shiori. And in you," he said. "Magic has been gone for so many centuries our people don't remember the good it can do."

"Like making moldy radishes new again?"

"Like this," Takkan said, gesturing at the wildflowers that had bloomed where my hand touched the earth. Gen was right about me needing to practice my magic—I hadn't even noticed.

"Flowers aren't going to win over Kiata," I said, thinking of how the palace servants avoided me now, as if my magic were a disease. "People are more afraid of me than of Bandur. That fear won't change even if we defeat him." The flowers wilted and vanished as I yanked back the threads of my magic. "Too many people have been hurt on account of me." I swallowed hard. "Maybe I *am* a menace to Kiata."

"The way you say that, I know there's more on your mind." Takkan leaned close, and his sleeves brushed mine. "Are you pushing me away because you think you'll put me in danger?"

How did he know me so well?

I stared at the ground until he tipped my chin up. "There it is—that displeased grimace. You're a skilled liar, Shiori, but your mouth gives you away."

I was about to protest, but Takkan wasn't finished: "You forget I spent an entire winter watching it. Observing every smile, every frown, every twist and tug for a window into your thoughts. Now that I can see your eyes, there isn't much you can hide from me.

"You always worry about others being safe," he went on. "Let me do the worrying for once. Will you tell me what's been troubling you?"

Guilt gathered under my skin. Tonight was the last chance I'd have to tell him about my vision before our betrothal ceremony. I parted my lips, readying an admission, but my ribs tightened and my mouth went dry. The words wouldn't come.

I'd already lost Raikama, and the possibility of losing

Takkan hurt more than anything. Better he hate me than die. Better we break off the ceremony altogether.

I pinched my eyes shut. "Maybe you should go back to Iro. Maybe we should annul our betrothal."

There. I'd said it.

I waited for Takkan to get angry, for his pride to overwhelm his senses, the way it had when I'd run out on him a year ago.

But he was quiet, and though his shoulders had gone rigid, he didn't stir from my side. "If you're going to say something like that," he said at last, "I think I deserve a better explanation."

I'd never been a coward, but I felt like one now. My back was to Takkan. I couldn't even summon the courage to face him properly.

Didn't you used to say fear is a game? Kiki had scolded me this morning. *You win by playing, not by running away. Which is what you'd be doing if you don't tell him.*

She was right.

I stared down at my scarred hands. "I saw you die," I admitted at last, in my smallest voice. "The Tears of Emuri'en showed Bandur killing you on Lapzur."

Takkan turned me slowly by the shoulders. "That's why you want to break the betrothal. That's why you want me to leave."

"Yes." A pause. "Will you?"

"No," Takkan said, as though he couldn't believe I'd ask such a thing.

"You have to leave," I said. "Bandur knows you're my weakness. He'll kill you!"

"No," Takkan said again in a steely tone. He took a breath. "Do you know what it was like for me, staying behind when you left for Ai'long? Every day wondering whether I'd ever see you again. After an entire winter of not hearing your voice and not being able to see your face, I wanted to hear you laugh. I wanted to . . ."

"To what?"

Ever so tenderly, he brushed aside the hair at my temple and tucked the strands of silver behind my ears. His eyes were on mine the entire time, causing my cheeks to burn and my nerves to tingle. If he kissed me right now, I'd make us—no, the entire courtyard—fly, and then the ministers really would arrest me. But he let go and settled his hand on the earth, so close to mine that I could feel the electricity between our fingers.

"You aren't a bird in a cage, Shiori. Neither am I. I'm coming with you."

"I didn't say you—"

"I appreciate that you're afraid for me, because now I know to take every caution." He narrowed the space between us, just an inch. "So . . . when do we leave?"

I gave him an arch look. "I still didn't say you could come. You'd be too heavy for my brothers to carry, anyway."

"You could turn me into a crane."

"Absolutely not!" I gawked at him. "You don't know what you're asking."

"I do. You'll have to tie me up if you want me to stay in

Gindara. I'll not stand by and watch you put yourself in danger, Shiori, not ever again. Whether I am your husband, your betrothed, or simply your friend."

"You're impossible," I said, harrumphing. "Fine. If you want to come, I won't stop you. But I'm not turning you into a crane."

"Very well," Takkan conceded. He'd won, and he was trying hard not to smile.

"You aren't to be recklessly brave," I went on. "If you get yourself killed, I'll never forgive you. Do you understand?"

"Does the same rule apply to you?"

I huffed. "I'm naturally reckless."

"And I'm naturally brave."

"Takkan!"

"I promise," he said, serious now. "But it's rather selfish, don't you think, to make me swear when you will not? I need you too, Shiori."

I need you. A sea of heat came over me, scorching away any retort I might have mustered. Gods, he was going to be the doom of me. "All right, I promise."

"Good," said Takkan. He pulled from his cloak a small package that fit neatly in his palm. "There's another reason I wanted to see you today."

A gift? It was wrapped in peony-print cloth and tied with a gold cord I recognized from one of Gindara's most famous shops. "You bought this for me?" I asked.

"No. I mean . . . no." He cleared his throat as I stared at him curiously. Was he nervous? "The wrapping's from Qinnia. I didn't have any of my own."

I was growing more mystified by the second. Qinnia had helped? "What is it?"

"Open it."

Typically, I would have ripped through the cloth, but I lifted each fold as gingerly as if it were a butterfly's wing. Inside was a simple comb, exquisitely carved and polished. I raised it to my nose, inhaling the scent of pine. "The wood's from Iro."

"How'd you know?"

I smiled coyly. "It smells like you."

Usually, Takkan was good at hiding his feelings, but I caught the faint flush creeping up his neck, peeking out of his high collar. "Turn it over."

Painted on the other side of the comb was a rabbit holding a red-stringed kite etched with flying cranes. The very kite Takkan and I had almost made together when we were children.

"In legend," Takkan spoke, "Imurinya's suitors brought her jewels and gold, riches from all across Lor'yan. But the hunter gave her a simple comb to put up her hair so he could see her eyes and light them with joy."

My face warmed. I hadn't thought of how that part of Imurinya's story was like my own. For an entire winter, Takkan couldn't see my face, and he'd tried valiantly to lift my spirits, even when he didn't know who I was. Now, months later, to give me a comb, as the hunter had, was a promise. Of devotion. Of love.

I could hardly breathe as Takkan took the comb and tenderly set it in my hair.

"I know it's been years," he said, the tempo of his words

accelerating a nervous notch, "and you never had any say when we were children, but I wanted to ask you now, before we—"

"Stop rambling, Takkan," I blurted. "Are you asking if I'll marry you?"

I'd rendered him speechless, at least for a second. He recovered admirably, and I wanted to kick myself for being an impulsive fool. But fool or not, I was still curious.

"I was going to ask more formally," he said slowly, "if you'd . . . if you'd be betrothed to me." He flashed a wry grin. "I suppose, in the end, the meaning is the same."

It took all my control to keep my voice level and even. "In legend, the hunter gave Imurinya a comb to try and win her heart." My hands were shaking as I spoke. "But mine's already been won. So the answer is yes, Takkan." I looked at him, trying to hold in the joy that was exploding inside me. Then I flew into his arms, all of me beaming with happiness. "Yes."

He rose and hoisted me up with both arms, holding me close so our noses touched, and his breath tickled my lips.

"Are you finally going to kiss me?" I murmured cheekily.

Takkan touched my chin, and I half closed my eyes, ready for him to lean in and take my breath away.

Only he chuckled softly. "You'll find out tomorrow," he replied, with equal cheekiness. On my nose he burned a kiss into my skin, then set me down. "Incentive to actually show up this time."

Incentive it was. I didn't take Takkan for the sly and brazen sort, but he must have learned a lesson from me.

I liked it.

"I'll be there."

CHAPTER TWENTY-SIX

At last, it was the morning of my betrothal ceremony. I was already awake when my maids arrived to dress me, and I was in my brightest mood. Without complaint, I sat on a cushioned stool, patiently allowing them to swaddle me in a dozen layers of silk and brush my hair until it shone.

"Please wrap this in my hair," I said, passing them the red thread I had taken from Raikama's sewing chest. If she couldn't be here today, I would still honor her.

Dressing me took all morning. I had many shortcomings, and though vanity had never been one of them, I had been self-conscious lately about the lock of white curling over my temples. My maids tried desperately to dye it black, even powdering it with charcoal and trying to paint it with lacquer, but nothing would take.

I tilted my head toward the mirror and stared at my hair. In an odd way, it suited me. "Let's leave it," I said finally.

"But, Your Highness—"

I have nothing to hide, I wanted to say. Everyone already knew I was a sorceress. But I wisely held my tongue and instead handed them Takkan's comb. "Let it be."

The maids bowed in silent acquiescence. In the end, they pinned the lock back and hid it behind my headdress. I smiled, wondering whether Takkan would notice his comb behind all the feathers.

My face was painted a ritual white, my lips and cheeks stained rouge, and my lashes coated with kohl. Strings of rubies, opals, and emeralds dangled from my hair, and disks of jade tinkled at my ears and wrists. Then came the final garments: the ceremonial coat and gown.

One year ago, I had worn these very robes—the same embroidered jacket, the same laborious skirt with a train that swept the ground behind my heels, the same gold-trimmed collar and cuffs. Yet the robes didn't feel as heavy as they had before. Perhaps because I was stronger now. Or perhaps because I was actually eager for the ceremony.

"You look beautiful, Shiori'anma," my maids gushed once I was dressed. "A true princess."

A smile tugged at my lips, and as I gave a nod of thanks, Kiki flittered out of her hiding spot behind a vase.

They're lying, she said, perching on my shoulder to survey my appearance. *Your face is whiter than an eggshell, and you look more like a heap of laundry than a bride.*

"So glad I can count on you to boost my confidence," I replied.

I wouldn't lie to you. Kiki sniffed. *I'm just amazed you were able to walk in all that silk, let alone run off to the Sacred Lake last year.* She leaned against my neck as if I were a tree. *You're not planning to do that again, are you?*

"Of course not. I told Takkan the truth last night."

Really? The disbelief on her paper face was almost human.

"It's true," I gloated. "You can ask him yourself."

Hasho arrived to escort me to the temple. When he saw I was dressed and ready to leave, he tilted his head. "Miracles of Ashmiyu'en, are you going to be early?"

"You're lucky this headdress obscures my eyes, brother. They are rolling at you."

Hasho laughed. "Kiki in your sleeve this time?"

"In my collar today." I bent my neck so the paper bird could return to her spot. As my headdress tinkled, Hasho gave Kiki a wink.

"Wait," I said, reaching for the round pillow on my divan. Behind it, I'd stashed my satchel. "Do me a favor and watch over the pearl during the ceremony."

Hasho quailed. "You can't hide it under your bed?"

I'd tried. Tried stashing it in my closet, tucking it under my bed, even burying it under the chrysanthemum bushes outside my window. But I never felt safe unless it was close by, especially now that I knew Bandur wanted it.

"It isn't a pea, Hasho. It's a dragon pearl."

"I'd be more comfortable watching over Kiki. Maybe you should give the pearl to Gen."

"Can't." I pressed the satchel strap into my brother's hands, trusting him to find a way to hide the bag under his own copious robes. "I sent him away."

"Away?"

"For his own good."

I wouldn't say more. It *was* for Gen's own good. After the council meeting I'd observed in the mirror, I had sought the young sorcerer out as soon as I could.

"I want you to investigate where the amulet is hidden," I told him. "Benkai will be at the Holy Mountains. Help him while everyone else is at my betrothal ceremony."

"Does this mean I'm not invited?"

"You're a sorcerer, Gen. Hawar and his ministers wouldn't dare hurt me, but the same isn't true for you. Stay out of the palace until someone can keep an eye on you."

Gen sniffed. "Who will keep an eye on you?"

"Don't worry about me. Just find the amulet." I gave him the mirror of truth as a bribe. "Use this."

His blue eyes lit. "Do I get the pearl too?"

"No."

A grumble huffed out of the boy's lips, but to my relief, he obeyed.

When I arrived at the temple, I was sure that sending Gen away had been the right decision. Every minister and lord of the first rank had come. They were fanning themselves in unison to combat the heat. They reminded me of the dragons, thirsty for a spectacle. The worst was Chief Minister Hawar. Here he was, buzzing merrily with his other hornets, as if he hadn't called for my death only yesterday.

When the procession delivered me to the red cushion opposite Takkan, I sagged into my spot as though I'd traveled for hours, not minutes.

He slipped me a smile before we assumed our customary positions. How silly we both looked. Takkan with silver and gold tassels dangling in front of his eyes, me with my burdensome headdress and veil. And our robes! We looked like caravans.

It was adorable—and strangely fitting that we were suffering through the ceremonial rigmarole together. I wished I could reach for his hand and tell him so.

"On this ninth day of the firefly month," High Priest Voan began, "we assemble to bind together the fates of Shiori'anma, beloved princess of Kiata and only daughter of His Imperial Majesty, Emperor Hanriyu, and Lord Bushi'an Takkan, son of and heir to the prefecture of Iro."

The palace priests and priestesses surrounded Takkan and me, carrying a long red ribbon and chanting prayers in Old Kiatan. I wanted to hear what they were saying, but it was impossible over the drumming.

Around and around, the priests and priestesses spun, whirling the ribbon over our heads. Nine times they would walk around us, the number of eternity. During our marriage ceremony, that same ribbon would be knotted to seal our promise to one another.

The spinning was starting to make me dizzy, so I focused my attention on the window behind Takkan. A cloud drifted over the sun, and darkness slithered into the temple, accompanied by a rhythmic rushing that made the roof shudder.

No one else seemed to hear it. Or feel it. But the sweat beading at my neck soon evaporated, replaced by the same icy chill I'd felt in the Holy Mountains.

Kiki? I reached out with my mind. My bird had decided at the last minute to sit with Hasho instead of me. *Tell me you feel that. The cold.*

Cold? she buzzed. *My beak is getting soggy from all this humidity.*

I wasn't listening anymore. Darkness unfurled through the temple, black as ink and heavy as a shroud. Too soon it enveloped Father, the high priest, even Takkan.

I was next. My hands were clasped primly over my skirt, and as I looked down at my lap, a tide of shadow crept upon me, drowning the embroidered cranes and staining the beaded flowers black.

Congratulations, Shiori'anma.

The voice came from Father's direction. I looked up in dread. Smoke from the braziers outside curled in through the windows, its tendrils hooking around the emperor's throat until his eyes were red.

I stared in horror. I started to rise from my knees, but the priests were still performing the ribbon-wrapping ritual. My headdress jangled, its jeweled strands chiming like alarm bells.

With a blink, Father's eyes were his own again. But my heart was racing, and I reached instinctively toward my hip, forgetting that I'd given my satchel to Hasho.

What's the matter? Takkan mouthed. His eyes swirled dark with worry.

I needed to stay calm. Everyone was watching. I couldn't make a scene.

Nothing, I mouthed back.

I bowed my head low, trying to convince myself I'd imagined it. Determined to focus on the ceremony.

Six, I counted, marking the times the ribbon had crossed Takkan and me. *Seven.*

During the ninth and final turn, a lash of cold caressed my cheek, and muscle by muscle my body went rigid.

No pearls on your betrothal day? Bandur purred. His voice sent shivers down my neck, like a chilled blade pressed to the skin. *A pity; they become you. One in particular.*

My eyes flew in every direction, but I couldn't find him. Where was he? *Who* was he?

I clenched the edge of my skirt. *You're brazen for coming here. This is sacred ground. The high priest and—*

Their pitiful prayers might ward away a common demon, but I am a king.

Hardly a king when you're tethered to the mountains, I retorted. *Even if I gave you the pearl, you wouldn't be able to hold it.*

Bandur snarled, finally manifesting behind Father's throne in a plume of smoke. *I would learn some respect if I were you.* He slunk a paw over the emperor's shoulder. *Or this betrothal ceremony just may become a funeral.*

You wouldn't dare.

Wouldn't I? It wouldn't be the first time I've killed a king.

It took all my control not to jump up and tackle the demon. But he was only a shadow. No one, not even my father, noticed him. Whereas Chief Minister Hawar was silently recording every move *I* made with his hooded eyes.

All of it was kindling for Bandur to torture me further.

I could arrange it so it appeared that you murdered the emperor, Shiori, the demon mused. *You'd be put in prison, easy to collect and take to the mountains.*

Hate flooded my thoughts. *No one would ever believe that I killed my father.*

You'd be surprised what a few well-placed knives can do to change people's minds. Especially with your reputation. Bandur clucked. *The ministers would jump at the chance to put you in chains.*

I hated that he was right. Most of all, I hated that I could do nothing.

Bandur floated away from Father's throne toward Takkan. *But why bother, when I know your greatest weakness?*

Anger and fear converged in my throat. *Leave Takkan alone.*

What a peculiar emotion, human love, said Bandur, circling Takkan from behind. *I never felt it when I was one.*

At this I began to rise, ignoring the priests' frowns. *I warn you. . . .*

No, I warn you, Shiori. You saw your fate in the waters. Deny me what I want, and I will kill the one you love most. Sickle-sharp nails shot out of Bandur's paws, scraping against Takkan's jawline. *In the end you will still bleed.*

Then, in one slick motion, Bandur sliced across Takkan's throat.

"No!" I screamed. "Takkan!"

"Shiori!" Father bellowed. "What are you—"

My heart roaring, I turned to Takkan. He was kneeling, his head slightly bent in prayer, as mine was supposed to be. No blood, no gash on his neck. He caught my eye, his brows knit with confusion.

Somewhere in the background, Bandur howled with laughter, knowing he'd fooled me. My horror fled, dissolving into stone-cold panic.

"Shiori, sit down," Father barked. "At once!"

I hardly heard him. The room was spinning, and everyone was whispering, gossip starting to spread. I could read their lips easily. "Why did she scream?" the ladies said to each other. "Look at her eyes, all wild." The lords, murmuring, "Most unbecoming. Hawar was right—there's something off about her." And Hawar himself was gleefully nattering to those beside him: "What did I tell you? She's dangerous."

It was too late to sit back down. I had to deflect attention away from any talk of magic or demons. I had to act like the Shiori they'd once known—impulsive, rash, and completely unpredictable.

Without another thought, I threw off my headdress and kicked away the red ribbons encircling my feet.

"I will not marry Bushi'an Takkan," I declared in my most impudent tone.

My words stunned the room into silence. I supposed that was a victory.

The confusion on Takkan's face had shifted into a dismayed understanding. *Shiori, don't.*

I took a breath for courage. "I will not complete this ceremony," I said, stomping my foot for emphasis. "I will not be tied down to a barren wasteland, shipped so far north that the sun is but a pebble in the sky. Lord Bushi'an Takkan will return to Iro at once. The betrothal is no more."

I hiked up my skirt, ready to flee. No one was more surprised than Takkan when I hooked him by the arm, dragging him to his feet.

"Run!" I ordered, and he shot me a look of utter bafflement. But thank the Eternal Courts, he didn't waste time. He ran.

CHAPTER TWENTY-SEVEN

I could hear my brothers being dispatched after us, so I cut through the gardens, veering off the paths and disappearing into the orchard. I didn't know where we were going, only that I needed to get us as far from the temple as I could.

We'd reached the peach trees when I felt a yank at the end of my sash. I called upon my magic, thinking to make the fruits fly off the branches and pelt whoever was behind me. Then I saw who had come.

The peaches tumbled to the ground.

It was Hasho. He was out of breath, but that didn't prevent him from lecturing me: "Don't you cast your magic on me, little sister. I won't have it."

"I'm not going back," I said, yanking my sash free.

"Then explain yourself."

What were you thinking? Kiki shrieked. *Honestly, Shiori, I thought you'd stopped being so stupid since breaking that bowl on your head. But clearly I was wrong.*

"Enough," said Takkan, standing between my brother, Kiki, and me. "That's enough."

"Did Bandur possess you?" Hasho demanded. "Because that's the only reason I can think of to explain what you've done."

Sweat made the white paint on my face drip down my forehead and cheeks, stinging my eyes and coating my lips with a bitter veneer. I wiped my eyes with the back of my hand. "That's not far from the truth."

Startled, Hasho's hands fell to his sides. He let out a sigh that turned into a rueful laugh. "I should've let one of the others catch you. Canceling the ceremony but running off *with* your betrothed—how am I going to explain that to the court? That's a new one, even for you."

I despised both Kiki and Hasho for chuckling.

"Go and find someplace to hide," Hasho said, waving Takkan and me away. "I'll straighten things out with Father."

And you straighten things out with Takkan, Kiki added before she left with my brother.

I turned to Takkan, who had gone so quiet it made me nervous.

"I'm guessing another tapestry won't be enough to serve as an apology," I mumbled, not sure what else to say.

"Your time is better spent away from a needle and thread," he replied. He folded my jacket over his arm. "Are you all right?"

"Am *I* all right?" I eyed him in disbelief. "Are *you* all right? I've just mortally humiliated you in front of the entire court. *Again.* Shouldn't you be furious with me?"

"No," said Takkan simply. "You didn't run out on me. You ran out *with* me. It's quite different."

"Don't you want to know what happened?"

He held my chin up so he could dab off the paint running down my face. It tickled. "You've told me enough," he said. "Let everyone else puzzle over it. It's a beautiful day and we ought to enjoy it. Like he is—"

Takkan waved awkwardly at someone behind me. "Good morning, Mr. Ji."

Mr. Ji, as it turned out, was a gardener who'd been picking up fallen fruit in the orchard and was now staring at us, slack-jawed. At Takkan's greeting, he swiftly tumbled into a speechless bow.

I was horrified. I grabbed Takkan by the arm and dragged him across a wooden bridge that led deeper into the gardens. The kitebirds were chirping, and the cicadas were as loud as they were shrill, but at least we were far from prying eyes.

Takkan was laughing.

"It isn't funny," I said, sincerely distressed. "Gossip in Gindara spreads faster than demonfire. Everyone in the whole city probably knows what I've done. And your family!" I wanted to bury my face in my hands. "Your family is going to despise me."

"Iro is quite a ways from Gindara," Takkan reminded me. "They won't hear for a few days at least. Besides, there's nothing you could do that would make Megari despise you."

"Your mother will be a different story."

"My mother will be appeased if ever there are children. And my father will be appeased when she is appeased."

His eyes twinkled, and I couldn't tell whether he was speaking in earnest or in jest. "Children?" I repeated as my stomach somersaulted. "I did say the betrothal was over."

"Well, if that's the case, maybe you *should* make another apology tapestry."

I gave him my fiercest scowl, but I couldn't fight the twitch nagging at my lips. "How can you make light of this?"

Takkan set my jacket on the bridge railing. "I make light because I don't care what others think of you or of us. Even if they never learn the truth, it matters not to me.

"There will be many trials and misunderstandings in our future, Shiori. We're bound to quarrel, and sometimes I may be too angry to run after you. Let alone with you." He chuckled. "But I have faith that we'll always laugh together in the end. I have a feeling we'll laugh about today years from now."

Years from now. The way he said it made my eyes misty.

Locking my hands with his, I drew him deeper into the gardens, far from the temple, until we found refuge under a forgotten wisteria tree. There, I reached for his comb in my hair and brushed it down to loosen one of the beaded threads dangling against my cheeks.

"What are you doing?" Takkan asked.

"Picking off the beads," I said, my fingers working deftly. "They'll have cleared the temple, so we can't go back. But that doesn't mean we can't finish the ceremony." I combed off the last bead and displayed the bare red thread on my palm. Then, realizing what I'd said, I blushed. "I'd . . . I'd prefer here, anyway, over that suffocating temple with every gossip in court watching."

Takkan smiled at my blasphemous language. "Are you sure you want to link your fate to mine?" he questioned. "A lord of the third rank from a wasteland so far north that the sun is but a pebble in the sky?"

My cheeks heated with shame. Those were my words. "I didn't mean it like that."

Amusement edged his voice. "I know."

"Takkan . . ."

"Your brothers warned me that a lifetime with you would mean plenty of jabs to my pride. But my love for you is far greater than pride, Shiori. Far greater than anything." He tilted his head and held me in a tender gaze. "Now, what did you say about finishing the ceremony?"

It was the profoundest magic how Takkan could cast away all the darkness that plagued my mind. How he turned the shame heating my cheeks into joy, and how that joy radiated across my body, seeping from pore and hair until I could have rivaled the sun with my brightness. Even my insides were beaming.

I unwound the red thread in my hand and met his eyes. "Surround yourself with those who'll love you always," I began, "through your mistakes and your faults. Make a family that will find you more beautiful every day, even when your hair is white with age. Be the light that makes someone's lantern shine."

Those had been Raikama's words to me—a last wish for my happiness.

With great care, I started wrapping the thread around his

wrist. "This is how Imurinya bound herself to the hunter so they could journey to the moon together—did you know?"

A foolish question. Of course he knew—Takkan was a scholar of tales.

I wound the thread around him once, twice, thrice. "I bind you to me, Bushi'an Takkan. Not because my father or my stepmother or my country asks me to do so, but because I wish to do so. I would always choose you. You are the light that makes my lantern shine."

I tied a knot. Then Takkan took up the thread, knotting the other end around my wrist.

"I bind you to me, Shiori'anma," he said. "Let our strands be ever knotted as we weather joy and sorrow, fortune and misfortune, and pass our years from youth to old age. We are of one heart, honor-bound, and one spirit, whether on earth or in heaven. From now until ten thousand years forth."

I tipped his chin toward me. "And now, don't you have a promise to keep?"

With one step, he obliterated the gap between us, and then his lips fell on mine in a kiss. Not a quick, shy peck on the cheek or forehead, like he'd given in the past. Not even the tender kiss he'd placed on my nose just last night. A real kiss, of lips to lips and breath to breath, that made my knees knock together and the world sway—just as I knew it would.

I rose to my toes unconsciously as Takkan pulled me close, our arms entangled and fingers intertwined—still tied together from the ceremony. We kissed again and again, until we were drunk on each other and our toes had left deep imprints in the earth and purple wisteria petals crowned every inch of our heads.

"Your fate is bound to mine now," I whispered, my lips against his. "Your heart is my own, and where you are is my home. Whatever we face, we face it together."

"Together," he echoed firmly. "Always."

Takkan was the end of my string. No matter how far my kite wandered, it would always find its way back to him. And though the impossible still awaited us, my heart rested a little easier knowing he would never let go.

CHAPTER TWENTY-EIGHT

Regardless of how I wished it, Takkan and I couldn't hide in the gardens forever. Sooner or later we had to face the palace. For once, I chose to go first—and Takkan went to look for Gen, who still hadn't sent word from the mountains.

There you are! Kiki said, flittering over my head as I emerged onto the garden pathways. *Your brothers are waiting for you in the Dragonfly Court. They've prepared an explanation that— Shiori! That's the wrong way! Where are you going?*

"To see my father."

Isn't he angry with you?

I faltered. "I'll find out." I touched my bird's wing. "You stay. It's something I have to do alone."

My mother's shrine was in the northeast corner of the imperial gardens, surrounded by willow trees. This was the quietest part of the palace grounds, and many assumed I didn't respect my mother because I didn't visit often, but that wasn't it. Coming to this place was like reopening an old wound.

Father was already there, ascending the wooden stairs. Pale rays of sunlight shone upon his back, and when our shadows overlapped, he didn't acknowledge me.

"May I join you?" I asked.

He looked up warily, his expression guarded. I trusted that Hasho had offered some explanation for my abrupt departure at the ceremony, but he still looked displeased. Duly so.

"Please, Father?" I said softly.

Finally, he gave a nod.

I followed him into the shrine. It was cool inside, in spite of the open doorway and the afternoon heat. Ivory banners hung from the rafters, wishing my mother safe passage to heaven. There were three priestesses tending the shrine's fire, a blazing pit that would burn forever in the empress's memory. When they saw us, they bowed and dutifully shuffled outside.

Behind the offering of rice, gold, and wine on the altar, there was a wooden statue of my mother. Father often told me I looked like her, but I saw little resemblance, except for our long ebony hair and pointed chins. Her eyes were round and kind. Mine were sharp, defiant.

Father bowed deeply to the statue and murmured his prayers.

I bowed too, but no matter how hard I tried, I could not think of any words for my mother. The few memories I had of her weren't even real. Raikama had planted them in my mind to bring me peace and happiness, but now that I knew the truth, I felt only remorse.

"What was she like?" I asked when Father rose.

It was a question he'd always deflected by saying something vague, like "She was very kind. Very beautiful."

I expected the same today, but Father made one last bow before the altar. Then he replied, mistily, "She hated incense because it made her sleepy. Once, she fell asleep during Andahai's naming ceremony."

"Really?"

"Yes." Father turned for the stairs. "She was more like you than you know."

The reproach brought a pang to my chest. "I'm sorry about what happened this morning. My behavior was . . . inexcusable."

He stopped abruptly. "It is fortunate that Bushi'an Takkan is a patient man. A good man. For I can name no other who would take you, princess or not, after you have dishonored his family thus."

I dipped my head, bearing the rebuke. I wanted to argue that I hadn't dishonored his family as much as before. I had run out *with* him, after all. Wisely, I kept my thoughts to myself.

"You disappointed me, daughter. I expected that you would have a stronger sense of duty. Especially after everything that has happened with you and your brothers."

His pause was deliberate, giving me a moment to wince.

"I will not rebuke you further at your mother's shrine." Father crossed his arms, long sleeves folded so as not to sweep the sacred ground. "All I will say is that I planned to send you away as punishment, but your brothers begged me to reconsider. Regardless, it is not my forgiveness you should seek, but Lord Takkan's."

I looked up, perhaps a little too eagerly. "Yes, Father. Of course you are right."

My agreeableness made him frown. "Rare words from my only daughter. I take it from your earlier . . . sprint that you've already spoken to him?"

When I gave a careful nod, he let out a harrumph. "May the gods reward young Takkan for his forbearance." A sigh. "Come. Walk the gardens with me before the rest of the palace discovers we are here."

The setting sun lit up the treetops, painting them a wild red. I savored the sight, knowing it'd be gone in a matter of minutes. Then I swallowed, wondering if Father used to walk this path with my mother. "Do you miss her? My mother."

"Your mother was bound to me by Emuri'en. If the gods are kind, I'll find her again when I ascend to the heavens."

"I wish I'd known her better."

Father walked on, and I thought that it would be the end of the subject—until he stopped on the wooden bridge over a pond of carp. "Your mother was stubborn, like you, and often impertinent, like you. But she always considered others before herself. When she fell ill, I swore never to marry again. She wouldn't hear of it. She wanted you to grow up with a mother. Even if it meant you'd forget her."

A lump swelled in my throat, making it hard to speak. "That's why you remarried."

"My marriage to your stepmother was not a love match, but we were friends. Seeing my children take to her, and her to them, eased some of the pain of losing your mother. It helped your stepmother as well."

"She was grieving, too," I murmured. "For her sister."

"She told you that?"

"Yes, before she died," I said thickly. "Didn't you find it odd that she never spoke of her past, that she didn't even have a name?"

"She had a name when I met her, but she wanted to forget it. Her life back home wasn't a happy one. I met her only because her father was trying to marry her off in a—"

"A selection ceremony," I murmured.

"Yes." Father looked surprised that I knew, and I averted my eyes as he continued. "Kings and princes who had heard of her beauty gathered in Tambu with offerings of jewels and gold. Initially, I went too. I'd heard she was kind and compassionate, and I'd hoped to find a new mother for you. But I was unsettled by the contest, so I left."

"Then how did she come to marry you?" I asked.

"It is a long story," replied Father. "The contest lasted many months, causing strife between the suitors. One of Tambu's great kings feared a war would break out. He asked that I return to aid her in making a decision.

"When I met her again, she was in mourning for her sister. The poor girl died not long after the selection began."

I lifted my head, my breath going shallow. "Did you ever meet her?"

"Once," said Father. "But I don't remember it well. Your stepmother never liked to talk about the past. Especially not about her sister."

I retreated, sensing Raikama had something to do with the gaps in Father's memory. But then he spoke again.

"What I do remember is that she had the loneliest eyes I had ever seen." Father's voice drifted, as if skimming off memories. "And she had a snake at her side. I always supposed that was why your stepmother found solace in snakes. Because they reminded her of her sister."

My chest hurt, and I had to look away, pretending to be fixated on a honeybee flitting from flower to flower. There was so much about Raikama that Father didn't know. One day, perhaps, I would tell him that she had been a powerful sorceress, that she had been the one to send my brothers and me away to protect us from Lord Yuji and Bandur—but I would never tell him the whole truth. The last of my stepmother's secrets would die with me.

That it was the lost sister Father had married. And her name had been Channari.

"Our grief bonded us," he said quietly, continuing the story, "and we became close. One night, the night before she was to select her husband, she asked me a peculiar question: whether there truly was no magic in Kiata."

In spite of the pain in my chest, I leaned forward. Father had never told me this.

"When I said it was true, she explained that it was magic that had killed her sister, and that she wished to get as far away from it as she could. She told me she had decided to choose me, if I would consider renewing my suit." He inhaled. "It was the last thing I expected."

"What did you say?"

"I told her that a hundred of Lor'yan's sovereigns had spent months declaring their undying love for her." He laughed quietly. "I told her that she should choose one of them, for my heart belonged to my children's mother. But her mind was made up. 'The fractures in our hearts will never heal,' she said. 'But I seek to make mine whole again. It is not a lover or even a husband who can do that, but a family. Let us be family for one another.'

"She made true on her word," said Father. "Do you remember when you first met her, you called her Imurinya?"

"Because she glowed," I said. "Like the lady of the moon."

"That was the happiest I had ever seen her." The ghost of a smile touched his mouth before he turned solemn once more. "The rift that came between the two of you wounded her deeply, Shiori. She loved you. Very much."

Heat flooded my nose and eyes.

"I miss her, Baba," I said through the ache in my chest.

I so rarely called him Baba. It had always felt odd, knowing he was the Emperor of Kiata, a man who was revered, loved, and feared—even by his children. But in this moment, he was my father first and emperor second.

In my lowest voice, I said, "Is it terrible that I miss Raikama more than Mama? Mama had six sons who knew and loved her. In my heart, I love her too—but I was too young to know her. Raikama . . . she had no one. Except me."

"She loved you as her own. You were the daughter of her heart."

Father couldn't have known those were Raikama's same words to me before she died. My self-control collapsed, and tears flooded down my cheeks before I could stop them.

Father leaned over the bridge, gazing at a carp nibbling on algae. His voice was faraway, thoughtful. "She chose him for you—did you know?"

"Who?" I blinked. "Takkan?"

"I'd planned to marry you to a king abroad, or one of Lord Yuji's sons to strengthen the warlords' support for the throne. Your stepmother fought for you to choose your own match, but the council wouldn't have it. So she swore that your marriage would at least bring you happiness."

"I thought she meant to send me as far from Kiata as possible."

Father gave a wan smile. "I seem to recall you thinking Iro was the darkest corner of the world. Wasn't it only a few hours ago that you called it a wasteland?"

I shrank back with embarrassment. "I suppose it *is* rather far. But why Takkan? He never even came to court."

"He did, once. I told you before that Bushi'an Takkan is not the sort of boy who would fare well in court. I suppose I never explained what I meant."

He hadn't, and I had assumed Takkan was a tactless barbarian, a lowly lord of the third rank. How wrong I'd been.

"His father has never cared about power," explained the emperor. "Something I've come to value the longer I reign. The same is true of Takkan. Even as a child, he lacked the artifice necessary to charm the nobility."

"He's too honest," I said dryly.

"Indeed," Father said. "A trait I wish you shared."

I winced.

"During his visit, he managed to impress your stepmother."

"Raikama?" I frowned, the wick of my curiosity lit. Raikama had been infamously cold toward the courtiers. "How?"

"It was unintentional, I'm certain. One evening, the court children gathered around her. Their parents had instructed them to fawn over her beauty, and so they did, but you know how that irritated your stepmother. So she asked what they thought of the scar on her face. All the children lied that they barely noticed it."

"Except Takkan," I whispered. Takkan wouldn't lie, and Raikama's scar was the first thing anyone ever noticed when they saw her. Long and striking, it had cut diagonally across her face, but not once did she hide it or lower her head in shame.

Father nodded. "He hadn't said a word until that moment, but I will never forget his response. 'If you wanted to be told you were beautiful, you would hide your scar. But you don't. It tells your story, a story that's meant only for those worthy of hearing it.'"

"Oh, Takkan," I murmured. I tried to picture the encounter, of Takkan all but insulting the imperial consort, and Raikama giving no hint at all of her thoughts. "His parents must have been mortified. His mother, especially."

"She was." Father chuckled. "For months, she sent us apology tapestries and an alarming number of rabbits carved

279

of pine. Your stepmother had them all thrown out. So imagine my surprise when she chose him for you. To this day, I don't know why those words endeared him to her."

I didn't, either. Raikama's scar was still a mystery to me. "Why did you agree to it?"

"I trusted her judgment. She was always full of secrets, but regarding Takkan, she made a cogent case for him. Once I agreed to consider the boy, she made me promise not to tell you. She knew you wouldn't give him a chance."

"She was right," I whispered. But fate had found a way to bring us together anyway. I wondered if Raikama had known it would be so.

"She was." Father walked to the end of the bridge. "She often had great foresight. When you and your brothers were away, she sensed that some dark enchantment had fallen upon you, but she never lost faith that you would return home one day."

The irony of his words should have made me wince, but I believed them. Raikama had cursed my brothers and me, exiling us to the farthest outskirts of the country—but she'd done it to protect us. How it must have pained her.

Father's voice went low. "I do not wish you to leave again, but you are not safe in Gindara." I made as if to speak, but he silenced me with a hand. "Do not argue with me, and do not even speak of going back to the Holy Mountains."

I bit my tongue. Father knew me too well.

"The soldiers there know of the Demon King's plans for you. If they see you near the breach, they will assume that he has invaded your mind and taken you prisoner."

My eyes flew up. "Is that necessary?"

"All precautions are necessary, Shiori. The people blame you for the demon's attacks, and the council presses me to banish you from Kiata."

So much for telling Father we were going to steal Bandur's amulet and take him to Lapzur. My brothers had been right—there was no chance he would approve.

"There is some good to come out of your outburst today," Father said. "People are confused by what happened, even those sitting closest to you and Lord Takkan. They will assume I'm sending you to a temple—to reflect upon your behavior."

"In reality, I'll go to Iro," I said. It was a lie that I had practiced, but as I spoke it now, my voice grew hoarse with emotion. "Castle Bushian is well fortressed, and I condemned it enough during the ceremony that no one would expect me to go there. Not even Hawar."

Father considered. "Take one of your brothers at least. I would feel more at ease if one accompanied you north. There are many who wish you harm, daughter." His voice grew tight, and I knew he was thinking of Hawar and his mutinous hornets. "Leave as soon as you can."

I gave a nod and said, "We'll go tomorrow."

It was a lie, of course, and I hated myself for it. For making him think he was sending me off to Iro—to a place of sanctuary—when really it couldn't be further from the truth.

I *was* leaving tomorrow. Only I wasn't running from danger—I was freewheeling straight into it.

It was a touch past dusk when I returned to the residential grounds. My stomach grumbled cantankerously, and I was more than ready to eat. I burst into the hall my brothers and I shared, ready to shout at their rooms and summon them all for dinner, when I saw Takkan in front of my door.

"Shiori—" He took my arm. "Hurry."

My lips parted with surprise. I started to ask what was going on, but Kiki flew wildly out of my room, biting my hair and dragging me inside.

We have to hurry! she cried. *Hawar took him!*

"Who?" I said, blinking with confusion. "Kiki! Who did Hawar take?"

Without explanation, my paper bird dove between the cracks of my doors, still frantic.

Takkan and I followed her, and my heart nearly stopped.

Gen's hawk lurked outside my latticed window, a mirror shard glinting in her arched talons. Her round yellow eyes blinked, and she made a loud cry as she dropped the shard into my grasp.

The glass was smeared with blood, and a heavy foreboding twisted in my gut.

"Gen," I breathed. "They've arrested Gen."

CHAPTER TWENTY-NINE

The hawk vaulted into the clouds, where crowds of birds had gathered. They thronged above the southwest gate—close to the imperial dungeons.

Gen really does have an affinity for my kind, Kiki remarked approvingly.

"Yes, and from the way they're shrieking, it sounds like he's in trouble," I said as I tossed her out the window.

"Get my brothers," I instructed her. "Find Benkai first." My second brother was soon to be high commander, and every sentinel, soldier, and guard was under his authority. "Takkan, come with me."

A large troop guarded the dungeons. An irritated muscle ticked in my jaw when I spied Chief Minister Hawar, surrounded by a handful of my father's sentinels.

"Release the boy," I demanded.

"My apologies, Princess Shiori," said Hawar with a curt bow. "I assume you refer to the sorcerer? Regrettably, he is detained."

"On what charge?"

"The boy was found casting dark magic over the breach," replied Hawar. "For all we know, he could be colluding with the demons of the Holy Mountains—to harm you, Your Highness."

My nostrils flared. "You know that's a lie. Gen came here—he was *invited* here—to help. I'm the one who sent him to the breach."

"Then that is most unfortunate," Hawar said. "Your father *and* Prince Benkai have made it clear the area is restricted. If you wish to contest their orders—"

"My brother is already on his way," I said angrily.

"I do hope he hurries. Sadly, I cannot guarantee the young sorcerer's welfare."

I balled my fists. "If you've hurt him . . ."

"We endeavored to treat him with the utmost kindness, Your Highness, but the boy put up quite a fight."

Another lie. "What fight could a thirteen-year-old boy put up against a regiment of trained imperial guards?"

"Look above you," said Hawar silkily. "Even now, he works potent magic."

"They're only birds!" I spat. I faced the sentinels scattered among the crowd. "Does Hawar have you all in his purse? What happened to your loyalty to the imperial family?"

"The sentinels are under oath to protect Kiata before all," Hawar replied. "Kiata is under threat."

Takkan grabbed the chief minister by the collar. "Let the princess into the dungeon. Now."

Caught by surprise, Hawar flailed and swatted his fan at

Takkan's head. "Unhand me at once! At once, Bushi'an Takkan! How dare you? Your father will hear about this! I'll have the entire court denounce your family—"

Takkan had had enough. He seized the minister's fan and snapped it in half with one hand. "You've already made it clear what you think about my family," he said icily. "The North is full of brutes and barbarians, you say?" He dropped the broken fan so he could unsheathe his dagger, and he prodded its blade against the wobbling bulge in the minister's throat. "I'm happy to prove your point. Now let Shiori inside!"

It was the wisest thing I'd ever seen Hawar do: flick his fingers to bid the guards step aside. I barged into the dungeon.

"Where's the sorcerer?" I demanded. One of the guards pointed to the stairs. I rushed down and found Gen in the first cell to my left.

The boy's face was bruised and bloodied, his nose broken again. He lay on a bed of straw, his black hair a curly mess. When he saw me, he raised a hand and waved—a greeting and a reassurance that he was alive.

"Here everyone says *I* have a knack for getting into trouble," I said, helping him up. "You're not much better."

"Trouble follows power," he mumbled, touching his nose to assess the damage. He groaned. "Damn it, I didn't get to finish healing, and now the bridge is going to be crooked forever."

"This isn't the time to be vain. Can you walk?"

He let out a whimper but nodded.

"That was clever, calling for the birds." I tried to cheer him up with a grin. "Kiki was impressed."

"I knew she'd be" was all Gen said.

Outside was pandemonium. While I'd been in the dungeon, Kiki had led the army of birds against Hawar and his men. Eagles and falcons battered the soldiers, and crows were pecking at Hawar's nose and ears. The chief minister resorted to picking up a wooden bucket from the ground to shield his face as he scurried for an escape.

"They're only birds," Kiki said, mimicking what I had told Hawar. Her papery chest puffed up proudly. *I don't think you'll be able to use that excuse ever again.*

"I hope I won't need to," I replied, but I patted her head affectionately. "Well done."

I rather liked leading an army, said Kiki. *I might do it again. We could use more wings.*

She flitted off right before Benkai and his men arrived. I wished I could stay and listen to my brother reprimand the dungeon guards, but Gen needed help. Ignoring the boy's protests, Takkan and I took him to the infirmary for bandages, then to Takkan's chambers for new robes and some rest.

Stacks of books, scrolls, and papers were strewn about the wooden floor, and unwashed writing brushes were scattered all over his desk. I sent my betrothed a curious glance. His rooms in Iro had been obsessively neat.

"I've been researching" was Takkan's sheepish explanation.

"Demons?" asked Gen. He lifted one of the scrolls and

skimmed its contents. "Kiata's knowledge on the matter is woefully out of date."

"Thankfully, we have you," I said, plopping onto a cushion.

Gen set down the scroll. "I wasn't able to get the amulet," he said finally. "I got close, but then—" He hesitated. The failure was obviously a blow to his pride. "Then I got afraid."

"Of the sentinels?" asked Takkan.

Gen scoffed. "They hardly noticed me." His voice dipped. "But Bandur did."

"He's inside the breach?" I asked.

"Don't worry, I didn't tell him anything," Gen said quickly. "I was well clear of the breach before he could get to me. I figured your sentinels were the far lesser evil. Didn't know your chief minister had them in his pocket."

I flinched. "I don't think Father knew, either. I'm sorry, Gen. I shouldn't have asked you to go."

"Better *I* face Bandur than one of your brothers," he said. "Besides, I know exactly where the amulet is now. You got the mirror back, didn't you?"

"Your hawk delivered it," I replied, fishing the shard out of my satchel. I'd been in such a hurry to save Gen I hadn't even taken the time to wipe the blood off the glass. Now I saw it wasn't blood at all, but a strange coppery dust that glowed faintly on my fingers as I rubbed it.

"There's a small puncture in the breach that's different from the rest," explained Gen tiredly. "The rock there's darker, almost crimson. It looks like the pupil of an eye.

According to the mirror, Bandur's amulet is wedged under the layer of rock."

No mere rocks could stop me from defeating Bandur. "I'll find it."

"You shouldn't be the one to do it," Gen said. "That's what he'll want. He'll lure you into the mountains and take your pearl."

Takkan had been silent this entire time, but the moment he opened his mouth, I knew exactly what he was going to say. "What if I—" He stopped abruptly when he caught sight of my face.

You aren't getting anywhere near the amulet, my glare informed him. *You aren't even to think about it.*

Takkan withdrew, but his lips were pressed into a thin, unyielding line. This wasn't the end of our dispute.

"Whoever takes the amulet needs to be careful," continued Gen, his eyelids drooping with exhaustion. "Being so close to Bandur will be a terrible burden. It will chew on your soul and weigh you down."

"Thank you, Gen," I said, starting to tow Takkan out of the room. "My brothers and I will discuss this tomorrow. You get some rest."

Before the young sorcerer could protest, I closed the door on him. Takkan and I settled in the adjacent room. I sighed. "This must be how my father feels when he worries about me."

"I'll watch him," said Takkan. "I fear the princes' guards cannot be trusted. Nor yours."

"Thank you." My shoulders dropped, as if I'd been bearing the weight of the world, and I peeked inside at Gen. He was sound asleep, chest shuddering as he breathed in and out.

"It's not safe for him here anymore," I said to Takkan. "I'm going to send him home. First thing tomorrow."

"He won't like it."

"I don't care," I said. My decision was made. "I'll ask Andahai to charter him a ship. It'll leave from the Sacred Lake. Quietly." An idea came to me. "I'll tell Father that I'm on the ship too, en route to Iro for my exile."

"In reality, we'll head to the Holy Mountains," Takkan said, understanding my plan.

"The timing is perfect."

He agreed. "Two birds, one stone. Clever, Shiori."

It *was* clever. But cleverness didn't used to make me feel so guilty. I wished I didn't have to lie to Gen, or to my father.

I shrugged off my conscience. "We should talk about the amulet," I said, sensing it was still on Takkan's mind.

Takkan perked up, naively assuming I'd changed my decision. "I should be the one to get it."

"Absolutely not," I said in a tone that brooked no disagreement. "I told you what I saw in the waters, and you promised you wouldn't be recklessly brave."

"This has nothing to do with being reckless or brave. I'm the only one who can do it."

"I have six brothers," I said firmly. "If I can't go, one of them will."

"They'll be cranes," Takkan argued. "How can they guard Bandur's amulet?"

"They have experience with magic. You don't."

"I don't see how that's relevant."

"It is extremely relevant," I said with more conviction than I could explain. Gods, I'd forgotten how stubborn we both could be.

I reached out to touch his arm. "Trust me."

He released a quiet exhale. "I do trust you," he said. "Although the last time someone asked for my trust, I got a snowball in the face."

He said it so deadpan that I blinked. "Megari?"

"Who else?"

I laughed, picturing his sister washing away one of his stern moods with a well-aimed snowball. Megari and I were of the same ilk, wise but depraved souls. "No wonder we're your favorite people."

"So you are," he replied with a grin, "though my sister often makes me regret it."

"I won't," I swore. "I've no snowballs up my sleeve. Only . . ."

"Paper birds?"

I smiled. "Only paper birds."

My hand was still on his arm, and Takkan took it, interlacing my fingers with his own. In that simple gesture, we were reconciled. And though the silence between us grew, I found strength in the words we left unspoken.

Gen looked much better the next day. He sauntered alongside Takkan and me, the wind mussing his curls, a touch of sunburn on his cheeks. If he had any inkling that I was up to something, he said nothing. Which worried me. I'd grown used to his incessant chatter.

"Shiori!" Hasho shouted as we approached the Sacred Lake. "Did all those cookies at breakfast turn your legs into jelly? We've been waiting for you!"

My brothers were assembled in a line. On each of their faces was a variation of the same proud grin, and when I drew close, they parted to reveal their creation.

"Behold," declared Yotan, gesturing behind him. "It's finished!"

It was a flying basket!

Mostly round and shaped like a large fishing creel, it looked far sturdier than the old basket we'd flown to Mount Rayuna: its sides were constructed of a simple weave of thin bamboo strips, while the base was reinforced with cedar planks.

"It's beautiful," I breathed. "Looks tough, too."

"You haven't seen the best part yet," said Yotan. "Gen!"

Right on cue, the young sorcerer shouted, "Fly!"

Six richly woven ropes jetted up from inside the basket, their ends rising into the sky and bending with the wind.

I clapped, marveling. So that was what Qinnia had done with all those silk robes. "It's a kite!"

Gen smirked. "Reminds me of Solzaya's octopus."

I saw the resemblance, now that he mentioned it, and it made me laugh.

"We figured there was no Summer Festival this year," said Hasho, "and it *is* tradition for us to make a kite together.

We've waited for you to make the last knot." He passed me a silken rope. The seventh and last to be tethered to the basket.

The request was a nod to my name, which literally meant "knot." My mother had named me thus, knowing I was her seventh and last child, the one who would bring my brothers together no matter how fate pulled us apart.

I ran my hands along the rope's woven red cloth, recognizing my old winter robes. A pair of embroidered crane eyes peeked at me from the silk, which made me smile as I tied the last knot to the basket. Then, after a breath, I let go.

As if it had wings, the seventh rope flew up to join the others. I knew it was Gen's magic that carried them, but the sight still filled me with awe. I lifted my arms to the sky, mimicking the ropes and reaching as high as I could.

"What are you doing?" Hasho asked.

"Stretching," I said. "Taking a moment to breathe and listen to the wind sing. Remembering what it's like to be home and bask under a familiar sun."

I settled my arms back at my sides. Near my feet was a crate of supplies Wandei had brought, and I bent down, picking up a handful of paintbrushes. I tossed a brush to each of my brothers. "The basket's looking a bit plain," I said with a wink. "How about we do some painting, like old times?"

The rest of the afternoon, we decorated the basket with designs from kites we had built together over the years—a turtle, catfish, fox, and rabbit. And on the bottom of the basket, Takkan wrote, in elegant calligraphy, *Seven knots strong*.

No one said anything about demons or priestesses or pearls; it really was like a Summer Festival day, except without all the food. I didn't mind. Simply being with my brothers again, the way we'd been before the curse, was precious.

At some point, Gen retreated alone toward the Sacred Lake. I made an excuse to my brothers and followed after him. If Gen noticed, he didn't turn around. He kept walking along the lake, and I skirted the bank to peer beneath the water.

Did you bring rice cakes? I could almost hear Seryu asking. *No? Then you'll have to wait a while longer to see me, Princess.*

His voice, his smirk, his usual disdain were all in my imagination. No silver horns pierced the water, no serpentine tail glittered with emerald scales. No Seryu.

I'd barely been back a week, and already my days in Ai'long felt like a lifetime ago. Lady Solzaya, King Nazayun, and Elang were little more than a dream. Seryu's friendship, a distant memory. I wondered whether Gen's would be too.

The boy had claimed a spot on the bank and was tossing pebbles into the lake. Once, twice, thrice they skipped.

I sidled up to him. "Looking for dragons?"

The lake rippled at the sound of my voice, and Gen met my gaze through our reflection. "This is where you met Seryu, isn't it?" he asked.

"Where he saved me from drowning, yes. Afterward, we used to meet here for magic lessons."

"Doesn't seem like he taught you much."

I glowered, and Gen put up his hands. "I'm joking! Mostly." He sighed, fidgeting with the new bandage on his nose.

293

"What's the matter?"

"It's probably for the best that you aren't taking me to Lapzur. For a great sorcerer, I seem to need a lot of saving."

It was my turn to sigh, and I pulled him to his feet. "Come now, there's no use in moping. It's a glorious summer afternoon, not too hot, not too humid. We should enjoy it."

I kicked gently at his shins, forcing him to walk along the lake. "Why did you seek the dragon realm? You never finished your story, after the part where Elang asked you to steal Solzaya's mirror."

My question won a small grin from him. "It started with a dare," replied Gen. "No one's seen a dragon in centuries. My friends at school said they didn't exist anymore. I disagreed. So they dared me to dive into the sea and bring back proof of one."

"You sought Ai'long out because of a dare?"

"Because of honor!" Gen said with panache.

"And a dragon pearl, if I recall correctly."

Gen cracked his knuckles. "It's one of the only ways to gain power without taking an enchanter's oath. No sorcerer's been able to acquire one."

Bandur did, I thought. *At least for a short while.*

"It took me over a month to plan," he went on. "I read every book I could get my hands on, but most of what I learned was misinformation. I read that eating molded white seaweed under a full moon lets you breathe underwater."

"It doesn't?"

"Not long enough to reach Ai'long," Gen said. "Only sangi can do that, and I didn't know how to make it. So I tied my arms to a turtle's feet. They're slow on land but remarkably swift underwater. That's how Elang found me. The rest you know."

So I did.

"He was supposed to teach me dragon magic in exchange for that damned mirror." A long pause. "Did Seryu teach you anything useful?"

"Just a sleeping spell," I replied, my eyes gravitating to the lake. A bloom of algae floated on the surface, and I kept thinking it was a certain dragon's hair. "I haven't used it yet."

Gen glanced back, noting the distance we'd traveled from the others. He picked up another pebble and tossed it in the water, watching it skip three, four, five times. "You should have used it on me last night," he said. Then he looked at me with new intensity. "When's the boat coming?"

I flinched, giving myself away. "What boat?"

"Don't lie to an enchanter, Shiori."

"You're not an enchanter yet."

"I heard you and Takkan talking last night through the door."

Of course he had. I wanted to kick myself. What an awful liar I had become.

Gen crossed his arms. "Let me stay—at least until after you've got Bandur's amulet. None of *them* have magic." He gestured at Takkan and my brothers by the basket. "You'll need my help."

I wouldn't be swayed. "You've done enough for us, Gen. More than enough. I would never forgive myself if Bandur hurt you."

He said nothing, turning instead toward the lake. A ship with bright orange sails skated across the water, its wooden dragon head regarding us with a carved smirk. "At least it's an impressive boat."

"My father thinks the boat's for me," I confessed. "It's supposed to take me across the lake into the Taijin Sea—to Iro."

"Shouldn't the emperor's daughter have more of an entourage seeing her off?"

"It's a secret send-off," I said, kicking at my skirts. They were overly long, meant to be worn with heeled sandals instead of boots, but their frothy hem covered my trousers nicely.

"I wasn't sure if I'd have a chance to go back to the palace before tonight," I explained, patting the round satchel at my hip, just the right size for transporting my mirror shard and the pearl. "Don't worry, I'm not going to face demons in a dress with lantern sleeves."

"I *was* wondering," mused Gen. "Well, I hope this boat really is headed for somewhere warmer than Iro. Though I suppose a frigid climate is preferable to a desert's."

"My brothers chartered it to take you home"—I faltered, remembering that Gen had no home, that his family had died long ago—"or wherever you wish to go. Your belongings are already on board."

He didn't thank me. "Looks hard to sink," he said instead. "I had to enchant a shrimping dinghy to get to Gindara. This will be much nicer."

"You're not going to put up a fight?"

"I know when I'm beaten," he replied. "You're more cunning than I took you for, Shiori. If I fought you now, you'd cast Seryu's sleeping spell over me."

I gave my signature twist of the lips, but I didn't deny it. "Guess it *is* useful."

Gen harrumphed with a note of grudging respect. "Your magic is greater than it looks."

"Thanks," I said sarcastically.

"Kiki's animation is particularly impressive, and I'm guessing you could perform some telekinesis with ease, maybe even resurrect a dead flower or a tree. But you could do so much more. . . . You could study with the masters and drink the blood of stars, become a real enchantress. Kiata will need enchanters now that magic is reawakening. You could be the first."

I hated the glimmer of temptation that sparked inside me, a flutter in my belly from wanting something I knew I shouldn't. I'd tasted magic plenty of times. I could see how it'd be easy to crave more, to believe that I'd been given a gift to do something good for the world. I wished now I had more—enough to seal the mountains and send Bandur so far away he wouldn't even *remember* Kiata.

I gave a vehement shake of my head. "If you'd asked me a year ago, I would have said yes. I would have run away to become an enchantress so I could see the world and live long enough to witness new ages come and pass. But I have my father and my brothers, my country. I want to spend my days here, with them." My voice softened. "I would wish to live a quiet life. Somewhere in the North with plenty of snow."

"Like Iro?" Gen smirked knowingly. "I'd never be happy with such a life. I was born to become an enchanter, to help great leaders and do great things. I'm going to be a legend."

"But in a thousand years, everyone you know will be gone. You'll watch everyone dear to you die."

"I don't have anyone dear to me."

"You might one day."

Gen scoffed. "Enchanters don't fall in love."

There was nothing I could say that would convince him. I recognized the dogged glint in his eye, the set of his jaw. He would make his own mistakes, just as I had.

"All legends have a spark of truth" was all I could manage. "Sometimes more than a spark. Don't forget who you are along the way to becoming one. A legend, that is."

"Thank you, *Aunt* Shiori. I won't."

In spite of his flippant tone, Gen plodded toward the boat. "What is it?" I asked.

His long black bangs fell over his eyes, and he became suddenly pensive. "The price of an enchanter's oath is one only a few are willing to pay. I had six brothers too, like you, once. They didn't care about me half as much as yours care for you, but if they were still alive . . . I wonder whether I'd seek a quiet life too."

He sounded so old. Then again, he had already seen more than most would see in ten lifetimes.

I nudged him. "Come on, let's get you to the boat."

Gen wasn't finished. "War is a terrible thing," he murmured. "Maybe even worse than demons. I pray you will find a way to save Kiata from both."

"I pray so too."

Together, we approached the lakeside where my brothers and Takkan waited. Gen made his farewells to each of them, then paused before wishing me goodbye. "Teach me that sleeping spell before I go. Cast it on me."

"Now?"

"If I can't prove that I was in Ai'long, some dragon magic will have to do." He shrugged. "Besides, I loathe boats, and I can't swim much. I'd rather be asleep anyway."

"It's an easy one," I said, recalling Seryu's instructions. "All you do is touch someone on the forehead and think sleepy thoughts."

"That's all?"

"Well, the dragon said it also helps if the spell's not expected."

Gen sniffed. "I guess it isn't going to work on me, then. Maybe you should try lat—"

He didn't get to finish his sentence. My hand shot out to tap his forehead. As his heels rocked backward, Takkan caught him neatly and carried him aboard the ship.

I didn't follow. My feet were rooted in place, anchored by the sudden heaviness in my chest. First Raikama, then Seryu, now Gen. I'd said too many farewells of late, and each was a weight on my heartstrings.

"You look sadder than the boy," Takkan observed as he returned from the ship.

If he'd only waited a moment longer, I would have collected myself. But when I turned to him, my eyes were swollen from holding back tears.

My words came out raw, soundless. *Stay with me.*

Takkan immediately understood. He slipped an arm around my shoulders and held me close. "I'm not leaving you. I promise."

I knew he believed it. Emuri'en's strands of fate bound us, after all. Threads that transcended time and place, knotting us from one life to the next.

But threads could be cut, and the threads of fate were no exception.

For what was chaos but a knife slashing across the fabric of destiny?

CHAPTER THIRTY

Twilight crept over the Holy Mountains. The moon was a crown faint against the coal-black sky, but the breach glowed a deep, visceral red. A stark reminder that the Demon King was inside, waiting for me.

Father had spread the rumor that I was being secretly exiled to Iro, and I'd left the palace unannounced, with all my brothers pretending to see me off. So far, no one we encountered had questioned where we were *really* going. But someone must have noticed that we never made it to the roads and had veered instead toward the forests.

I crouched in front of a pine tree, my fingers anxiously pressing into the moist dirt while my brothers went over our plan one last time. As the fastest, Benkai would climb to the eye of the breach and extract the amulet. I'd summon Bandur, then turn my brothers into cranes, and we'd fly to Lapzur.

My brothers sounded as matter-of-fact as cooks steaming the daily barrel of rice. As if nothing could go wrong.

Seryu had warned me once that my emotions affected my

abilities, but never had it been so apparent as now. Magic sparked wildly under my hands and feet, causing leaves and blades of grass to sprout from nothing, then shrivel the next moment, as if they couldn't make up their minds whether to live or die.

Calm yourself, Kiki rebuked. *You're going to give us away to the demons.*

Chastened, I clasped my hands in my lap. Everything I held dear was at stake tonight.

"We must be alert," Benkai was saying. "We've made an enemy of the chief minister, and I suspect he doesn't believe Shiori left for Iro this afternoon. He'll make a nuisance of himself if he finds us here."

"We'll be on our guard, commander," said Wandei. "Shiori won't step foot anywhere near the breach, will you, sister?"

I gave a numb shake of my head.

"Good," said Benkai. "Then we begin?"

One by one, my brothers clasped their hands and dipped their heads to show their assent. But when it came Takkan's turn, he set down his lantern.

"Takkan!" I whispered, grabbing his sleeve as he rose. "What are you—"

"Let me go in your stead," Takkan said to Benkai. "You're needed to fly as a crane. If something happens to you, Shiori will never make it to Lapzur."

Benkai eyed my hand on Takkan's jacket. "You speak as though you are expendable," he replied. "You aren't. Especially not to my sister."

Takkan wouldn't give up. "Bandur will attack you the second he senses you're after the amulet."

"Then I'll be quick," said Benkai. "Don't look so fraught, Lord Takkan. My brothers and I are no strangers to dark magic. All we ask is that you protect our sister."

With that, Benkai mounted his horse and rode off to the breach. Kiki, too, had gone to gather feathered reinforcements for the journey ahead.

I went to Takkan's side. His jaw was tense, and I could practically feel the frustration rolling off his shoulders. But he didn't complain.

While he and my brothers made last-minute adjustments to the basket, I leaned against the tree and pulled out the mirror shard from my satchel. "Show me Benkai."

True to his word, Benkai had been swift. He was already scaling the mountain, keeping to the shadows and moving so quietly that not even his soldiers below noticed his presence. I prayed the Demon King didn't, either.

"Hurry," I whispered as he climbed, using his dagger as a pick when he couldn't find a crevice or foothold. He kept about an arm's length from the breach; its enchantment cast a scarlet glow over him.

With a grunt, Benkai settled himself on a ledge about halfway up the mountain, and he began to search for the amulet. I held my breath until he found the tiny patch of dark crimson rock—the pupil, as Gen had said. There, with all his strength, he stabbed his dagger into a fissure, and the earth released a groan.

Benkai worked quickly, carving around and into the eye, searching. I gripped the mirror, my shoulders tensing—until finally, his blade clinked against the metal.

My brother withdrew his dagger and stuck his entire arm inside. He tugged. A chain jangled, and a sliver of black pierced through the crimson rock.

I gasped. That was it! The amulet.

He chipped away at the breach and pulled harder, but the amulet was caught on something. As he cut deeper, black smoke hissed out of the breach.

With a growl, the smoke shifted into the shape of a wolf. *Just what do you think you are doing, mortal?*

To his credit, my brother kept his composure. He pulled again and again, but the amulet would not give. Bandur snickered. *Stuck, are we? Perhaps you need to cut deeper.*

Before Benkai had the chance, the demon seized the rusted chain of his amulet. The moment he touched it, his body solidified into flesh and bone—and he grabbed my brother by the neck.

Now, where is your sister? he rasped.

I stiffened. A chill prickled the back of my neck, and I didn't dare reply.

Shiori, I know you're listening, Bandur taunted as Benkai struggled to fight him. Every time my brother struck his dagger into the demon's flesh, mist and shadow patched the wound within seconds.

Come find me, Princess. Before you have only five brothers left. The demon pressed a sharp nail against my brother's chest. *Let's see if you remember how to fly.*

Then he pushed Benkai off the mountain.

The mirror went dark.

I felt too sick to scream. Impulsively, I sprang up to help him, but Andahai dropped a heavy hand on my shoulder.

"Don't go anywhere," he said. "Reiji and I will find him. We'll bring him back. Be ready for our signal to cast the curse."

I had to fight every instinct not to argue. "Hurry" was all I said.

As Andahai and Reiji made for the breach, I opened my satchel—just a pinch—to return the mirror. A loud hum came from the pearl, and it jostled the satchel, hard.

"Stop that!" I said, smacking my bag and warning the pearl to be still. Defiant streaks of light fanned through the seams of my fingers. "Stop. You'll give us away."

The pearl didn't listen. It writhed against my grip and wrestled out of the satchel. Wandei tried to grab it, Hasho too. Takkan threw his cloak over it, but the pearl wouldn't be stopped. It bludgeoned Takkan down and shot into the trees.

I ran after it, tracking its mercurial glow until it dipped into darkness. Where was it going? I'd lost the trail, and I scrambled through the forest until I skidded down a hillock into a clearing, practically knocking into it.

"Got you," I hissed, scooping the pearl back into the satchel. Raikama had been right about it having a mind of its own; best to keep it locked away before it got me into trouble.

No sooner had I snapped the satchel closed than I heard the crack of a twig behind me.

It happened so fast I didn't even have time to curl my hands into fists. A sentinel's arm came swinging at me, his metal gauntlets whistling in the air, and a moment later my back cracked against the pommel of his sword.

Down I went.

When I opened my eyes, I was a prisoner. Ropes secured my wrists and ankles, and a dozen sentinels raised their swords, fencing me in with their steel blades. From the grimaces they wore, they looked uneasy about their orders, but no one dared speak up.

Stupid, stupid, Shiori. I gritted my teeth and kicked at the dirt. My satchel was missing, of course. Where had it gone?

The only good news was that Benkai was alive.

I'd been planted across from him, no more than ten paces away. His black sleeves were ripped, and there were new scratches on his proud face, along with leaves in his hair. A tree must have broken his fall.

Benkai *commanded* the army. Why would his own men restrain him? Who had Bandur possessed this time?

I uncurled my fingers, willing the tiniest thread of magic into my ropes. But my head was still roaring from the strike to my back, and the world spun. I couldn't focus.

"I'm afraid that your release would be against His Majesty's law, Lord Commander," someone behind me was saying. "The only way I can explain your sister's presence is that the Demon King has taken her mind. Yours too, it appears, as you are her accomplice."

I strained my neck to find Chief Minister Hawar standing behind me. His long sleeves were folded back so the dirt wouldn't soil the pristine silk, and my satchel dangled from his wrist. He held it far from him, as if it contained locusts and bones rather than a magical pearl.

His eyes were clear. Bandur didn't reside in him. Still, I wished I could punch the smug expression off his face.

"Release us, Hawar," said Benkai. "Do you not fear my father's wrath?"

"Should I?" Hawar replied. "Perhaps we can speak to His Majesty together."

At that very moment, a golden palanquin arrived, and the emperor stepped out, his white mourning robes a stark contrast against the breach's scarlet light. The soldiers parted for him as he strode in my direction, worry and anger creasing his brow.

"Father," I appealed. "I can explain—"

My words died in my throat. The air went cold with an invisible snap, and smoke hissed out of the forest. It settled over Father and slid around his neck.

"No!" I whispered. Dread and horror festered in my gut as Bandur merged with the emperor's flesh. *Bandur, don't!*

Then Father blinked, and he was my father no more.

Bandur chuckled in a way my father never did, the laughter tumbling out of his throat in a slow, wicked roll.

That isn't Emperor Hanriyu, I wanted to shout. *That's the Demon King!* But I held my tongue. Rash decisions had brought me thus far, and no one would believe me if I said the demon had possessed my father. They believed *I* was the one possessed.

"I warned you not to come to the Holy Mountains," uttered Bandur through my father's mouth. "The demons want your blood, and you come here, practically offering it to them. What madness has overtaken you, daughter? And to bewitch your own brother into joining your treachery?" He glanced at Benkai, still in chains. "You must be taught a lesson."

The Demon King's stare bored into me, but only I could see the red in his eyes, taunting me. *Don't look so stricken, Shiori. I told you I wasn't your only enemy. Hawar did most of the work.*

Get out of him, I said, seething. *Get out.*

I have to say, I quite like being an emperor. The power, the respect . . . the effect on you. He forced my father's lips into a sneer. *You should have seen his face when Hawar told him where you'd gone. He raced a carriage here himself—he was worried I might come out and bite.*

Rage boiled in my chest, rising up white-hot. It hurt to hold it in, and I ground my teeth. Let Bandur taunt me, I would not give in. He wanted me to make a spectacle in front of the sentinels. I wouldn't fall for that trick again.

Instead, I reached out to Father directly. *Father!* I screamed into Bandur's mind. *Father, I know you're there. Fight him. Don't let him win.*

The emperor's chin lifted. He straightened and squared his shoulders, his eyes rolling lazily in my direction. It was no use. Bandur was too strong.

But I wasn't about to give up. "Father!" I shouted, lunging toward him. "Stop!"

As I moved, the ground trembled. Little rocks and pebbles spilled down the breach, which glowed brighter than before. The sentinels wrenched me away from the emperor, their blades now pointed at my throat.

Now, now, Your Highness, taunted Bandur. *You must control that temper. You're exciting the demons.*

"See how the mountains react to her presence?" Hawar cried. "It is as I warned, Your Majesty. She is calling the demons forth!"

Bandur pretended to be shaken by my attack. He staggered back and crossed his long embroidered sleeves. "You are right, Minister Hawar. It is time I taught my daughter a lesson." Bandur mimicked Father's smile, giving it a wicked slant. "It's time to come home, Shiori."

Everyone else thought the emperor was going to take me home, but I knew what Bandur really meant. The demons were waiting inside, their restless magic making the earth tremble.

Shiori! they cried. *Shiori, you've come. Free us.*

They sounded different than they had in the past, almost as if they were begging. But I was unmoved; these creatures were just as manipulative as their king.

And by the Eternal Courts, Bandur was *not* taking me back into the mountain.

I braced myself. Already the red-laced shimmer in Father's eyes was fading, like two embers into ash, and puffs of smoke seeped out of his nostrils. Bandur flew out of my father's body in a torrent of shadow and smoke—but I was ready. As I ducked, the ropes on my wrists came alive, lashing toward the chief minister to snatch the satchel back into my arms.

I ripped the bag open and released the pearl. It floated in front of me, the jagged fractures along its dark surface coming aglow.

Bandur laughed. *Well played, Your Highness. But if you use that pearl on me, you won't have the strength left to change your brothers.*

I'm stronger than I look, I said.

Perhaps. But is the pearl?

An outraged cry came from Chief Minister Hawar. Bandur was invisible to him, so all he saw was me holding the pearl aloft over the emperor's unconscious body.

"Shiori'anma has attacked the emperor!" Hawar shouted hysterically. "Kill her. Kill her!"

"Enough!" Benkai shouted, springing up. Andahai and Reiji charged to his side. "Arrest the chief minister."

Half the sentinels obeyed their commander, but the other half followed Hawar. Their swords flew out, only to clash against Benkai's chains, and those loyal to him.

I'd never seen my second brother in combat, and suddenly I understood why soldiers fought to join his command. The chains that bound him became a blur of silver, felling every man in his path. Not even the most seasoned sentinel stood a chance.

While everyone is distracted, you'll come with me, Bandur said, looping his claws around my wrist.

I thrust the pearl at him, ready to call upon its power. Then his body spasmed, smoke sputtering from his limbs and tail. Bandur growled, but he kept shuddering.

"You shall not touch her!" came a shout from the top of the breach. "Return to your vessel."

I had to squint to see who it was, and my heart skipped in alarm.

Takkan.

All this time, he'd been scaling the breach—and he had the amulet!

"Return to me!" Takkan shouted again.

Bandur's eyes turned liquid with anger, but he had no choice. He dissipated into smoke, and as the amulet sucked him back inside, the mountain trembled once more.

"We need to go!" Andahai shouted, dragging me by the arm as aftershocks rattled the forest. "Let's get back to the basket. Cast the curse."

"But Takkan—"

"Benkai and I will help him. He's on his way. Go!"

My heart roared in my ears, but I ran, stumbling as the earth quaked. My lungs were burning by the time I spied a slip of bright silk through the trees.

"Cast the curse!" called Hasho as he helped me into the basket. "Hurry."

Ducking into the basket, I ripped my satchel open. The pearl glowed at my touch. The last time I had wielded its power, I had barely survived. Gods knew what would happen this time.

It floated above my palm, dark and bright at the same time, as if it were eager to go to work. Before I lost my nerve, I spoke the words I'd rehearsed and dreaded: "Protect my brothers as you did once before. Turn them into cranes so we might return you to the Wraith."

I said it only once, imbuing every word with meaning, as if it were a sacred vow. In turn, the pearl listened. And miracles of Ashmiyu'en, it obeyed.

Its light flooded over my brothers, reaching even the ones farthest from me—Andahai and Benkai, who were still running into the forest with Takkan.

Tears pricked my eyes as I watched them begin their transformation. Their swords thumped to the ground, their human yells and cries cut short as their necks and limbs stretched, black feathers sprouting along their throats and tapered wings bursting from their fingers. Then, at last, six familiar crimson crowns painted their heads. Fully transformed now, they flapped frantically toward me, and in a brilliant flash, all of the pearl's light came rushing back inside. Its halves snapped shut, emitting a shock wave that sent me flying back against the basket.

As I pulled myself up, a legion of eagles, hawks, and falcons pierced the clouds. True to her word, Kiki had recruited dozens of birds to fly with us. Together with my brothers, they grabbed the ends of the basket's ropes in their beaks.

"Wait!" I shouted. "Wait for Takkan!"

He was close, and he leapt for the basket, fingers catching its woven edges.

I reached and grabbed him by the arm. "Got you," I breathed, pulling him up.

He landed on top of me, and the impact knocked us both to the floor. We'd made it.

Everyone's aboard! Kiki shouted to my brothers. They beat their wings and accelerated upward until we were soaring over the treetops. Their snow-feathered wings were a familiar sight, and the thrill of skimming past the clouds a familiar feeling. My ribs tightened as I watched my brothers fly. It was as if we'd gone back in time. I hoped they wouldn't regret placing their faith in me once again.

When the Holy Mountains of Fortitude faded behind us, I let out a long exhale. Using the pearl had exhausted me, and my body begged for rest.

I crawled over to Takkan. "That was the most reckless, most foolish—"

"Bravest thing you've ever seen?" Takkan finished for me.

He touched my cheek. He was breathing hard, and I bit back any further rebuke. "It *was* brave," I said.

I helped him to slip Bandur's chain over his neck and watched the amulet swing down over his chest. It was as black as obsidian, with a crack in the center not so different from the Wraith's pearl. A demon's instrument.

"Sleep," I said, sweeping my fingers over Takkan's forehead. And I couldn't tell whether it was my enchantment or his exhaustion that did it, but his breathing steadied and his pulse evened. His hand didn't let go of mine.

I lay my head on his shoulder, tucked my feet next to his, and spread a blanket over us for warmth. The last thing I saw before I too fell asleep was the glint of the amulet, and as my brothers carried us over land and sea, a demon's laugh echoed into my dreams.

CHAPTER THIRTY-ONE

I woke to the wail of the night sky breaking.

Thunder rattled the clouds, and lightning soon followed. We were riding on the wings of a gathering storm. The winds grew violent and chased us over the Cuiyan Ocean.

Shielding myself from the rain, I rose to my knees and peeked over the rim of the basket. Led by Kiki, twenty birds flew alongside my brothers, unfazed by the storm.

"Where are we?" I asked.

Kiki didn't glance back. *Not far from the Tambu Isles.*

"So quickly?"

The winds are helping. Only good thing I can say about this storm.

I rested my elbow on the rim of the basket and clutched one of the silk ropes as I gazed down. Dark clouds obscured my view, but if I stared through the gaps, I could make out the hundreds of islets dappling the storm-lit sea. Raikama's homeland.

A lump rose to my throat, and I swallowed it down, focusing on the distant horizon. We'd have to land before sunrise, or my brothers would lose their wings while still flying over the water.

The rain was growing stronger, and wind pounded the basket, twanging the ropes as if they were zither strings. My stomach dipped, and I ducked down again, reaching for Takkan.

His head lay by my feet, eyes pinched shut. Bandur's amulet weighed on his chest, heavy as a grindstone, dark and ominous. I wanted to free him of the burden, but I didn't dare touch it. Another lashing of thunder cracked the sky, but Takkan's breath barely hitched. I had a feeling whatever he faced in his sleep was far worse.

Gently, I brushed the rain from his cheeks. His skin was cold, and I rubbed his hands in mine, trying to warm them.

The last time I had tended to him like this, I'd hardly known him—in fact, I'd resented his very existence. I had stitched up his wounds with all the care I'd show a pair of old trousers. From the looks of it, he still bore the scars.

Heat rose to my cheeks. Thank the Strands, my brothers were too busy flying to notice me staring through the rips in Takkan's tunic at his muscles and smooth skin. I'd never hear the end of it.

"I should've known it was you," Takkan murmured, his eyelids blearily peeling open.

"What?" I scooted closer worriedly. "What did you say?"

"All those uneven stitches you made on me." The corner of his mouth quirked up. "Same as in the apology tapestry you sent. That should've been my hint that it was you, Shiori."

I couldn't help my reflexes. I punched his shoulder, probably harder than I should have.

"Did that hurt?" I asked, feeling immediately awful. "Are you"—my gaze went down to the amulet on his chest—"hurt?"

Takkan choked back a laugh. "No. I deserved that."

His eyes were open now, but they lacked their usual spirit. "You should take my weapons," he said hoarsely. "I won't let Bandur hurt you, even if he takes my body—but it's better to be safe, just in case."

I bit down on my cheek and gave a nod. I saw only the carved birch bow he'd carried when we'd first met. Painted on the widest part of its grip was Takkan's family crest: a rabbit on a mountain, surrounded by five plum blossoms—and a full white moon. I picked it up. "Anything else?"

"The dagger on my belt. Two knives in my boot."

"No sword?"

"Didn't bring it."

I gave him a narrow look. "What sentinel doesn't bring his sword?"

"The one you foolishly bound yourself to." A small smile touched his mouth. "I'm a better archer than swordsman, anyway. It would've been extra weight."

Fair enough. I stashed the dagger in my sash, then found the knives. I was starting to put them away when the amulet's chain began to twist around Takkan's neck.

"He's waking," he rasped. "Shiori . . . get away from me—"

Takkan covered the amulet with his hands, trying to hold

Bandur inside. All color drained from his face. His eyes flickered, earthy brown one moment, then red as demonfire the next.

"Takkan." I reached for his arm, trying to help.

A mistake. Takkan's gaze was bloodshot, and he grabbed my wrist with a wolf-like snarl. *You should listen to your betrothed, Shiori'anma.*

I hooked my elbow and sent it flying into his chin, but Bandur was too fast. He shoved me back, laughing gleefully as I fell against the side of the basket.

"Shiori!" Takkan's eyes flickered back to brown, and he grabbed the Demon King's amulet, trying once more to tackle him. But Bandur had already won.

Wisps of smoke unfurled from Takkan's fingers, and his entire body shuddered, all strength leaving him until he crumpled to his knees. Then the smoke flooded out of the amulet, coiling and steaming until it settled into the shape of a wolf.

I plucked Takkan's bow from the ground, fumbling with one of the blue-feathered arrows.

"He's stronger than he looks, your betrothed," Bandur said, prowling along the basket to stalk me. "But every mortal has his weakness. You are his."

The bowstring chafed against my knuckles, and I gritted my teeth.

"You know your arrows do nothing against smoke, don't you?"

I nocked the arrow and raised the bow. "Watch me."

"Here—I'll stay still for you." Bandur sat and wagged his

tail like a puppy. Even in his most nebulous form, he found a way to mock me.

With a laugh, Bandur dissolved into a shapeless haze. "Clever of the witch to bind you to the pearl," he said. "But if she thought that would buy you more time from me, she was mistaken. Look. See what you've done to it."

I didn't need to look. The pearl was more broken than ever, like two halves of a moon connected by the slenderest bridge.

"Will you reach Lapzur before it shatters?" Bandur asked. He blew a puff of air, loosening the streak of white from behind my ear. "It wears on you, Your Highness. I would gladly take its weight off your hands."

"And free yourself of your oath?" I spat. "I'd rather die."

"Fortune smiles upon you, then, for that is a rather crucial part of the plan."

The amulet trembled upon Takkan's chest, and Bandur began to speak, whispering words of dark magic I could not understand.

I crawled to Takkan's side and shook him. "Wake up! Wake up, Takkan. You need to return Bandur to his amulet."

While I tried to rouse him, the birds Kiki had recruited to help fly the basket let out bloodcurdling screeches. All this time, they had flown in harmony, but something had changed. They splintered off in droves, as if spooked.

"What's going on?" I yelled to Kiki. "Why are they leav—"

My question trailed into a scream. Caught in a tumultuous wind, the basket jolted, throwing me against Takkan as we plunged below the clouds.

The ropes jerked down, twisting and making the basket spin. I fumbled for something to hold on to while my brothers desperately tried to regain control. Even without the other birds, they should have been able to steady us. But something was pulling us down.

I could feel it. And my brothers could see it. They were just as agitated as Kiki's birds, only they didn't abandon me. They veered sharply, thrashing their wings.

The basket shuddered, and Bandur flashed a menacing smile. "Prepare yourself, Your Highness. They're coming."

Who was *they*? I couldn't even see what was happening. "Kiki!" I shouted. "What's going on?"

Demons! she cried. *From below!*

Dread coiled in the pit of my stomach.

The demons of Tambu arose as one teeming mass, the glow of their red eyes illuminating foxes, bats, tigers, and snakes. Their faces were garish, like the masks children wore to scare evil spirits away during the New Year.

They sounded like children too, squealing and laughing as they brigaded my brothers. Their tails curled around the ropes, and their wings batted excitedly against the underside of the basket. When their claws began to slash and tear, my heart tightened with fear.

Curled strips of bamboo flew off, a painted turtle eye and silken fox tail peeling into the sea of clouds, never to be seen again.

I swiped at the demons with my dagger. "Go away!" I shouted. "Get! Get!"

They snickered.

The dagger was useless. My magic was too. Every time I launched an attack, more demons appeared.

A winged tiger swatted a paw at Benkai's feathers, and a bat nipped its sharp teeth into Kiki's wings until my paper bird fled in terror. Others still were more interested in the basket, prowling up its sides and stripping it of parts.

Feeling cornered, I turned once more to the pearl.

It was humming a low song, the way it tended to in the presence of danger. As I drew it out of my satchel, its power fanned out beyond my control, ensnaring the demons in plumes of bright white light.

Their shrieks were like knives against glass, loud and shrill. Wings thrashed and tails whipped, claws and talons flailing as the demons struggled to be free of the harsh pearlescent light. I twisted around, watching the demons drop back into their teeming swarm and retreat to the islands below.

I expelled a sigh of relief. A *premature* sigh of relief, unfortunately.

I'd forgotten about Bandur.

He leapt into the basket, fur spiked and blood-red eyes piercing. This time he didn't wait. He pounced, and I braced myself.

The attack never came.

Takkan had stirred, and he held the amulet to the sky. It was nearly dawn, and the last threads of moonlight sieved through the clouds, touching upon the amulet.

"Return!" Takkan shouted. "Return, Bandur!"

At the command, Bandur's body began to writhe and contort, as if yanked by invisible strings toward the amulet. The demon spun angrily to confront Takkan. "You think you have the strength to best me?"

Takkan didn't reply, but he rose, standing face to face with Bandur. A silent war broke out between them, the demon pushing and striving against Takkan's control. Sweat beaded Takkan's temples. He took a step back and clenched his jaw, his eyes going white as he strained against the demon.

At last, Bandur jerked away. "I will have your soul for this," he swore.

In one last effort, his claw struck out and caught Hasho by the wing, ripping through feather and bone. Then, with a hiss, Bandur vanished back into the amulet.

The basket careened, the ropes slipping first from Hasho's beak, then from my other brothers'.

Down, down, we plummeted into Tambu, the origin of demons—and the birthplace of my stepmother, the Nameless Queen.

CHAPTER THIRTY-TWO

A leafy canopy broke our fall. Takkan and I tumbled out of the basket in opposite directions, crashing through a web of outstretched branches to the jungle floor.

Thud.

Insects skittered, leaves crunched, and branches snapped. Light shimmered in waves, glistening like hot oil, and sweat trickled from my pores.

With what strength I had, I scrambled onto my forearms, my elbows sinking into the warm, moist earth. Then I went still, remembering belatedly to scan for demons.

Nothing.

When I was sure it was safe, I pushed up to my feet, sweeping away the fronds that brushed against my waist. "Takkan?" I called out. "Kiki?"

The rain had ended, and sunlight yawned through the canopy, a sight that spurred me into motion. It was past dawn, so my brothers should be men again. But where were they? Their transformations weren't exactly peaceful and quiet. Surely I would have heard their cries.

A flash of red silk penetrated the fog, and I scrambled toward it. There, not far from the basket, lay Takkan. Kiki and my brothers, too—but they were still cranes!

Leaves and dirt clung to Takkan's skin. He was breathing, but unconscious. My heart pounding, I quickly inspected him. There were new tears in his tunic, exposing a tanned shoulder and more of the scars I'd left on his chest. But he was unharmed, thank Emuri'en. I propped him against a tree and dotted away the beads of sweat on his nose with my fingers.

A muscle in his jaw twitched. "Hasho . . . ," he mumbled, his eyes starting to peel open. "His wing . . ."

Not understanding, I twisted to face my brothers. There were only five of them, all squawking sounds I couldn't understand.

Panic seized me. "Where's Hasho?"

As soon as I asked, the fog lifted, and I saw.

My youngest brother lay curled, his entire body tucked against himself. His throat hummed painfully, and his belly shook with every breath. I crouched beside him, taking in the wings furled tightly at his side. His left wing was smoldering, its feathers charred.

"Hasho," I choked.

"It was Bandur," said Takkan, the tenor of his voice gone low. "I couldn't stop him in time. I'm sorry."

I didn't know what to say. My attention was fixed on the stripes of watery light caressing Hasho's black wing—

a sinking realization that he hadn't changed back to a man. None of my brothers had.

Andahai thinks the enchantment is different this time, said Kiki. *They won't change back and forth.*

I breathed in, my mind reeling. *That is good,* I told myself. In his state, Hasho couldn't endure a transformation. "We need to find help for Hasho. There has to be a village on this island."

I'll look, offered Kiki, jumping to get a view from above. A beat later, she was fluttering back to us, crying, *Snakes! Snakes!*

Out of the trees, the rocks, even the bushes, snakes beset us. The fattest ones hung off long tree branches, their mottled scales melding in with the lush junglescape. The sight reminded me of how Raikama's garden used to be. That was the only reason I wasn't afraid.

They look hungry, Kiki said nervously. *They're staring at me. Maybe my paper is tasty to these Tambun serpents— I am becoming more like a real bird every day, you know.*

"You're still far from being a real bird, Kiki," I replied. "Besides, cranes eat snakes, not the other way around."

"Then ask your brothers to eat them."

"No one's eating anyone. Have you tried talking to them?"

I've been trying. My paper bird lifted a fearful wing. *Wait—someone's coming.*

The snakes parted, making way for the largest serpent I had ever seen. Her scales blended into the palm leaves crinkling under her body, but as she slid out of the foliage, they transformed. Changing first to match the umber dirt, then fading to parchment white—the same shade as Raikama's snake face.

Only the great snake's eyes didn't change. They were like slivered diamonds against a liquid yellow moon. Mesmerizing.

She rose, standing high as my waist. A forked tongue darted out, and she gave a long hiss.

Kiki shuddered.

"What's she saying?" I asked.

She says her name is Ujal, and she asks if you are the daughter of Lady Green Snake.

"Lady Green Snake?"

The lady has been gone for many years, Kiki went on, *but Ujal can smell remnants of her magic on you . . . daughter of Channari.*

At the name, a note of grief hummed in my chest. "She knew my stepmother?"

"Her father did."

Raikama's past was a mystery I longed to unravel, but I bit my tongue, holding back the urge to ask the serpent more. Now wasn't the time.

I knelt, leveling my gaze respectfully with Ujal's. "My brother is injured. Do you know where we might seek aid?"

Her scales changed color once more as she slithered back in the direction she'd come.

By the time I rose and Takkan picked Hasho up, Ujal had disappeared into the dense undergrowth. I feared I had lost sight of her, but her snakes had waited. They showed us the way, moving as one and with impressive speed, like a billowing cloth rippling over the earth.

I kept my eyes on the ground. Thick roots bulged in our path, often hidden under a mantle of leaves and wildflowers. We passed a grove of black bamboo trees and too many waterfalls to count, but everything else was green. Ujal could have led me in circles and I would never have known.

The dawn burned into morning, and the sun turned harsh, stewing and thickening the air. My breathing had become a series of pants, and my clothes weighed on my skin, sticky with perspiration. Kiata's hottest days were nothing compared to this.

I stole a glance at Takkan. Usually he would have been at my side, making idle comments about the jungle to help distract me from the heat. Not today. His steps were heavy enough for me to notice, and his skin carried a tinge of gray. His eyes were shadowed by dark half-moons, and his broad shoulders sloped down, as if bearing far more than an injured crane. But his spirits were undampened. When he caught me looking, he sent a cheerful wave. Instead of waving back, I slid my arm through his, walking beside him the rest of the way.

We've arrived, Kiki announced when Ujal stopped before a short wooden fence. She wrinkled her beak. *This is the shrine.*

It was a lone building at the end of a dirt road: a wide house made of teak that had seen better days. Moss coated the walls, whose orange paint was faded from years of rain, and the hanging prayer signs were cracked and chipped. I ventured past the wooden fence, following the line of stone statues up to the threshold.

"Hello?" I said in my best Tambun. "Hello?"

There was a girl with sun-browned skin sweeping leaves from the courtyard, and she dropped her broom when she saw the snakes behind me.

"Uncle!" she screamed, disappearing into the shrine.

Not long after, a middle-aged man with an orange scarf and straw sandals appeared. He was slight in frame, no taller than me. Deep creases of irritation lined his brow; perhaps he'd been in the middle of a prayer when interrupted. His hard gaze swept past the snakes to the crane in Takkan's arms, then to the five others soaring over us protectively. None of this seemed to surprise him in the slightest.

I fumbled for the words in Tambun to request help, but I needn't have bothered. The shaman spoke Kiatan.

"They say a storm brings snakes into the home," he said. "What trouble do you carry with you, that the Serpent Queen herself should come to my doorstep?"

"We seek help," I said, gesturing at Hasho. "This crane is injured."

"The Serpent Queen brought you here for the life of a bird? Curious indeed." The shaman gathered his fraying sleeves and folded his arms. He didn't look curious at all. "Come inside."

As he turned on his heel for the shrine, Ujal and her snakes retreated toward the jungle.

"Wait!" I called, chasing after the Serpent Queen. Her skin had changed again, this time to match the gray stones of the road. When she stopped, I bowed and said, breathlessly, "Will I see you again?"

She rasped in reply.

She says the jungles are rife with demons, conveyed Kiki. *Do not venture into them with him.* Kiki cocked her head at Takkan. *Especially not at night.*

That wasn't what I'd asked, but the Serpent Queen had already slithered away, vanishing into the shrubs beside the road.

So it wasn't Hasho that had made the snakes uneasy. It was Takkan.

"You," the shaman said, pointing at Takkan as we re-entered the shrine. "Wait outside."

With great care, Takkan passed Hasho to me. My brother's feathers brushed against my elbows as I wrapped him in my arms. He was so light and fragile, almost like a child.

The room was small, furnished with a low table and an incense pot for repelling mosquitoes. Silently, I laid Hasho on a straw mat for the shaman to examine.

"The demon that marked him," the shaman began woodenly, as if he were speaking of a winter melon and not a living, breathing bird, "what was its name?"

"Bandur."

The shaman frowned. "That is not one I recognize."

"He is . . . newly made," I replied. "In Kiata."

The edges of his eyes constricted, and I could tell what he was thinking—that there were no demons in Kiata. That Kiata had repressed its magic for centuries, until even our gods were silent.

He let go of Hasho's wing and wrapped his fingers around

my brother's long neck. "It is best to let such things be, unfortunate as they are. A demon's mark is difficult to undo. He will be reborn into a better life."

"No!" I exclaimed, realizing in horror what the shaman was going to do. I lunged to block him. "No . . . please. He's my . . . my brother."

If I had uttered such words to anyone in Kiata, they would probably have thought me mad. But the shaman didn't even flinch.

Calmly, he let Hasho go. "You should have said so earlier. The crane's enchantment is not the demon's doing?"

"No," I said uneasily. "It is mine."

"I see." He was considering. "My acolytes will contain the demon's touch to just his wing. But I cannot guarantee that he will recover fully. You will find out only once he is a man again."

A pang of worry stabbed my chest. "Will he live?"

"Yes." The shaman glanced at Takkan, whose long silhouette stole along the walls. "It is this one I am more concerned about. He may not stay at the temple; his presence will attract demons. It has already, I gather."

"How did you know?" I asked.

The shaman offered Hasho water from a jug. "I speculated. Demons are drawn to those who bear their mark."

"You seem to know much about them."

"Tambu is the birthplace of demons. They are a part of our lives."

That idea was so foreign to me I needed a moment to let the words sink in. I believed it, though. Magic here wasn't buried, as it was in Kiata; it was woven into the very fabric of Tambu. I could feel—in the air, in the trees, even in the small lizards that scampered up the walls—the potential for wonder, for chaos, for miracles. Like most Kiatans, I'd never been abroad. I'd never been to a place where gods and demons and mortals lived side by side. That was unfathomable in my homeland. Yet here it felt like the most natural thing.

"You don't fear demons?" I said.

"I fear humans more than demons," the shaman replied. "There are many kinds of demons, but the majority are simpleminded. Most in Tambu stick to the forests, though one or two a year will cause mischief in the village: last month there was one who wouldn't leave the local well—kept making the water salty."

I tilted my head. Such mischief was far different from the experiences I'd had with demons.

"We teach the children to treat them like wasps," continued the shaman. "So long as we do not bother them or rouse their attention, they keep to themselves." He straightened the pleats of his sash, his tone so bland he might as well have been talking about the laundry. "Rare is the demon with the cunning and power to cause great harm. But this Bandur . . ."

"He was an enchanter," I whispered. "Before he turned."

"As I thought," he replied. "Demons are drawn to power, weak ones to strong ones. It is their nature to bring ruin and chaos, but they tend to follow by example. So when an enchanter turns demon . . . the combination of his human greed, his enchanter magic, and his demon hunger brings many into his thrall. As you witnessed when you arrived."

The shaman's eyes were on Takkan, and I understood what he was thinking. "Takkan isn't a—"

"I know he is marked," the shaman interrupted, "and I know what he bears in that amulet. There is a place not far that will be safe for him. I will take you there while my acolytes tend to your brother."

I swallowed, uneasy about leaving Hasho alone.

Your brothers will watch him, Kiki said. *Don't worry, they'll make sure nothing happens.*

The shaman was still waiting for my answer. "Thank you . . ." I faltered, not knowing what to call him.

"Oshli is enough," he said. "There is no need for honorifics."

Without another word, Oshli led me behind the temple and down a winding dirt road. The houses we encountered on the way were in ruins, their tiled roofs blanched by the sun and their gardens left to rot. They looked long abandoned.

"Is this the main road?" I asked.

"It was once," replied the shaman. "People only come down to Puntalo Village on their way to visit the shrine. The area is believed to be cursed."

"Cursed?"

He did not smile. "It is superstition. I have lived here all my life, and I am well enough."

He ushered us into the last lot on the road. "In here. The demons will not come to this place."

It was a small plot of land, deserted years ago, with weeds thriving in the cracks of the stone path. Three wooden huts stood in the open yard, overridden by cobwebs and moss.

A kitchen, a bedroom, and a storeroom, I guessed. Village houses in southern Kiata had similar layouts.

A flicker of movement drew my eyes to the largest hut—inside, a muslin curtain undulated in the warm wind, and through the broken windows I could make out a wobbly stool. There was no one else here, yet I could hear someone singing faintly—the lilting melody of a song I'd known since childhood.

"Why do demons not come here?" I asked. "Whose home is this?"

Oshli must not have heard my questions, for he didn't reply. "This tree is descended from a sacred grove," he was saying. "Every house on this street once bore such a tree, but only this one still lives. When dusk falls, you must tie your companion to the tree and light the braziers."

"Tie him? To the tree?" I repeated, appalled by the instruction. "I thought demons wouldn't come to this house."

"They won't come in," replied Oshli, with an edge to his tone. "But the one inside him may come out."

"Is there any way to subdue Bandur?" Takkan asked evenly.

Takkan's calm rivaled the shaman's, and only I winced.

"Demons are immortal; only magic can kill them." Oshli paused. "But we humans are not without defenses." He circled the tree, his gaze never leaving Takkan. "I'll return with incense and rope before sundown. Do as I bid you, and Tambu's demons should let you alone. I cannot speak for the one within him."

Sensing that his presence wasn't entirely welcome, Takkan lingered by the tree. "I'll wait here while you acquaint Shiori with the house."

Before I could protest, he backed into the courtyard, leaving me alone with the dour-faced shaman.

Thanks a lot, Takkan, I grumbled in my thoughts.

Oshli entered the hut on our right. "You may stay in the kitchen tonight," he said. "There's a bed on the other side of the curtain, and some food left in the pantry for nourishment. Not much, but it should sustain you until I return."

"I thought no one lived here anymore."

"I come sometimes, to pay my respects." The slightest flicker in his brow perturbed his calm.

"Who lived here?" I asked again.

A beat of hesitation. "The owner left many years ago for the capital," he replied. "Only I come, sometimes, to bring offerings to the tree."

That explained the food in the pantry. "Offerings to the tree?"

He wouldn't look at me. "For the two sisters who once resided here."

The hairs on the back of my neck rose. "What happened to them?"

"They were both lost to Tambu, but in very different ways."

My eyes flew up to meet the shaman's. Two sisters. "This was *their* house, wasn't it? Vanna and . . . Channari's."

Channari. Every time I said the name, my heart gave a twinge. Channari was the name of my stepmother's true self, a secret she had kept from everyone—even my father.

"This was their house," I repeated. "You knew them."

I'd finally broken the shaman's composure, and he pursed

his lips tightly. "Everyone knew them. The beauty and the snake."

There was no malice in his reply, but I still flinched. "Were you friends?"

"Channari had no friends." A pause. "But I knew Vanna."

"What was she like?" I said.

The hard lines bracketing Oshli's mouth softened, giving me a glimpse of the boy he'd once been. "She was kind and generous and gentle. She had the power to make anyone adore her—even her stern adah could never say no to her. The girls in the village used to fight over who could brush her hair, and the boys vied simply to touch it."

"Softer than waterbird feathers," I murmured, remembering Raikama's hair.

"Yes."

I regarded him, and the wistfulness on his face shuttered a beat too late.

"Were you in love with her?" I asked, surprised by my own brazenness.

To his credit, he did not falter. "We all were. Everyone worshiped her. They used to think the mysterious light in her chest was a gift from the gods. She was born with it, you know. When she laughed, it would emanate through her clothes like the sun. The Golden One, they used to call her."

Oshli's face became a mask. "My father was the shaman then, and he asked me to keep her from unwanted attention until she was married. That was how we became close. She trusted me." A breath. "But after Channari died, she changed. She stopped speaking to her friends—even me."

His hands fell to his sides, and I wondered at the stories he was leaving untold.

"What changed?" I asked.

"The light within her shone differently, her spirit became . . . stronger. No one else noticed, but I knew Vanna. For all her radiance, she'd never been as strong as her sister. People thought me mad, but I've always wondered whether it was truly Vanna that her father buried in the jungle." Oshli's expression turned hard once more. "Today, when the Serpent Queen brought you here, I at last had my answer."

I whispered, "My stepmother's true name is a secret I promised to keep."

"I will keep it as well," said Oshli solemnly. "There are few that remember Vanna as well as I do. Or Channari."

He'd said himself that he'd been Vanna's friend, but not Channari's. Why did he remember them both, when others did not?

"Months ago, the Nameless Queen's ashes arrived at my shrine," said Oshli, bringing up Raikama's name as if he'd read my thoughts. "You sent them, didn't you?"

I nodded.

"I thought so. I considered taking them to the King of Tambu, to be buried in his palace, but now that I know it is Channari's spirit within . . . I will bury her by the sacred tree in the jungle. It is not far from where Ujal and the other serpents dwell."

"She would have liked to be with the snakes," I agreed. "I should like to join you if there's time."

"Tomorrow, then," said Oshli. "It is no coincidence that

you landed in Sundau. The strongest spirits live even after death, and I suspect Channari's brought you here."

"Why?"

"Who knows. To find answers? To protect you? Only time will tell." He stood by the threshold. "Fate watches you closely, Shiori'anma, as it did her. It never favored her. Do not assume that it favors you."

His words were grave. I meant to ponder them with the weight they deserved, but the moment the gate swung open and Oshli left the compound, my stomach let out a loud, fat growl.

I glanced outside, spying Takkan asleep under the tree and Kiki buzzing about the huts. My hand came to rest over my stomach. How long had it been since I'd eaten? Hunger rolled inside me in a torrential wave, and it was a good thing Oshli had mentioned food in the pantry.

Fruit flies and gnats buzzed over a bowl of rotting coconut flesh, but inside the cupboard, I found a stalk of sugarcane, a jar of peanuts, and two raw cassavas. A tincture of pandan juice and ground sesame too. Spices that would have cost a fortune in Kiata but were commonplace here.

I spent a few more minutes raiding the pantry, then I set everything I'd found on the table next to the stove. I knew just what to make.

"Channari was a girl who lived by the sea," I sang, "who kept the fire with a spoon and pot. Stir, stir, a soup for lovely skin. Simmer, simmer, a stew for thick black hair. But what did she make for a happy smile? Cakes, cakes, with sweet beans and sugarcane."

When I finally looked up, holding my bowl of batter, Takkan was outside the window, arms folded over the sill, with Kiki on his shoulder. Listening intently.

I nearly dropped my batter, but Takkan reached through the window to grab the rim of the bowl, steadying me at the same time. Then he inhaled deeply, taking in the smell of the coconut and peanuts pervading the kitchen.

"How long have you been standing here?" I demanded.

"Standing? I was guarding that bowl with my life. A good thing too."

It warmed me to hear humor in his voice, even if it was only a shadow of his usual mirth. I slumped my shoulders. "I thought you were sleeping."

"I was, until I heard you singing. I didn't mean to stop you."

You should keep at it, Kiki quipped. *That song of yours scared away all the birds. And all the demons too, I'd bet.*

I glared at my bird, glad for once that Takkan couldn't hear her. "It's just a silly song. Something Raikama used to hum. I probably have all the notes wrong."

"There are no wrong notes when you're happy," Takkan replied earnestly. "You sound happier than you have in days."

"I . . . I like it here," I admitted. "It's almost like she's still here with me."

A rush of grief sprang to my chest, and I focused intensely on stirring my batter.

Takkan touched my hand. "Will you teach it to me when we go home?"

"The song?"

337

He nodded, and I suddenly wanted to hug him and cry in his arms at the same time. I turned to wipe my nose on my sleeve. "Lunch will be ready in an hour. Can you wait?"

"Of course." He picked up the two empty buckets tipped against the walls. "That's just enough time to search for a well."

"You're going out in this heat?"

"I don't mind."

His voice was light, but it carried an edge. One that made me notice the distance between us. The fact that he hung back from me, that he still hadn't come inside the kitchen.

What I wouldn't give to chase those shadows out of his eyes. It would do Takkan good to occupy himself with an errand, I decided, if only to keep his mind off Bandur.

"Very well," I said. "But take Kiki with you."

And if there's any sign of Bandur, come tell me immediately, I instructed my bird.

She gave a sharp nod. *Oh, don't worry. You'll hear my shrieks from across the village.*

338

CHAPTER THIRTY-THREE

By afternoon, the island's heat had swelled past the point of unbearable, and I felt like the biggest idiot in Tambu for deciding to steam cakes over an open fire. Even the gnats had fled the kitchen in favor of a cooler haunt.

This was how Oshli found me—fanning myself in the corner, watching my batter cook.

He set down his bag with a displeased thump. "You're alone."

"Takkan went in search of a well. You said he only had to stay by the tree after sundown. Dusk is hours away." Seeing Oshli frown, I quickly changed the subject. "How is my brother?"

"The crane is convalescing and should be able to fly again by tomorrow. However, the other five squawk endlessly, and their feathers have molted all across the shrine." His frown deepened. "It is quite a chore for my niece to clean."

"I'm sorry—"

"Save your apologies," said the shaman curtly. "She

hardly minds. She's taken to the birds as a way to shirk her prayers." A harrumph. "You will be leaving tomorrow anyway, I gather. Sundau is no one's ultimate destination. It hasn't been since the Golden One's selection."

Again with that name, the Golden One. I knew it referred to Vanna, but hearing the title made me flinch.

"In Kiata, we called her Your Radiance." I paused, not sure where I was going with this. "How did you learn Kiatan?"

"The king asked me to. When the Golden One left for Gindara, he thought she might send for me. She never did."

Oshli began unpacking the items he'd brought: a sheaf of incense, rope, a short sack of rice, two sugar apples, eggs, and half a carp. He sniffed. "What are you baking?"

"Cakes," I replied. "Would you like to try? They're almost ready."

Oshli lifted the steamer's lid, peering inside at the rising little lumps. He took one cake and chewed. "It's tougher than I remembered. Tambun cakes are meant to be soft and sticky." Another bite. "But I suppose the flavor is there, vaguely."

"You've had them before?" I asked.

"Vanna used to bring cakes like these. She would cut them into the shapes of flowers and decorate them with rose petals."

I set aside a plate for Takkan, then sat with Oshli at the table. All afternoon, my mind had buzzed with questions about Raikama. "Will you tell me about Channari?"

"What is there to tell? We weren't friends."

Oshli's reply was brusque, a clear signal to talk about

something else. But I'd never been known for my tactfulness. I pushed: "Anything. Please."

He set down the cake. His face had turned hard, and I didn't think he'd actually speak. "The other children and I used to throw turtle eggs at her when she walked down the road. We called her a monster, a snake demon, a witch. Many other names that were far more cruel."

The shaman closed his eyes. His words were heavy, and I could hear that the past had long been a terrible weight on his conscience. "Her adah forced her to wear a mask wherever she went, even at home. I could hear him beating her when she disobeyed. He was the only person she ever feared, I think. He worked her hard, giving her chores to keep her out of sight. She had the face of a snake, you see. Her eyes . . . her eyes alone would make grown men cower."

"She was cursed," I said.

"She was a sorceress," said Oshli. "Rumor had it that she could make you change your thoughts with a flicker of her eyes and could call the snakes to do her bidding."

They weren't rumors. My brothers and I had witnessed the hypnotic thrall of Raikama's magic many a time.

"We used to say Channari ensorcelled Vanna to love her. Vanna was the only one who was kind to her, the only one who mourned her when she died. Though now I suppose it was the other way around."

"How did she die?" I asked. "How did you *think* she died?"

"There was an attack," answered Oshli. "A demon came for her in the middle of the selection ceremony. Only Vanna witnessed it. She said Channari tried to protect her and, in doing so, was killed."

My chest constricted at the lie. Raikama had told me the truth just before she died, that the demon had killed Vanna, not Channari. And while Channari mourned, the pearl in her sister's heart rooted itself to her—fulfilling her wish to be beautiful in the most awful way: it gave her Vanna's face.

"When she emerged from mourning, she had changed." Oshli looked away, his shoulders pinching. "She was colder, her light muted like the moon's. Some worried that she'd gone mad. She cut herself, you see. Straight across the face."

Revelation dawned, and a tingle shuddered down my spine. The mysterious scar across my stepmother's face— why she had borne it so visibly had been a source of gossip in the palace for many years. Even I had wondered where it had come from. Now I knew.

"I hated seeing my sister's face in the mirror," Raikama had told me before she died.

She had *intentionally* given the scar to herself. As a reminder of her life as Channari.

"Her adah was furious about it," Oshli went on, "but it did little to deter the suitors. They vied for her hand, going on impossible trials for her, obtaining things like mosquito hearts and gold from the bottom of the sea. That weeded most of them out. In the end, she chose the most unlikely of the men."

"My father," I said.

"He wasn't even a suitor. But she left with him one evening, so quietly and swiftly that no one noticed until they were long gone. We thought all the kings and princes would wage war against Kiata, but it was as though a haze had fallen upon the suitors. They all forgot about her. *Everyone* forgot about her."

"Except you," I said.

"My memory is not untouched. But yes, as I said before, I remember more than most."

After all these years, Raikama's magic held strong.

Still, there was a piece of the puzzle that didn't fit. "The demon that attacked Vanna—do you remember anything about him?"

Oshli shook his head. "Only that Channari fought him with a spear." He began to rise. "It broke during their battle, but I've kept it. Do you wish to see?"

Of course I did. I followed him outside to the tree in the courtyard. Leaning against the trunk was a long spear, its wood dark with age.

Oshli picked up the weapon and held it upright. It was as tall as I was, but its end had been split off.

"She slew a tiger with it once," Oshli said. "It came into the village and slaughtered the four men who tried to fight it, and the rest of us ran away. Channari stayed. Not for us, but for Vanna—I doubt she would have cared if the tiger had devoured us."

With both hands, Oshli carefully passed me the weapon. "That was the first time I glimpsed the true Channari, whom even tigers feared, and not the girl who sat on a broken stool peeling taro root all day in her mask. She was exceptionally strong, and bold, and loyal. That was the woman who became your stepmother."

I was quiet before I spoke. "Thank you."

Oshli gave a slow nod. For a moment I thought he might speak again—for his lips were parted. But before I could query what had been on his mind, he turned for the road and took his leave.

I wasn't alone for long. Soon enough, Kiki returned, and I spied Takkan's silhouette not far down the road. The paper bird landed on my shoulder, and I let her poke into my thoughts, catching up with what she'd missed while away.

I said nothing and rolled the spear in my hands, tracing its grooves and edges. Even broken, it was heavy—I could hardly heave it past my shoulders without straining. That Raikama had wielded it against a tiger was a testament to her strength—and a reminder of how twice she had lifted me off my feet, as if I weighed little more than a doll.

I had thought that coming to Raikama's birthplace would give me answers about her past. Instead, I had more questions than ever.

Blood stained the broken end of the spear. It was dried, blackened by time. I could not tell whether the blood was my stepmother's or someone else's.

I dipped into my satchel for the mirror of truth. "Show me whose blood is on this spear."

Seconds passed, and the glass only misted over with humidity.

Kiki wrinkled her beak. *Some magic mirror. I hope Elang is getting more use out of it than you.*

I shrugged. "Lady Nahma told me it would show only

344

what it wants me to see. Perhaps the past is better kept in the past."

Is it? I never took you for a sage, Shiori.

My face crinkled into a small, tired smile. "Not that I don't have suspicions."

You think the blood is the Wraith's.

I did, and I finally lowered the spear. Takkan had returned, carrying two buckets of water.

"That looks like it's impaled a demon or two," he said, gesturing at the spear.

"It was Raikama's," I replied. "Oshli says she wielded it to fight the demon that killed her sister."

Before he could ask more, I steered him into the kitchen. "I saved you cakes. Eat them before they spoil."

Takkan picked one up from the plate. "These are Channari's cakes. From the song."

I nodded, impressed that he remembered. "Of all the islands and all the villages in Tambu, we came to hers," I murmured. "And here I am, baking her cakes in her childhood home."

"Your strand of fate is tied more closely to hers than anyone's."

"Even yours?" I teased.

Takkan parted his lips, but no reply came. Dusk was fast approaching, and the shadows grew bold. They crept out of the cracks in the walls, draping a film of darkness over the house. When they touched Takkan's eyes, his gaze blackened, like a light extinguished.

He set down the cake and took a step back, resuming his distance from me. "You should get the ropes."

I didn't waste a beat. I grabbed the ropes and incense Oshli had left. Together, we tied him to the tree in the courtyard. I couldn't help but think of the threads we'd tied around our wrists just days before. About how those knots had been made with love and laughter, while this one, which I tightened against Takkan's chest, was made with fear.

Were he in my place, he'd find some story to tell to ease my mind and distract me from my ordeal. Stories about monkeys with magical hair, carp that granted wishes, and brushes that painted objects into life, as in the letters he'd written me. Yet I was useless. My throat had constricted in worry. All I could say was "I'll prepare a fire to light the braziers."

He didn't even eat, remarked Kiki as I returned to the kitchen.

I swallowed hard, picking up his untouched cakes. *Let him be.*

I was looking for something to strike a fire with and accidentally yanked aside the muslin cloth hanging against the wall. Behind the curtain was a broken stool—the very one Oshli had mentioned. I leaned my stepmother's spear against the wall, giving my shoulders a break from its weight.

Don't look so dour, Kiki said, trying to cheer me up. *With Takkan tied up to that tree, you'll get the bed all to yourself. There's only one in this whole house, and—*

I didn't know why I flushed. "That isn't it," I said curtly.

Is it the blood, then? Kiki was in a gossipy mood, which was nothing unusual. She landed on the spear, pecking at its

346

warped grooves as I searched the room. I could have sworn I'd seen a stash of flint somewhere.

You really think Vanna was killed by—

Too late, I felt a stab of panic. "Kiki, don't say his na—"

Khramelan?

Too late. The name had been uttered, and I shot up to my feet, adrenaline rushing to my head. I clamped down on Kiki's beak and glanced outside, heart speeding in my chest. The sun was nearly sunk, and Takkan's back was to me.

What's the matter with you, Shiori? Kiki trilled. *Takkan can't hear me anyway.*

"It is not Takkan I'm worried about."

A tuft of smoke had puffed up from the candle by the window. Except that candle had never been lit.

A terrible certainty welled within me.

From the window, I saw smoke drift up from the amulet around Takkan's neck. It slipped between the knots that held Takkan fast, then seeped into his mouth and nostrils. "Get the spear!" he shouted. "Now, Shiori!"

With a gasp, I lunged for Raikama's weapon. I'd made it to the door when Takkan appeared, ropes still dangling from his waist, eyes flickering uncontrollably from brown to red. He blocked me, a smirk distorting his features.

I swung, but Takkan evaded the spear easily and caught the shaft in one hand. His eyes blazed red as wolfberries as he pushed me against the wall.

You know, I've always wanted to meet the Wraith. Bandur's voice stabbed into my thoughts. *And now I know his true name, thanks to you.* He rammed the spear against

347

my shoulder, and a firework of pain exploded in my collarbone.

Kiki launched herself at the demon, but I caught her by the wing and hurled her out of the window—she had no chance against Bandur. Not that I did, either. I couldn't even look away as the Wolf misted into being, his horrid visage superimposed over Takkan's.

"Clever of you, seeking to pit the Wraith against me. But you make a mistake, Shiori'anma. You imagine he'll be like me, open to reason and conversation."

"You? Open to reason and conversation?" I scoffed. My hands were on the spear, but little by little, I was stepping toward the kitchen, trying to reach the unwashed bowls I'd left on the table. "Don't make me laugh."

"He is called the Wraith for a reason. There is a dark side to his nature, and his time on Lapzur has surely eroded whatever good there once was. He will be demon to the core—only with a dragon's strength. You'll see soon enough."

"Yes," I said through my teeth, "I will." Letting go of Raikama's spear, I smashed a bowl over Takkan's head.

The room went silent as he slumped to the ground, unconscious. Bandur was gone, at least for now.

I didn't have a breath to waste. With my heart pounding, I dragged Takkan back to the tree. His whole body clenched as I retied the ropes, wincing to see the knots dig into his skin. Just when I thought to loosen the ties, a snarl escaped his lips. I didn't know if that was Takkan subconsciously helping me or if he was actually fighting off Bandur. But I gritted my teeth and tied them tighter. Then I lit incense around the tree and started fires in each brazier. By the time I was finished, it was nightfall.

I was exhausted, and I collapsed onto Raikama's broken stool. I leaned my head against the wall, trying not to worry about Takkan and instead imagine my stepmother's former life. At my side, the mirror of truth lay beneath a damp pile of sweat-ridden clothes.

"I wonder if she used to sit here," I murmured aloud to it, "and just stare out the window. Not much of a view. I bet it helped her sleep."

As I spoke, Ujal slid into the hut, crawling noiselessly to my side.

She's telling you to sleep, said Kiki. *You'll need your rest for the battles to come. Her kind will watch Takkan tonight.*

"I'm not tired."

The Serpent Queen's words were not a request. Her yolky eyes glowed like Raikama's, and a lull fell over me, forcing me to obey her wishes.

If only I'd asked Seryu how to break the sleep spell. "Dragons and snakes really are cousins," I mumbled before I slumped over the broken stool, my head tipping against the wall.

As I nodded off, I was dimly aware of Ujal and her snakes surrounding the tree, layering themselves in a protective circle around Takkan.

What I didn't notice at all was the mirror of truth, glimmering under my arm.

In my dreams, I hadn't been born yet, and this house hadn't been abandoned. It belonged to a family of two sisters. The first was a girl a little older than me, tanned and sinewy, her limbs as muscular as a seasoned sentinel's. Her hair was in a long and messy braid, but when she turned, I saw her face covered by a thin wooden mask.

Channari.

The broken stool was broken even then, and it wobbled as she sat. Her hands worked deftly, peeling a taro root, but her thoughts roamed far away, as far as she could get from her adah's kitchen, from the four walls that surrounded her like a cage. What she wouldn't give to run free of this place forever and disappear into the forests.

What she wouldn't give to live among the trees and wild beasts. Only there did she feel safe. Only there did she forget that she was a monster.

She reached for the next taro root to peel.

"It's such a shame, isn't it?" her sister was saying, oblivious to Channi's thoughts. "You know Adah's going to pick the richest one, but all the rich ones are so ugly. And old."

"Did you have someone else in mind?"

Her sister flushed, but she said, far too quickly, "Of course not."

Channari said nothing. Secretly, she was sure her sister had a lover. The other day, she'd found a note in Vanna's pocket. *You are the light that makes my lantern shine,* it read, but she didn't see the point in bringing it up.

"You'd think all the gold in the world could buy beauty and health, but it can't."

"No." Channari's jaw ticked. Nothing would smooth away the scales of her face into flesh. She'd tried. She'd tried to cut off the thick splotches along her cheeks, chewing on a chunk of wood to keep from screaming and ignoring the scorching flashes of pain as her steady hand nicked next at the rough grooves between ears and neck. But overnight, her skin grew back the same. Only the pain remained, seared deep within her.

Nothing would make her beautiful. Not all the gold in the world.

"No," she said again. "I would know."

"I'm sorry, Channi," Vanna pleaded. "I didn't mean it like that. You know I didn't."

The words crawled out of Channari's throat: "I know."

Vanna wrapped her arms around Channari's shoulders and pressed their cheeks together, the way she used to do when they were little. Her cheek was always too warm, and Channari's always too cold. Together, she'd say, they were just right.

Her sister lifted her cheek and squeezed Channari's hand. "When I become a princess or a queen, I'll get you the best creams and paints money can buy."

Vanna meant well, but the words stung all the same. This time Channari could not force a smile. "What about my snake eyes?"

Vanna giggled, not hearing the bitterness creeping in her voice. "You can use them to mesmerize our enemies."

"If I had that power, I'd just make everyone forget I was there," Channari replied softly.

Vanna didn't hear. Someone was calling for her outside.

Channari exhaled, relieved when Vanna slipped out. Sometimes . . . sometimes she couldn't tolerate her sister's blithe optimism. Sometimes she wondered whether it would be easier if Vanna thought her a monster. It would hurt less— for both of them.

Channari crept off her broken stool, accidentally catching a glimpse of herself in the washpot. Taro pieces floated in the water, hiding her eyes and her nose. A breeze pushed them apart, and she shuddered.

To see the monster in her reflection instead of the girl she should have been—one with black braids, copper eyes, a soft nose, and full lips. She thought that pain would have eased over the years, but it hadn't. It'd only dulled and become a part of her, stitched deep into her soul.

In her dark, secret heart, what she yearned for, even more than for her face to go away, was for someone to love her. For someone to look her in the eyes and make her feel beautiful, even if she was not. For someone to take away the loneliness etched in her heart so she could laugh without tasting the bitterness on her tongue once the sound faded.

She wanted to be the light that made someone's lantern shine.

But that would never happen. Not for her.

She hit the water with her fists until her reflection was no more.

CHAPTER THIRTY-FOUR

Come morning, the fires around the tree had gone out, the incense sticks were burned to charred nubs, and the snakes that had arrived to safeguard Takkan were gone.

The heavy rain that had come in the night had dwindled to a drizzle, and as I walked into the yard, Takkan barely stirred. Even in his sleep, he grimaced, clutching Bandur's amulet in one hand as if he were trying to shatter it in his fist.

In the two days he'd carried the amulet, it had already extracted a toll. He was noticeably thinner, new hollows appearing in his cheeks when he wasn't forcing a smile. His eyes too became duller and more sunken by the hour, especially past dark.

Takkan let out a faint wheeze as I pulled him toward the hut. Once we'd taken shelter, I brushed aside his hair and wiped his skin dry. That was when I saw the scorch marks along his sleeve.

"What happened?" I whispered.

A low hiss drew my attention to the window, where Ujal lounged against the warped shutters.

"The demon was stronger than I anticipated," she said as Kiki translated. "But my kin were born to battle his kind."

"Thank you." I hesitated. Ujal sounded worn. "Was anyone hurt?"

"Your gratitude is not necessary, nor is your concern. We see it as an honor to fight for Channari's daughter and guard her betrothed."

My head was dipped in respect, but I lifted it now, surprised. "How did you know he was my betrothed?"

"Snakes are sensitive to magic. We always have been. And the two of you are bonded." A pause. "He fought well. Not many can endure a possession as powerful as Bandur's."

"Channari chose him for me," I said before thinking. But it was the truth.

The Serpent Queen was quiet for what seemed a long time. "My father said she was a good judge of character," she replied at length. "She could see the light in others, whereas they saw only the darkness in her. That was her greatest pain."

I had felt a bit of that pain last night, in my dreams. My heart still ached from it.

Ujal started to slither down the other side of the wall, but I called out to her: "Wait!"

One last question had been pecking at the back of my mind. "Oshli told me that a demon killed her sister. Was it—" I halted, knowing better than to say Khramelan's name aloud. "Was he a half dragon?"

Ujal dithered, letting out a long hiss before she skated across the weeds and wildflowers and out the gate.

I turned to Kiki. "What did she say?"

That their fates were once entwined, then they diverged. Kiki shrugged. *Whatever that means.*

I didn't understand, either. I'd have to see if Oshli knew more.

Back inside the hut, Takkan was stirring. Sunlight poured over his face, chasing away the shadows in his eyes and bringing a trace of color to his cheeks. I dared think it meant he was better.

I hovered over him, feeling bad as he rubbed his head. "If you're wondering about why it's sore," I said, "I gave you a big thwack on the skull with a bowl."

"Ah." Takkan gave a sheepish look. "That would explain it."

I offered him some water. "I saw the scorch marks. Are you hurt?"

"I'm fine," he assured me. "The snakes helped. So did the ropes. I'll tell you about it another day, when my ears aren't ringing quite so much."

He was trying to sound wry, but there was an undertone of pain that made my heart both heavy and light all at once, and I bumbled for something to say. Failing at that, I kissed his cheek.

His skin was warm. Warmer still when my lips left it. I basked in the astonished look he gave me. "What was that for?"

"To make sure you haven't turned into a demon." I pinched his chin playfully. "Demons don't blush."

A corner of his mouth lifted, and I felt a sense of triumph.

Now I know what it was like for him all of last winter, trying to make me smile, I thought.

He rocked forward to get up. "Are there cakes left? Seems I forgot to eat yesterday, and battling all your demons has burned a hole in my stomach."

"All *my* demons?" I crossed my arms. "You're the one they're attracted to, and you had an army of snakes helping you." I bit down on my lip. "You're actually hungry?"

"I could eat. I *should* eat."

"Have some, then," I allowed. "But have more than cakes—too many sweets for breakfast will make you slow, and how will you defeat all my demons if you have indigestion?"

Humor flecked Takkan's eyes.

"Eggs will be good for you," I went on, encouraged. "Oshli brought some yesterday, along with fish. I was planning to prepare them for our flight to Lapzur, and I could use some help. That is, if your lordship learned to cook while growing up in Iro's tundra?"

"All of us sentinels learn the basics."

"Good. Then you steam some rice and eggs while I make the fish. Kiki'll chase away the lizards and fruit flies." I rose, passing him the sack of rice and nudging him toward the stove. "I'm not letting us face any more demons on empty stomachs."

Overnight, my brothers had become Sundau's most popular attraction. When Takkan and I arrived at the shrine, half a dozen village children were crowded around the cranes, feeding them berries and rice kernels.

Hasho was among my brothers, and he clamored for his share. It buoyed my spirits to see him so animated. If not for his darkened wing, I would have forgotten about Bandur's attack.

He looks well, remarked Kiki. *Fatter than yesterday, too. Maybe I should've stayed in the shrine instead of loafing about in that old haunted hut with you.*

As I glowered at her, Oshli appeared.

"I was wondering when you'd show up," the shaman said. A cloth bag hung over his shoulder, and he tucked it to the side. "Make haste. The children may delight in your brothers, but I assure you, their parents are already plotting to stew them for dinner."

That got me moving, and quickly. I whistled for my brothers to follow.

It wasn't easy herding six overstuffed, excitable cranes into the jungle, but once their breakfasts had digested a bit, their minds seemed to sharpen.

The opposite was true with me. The deeper we ventured into the forest, the more my thoughts wandered. I felt clumsy here, tripping over the looping vines and meandering ferns—and my flesh was bait for the mosquitoes. I couldn't have been farther from home, from what I knew and loved. And yet, part of me wasn't ready to leave.

One day in Raikama's homeland had only ignited my curiosity about her past. I wanted to stay and learn about the girl she had once been, but the pearl couldn't wait. Neither could Takkan.

"What's on your mind?" he asked, walking by my side while my brothers flew ahead. "Raikama?"

I grimaced. "Am I that easy to read?"

"Easier than when you had a bowl over your head."

"You're never going to forget that, are you?"

"Never."

That earned a laugh from me, but my amusement was fleeting. I chewed on my lip. "I was thinking about how I used to beg her to tell me where she was from. She never spoke of her home, not even once. I didn't even know her name . . . until the end."

My voice softened. "I dreamt about her last night. To be honest, I can't remember most of it." I swallowed hard. "But when I close my eyes, I can still see the island as she did. I don't want to lose that."

"Then tell me," he said. "Let me help you remember."

I drew a deep breath, trying to summon Channari's yearning to escape into the jungle. "She had names for everything, even the flowers that cling to the trees like strings of beads and pearls." My voice grew thick as I went on. "She knew which barks cured stomachaches, which ferns tasted sweet if you fermented them long enough, and which petals turned bitter when you boiled them. She knew where to find orchids for every color of the sunrise, and how to soften palm fruits to glean their precious oil. She even knew where to find fireflies at night—by the low grassy hills beside the jungle—so that if her lantern were to go out, she could still find her way back to her adah's house."

I faltered then, my mouth going dry. "This was her home. After all these years, I finally know where she came from."

Takkan said nothing, but he reached for my hand. I found that was all the comfort I needed.

The sacred tree wasn't far from where our basket had landed, but I never would have found it without Oshli. He led us through a narrow ravine overgrown by bamboo and palm trees.

There, among a thicket of pale-barked birch and a sprawling field of white moon orchids, was a withered tree, little more than a stump.

I blinked. "This is the sacred tree?"

"This is all that remains," said Oshli. "The tree itself died years ago."

"Yet you remember."

"It is my duty to remember what others have forgotten," he said solemnly. "But I am simply a vessel. Some memories slip even my tightest grasp."

I knew he was referring to Raikama.

The shaman gestured at the orchids, and a pair of butterflies fluttered up from their petals. His voice fell soft, almost tender. "They were Vanna's favorite flowers." A pause. "Channari's too. The sisters were like the sun and moon, different as day and night, but they both loved orchids."

"Vanna is buried here," I said.

It wasn't a question, and Oshli said nothing as he settled his lantern before Vanna's grave. My brow furrowed, seeing that the lantern was lit though it was still day. Its light shone upon the orchids, steady and unwavering. Then my heart pinched as if struck.

The lanterns, the light—they confirmed what I'd suspected all along.

He'd loved Vanna. That was why he'd never left Sundau. That was why he had stayed.

"Let their spirits be together at last," Oshli said to me quietly, giving back a wooden box that I recognized. Inside were Raikama's ashes, as well as the tokens my brothers and I had placed within to accompany her journey to the gods.

The red thread I'd tied around it was still there, its color dulled by time and sun. Seeing it, I felt my heart swell with emotion. I had sent the box all the way from Kiata, certain I would never see it again. Now here I was—halfway across Lor'yan, in Raikama's birthplace—reuniting her with her sister, and her home.

Even after death, Raikama's fate and my own were knotted.

"You are her daughter," said Oshli, "and a sorceress in your own right. It is time to undo the curse that was set upon the sisters, and right the wrongs cast upon their souls."

He departed before I could speak with him again, and I sank my knees into the flower beds. My brothers surrounded me, bowing their long necks in turn.

They want to give you a moment alone, Kiki said, sitting on my arm. *We'll finish patching up the basket, and torment some local birds until they agree to come with us.*

I gave a wordless nod.

She touched my cheek with her head, then flitted off.

When I was alone, I set the box on the earth, among the gently swaying moon orchids. Using Raikama's spear, I dug a small hollow and buried the box inside.

I bowed low, pressing my forehead to the earth. When my stepmother lay dying, I hadn't had time to forgive her for all she had done. I had barely understood the sacrifices she had made for my family. Our family.

"I wish I could ask for your forgiveness," I whispered to the earth, believing that, somehow, Raikama could hear. "And I wish I could forgive you in return. I wish I knew more than a sliver of your story." The words burned in my throat, and I punished myself by swallowing. "I'll always miss you."

The smell of orchids flooded my nose. Raindrops shimmered on the white petals, and I plucked the loveliest blossom and laid it over Raikama's ashes. "May your spirit find peace, Stepmother," I said. "Whether you choose to stay here, among your snakes, or find your way to heaven."

I bowed once again. Then, as I rose, dusting my sleeves, seven paper birds rustled out of the flower beds. The very same ones I had enclosed in Raikama's box to accompany her to wherever she took her final rest.

They took flight, circling me as I stood.

They're coming with you, spoke Ujal, camouflaged among the orchids. She slithered into view. *What task did Channari set upon you, that she should watch over you even after death?*

Was she truly watching over me?

I started to answer, but my jaw fell agape when I realized Kiki wasn't here. No one was translating. "How . . . how am I understanding you?"

The tongue of snakes is understood by those we regard as kin, Ujal replied. *My father shared with Channari an unbreakable bond. He was to her what your bird is to you. In a way, we are family—you are her daughter, I am his. But I couldn't trust you until I understood why you carry that accursed gem at your side.* Ujal's sulfurous eyes fell on my satchel. *The heart that cursed the Golden One, who cursed Channari in turn.*

Ujal was speaking of Khramelan's pearl.

"She asked that I return it to its true owner," I replied. "That was her last request."

Its true owner . . . Ujal let out a long, angry-sounding hiss. *Is that what she called the demon?*

Half demon, I corrected in my head, but I wisely left it unsaid.

Ujal's tail snaked around Raikama's spear, her scales turning red and black to match its dried blood. *You asked about the demon she fought. My father warned her not to trust him, but she thought he was her friend. That was her one mistake.*

She spat her next words. *In the end, he betrayed her.*

I'd already suspected, but now . . . I finally confirmed the truth.

"The Wraith," I whispered. "He was the demon that killed Vanna."

Yes, needlessly. Channi had sworn to give the pearl to

him when her sister passed naturally. *But that agreement was broken when he killed her, so the pearl doomed him to his current fate.* Ujal paused. *He won't be happy to see you, Shiori'anma. Far from it.*

"But a promise is a promise," I said softly. "Not a kiss in the wind, to be thrown about without care. It is a piece of yourself that is given away and will not return until your pledge is fulfilled."

I looked into Ujal's eyes. "Channari still has a part of me. I must return the pearl so I can claim it back. So she may rest."

Ujal's anger faded, and she gave a slow nod.

Then the seven paper birds fell, landing lifelessly among the folds of my robe. As I gathered them up, Ujal let go of the spear. It began to sink into the earth, disappearing into the flower beds.

She watches you, her daughter, said the serpent as she too blended into the orchids. *My father would have been happy to know that she found a family in the end.*

Long after I'd departed Tambu, her words stayed with me. Remembering them never failed to make me weep.

CHAPTER THIRTY-FIVE

We left Tambu on a headwind of luck, our basket breezing along in a warm gale over the Cuiyan's emerald waters.

I should have known it was too good to last.

"Look," Takkan murmured, pointing at a blanket of mist unfurling over the water. "That must be Lake Paduan."

Where the mist touched the Cuiyan, its emerald waters went dark. As my brothers dove nearer, the air turned cold, as if we'd pierced a hidden veil.

Far too early it was twilight, and streaks of black and violet painted my brothers' wings before steeping the world entirely in darkness. It was beautiful at first. Not a star blinked, and the moon was lean, like a scythe scraping the clouds. When it grew too dark to see, I took out the pearl. At my touch, it opened a hair, emanating the light of lost stars to guide our way.

I wished I could say the rest of the journey was peaceful, and that whatever darkness awaited us I banished with the pearl. But that was not so.

Before long, the birds Kiki had recruited began screeching and flailing their wings.

Not again! Kiki cried as they abandoned us, winging back the way we had come. *Cowards! Come back here. Come back!*

Without the extra birds to help, the basket teetered against the wind. My brothers bit deeper into the ropes, their necks stooping as they strained to carry us. But it was no use. We dipped lower and lower, and my stomach made a hard swoop as I held in my screams.

"Help us!" I cried, turning my attention to the pearl. Light blinked from its crack, but instead of helping, it spun off into the clouds. Leaving me in the dark.

Scourge of my existence! I started to hurl a curse after it, but the basket made another drop, and my throat fell to my stomach. Enough with the pearl. I had to help my brothers.

I tossed Raikama's seven paper birds into the sky. "Awaken!"

One by one, they quivered to life and picked up the basket's ropes with their beaks. Their aid wouldn't keep us from falling, but it'd buy us time. Enough to reach Lapzur, if we were lucky.

We had to be close. The Forgotten Isles sprang up from below, their waters pockmarked with jagged rocks and hanging cliffs.

The winds gathered strength, and Lake Paduan thrashed hungrily. It was under the guise of this gathering storm that the darkness birthed a shadowy behemoth. None of us saw the guardian of Lapzur creep upon us, his black wings skulking beneath the clouds.

Until he smashed our basket.

I slammed into Takkan as the world shook, wooden debris and shredded silk exploding in every direction. Somehow, while the world around us fell apart, I managed to grab hold of Takkan's hand—or maybe he grabbed mine, I couldn't tell. A scream had knotted up my throat, and I bit down on my tongue until my mouth filled with blood. Its iron tang was all I tasted as we fell.

In the darkness I crashed against feathers and beating wings. My brothers! They'd found me, and they threaded their necks between my arms.

That was close! Kiki cried, hanging onto Andahai's neck.

Close indeed. I caught my breath, glancing back at Wandei, Yotan, and Reiji. They'd rescued Takkan too, but they were struggling to hold him. At first I thought it was because he was heavier than I was, but then I saw Bandur's amulet rattling against his chest, juddering violently as smoke seethed out. . . .

Takkan's eyes met mine, an unspoken apology on his face.

Adrenaline shot like a lightning bolt through me. *Takkan, don't you dare—*

I didn't know whether it was Takkan or the amulet that made him act, but he flung himself free of my brothers' backs—and plunged into the sea.

I lurched after him, but the pearl suddenly returned. It slammed into my ribs and yanked viciously, tearing me from my brothers. While Takkan disappeared into the depths of Lake Paduan, the pearl spirited me soundlessly away.

We soared over the water, under the black night, to a city so old it was the color of ash. A city sculpted of despair and decay.

Lapzur.

~

The pearl dropped me on a promontory overlooking the thrashing sea. I turned away from the water, only to find myself face to face with an army of ghosts, all standing silent as tombs. Something told me that they'd been awaiting my arrival.

My knees scraped against the ground as I pulled myself up. Behind the ghosts were the ruins of Lapzur: cracked walls and battered roofs, roads that came to ragged ends like broken bones, cemeteries of headless trees. Its skyline was low, except for one tower in the center, so violently tall it looked like a sword staked into the island's heart.

It was the same tower as in my vision. At the top was where I'd seen Takkan die.

I ran to the edge of the cliff. "Takkan!" I cried. "Kiki! Brothers!"

Only the pounding waves of the ocean answered. Kiki, Takkan, my brothers—they were nowhere to be seen.

The wind susurrated against my neck, and I whirled at the sound, trying to hold on to my courage despite the sinking feeling in my gut. More ghosts had gathered on the cliff.

Their presence turned the air sour. Strips of dead flesh dangled off their skeletal frames, white hair matted against their spines. Those with eyes greeted me with smoldering glares. Those without stared vacantly ahead through holes gouged in their skulls.

They began to soldier forward until I was cornered, steps from the edge of the promontory.

I didn't dare fight. I knew what would happen if they touched me: I'd become a ghost like them. Trapped here without a soul. For eternity.

"Khramelan!" I shouted, scanning the swarm of hollow faces for the half demon. Where *was* he? He'd just tried to kill me over Lake Paduan. He had to be here somewhere. I held the pearl high. "This is what you want, isn't it? Come and take it."

As my words echoed into the hollow night, the ghosts came to a halt. They craned their necks.

At first I thought Khramelan had come. But when I looked up and saw the smear of red light in the sky, a chill came over me. The color was strident—a gash in Lapzur's monochromatic landscape—and it was our only warning before the demons descended.

They took the form of many different beasts crudely patchworked together: gray-furred bears with lizard tails and webbed bat wings, tiger heads with snake bellies and shark fins. Some even had distortedly human features. But unlike the demons of Tambu, they were made of shadow and smoke, turning to flesh only when they touched the earth. They were bound to Lapzur the way the demons at home were bound to the Holy Mountains.

I dropped to my stomach and scrabbled for my knife. But

the demons ignored me and rushed for the ghosts—spearing their throats and clawing at their eyes.

High-pitched screams broke the island's silence. This was my chance to escape, but I couldn't look away. The demons and ghosts were at war, ripping at each other's heads and throats. What was happening?

I swear, Shiori, it's a miracle your curiosity hasn't gotten you killed. Kiki shot into view with the seven paper birds trailing. *What are you doing, gawping like that? Come with me—this way!*

Following her lead, I raced into the city, instinctively using the tower as my compass. Road after road led to a dead end, and I swore the buildings moved. I set one with sloping clay roofs and arched windows as my target, but try as I might, I couldn't reach it.

The city was a labyrinth, one that shifted so I could never find my way.

Only the tower never changed. Each time I saw it, I cowered, thinking of the fate it held for Takkan. But finally I looked at it head on. *Really* looked. At the top there loomed a winged demon, partly submerged in darkness. He was as still as the parade of statues that surrounded the tower's base, only I knew he was no statue.

"Khramelan," I whispered.

Kiki wailed. *Just give him his vile heart so we can find the others and get out of here!*

I was trying. I shouted his name and charged toward the tower, but I couldn't get past the God of Thieves statue guarding the stairs up to the base. Whenever I approached it, whorls of smoke misted out of his eyes, and the island's dark enchantment would take me back into the outskirts of the city.

It was as if Khramelan didn't want me to reach him. As if he wanted me trapped here, to be devoured by ghost or demon, whichever got me first. Now that the pearl was on Lapzur, it would find its way to him regardless of whether I lived or died.

My blood heated. Well, *I* certainly had a preference.

I leapt over a crumbled moon gate into an alleyway, ducking behind the half-crumbled wall to avoid detection. Hands shaking, I crossed my satchel over my body and took inventory. My mirror shard, the pearl—which had gone numb since bringing me to this accursed place—two dull knives I'd taken from Sundau.

I stole a glance at the tower. Was it safe to make another run? It wasn't. The demons were winning the fight, and now they stalked the streets, stomping on broken skulls that still moved and clutching clumps of white hair in their jaws like trophies.

A winged pair glided overhead. "We have our orders," they announced to all below. "Track the human. She can't be far."

The demons nodded their assent in unison. I had to move. Now.

I hoisted myself up a wall, using the broken bricks as footholds, then slid down onto the next road and ran.

I might as well have been a fly caught in a web. The two

winged demons had been trailing me, and they swooped down to corner me. One by one, demons plucked Kiki and my paper birds into the shadows, and before I could scream, I was surrounded.

"Silly Princess," the demons spoke as one, a perverted chorus of every voice I had ever known and cherished. "You don't want to go to the tower. The guardian is there, and he's no fun at all. Always kills everyone so quickly. . . . Come with us . . . we'll take you to the king. But first, a little sport."

The two demons shuddered, and their eagle wings shrank away as their tiger-striped faces shifted into Hasho's and Andahai's. They were expecting me to be shaken and disturbed, but honestly, I'd become inured to such trickery. And besides, I'd fantasized plenty of times about punching Andahai in the gut.

I slashed at Hasho first, cutting him across his chest. Inky smoke rippled from the wound. I knew it'd close up again soon, but I'd bought myself a few seconds.

I slammed my knife into the back of Andahai's skull and drove the blade in. The flesh yielded easily under my knife, as if his head were a boiled turnip.

Andahai snarled in pain. The demon snapped at my ankles, laughing as I jumped back. "We have a fighter," he growled. "Fighters have delicious souls. No wonder the king wants this one."

I had better things to do than listen to demon gossip. I spun, brandishing my knives at the fiends that had captured Kiki and my paper birds, but as soon as I freed my friends, the false Hasho and Andahai grabbed me once more. They were done playing, and they hoisted me with them into the air, slipping back into their original forms as they flew.

Two arrows fired from below pierced their wings. The demons howled in pain and dropped me—straight into the arms of a monster wearing Takkan's face.

His hand clapped over my mouth, smothering my cries. He pulled me into the shadows.

I struggled, but no claws dug into my skin, no teeth bit into my flesh. His heart was racing, same as mine.

I twisted to glance up at him. In the dim gray light of Lapzur, his features were harder and harsher than I'd seen before. But then I took in the birch bow hung over his shoulder, the hair slick with seawater, the thin gash of blood smudging his cheek.

My heart stopped. It was the real Takkan, not some illusion.

"You're alive!" I breathed in astonishment.

He inclined his head, making the smallest nod of acknowledgment. He led me down a narrow alleyway and into an abandoned house with crumbled gables. The demons had circled back and were marching toward our hiding place—with reinforcements.

"Where are you, bloodsake?" they growled. "We have your brothers surrounded. Come out before we tear apart their flesh, feather by feather, and feast on their souls."

I leaned back against Takkan, sliding my arm under his and restraining every urge to jump out and search the sky for my brothers. I wasn't a fool.

Once their taunts passed into the distance, I twisted to face Takkan. I was brimming with questions.

He put a finger to his lips. His face was gaunt; the amulet's strain on him here was painfully strong.

"The demons are under orders to bring you to Bandur," he whispered. "He's told them that if he, not the Wraith, acquires the pearl, he will free them from Lapzur."

I stilled. So *that* was why the ghosts and demons were fighting. The ghosts were loyal to Khramelan, while the demons were mutinying against him.

Demons are drawn to power, weak ones to strong ones, Oshli had said.

Yet something didn't make sense.

Why did Bandur think the pearl would choose him over Khramelan? True, it hadn't exactly leapt into Khramelan's heart the moment I'd set foot on Lapzur, but why?

What was I missing?

"I've been trying to find Khramelan," I said. I started out of our hiding place, but Takkan pulled me back.

"Bandur will be expecting you. Let me go first."

I shot him my fiercest look. "You promised you wouldn't do anything heroic and stupid, Bushi'an Takkan, yet you leapt into the middle of Lake Paduan like a fool. Don't think I've forgotten."

"Jumping off your brothers' backs wasn't heroic *or* stupid," he replied. "It was a calculated move to get Bandur away from you."

"You could have died!"

"But I didn't." He touched his nose to mine tenderly. "Nor did I leave you."

My lips parted. I wanted to argue that he was weakened, that Bandur would kill him. But trying to reason with him would only waste precious time. For I knew he would come with me no matter what I argued. So instead, I compromised. "We'll go together."

"Lead the way."

I grabbed his hand and ran. Our steps echoed behind us, and my breath grew heavy as we wove our way into the heart of Lapzur, making for the tower. Around us, the buildings flickered, but I ignored the dark illusions they tried to present.

At last, we approached the statue of the God of Thieves, and Takkan clutched Bandur's amulet over his chest. I didn't see the Demon King, but he had to be near. The amulet was tugging us forward, as if by a string. It allowed us to pierce the invisible barrier that had blocked me before, and we ascended the stairs to its courtyard.

There was Bandur, surrounded by Lapzur's demons. So it was true—he had won them over to his side.

At the sight of me, he picked himself off a dead and crooked tree and swaggered to life. He was smoke no longer but a fully fleshed wolf with gray fur, blood-red eyes, and razor-sharp claws.

"There you are, Shiori'anma, as expected," he said in greeting. "Why so sullen? I told the demons you were clever, and I even spared you their usual tormenting. Do you not appreciate my thoughtfulness?"

Takkan's hand went to Bandur's amulet. "Return!" he shouted.

Bandur's body convulsed, smoke fraying from his arms and pointed ears, but he resisted. "You bore it well, Bushi'an Takkan," he said calmly, "but alas, it has no power over me here—in the heartland of darkness!"

To prove his point, Bandur summoned the amulet back to his possession. He chuckled as Takkan and I stepped back, both stricken. "Let us pass," I demanded, hating how my voice shook. "Khramelan must be reunited with his pearl."

"I heartily agree, Shiori. A promise is a promise, after all. Don't let me keep you from honoring it." Bandur gallantly moved aside from the tower entrance. "Go on ahead."

These were the last words I expected from him.

It was a trap. I knew it was a trap, but what choice did I have?

"Don't," Takkan whispered.

I forged on, and together Takkan and I ascended the tower, scrambling up the hundreds of steps two at a time. When we finally reached the top, the pearl was humming louder than it ever had, and it beat like a drum against my hip.

The Wraith was still there, sitting on the edge of the roof. Darkness wreathed him, making it impossible for me to see more than the outline of his back as I approached.

I opened the satchel one last time for the pearl and held it up. "I have brought you home," I told it. "As I promised."

At the sight of the Wraith, the pearl swiveled out of my hands and emitted a brilliant light. But it did not go to him.

Instead, as fast as a comet, it shot out into the fathomless dark of the night.

Khramelan finally turned then and raised a thick black talon. In one swipe, he wrapped it around my waist—and leapt off the tower.

CHAPTER THIRTY-SIX

Up swooped the dragon, and the Thief's Tower disappeared beneath the clouds. Wind pelted my face, stinging my eyes so fiercely I could barely see.

"Khramelan!" I shouted, thumping my fists at him.

His beating wings overwhelmed my cries, and we flew higher, pivoting until his massive back was to the moon. There he hovered, allowing Imurinya's silvery glow to limn his dark form, from horn to talon, glinting off the jagged ridge of his spine.

Smoke curled along the tips of his wings, which folded seamlessly into the starless night, and each of his onyx-black scales was edged like the tip of a spear.

His eyes were mismatched, as Elang's had been. One was deep red and merciless—like a demon's. The other was blue as the sea—his dragon eye. In their centers glittered two broken pupils, each split in half like the pearl.

"Khramelan!" I shouted again.

This time, the dragon growled. The sound made his entire

body tremble and set my ears ringing. Everything hurt, as if I were inside a drum that had just been struck.

"That name is not yours to speak," he snarled. "Say it once more, and the dust of your bones will join the other imbeciles who dared trespass on my island."

"You would have killed me already if that were your plan," I said, finding courage by focusing on his mismatched eyes instead of his hulking figure. "But I came here with your pearl. It must be calling for you." *Wherever it is.*

He did not reply. He didn't even acknowledge that he had heard me, though I knew he had.

"Khramelan!" I cried. "Take your pearl back!"

In a rush that made my stomach leap, he lifted me, dangling me before his broken eyes.

"Did you kill her?"

Her? Is he talking about—my stepmother?

"No, no!" I cried. "I'm her—"

"It matters not who you are." His fangs grazed his bottom lip as he glowered. "You think because my darkness is lifted, I will take mercy upon you? Stupid, brazen girl. Never in all the ill-fated years of Lapzur has anyone dared bring another demon here."

My breath caught. Of all the preposterous things— Khramelan thought Bandur and I were allies? "You misunderstand."

"There is nothing to misunderstand. You are not the first to come here since *her* death. So long as I am guardian of this island, it matters not how darkly I see. I spare no one."

"No!" I shouted. "I brought Bandur here to make *him* the guardian—and free you!"

"So you gave him my true name, which has allowed him to lead my own demons against me? Helpful indeed!"

"That . . . that was a mistake," I admitted. "But if you reclaim your pearl—"

Khramelan's demon eye glowed noticeably brighter than the dragon one. "The pearl won't take me like this."

Like this? What did he mean by that?

"Channari wanted me to give it to you," I whispered. "She sent me. I'm her daughter."

Khramelan flinched at the name. There was power in names. Channari's still meant something to him.

"The pearl, Khramelan," I cried out. "You need to get it before Bandur—"

"As I said," he interrupted, "so long as I am guardian of this island, I will spare no one. Channari is dead. You will join her shortly."

He dropped me into the sea.

CHAPTER THIRTY-SEVEN

It was a special kind of terror—knowing that within seconds, my bones would shatter into a million pieces and my entire life would be reduced to a bloody puddle. Even now, I couldn't tell my gut from my lungs from my heart. My body moved faster than my thoughts, and all I could feel was the screeching panic that every moment might be my last.

"Kiki!" I wasn't ready to give up. *"Brothers!"*

No response.

My satchel slipped off my shoulder. I watched in horror as it disappeared into the mist.

Needles of icy spray rained upon my skin as I plunged for the furious sea. It hurt like demonfire, but I couldn't scream. My lungs felt like rocks in my chest, dragging me down, and all the air inside me had gone out. Even if I could yell, what use would it do? No one could hear or see me in this darkness.

I had nothing.

Nothing, except the magic in my blood.

It was excruciating, trying to concentrate while I fell. I stretched my senses, reaching out for something, anything: leaves caught in the fists of the wind, twigs from Lapzur's shrunken trees, specks of stone. A slip of silk.

My heart leapt. It was red silk from my birthday robes. I reached out to it, wrapping the strands of my magic—my soul—around it, pulling it closer, closer. In my delirious state, I could almost hear the cranes embroidered in the jacket bellowing and squawking.

Against the roaring wind, cranes *were* bellowing and squawking. *Real* cranes, their wings batting Lake Paduan's spray as they pierced the mist.

Could it be?

"Brothers!" I choked.

I saw Kiki first, sailing triumphantly at their helm. Moonlight clung to the silvery-gold patterns on her wings, making them gleam. She let out a whoop, and six cranes dove under me, catching me with their long necks. In their beaks were the remains of my birthday jacket and gown, spread just wide enough to hold me.

I rolled onto my old robes, clasping their folds. "Kiki, I've never been so happy to see anyone!"

I told you to always call for me first, she said smugly. *Can't have you dying. That'd be the end of me too.*

Something like a laugh climbed up my throat. "Thank you, my dearest friend."

It was like old times again, me clutching the edges of a tattered blanket, my brothers testing the fringes of life and death. But usually we were running away. Not so today.

"We have to go back!" I yelled to my brothers. But I needn't have said anything.

They were already on their way.

Sea foam curled up against the coast of Lapzur. From the air, the island looked like a ghostly hand, with five skeletal fingers extending off the mainland. Instead of bones and knuckles were escarpments and cliffs and veins of icy lake water that churned between the land masses.

Winged demons loomed over the crags as we approached the tower. They'd been slavering with anticipation for us to return, and once we pierced the fog into the island, they barreled forth.

The demons were fast. My brothers had no chance of outflying them, or of fighting them—not while they bore my weight. Andahai was commanding the other cranes to fly higher and faster and me to lie low. But I couldn't stay. I had to face Bandur.

I whistled for Kiki and the seven paper birds. Before I lost my nerve, I leapt.

Kiki and the birds caught my feet with their wings. They rearranged themselves into a tenuous bridge, and I sprinted to the tower.

I vaulted onto the roof, landing steps away from Takkan. He was floating over a stone well. Dark blood streaked his face, a gold and silvery light shimmering around his silhouette.

My stomach dropped. This was the moment I'd seen in the Tears of Emuri'en.

When Takkan saw me, his fingers uncurled at his side and his lips parted. But he didn't speak. He had not the strength.

"Let him go," I choked, spying Bandur lurking behind the well.

"Were I still human, I might be touched by this sentimental display," replied the demon. "But alas. Don't look so pained, Shiori. I haven't taken his soul yet. Not that the boy hasn't offered—he would give up his life for you. Unfortunately, it is not his life that interests me."

It was mine.

"Will you come to me now in peace?" Bandur asked mockingly as he flexed his claws over Takkan's throat. "Or will you spring at me in vengeance when I rip him apart?"

"Shiori," whispered Takkan hoarsely. "No!"

"Give me your word that no demon will harm Takkan," I said through gritted teeth. "Or my brothers."

Bandur touched his amulet. "This I can promise."

The chains holding Takkan vanished, and he dropped onto the flagstones. I didn't get a chance to go to him before the demons tossed his limp body to my brothers in the sky and invisible shackles bound my wrists and dragged me to the well.

"Takkan!" I screamed.

I was lifted high above the well and tipped forward so I could see the dark abyss swirling beneath, awaiting my fall. I couldn't twist, I couldn't turn, and when I tried to summon my magic, the chains around my neck tightened until I couldn't breathe.

Bandur stalked up from behind and pressed his cheek to mine. At his touch, I went hollow. His fur prickled like icy needles against my skin, numbing my every sense.

"I will say," he drawled, "all that time in the mountains gave me many hours to think." His amulet swung from his neck, taunting me as I reached for it in vain. "It was a puzzle figuring out how to deal with that pearl of yours, but my patience has been rewarded."

I wasn't listening. I was silently calling for the pearl, over and over. It had to help me against Bandur—the way it had against Lady Solzaya. But where was it?

"Are you paying attention, Shiori'anma?" Bandur tugged on his amulet, and the chains around me tightened until I arched with pain. He snickered. "I've been told you were not a diligent student of history. Yet you know what lies within this well, don't you?"

I had no choice but to look. The stones seemed to stretch forever—deeper even than the tower was tall. Gen had been so impassioned about the blood of stars, I'd expected something spectacular of its well. A dazzling display to eclipse the beauty of winter's first snowfall, to carry the colors of the universe.

But it looked like soup. Thick soup, bubbling slightly with the color and density of black sesame paste.

"The blood of stars is the source of the greatest magic in Lor'yan," Bandur was saying. "The greatest that mortals can attain, anyway." He cracked a wide, feral smile. "Within its well is the power of the gods, where oaths are made and bonds are broken. But we won't be needing its power today."

I went cold all over again. "What are you talking about?"

"The pearl, Shiori. Your promise was fulfilled the moment the Wraith laid eyes on it. Your bond to the pearl is broken—it no longer protects you."

Dread curdled in my throat. I couldn't speak.

"Don't believe me?" He swept his hand across the sky, as if indicating the pearl's absence. "Where is it now, when you need it most?"

Nowhere. The pearl was nowhere.

"That can't be," I whispered. "Khramelan hasn't taken it."

"As I told you before, the guardian of Lapzur has long succumbed to weakness and obsolescence. Even his own pearl doesn't recognize him. It doesn't want him. It is free to choose a new keeper."

"You're deluded if you think that'll be you."

"While you and the Wraith live, I do have some competition," Bandur admitted. "But once again, the solution is an exquisite gift of fate." He licked his lips. "Your soul is strong and bountiful, Shiori'anma. One of the finest I've ever smelled. It will sustain my army and give us the strength we need to slay a dragon." His voice rose as my heart sank. "And once you and Khramelan are dead, the pearl will be mine, along with the demons of Lapzur. We will be free."

Revelation punched me in the gut. "You *wanted* to come to Lapzur! You . . . you planned this?"

"Guilty," Bandur purred. "I even left you my amulet at the front of the breach so you'd be sure to find it. You really ought to thank me." He sneered. "My only regret is leaving your Kiatan demons to languish in the mountains. They were such hospitable hosts. It pained me to lie to them. But they were so desperate, so willing to believe anything I told them. Like you."

A shot of anger seized my muscles, and I struggled against my chains, trying to strike the demon.

"One little vision in the waters, and you were almost ready to give the pearl in exchange for the sentinel's life. I never understood what you saw in him, Shiori. But since you seem to value his life so highly . . ."

He jerked his chin at the demons standing guard behind him. "Find the sentinel and kill him. The cranes too."

"No!" I cried. "You made an oath, you—"

Bandur leaned close. "A word of advice," he said darkly. "Next time you make a bargain with a demon, be sure to seal it with your soul."

Hatred boiled out of me, and I convulsed, twisting with all my might. But I couldn't even touch Bandur. So I spat.

Bandur didn't flinch as my spittle dribbled down his cheek. "No need to rile yourself, Shiori. I kept my promise to you—you will still bleed." He seized my hand while I struggled and slowly, reverently, turned it palm up. "After all," he said as his nail skated deep across the veins in my arm, "nothing agitates the soul like pain."

Blood pooled bright against my skin. It ran in a thin river at first, staining the yellow trim of my sleeves, before branching off into little streams that trickled down my arm. My knees buckled as it rushed out of me, and the world swayed. *Focus.* I crushed my jaws together. *Focus, Shiori.*

"Always so good at keeping silent," said Bandur. "Don't be afraid to cry. There is no shame in agony."

I wouldn't give him the pleasure. My body hurt like demonfire, but I was used to holding in my voice. Used to holding in the pain too. *Khramelan!* I shouted in my mind. *Where are you?*

Bandur dragged his nails against the stone wistfully. "It's rather poetic, don't you think? I came here once to consume the blood of stars. My passage here marked the end of one life and the beginning of another. So it shall be for you."

CHAPTER THIRTY-EIGHT

My blood started to spill faster. It fell in swirls of crimson, spinning off like raindrops to the bottom of the well. Then Bandur hooked a claw into my heart—as Lady Solzaya had done once—and plucked out a strand of my soul. As it stole out of me, like a thread unspooling, my body began to shimmer silver and gold. One strand multiplied into dozens, spiraling down and down until I could see the darkness beneath begin to churn.

Bandur beckoned the demons closer, waving the strands of silvery gold in their direction. "Drink. Take her strength, and wield it against your former guardian. Once he is dead, I will free you all, and we shall take the world for our own. Let this be your last hour on this accursed island!"

Their growls went silent, and that was the most chilling sound of all. My eyes rolled back, and I held on to whatever reserves of strength I had left. I wouldn't give up without a fight.

"Her soul is too tough," the demons complained. "It won't cut."

"Then bite harder!"

The chain of Bandur's amulet rattled over the well, but I was too weak to even reach out for it. All I could do was whisper, "Khramelan. Khramelan."

I could feel the power of Khramelan's name as I spoke it, over and over until the wind carried it across Lapzur, until the sound sank deep beneath the stones of the tower, until the word edged along the dark that rippled inside the well of the blood of stars.

Bandur had wielded the name as a weapon against Khramelan to win over Lapzur's demons. I would use it to summon him back.

"Khramelan. Khramelan."

Bandur's ruff bristled, and the amulet sank into his fur, no longer humming. Something had caught his attention.

It was the pearl. It had returned, a crack of light slipping out of its broken center. The sight made me dizzy. The color in my world had washed out, and I could barely keep my eyes open.

"Go to Khramelan," I beseeched it weakly. "Reunite with him."

The pearl didn't respond. It skulked in my shadow, a numb observer.

"So you've come at last," Bandur said, turning to the pearl. He clasped it. "And you will choose me!"

"No," growled the guardian of Lapzur. "It won't."

The pearl flew out into oblivion again, the way it had when Khramelan crashed onto the tower. His wings alone spanned the expanse of the entire rooftop, and he dwarfed Bandur easily.

"Bow down," Khramelan ordered the demons, but they no longer obeyed. They were Bandur's to command now. And Bandur had commanded them to kill.

They shot up to attack, biting and gnashing at their former master. Khramelan knocked them away with his wings, but still they did not bow. More demons came, in relentless waves, and as formidable as Khramelan was, I sensed with dread that Bandur was winning.

Blood the color of tarnished gold smeared the folds of Khramelan's wings: deep, diagonal cuts and scratches that the demons had given him. In this condition, he couldn't hold them off forever.

The ghosts rose to Khramelan's aid, and in a soundless clash, a great battle was fought. Humans and cranes and paper birds had no place in this fight, would only die in this fight. But I couldn't do anything to help them.

"Get out of here!" I cried when I saw my brothers dip through the mist. They had returned, and bit at the invisible chains that held me.

"You fools," I whispered through the relief in my heart that they were alive. "Leave before the demons kill you. Go!"

Of course they ignored me. So did Takkan. My vision was too faint to make out his face, but I recognized the soft tap of his footsteps, the warmth of his hand on mine.

"I've one arrow left," he told me. "Your brothers and I think if I shoot Bandur's amulet, we can free you."

"Do it," I whispered. "I'm ready."

Takkan was swift. I couldn't imagine how he would pick

out one demon amid the horde, but I heard the snap of a bow-string and the whir of his arrow flying.

Then, a beat later, I dropped. His arrow had found its mark.

My brothers caught me as my fingers scraped against the lip of the well. Takkan reached for my arms, and Kiki grabbed my hair, the seven paper birds nipping my sleeves and collar.

Six princes, eight birds, and one lordling, all here to catch you from falling into a well, said Kiki, shaking her head at me. *Not your finest day, Shiori.* She landed on my shoulder, the glint of gold and silver on her wings shining brighter than ever. *But we've been through worse.*

"So we have," I replied as I took Takkan's hand and slowly pulled myself up.

Spinning out of a hidden corner, the pearl crept toward me.

I crossed my arms. "You're no more than a child, aren't you?" I scolded it. "I brought you halfway across the world, nearly getting killed a dozen times, and you're too afraid to go back to him?"

The pearl pulsed—rather ruefully, it seemed. It didn't come out of the shadows.

Irritation radiating from my core, I limped toward it and scooped it under my arm. "Your home is his heart, and his heart is your home. You don't belong to anyone or anywhere else. Whatever has happened between you, you two must sort out. Help him now—or Khramelan will die."

A wink of the pearl's light bathed me, which I took as

assent. "Come," I said to it firmly. "We know what we have to do."

There was little time. Powerful as Khramelan was, he couldn't defeat Lapzur's demons on his own. Already, Bandur was starting to howl his triumph.

I clasped the pearl in both hands. Its halves began to open, sparks of light dancing out like fireflies, but I didn't flinch. I wouldn't even blink.

"Free Khramelan of this island," I commanded the pearl. "He is the dragon you belong to, and you are the heart he seeks. The island and all its demons and ghosts will be Bandur's. Make it so."

In a searing burst, the pearl's power exploded over Lapzur. The pearl floated above my hands, spinning faster than ever, the great fracture in its center crackling like lightning.

That's enough! Kiki exclaimed. *The pearl—it's killing you!*

I barely heard her. Light and wind and heat gushed from the spinning pearl, and my back arched as it tugged at the glimmering silver-gold threads of my soul.

Brighter and brighter the pearl shone. My pupils burned just from looking at it, but I couldn't turn away. By now, its light encompassed the entire island, casting a net over every demon and ghost, even Bandur. I could feel it was on the verge of breaking, its center splintering a hair further with each moment to emit more light, more power.

"Stop," I told the pearl. "That's enough."

Of course it didn't listen. I reached up to hold it, to stop it from cleaving in two.

It was like holding an exploding star. Heat scalded my cheeks, and my hair came undone, flying wildly. Before my eyes, every strand turned silvery white . . . until I couldn't tell my hair from the light. Just before it became too much to bear, the pearl whizzed out of my grasp to Khramelan's side.

A firework of light rocked the sky, and the demons snapping at Khramelan's wings and stabbing at his flesh blew apart. Khramelan emerged from the frenzy, his claw curled around the pearl, and he let out a deafening roar.

The island's ghosts rose once more. They picked up their fallen skulls and hacked bones and thronged into one teeming mass that tore into the demons. Khramelan too found his strength.

Launching from the sky, he dove and landed on Bandur's back, pinning him to the ground. "You wished to become the King of Demons," Khramelan boomed. "Welcome to your domain. From now on, your power extends not past these waters. My reign is done, and now yours begins. I bind you to the Forgotten Isles of Lapzur."

Bandur began to writhe, his fur blurring into smoke as the magic of the island seized him. "No!" he cried. "No!"

The demons of Lapzur squealed as the feast began, and the ghosts stretched open their gaping maws and consumed each of them whole. Championed by the power of Khramelan's pearl, the ghosts wielded their cursed touch, and every demon on the island transformed into a ghost. It was a fitting punishment for betraying their former guardian—and ironic for Bandur, for now he would be the lone demon of the Forgotten Isles.

With magnificent strength, Khramelan grabbed Bandur by the tail and flung him into the well, sealing it shut with a flare of demonfire.

The tower made a great and terrible shudder as Lapzur claimed its new guardian.

Takkan and I had fled to the tower ramparts, but now the stairs were blocked by demonfire. There was no way out.

"We have to jump!" I shouted. My brothers hovered below, assailed by ferocious winds.

You'll never make it home without the basket, wailed Kiki.

I gritted my teeth. She was right, but getting off this island was my primary concern. I'd worry about Kiata later.

Hand in hand, Takkan and I dove off the tower.

As we plummeted toward the sea, my brothers swerved to catch us, but the winds were too strong and buffeted them off course.

Out of the darkness, Khramelan swooped into view. Takkan and I tumbled onto his wing, rolling from the impact until we hit against the spikes along his spine.

"Hold on!" I yelled to Takkan, grabbing a spike and clinging on with all my might.

Faster than the sons of the wind, Khramelan surged past Lapzur, piercing the mist that shrouded the Forgotten Isles. I held my breath, waiting until I caught sight of six crimson crowns in our wake.

Had every muscle in my body not been utterly spent, I would have let out a jubilant whoop. But I settled for a ripple of satisfaction in my heart.

We'd won. Bandur was now trapped on Lapzur—forever, I hoped. I watched as the island receded behind us, blanketed by sea and mist until it became as small as a grain, a speck. Then nothing.

"You should rest," Takkan said as we settled into the crook of Khramelan's wing. He ripped his sleeve to begin wrapping my arm. "You need to heal."

I parted my lips to protest, but Takkan cut me off. "I might not be able to cast sleeping enchantments, but I have a spell of my own."

I was mystified until he smiled and began to sing:

Let the sleep spirits come
to dance in your dreams.
May you dance with them
and awaken to a brighter world.

It was an old lullaby every child in Kiata knew, one I hadn't heard in years. Takkan's voice *was* magic, and it was what I needed.

For once I was obedient. I laid my head on his lap and let him cast his spell.

CHAPTER THIRTY-NINE

Dawn opened over the Cuiyan's pale waters. Khramelan had hardly said a word during the entire flight, but I recognized my homeland's shores long before I saw the fishing skiffs and shrimping boats dotting the sea and before the scent of summer pine sharpened in my nostrils.

It was the sun upon my brothers' feathers—its light tender and familiar, the same as it'd been a hundred other mornings when they were cursed. Its warmth seeping under their wings and lingering on their crimson crowns was what told me we had returned to Kiata.

I was half awake when Khramelan flung Takkan and me carelessly onto land. It was a rude awakening, and I nearly rolled off the cliff into the sea.

Takkan grabbed me by the arm, pulling me safely away from the brink. As my hair whipped about me in whorls of silvery white, I flew into his arms, laughing and laughing and unable to stop.

He was trying hard to look stern, to smother the clumsy smile that threatened his seriousness—and failing adorably. I didn't care that my brothers, who had landed on the same cliff, were barely a stone's throw away. I didn't care that Kiki was soaring above us, yelling orders at her new little legion of paper subordinates to poke the passing pigeons. All I cared about was Takkan.

I grabbed him by the collar—and kissed him.

Our lips were cracked from the wind and the cold, our hair mussed and windswept and badly in need of washing, and I was sure my breath was anything but sweet. And yet, as he pressed me against him, deepening our kiss with the same rawness and passion, I wished for every day to begin just like this.

"Someone must be feeling better," remarked Takkan when we finally surfaced for air. "What was that for? Not that I'm complaining . . ."

"For being you," I replied, planting more kisses on his nose, his cheeks, his teeth—by accident. We laughed together. "For being mine."

Takkan sat up and leaned on his elbow. With one strong arm, he pulled me close. "I was always yours. You just took a long time to see it."

"So I did," I murmured, a beat from kissing him again—

"Are you finished?" Khramelan interrupted.

Like children caught making mischief, Takkan and I quickly snapped to attention. I sprang to my feet just as Khramelan landed.

Sunlight dappled his back, gilding his scales. He tipped his head to face the sun directly. Taking in its warmth as if he hadn't felt it in years. And I realized he probably hadn't.

The pearl lurked in his shadow. Like his eyes, it was still broken. I started to ask him about it, but before I had the chance, he tossed a piece of glass at my feet.

"This is yours," he said gruffly.

It was the mirror of truth.

"Don't get in the habit of scattering your belongings in Lake Paduan. You won't get them back."

"Thank you," I said as I dusted the shard and wiped it on my sleeve.

Khramelan was moving toward the edge of the cliff, his wings already spreading, when I ran after him.

"Wait!"

He growled, and only narrowly did I avoid being hit by his wing.

I staggered, wisely leaving some distance between us. "My brothers . . . ," I began. "The pearl turned them into cranes so I could reach Lapzur. Please, change them back."

Khramelan barely glanced at the six cranes waddling in the sand. "What you did with the pearl is none of my concern."

"But—"

"You humans are all the same. I do you one favor, and you ask for another."

My jaw locked. "It isn't a favor. They risked their lives to help save you."

"Their lives will be better spent as cranes than as men."

Fury boiled in my throat, but I swallowed it, knowing it'd do no good to lash out at Khramelan. He'd only fly away, and my brothers would be trapped forever as cranes. So I chose my next words carefully. "Humans treated you like a monster, and you hate them," I said. "I understand that. They were the same to Channari."

Khramelan didn't flinch this time when I spoke my stepmother's name. Undeterred, I ventured a step toward him. "You were friends. A long time ago."

"Your stepmother made the mistake of thinking so," he replied. "It cost her."

"So I've heard," I said, remembering Ujal's words. "I'm sure she hated you. But you must have deserved it."

At that, Khramelan fell silent.

Sensing an opening, I said, quietly, "Why did you kill Vanna?"

Khramelan gave me a dark look. "Channari and I had an understanding," he replied, speaking through locked teeth. "I promised her I would not harm the Golden One, and that I would not claim the pearl in her heart until she died. I am immortal, after all. A few decades of waiting is inconsequential."

"What happened?"

"Obviously, I didn't wait." Khramelan stared straight into the sun. "I was tricked into attacking Vanna. Channari failed to protect her sister from me. She had a chance to kill me, but she hesitated. Another one of her mistakes."

My eyes fell on a stab wound in his chest. Unlike the wounds he'd incurred while fighting Bandur's demons on

Lapzur, this one had not healed. It was deep and old, pale against his night-black flesh, and gravely close to his heart.

So that was how Raikama's spear had broken.

"It still hurts from time to time," said Khramelan thickly. "As you say, I deserved it."

I was quiet, filled with pity and remorse for all the wrongs of the past—and a sad wonder that they had all led to this moment.

But a few things still didn't make sense. "If Vanna died, shouldn't the pearl have gone to you?"

"I broke my promise to Channari," said Khramelan. "When an immortal breaks his promise, he loses a piece of his soul. The pearl found me . . . unworthy."

I eyed the pearl as it lurked in the half dragon's shadow.

"It chose Channari. It burrowed itself inside her, forcing me to wait until she died." A pause. "She cursed me: 'Until I die, you will live in darkness.'"

"You felt it when she passed," I said.

"It was like waking up from a dream," Khramelan said. "The demons sensed my change too. That is why they were eager to follow Bandur."

I nodded, understanding. "What happened after my stepmother cursed you?"

"She disappeared to Kiata, and the Dragon King trapped me into being the guardian of Lapzur." Khramelan bared his teeth. "For that, I will never forgive him."

"You'll seek your revenge."

"I will go wherever I wish," he said. "That is what it

means to be free, after all. For sixteen years I have been the guardian of Lapzur. Bandur will be there for much longer."

"I hope he'll be trapped in that well forever," I said.

"He'll find a way out. Even demons deserve to be free. Most of them, anyway." A grunt. "Demon magic created Lor'yan, same as the gods and dragons, and they are owed respect. Something your ancestors clearly forgot."

I met his glare with a frown. "My ancestors trapped the demons to keep Kiata safe."

"And for their lifetimes it worked." He growled. "Humans are selfish and shortsighted. But consider this: when the demons finally break free, they will be wrathful. They will inflict a thousand years' worth of vengeance upon your land. Ask yourself then whether your ancestors made the right choice."

His rancor took me aback, and I drew an uneasy breath. "You sympathize with them."

"Of course I do. I am half demon," he said. "My kind is not without feeling, and I can feel my brothers in Kiata. They are in anguish. In pain."

So much for hoping Khramelan might use the pearl to seal the Holy Mountains once more.

I took a step back, wary of his wings and how easy it would be for him to knock me off the cliff into the sea. "I'm sorry for all that my ancestors have done," I said, meaning it. "But if what you say is true, I cannot let them be free."

"Then why should I free your brothers, when you will not free mine?"

It was a good question, and I swallowed. "I don't know if I can answer that," I replied honestly. "Except that you know what it's like to be cursed, to be trapped between worlds."

"I know what it's like to be alone," Khramelan said. "Your brothers will have each other."

"You had Channari," I said softly. "Her last wish was for me to return your pearl. She didn't hate you in the end."

The words undid his wrath, and for the first time, he folded his wings to his sides, allowing the sun to drench him completely.

Gathering my courage, I nudged the pearl toward him. "Please," I said softly.

He stared at his reflection in the pearl's dark surface— even in the sun, its fractured light spangled his pupils, as if they'd reaped a net full of stars. Then his shoulders heaved, and he let out a fearsome growl.

"You asked for my help, Princess. Pray you don't regret it."

With no more warning than that, he threw Takkan and me over his wing once more and blasted up into the clouds.

CHAPTER FORTY

I *more* than regretted asking Khramelan for help. As he swerved away from the ocean and wheeled over the heart of Kiata, my stomach made a hard swoop of fear.

"Stop!" I shouted, desperate to get Khramelan's attention. "Stop! People will see you!"

I didn't know whether he heard me, but it couldn't have been a coincidence that he immediately did the opposite, dipping lower and picking up speed. Now, as we tore past village after village, I could hear the screams.

No one had spied a demon in a thousand years, and I could only imagine the terror and panic this hulking nightmare with wings wide enough to block the sun would instill.

"This wasn't what I meant by helping," I said to Khramelan. "Enough! Enough!"

This is what you get for trusting a demon, Kiki screeched from behind. *Hurry and jump on your brothers' backs before the lunatic drops you from the sky.*

Even if I had wanted to, I couldn't. My brothers couldn't

match his speed, and no one could predict where he would go next. He swerved and swooped every other second, as if encouraged by the shrieks that followed.

Please let this be a nightmare, I thought. *Maybe the demons got me on Lapzur, and I'm still asleep.* On second thought, I wasn't sure I'd prefer that.

What I *was* sure of was that half of all Kiata had seen Khramelan by the time he came upon the Holy Mountains. There, he finally slowed.

As he hovered, ignoring the legion of armed and alarmed soldiers by the breach, I could feel the wind change. Rubble spilled down the mountainside, and the forest trees juddered. I couldn't tell whether the demons inside were reacting to me or to Khramelan.

"Do you hear them?" Khramelan asked me, breaking his silence. "DO YOU HEAR THEM?"

Shiori . . . , the demons whispered. *Release us. . . .*

"Yes, I hear them!" I shouted. "Now, will you stop?"

Father's soldiers spared Khramelan from answering. Spears shot up at his wings, one or two bouncing against his knuckles and nearly impaling Takkan and me—praise the great gods for Khramelan's thick skin. He spiraled away until the weapons could barely touch him. Arrows came next, barraging the clouds, arcing and falling like dying stars.

Khramelan sped across the forest and over the palace. Home washed by, a blur of blue-tiled roofs, vermilion gates, and lush gardens speckled with pink-blossomed trees. I didn't want to think about how I was going to explain Khramelan's joyride to Father.

Our aerial tour of Kiata was over, and Khramelan had the gall to land in the middle of Gindara's commercial square—right in front of the capital's temple. The crowds parted in waves, screaming in terror as they ran. Carts toppled, mules and horses crashed into streetlamps, and boats in the canals rammed into one another, crates of precious cargo tumbling into the water.

The earth shook under Khramelan's feet, and lanterns and rusted green tiles fell from the temple's eaves. He deposited Takkan and me on a spice merchant's tent.

"You asked for my help?" he said amid the screams. "This is it. You are welcome."

"How is this help?" was all I could manage. My gut had gone up to my throat, and I could hardly hold in my nausea from Khramelan's erratic flying.

He turned his back to me. "I've lived in a nightmare for sixteen years, and your country's been in a dream for a thousand. Everyone needs to wake up."

Those were the last words he spoke to me before he vaulted back into the sky.

Stones and oranges and melons pelted after the demon, and I knew that once he was out of sight, they'd be aimed at me. Takkan and I had started to climb down from the tent when something rose behind the striped purple canopy.

The pearl. Perhaps it was a trick of the sun, but I swore that it slanted its crack to face me, and its light winked. A "you're welcome" of sorts, for all the trouble it had wrought upon my life.

Then it blasted after Khramelan, who was hovering just

below the clouds, and enveloped the half demon in a flash of light. At last, he began to transform.

His scales suddenly shone, turning from black as onyx to blue-green like a forest of sapphire and jade. The spikes on his wings were sanded away, and when his wings parted, I saw that his eyes too had changed. They were mismatched—one a crisp blue, like the sky above us, and the other still red, though no longer the demon blood-red it had once been. The color was warmer, deeper. An eye befitting a dragon.

The arrows came to a halt, the flying stones and oranges too. Fear slowly turned into awe, and adults and children alike crawled out of their hiding places to watch the sight unfolding.

"A dragon!" they murmured. "A dragon!"

A few people began bowing, and priestesses and monks from the temple prayed aloud. Drums pounded, and bells chimed, and some of the elderly were even crying.

"The gods have returned."

"Quick, make a wish. Wish on the luck of the dragons."

"By the Strands, a demon transforming into a dragon? It's a sign from the heavens!"

I flattened my palms against the tent to lean forward. My attention turned from Khramelan to the people; I was astonished by how rapidly their reactions had changed toward him.

"I guess Seryu was right about how much people love dragons," I remarked to Kiki as she perched lightly on my head. A bittersweet tightness returned to my chest. "Can you imagine how smug he'd be if he were here? He'd be insufferable."

He'd be collecting coins, said Kiki. She pointed a wing

at someone on the street. *Look, one person already is. I bet they'll be selling dragon masks everywhere by the end of the day.*

That made me chuckle.

"Shiori," Takkan whispered, nudging my attention toward the temple pavilion where my brothers had landed. "Look."

They were changing too, their enchantment finally undone. For the last time, their feathers smoothed into flesh, and their wings melted into human arms and legs. The crimson crowns on their heads blackened into mops of hair that badly needed to be washed.

"Andahai!" I cried, jumping down and running. "Benben, Reiji, Wandei, Yotan! Hasho!"

Before my brothers could even rise to their feet, I threw my arms around Wandei and Benkai—the closest to me—and hugged them tight.

"Our bones are still stretching, sister," Wandei said with a cringe. "We could use a moment."

I let him go, but only to hug Yotan and Reiji. Hasho kept his arm behind his back, but he smiled so widely I did not ask what was wrong.

In the distance, Khramelan gave a small, almost imperceptible nod. His wings were gone, but he could fly, his body kept afloat by the pearl, whole at last, shimmering in his chest.

He launched into the sky, threading into the clouds and disappearing among the birds—the same as he'd done in Channari's memory.

Dragon and pearl had been reunited, my promise to Rai-kama kept.

As I turned to join the others, a silvery ray of light danced over my arm, illuminating a bracelet of red threads on my wrist. Two shone brighter than the rest: the one connecting me to Takkan, and the other . . . to an unseen end high above the clouds.

"Stepmother," I whispered.

One of her paper birds perched on my palm, head tilted inquisitively. It didn't speak, yet I knew what it was asking.

There came a pang in my heart. "I'm ready," I said.

With a nod, the bird snipped Raikama's thread from my wrist—and the wind swept it away. I wanted to chase it, but I held my hand back. I watched as, with one last shimmer, the thread vanished above me, never to be seen again.

I hugged my arms to my chest. I was on my own now.

Raikama's paper birds landed on my brothers' shoulders—and Takkan's. And together, they opened their wings to me.

You are without her, the gesture seemed to say. *But you won't be alone.*

With that, the wind blew them away, and the seven paper birds drifted after the threads they had cut. I knew they weren't coming back.

The pang in my heart faded as I slid between Hasho and Takkan. I took Takkan's hand, but as I reached for Hasho's, he flinched. He was fidgeting with the folds of his cloak and tucked his arm under it quickly.

"Did an arrow graze you?" I asked worriedly.

"No, no. I'm just not used to wearing clothes. Takes me a minute to forget my feathers."

Always a bad liar, Hasho. "Is your arm—"

"I'm fine." Hasho took my hand, squeezing it tight as if to prove himself.

I wasn't convinced, but the distant clap of firecrackers distracted me. Around us, children sang and danced down the streets, waving colorful fans. Merchants and vendors returned to their stalls, and another round of firecrackers exploded. A few kites glided over the parks. If I hadn't known better, I would have thought it was a festival day.

People were already cleaning up the mess Khramelan had made, and for every mistrustful glare that was sent my way, there came a dozen beaming smiles. I told myself to focus on the smiles and not worry too much about the frowns—at least until we got home to Father.

My shoulders relaxed, and I forgot what I had been going to say to Hasho. I swung him and Takkan toward the rest of my brothers, tangling my arms around theirs until we made a knot.

"It's been a long journey," I murmured, hugging my family close. Cheekily, I looked up at the seven young men. "Is there time to get lunch before we go home?"

Visiting Gindara was always a treat, and I grew giddy as we made our way through the city streets. It was even rowdier than usual, thanks to the scene Khramelan had made. But within an hour, the crescent-shaped fishing boats were drifting down the canals again, and most of the merchants had cleaned up their stalls and shops. Carts loaded with rugs and earthenware from the Spice Road trundled along, silk lanterns hung at every street corner, and children raced into alleys to feast on their favorite snacks.

I could already smell Cherhao Street. Devoted entirely to food, it was one of my favorite places in all of Kiata. Coincidentally, it was also on the way to the palace, so we couldn't avoid it completely. I considered that a blessing from the gods.

Yotan bought a straw hat to cover my white hair. It was far too large and I felt silly, but it would be wise to try and stay incognito. Though we were blocks away from where we had started, almost every person was still talking about the dragon in the sky. Word about me would spread. And quickly.

"We have to hurry," said Andahai cautiously. He and Benkai were observing the glances that came our way. "Don't be picky about lunch, Shiori. Anything will do."

"Everyone's so happy. What is there to worry about?" said Yotan. "Maybe Kiata *is* ready for magic again."

"They think they witnessed a miracle," replied Reiji, ever pessimistic. "That doesn't mean they're ready for flying paper birds and princes who turn into cranes."

"Or maybe they are," Wandei said, agreeing with his twin for once.

Reiji was still skeptical. "We'll see what the council thinks about what happened."

I kept quiet. I didn't want to worry anyone, but with every few steps a rush of dizziness went to my head. Food would help.

"Are you all right?" Takkan asked. While everyone else had been observing the reactions to the dragon, he had been observing me.

I fidgeted with my hat. "Just hungry. And tired."

Takkan's brows knit, and he let go of my hand. "I'll be right back."

I frowned after him. It wasn't like him to leave without explanation, but I didn't puzzle over his disappearance for long. Food was a glorious distraction, and my brothers and I were passing a rice cake cart.

My favorite rice cake cart, to be precise. I had patronized it often in my old life. The chef and I were on friendly terms.

Keeping my head low, I went up to her. "I'd like two dozen of the half-moon cakes with peach filling, a dozen regular with lotus paste, another dozen with red bean." I paused, re-membering that I was traveling with seven boys who hadn't eaten in over a day. "Make that *three* dozen with red bean. And the peanut ones too."

In spite of my hat, my enormous order gave me away. "Princess Shiori, is that you?" Mrs. Hana exclaimed. "It is, it is! Welcome back!"

So much for staying incognito. Within minutes, cooks from other vendors were hounding me. Someone pushed a tray into my arms, and soon it was piled high with skewers of sizzling meat, eggplant stuffed with bean curd and shrimp, noodle soups with floating fishballs, and dumplings that wriggled and danced as I walked.

"I didn't realize how beloved you were by Gindara's food district," Takkan remarked as he returned to my side. He smiled wryly. "I'm starting to think I should have given you cakes instead of a comb."

"No." I set down my food, looking thoughtful. "Cakes, I relish only for a minute. Your comb, I'll treasure forever." I wiped sugar off my fingers and winked at him. "But I will take cakes over flowers any day."

He laughed. "Noted."

"Now try this." I stuffed a skewer of cumin-spiced lamb into Takkan's mouth. "I bet you don't have this in Iro." I offered him a spicy dumpling that dripped with chili oil, and then, before he had a chance to finish it, I planted the plumpest rice cake—oozing with red bean paste—on his palm.

Don't I get some? Kiki asked. *Or am I to stick with paper worms?*

I laughed at her. It was like I'd gone back in time to last year's Summer Festival. I was the carefree Princess Shiori again, famed for her discerning food taste and ability to conquer every dish at the festival.

Soon it wasn't just the food vendors swarming me. City dwellers did too. The joyful ones blessed me and cried: "The luck of the dragons is with you, Princess Shiori."

The curious ones asked: "Can you tell us what happened with the dragon? Why was he a demon before?"

And behind the crowds, fearful stragglers murmured: "So

it's true, the princess *does* have magic. . . . Look at her hair, like a ghost! What can it mean if a dragon is here? The demons must be growing stronger. . . . I'll bet it's her fault. . . . That's what my friend in Yaman said, that the spell that made us sleep all winter, the fires that have been raging across the forest—it's all because of Shiori'anma."

I swallowed the last fishball on my skewer and staked it into an uneaten rice cake. My appetite was gone, and I tugged my hat firmly over my head and hustled my way through the crowds, hating that Andahai had been right after all. We needed to go home.

Benkai had been whispering to the sentinels patrolling the city, and on his signal, they dispersed the crowds. Trained soldiers that they were, Takkan and my brothers surrounded me and shuttled me to the edge of the city.

I kicked a loose stone on the road as we waited for a carriage to take us home. "Who would've thought I'd miss that bowl on my head so much."

"I think your appetite gave you away more than your face," Reiji teased. "Seven dozen rice cakes?"

"I was ordering for all of us," I replied. "But I should've been more careful. I'm tired. I wasn't thinking." Suddenly exhausted, I sank onto a bench beside the public garden. "Sorry, everyone."

Yotan smacked his lips. "Don't apologize. After a week of mice and worms, I'm still coming out of my bird brain too. Besides, you needed food. You were looking like a ghost. And not only because of your hair."

I combed my fingers self-consciously through the silvery knots in my hair, and Takkan sat next to me. "Ignore him," he whispered. "Ignore all of them."

He could always read me. I made the barest nod. *I'll try.*

A hemp pouch dangled from his wrist, reminding me to ask where he'd gone earlier. "You went shopping?" I asked. "I wondered why you mysteriously vanished."

"I bought bandages and ointment for your arm," he replied. "I know the palace will have better medicine, but we're still an hour from the gates at least. And you lost a lot of blood." He started to open the pot. "This will help."

I wrinkled my nose. "Smells awful."

"That's why I waited until you'd finished eating."

I glowered, but much as I hated to admit it, the ointment really did help my arm feel better. When he was finished, I dipped my fingers into the medicine and smeared it over the cuts on his face. I cupped his cheek and said softly, "I'm not the only one who got hurt—so I'm not the only one who should smell like dung."

Takkan shook with laughter, and he kissed my fingertips, dung smell and all. He was about to say something more when Andahai ruined our interlude.

"Not in front of family," my oldest brother said crisply, and I swore Takkan's back went straight as a spear.

I crossed my arms. "Oh, come now. You'd be the same if Qinnia were here."

"It's time to go," said Andahai, ignoring me. "The carriage is nearly here. You need to rest, Shiori. We all need to rest."

Why did he flick his eyes at Hasho when he said it?

"What did I miss?" I glanced back at my youngest brother. He'd been quiet this whole time, keeping to himself and eating sparingly. A stray cat had trotted up to his side, and a sparrow perched on his shoulders, nibbling on leftover crumbs. He'd always been my most sensitive brother, and I assumed he needed extra time to recover from his transformation. "Is Hasho—"

"He's fine."

Andahai's curt response triggered my suspicion, and before my brothers could stop me, I pushed my way to Hasho's side.

"It's too hot to be wearing a cloak," I said, tugging on the heavy fabric draped over his shoulder. He flinched, and finally I understood why he had retreated from our company.

His right arm—the very one that Bandur had cursed—was still a wing. And black like a pocket of night.

"Hasho!" I exclaimed in shock.

Hasho lifted the wing, letting its ends peek out of the cloak. Its feathers were long and tapered, in a cruel imitation of fingers. A bird's arm, not a man's. Never could it grasp a cup of tea or write or draw or even fit into a sleeve.

"It's one arm," Hasho said, folding the wing to his side. "It could have been worse." He managed a half grin. "I only need one hand to beat Reiji at chess."

"Oh, Hasho," I whispered, a sob racking my chest. "Why didn't you . . . why didn't you say something? Maybe Kiki can track Khramelan down, maybe it's not too late and he can—"

"Nothing can be done," my youngest brother interrupted. "I've known it for some time. I've accepted it."

"But—"

Hasho stroked my cheek with his feathers. "This is hardly the worst of outcomes. I can still speak to the birds—and Kiki."

His tone was gentle, but firm. *Don't argue,* it pleaded.

My brother retracted his wing. "At least people will believe us when we tell them we spent our days as cranes."

"People are already starting to believe," I said through the ache in my throat. "And thanks to Khramelan, we'll have to confront that sooner rather than later."

I'd hoped Khramelan might help me solve Kiata's demon problem, but he'd only aggravated them beyond measure. I couldn't ignore the demons forever.

"Is it our right to keep them imprisoned?" I murmured, almost to myself. "Magic . . . and the demons. Maybe that was our ancestors' mistake in the first place."

"You can't free the demons," said Reiji. "That'd be madness."

It would. And yet . . . I couldn't bear the thought of Kiata suffocating for another thousand years without magic.

Maybe I was being selfish for thinking of how Hasho's wing would brand him the rest of his life, of how a touch of Raikama's curse would always haunt my brothers, of how *I* would never be able to traipse down Cherhao Street—or anywhere—without hearing whispers that I was a witch or a monster. Of how I so desperately wanted home to be home again.

Maybe I was being foolish for thinking I played any role in Kiata's fate at all.

Yet if I did nothing, who would? Was it worse to be a kite with no anchor, wandering lost on the wind, or a kite that didn't dare seize the wind and never flew? One at least had a chance of finding home, however slim. The other had none.

As I stepped into the carriage, I knew which kite I had to choose.

CHAPTER FORTY-ONE

"You sent for me?" My voice wobbled, and I bowed as low as I could, the way I used to when I knew I was in for a stern reprimand. The only time Father ever summoned me alone to his private chambers was when I had done something inexcusable—and riding a dragon into the middle of Gindara put all my prior mischief to shame.

My imagination went wild: I braced myself to be banished, married off to an A'landan prince, or put in a cell and only fed mushy rice with bitter tea.

"Are you rested?" said Father, interrupting my thoughts.

From his harsh tone, I knew that wasn't an invitation to rise. "Yes."

"Demons of Tambu, daughter," he grumbled then. "The commotion you've made in the last few hours . . ."

I'd never heard my father curse before. "I'm sorry. I know it's my fault. . . . I shouldn't have—"

"I want to see your arm," he said. "Your brothers told me what the demon did. That he . . . he injured you."

That wasn't what I expected.

I rolled up my sleeve carefully and undid my old bandage. I'd bathed since my return, but I still smelled strongly of the ointment Takkan had slathered over my skin, and it prickled my nostrils.

Father's jaw tensed at the gashes on my arm. It was a good thing Bandur was already locked away, because he looked ready to stab the demon and chop him into bits for stew.

"Your hands, too?" Father asked.

"Those are old wounds," I explained of the scars on my fingers. Usually in his presence, I hid them under my sleeves, but now my hands moved while I spoke, and the scars on my fingers tingled. I'd stopped paying attention to them sometime on my journey to Ai'long. They'd served as a painful reminder of the price I had paid to save my brothers. But lately, I was starting to see them in a different way—as a sign of strength and all that still must be done.

"The bandages will need to be changed," Father said. There was a bucket of hot water behind him, which made me realize he'd been waiting for me.

I started, but Father blocked me. "I'll do it," he said.

He chuckled softly at my surprise. "I wasn't always an emperor, you know. Like your brothers, I trained to be a sentinel. My father made sure I laced and polished my own armor, scrubbed my own bowls, stitched my own wounds— same as any other soldier. Hold still, this may hurt."

I bit down on my lip while he cleaned my wound, fixing my attention on the wooden window screen.

Father's quarters were sparse, with a simple rosewood

table, a matching shelf filled with scrolls and books, a long divan embellished with cranes and orchids, and a bronze mirror that had been in the palace since the reign of Kiata's first emperor.

After Mother died, his quarters became his private sanctuary, and guests were permitted only into the forecourt. Even my brothers and I could count on one hand the number of times we'd been invited into Father's residential apartments.

Yet here I was, shedding bandages onto a woolen carpet gifted by a king of Samaran, my wound stanched by raw silk that'd traveled the Spice Road from A'landi to Kiata, and my flesh sewn together by an emperor of the Nine Eternal Courts.

I couldn't help thinking how, without the armor of his ceremonial robes and his gold headdress and medaled belts, he looked simply like a father who'd stayed up too many nights worrying about his children.

"Relax those shoulders, Shiori. Did you think I sent for you to punish you?"

"It's no more than I deserve."

"Many would agree with you."

The ministers, obviously. Likely most of the court too. The whole of Kiata, actually. "Have you spoken to the council?" I asked carefully.

My question made Father's face harden once more. "It has been dissolved for the time being." A pause. "While you were away, Hawar confessed that *he* poisoned you."

"Hawar *confessed*?" That shocked me.

"He said his actions were justified," Father said with a dry laugh. "After you seemingly attacked me in the Holy Mountains, he thought it safe to admit that two cultists had approached him months ago with poison. He said he had refused to even consider harming a princess of Kiata, but when you showed signs of a magical affliction . . . he said he had no choice but to protect the realm."

I shivered. "What's happened to him?"

"He was executed yesterday," Father replied without feeling. "His accomplices have not been named, but I have faith your spectacle in Gindara will provoke a few to come forward."

I said nothing. I was wondering how many in the palace secretly agreed with Hawar that I was a problem. Maybe that was why the mirror of truth had not shown me my assassin's identity—because he hadn't acted alone.

Father made a grim face. "There are few I trust these days."

I could hear the words left unsaid: *Can I trust you, daughter?*

I flinched. "I'm sorry I lied. About going to Iro. About everything."

"Your lies I'm used to," said Father. "But not your brothers'."

The rebuke made me wince, but I deserved it. I bowed even deeper.

After a pause, he asked, "Where did you really go?"

"To the Forgotten Isles of Lapzur," I replied. "Raikama asked me to go there to fulfill her last wishes. I took Bandur with me, and he is trapped there. He will never plague Kiata again."

"That is welcome news," said Father. His tone betrayed nothing, and I didn't bring up how Bandur had possessed him in the Holy Mountains. I understood my father's pride; that would be a secret that died with me.

He gestured at my hair. "Is this the price you paid for our deliverance?"

I offered a small smile. "I'm not as changed as I look. Still impertinent, still not good at following instructions."

"I believe it." The emperor brushed his hand over my forehead, the way he had when I was little. "It'll take some getting used to, but it suits you. You always were a child of winter."

His hand fell to my shoulder. "No more lies. No more secrets. Can you promise me that?"

I took a step back. "Baba," I said quietly, instead of answering, "would you have protected all the bloodsakes the way you've protected me—or do you only care because I'm your daughter."

The question took him by surprise. He inhaled. "If I am honest, usually by the time word of the bloodsakes reaches the emperor, they are dead."

Perhaps that was why I'd been chosen this time. Because unlike the others born before me, I had the emperor's ear. I had a voice.

I had to use it.

"I will be honest too," I said. "I'm going back to the breach. I want to speak with the demons."

"Have you lost your senses?" Father's eyes constricted. "You are not permitted anywhere near that evil place. A law you knew well the first time you broke it. Break it again, and I will have no choice but to punish you."

"Had I stayed put, Bandur would still be in Kiata," I argued. "Let me deal with the rest of the demons."

"Demons killed your stepmother. I will not have them kill you too." The circles under Father's eyes deepened, and I noticed for the first time how much he had aged in the past year. "If you have children one day, you will understand. When you and your brothers disappeared, I would have given anything—my crown, my kingdom, my life—to have you all safe."

A lump hardened in my throat, and I did something I'd never dared to do even when I was a little girl. I reached for Father's hand, clasping it tightly.

I can make us safe again, I wanted to assure him. *I can stop the demons.* But those words wouldn't come.

Because no matter what I did, things could never go back to the way they were. The home I'd yearned for when I was under Raikama's curse was gone, and all I could do was build a new one. Somehow.

"Kiata is my home," I said instead. "Let me fight for it."

Father's eyes were mirrors of my own, reflecting the same stubbornness and resolve. "I'm not a fool, daughter. I understand what happened to Hasho." His fists clenched, and it took a long breath for him to regain his composure. "You could suffer far worse."

"Even if that is so, I am not afraid. This is what I was

born to do. For so long, I've ignored my role as a princess—a *daughter* of Kiata. Let me do my duty now."

Father's hands dropped to his sides. He knew I was using his old words against him. "I miss the days when you hid from your tutors in the trees. I didn't worry half as much about you then as I do now."

My mouth quirked into a knowing smile. "You won't keep me from the mountains?"

"I want to," he said thinly. "But I know you, Shiori, and I know you have your brothers behind you. Young Lord Bushi'an too. You've already sneaked out once before; you'd do it again without question. So better I equip you all with what you need than have you confront these demons unprepared."

"Thank you," I said, meaning it. Then my brow furrowed as I thought hard. "Are the priestesses captured from the mountains still alive?"

"One is . . . barely."

I almost pitied the woman.

"Could you arrange an audience?" I asked. "I wish to speak to her."

The priestess Janinha was a specter of the smug old woman I'd encountered in the mountains. Patches of blood crusted her cheeks, and her hair hung about her in straw-like clumps, marbled with dirt and mud. Without her wooden staff, she looked too weak to do harm, but I wasn't fooled. Not when her eyes cut into me like two scythes, freshly sharpened and devoid of remorse.

Are you sure I can't come too? Kiki had asked. *I didn't get to peck Hawar's eyes out—at least let me have at this priestess's.*

I almost wished I'd relented. But it was best if I spoke with the priestess alone.

The guards dragged her into the room and thrust her upon a black cotton sheet laid on the chamber's floor— placed there to protect the parquetry from her blood. There were no windows, but lantern light illuminated the welts and lashes on her sallow cheeks.

Yet beneath her hard gaze, I somehow felt like *I* was the prisoner.

"My father has sentenced you to death by a thousand cuts," I said coldly. "Answer my questions truthfully, and I will see to it that you are granted a merciful fate."

"I've been waiting to see you, Shiori'anma," rasped Janinha, completely ignoring my offer. "What is it you wish to know?"

I wouldn't let her dark eyes chill me. I said: "You possess knowledge about bloodsakes. Have the ones before me always been able to hear the demons?"

A whistle leaked from the gaps between the priestess's teeth. It took me a while to realize she was laughing. "Do not speak as if you can fight your fate," she replied. "Princess or not, you are prey, Shiori'anma. Either you die for us, or you die for them."

"Answer the question," I said harshly.

"Yes, all bloodsakes are drawn to the mountains. Do you think you are the first to spill blood for the demons?"

Wasn't I? My lips twitched with curiosity. She had my attention.

"The last time was forty years ago. The bloodsake before you was a silly girl who had no idea what she was until it was too late. When the demons lured her to them, she thought they were the gods speaking to her, promising her wealth and power and beauty. She gave her blood to them, creating a breach. A much smaller one than yours, but all the same . . . We let her do it. People were beginning to forget the wickedness of demons, and nothing prods the memory like a bit of blood.

"We lit her entire village on fire while she was sleeping. We told her it was the demons she had freed, and unlike you, she knew she had to atone." The priestess's face glowed. "We were only too happy to help."

"You monsters . . . ," I whispered.

"With her ashes, we sealed the mountains before a single demon could escape." The priestess dipped her head. "Such we can do again—with you, Shiori'anma."

I ground my teeth. "You *murdered* an innocent girl—an entire village! And framed the demons for your own sins—"

"If not for what we did, many more would have perished," Janinha said, cutting me off. "My order understands that sacrifice is necessary. We are willing to die for the good of Kiata. Are you?"

"The good of Kiata," I said. "What would you know of that?"

The guards wrenched her off her knees to take her away, but she reached into the back of her mouth and made a sharp twist. Out came a blackened tooth, covered in blood and rot.

She crushed it between her fingers. My heart gave a lurch as it crumbled in her palm, like dark sand. "Stop!" I shouted.

The guards unsheathed their swords, but the priestess tossed the ashes high, and their blades froze midswing, the edges clinking against her chains.

"No need to get up, Princess," she croaked as I sprang. "I am nearly finished."

One by one, the bronze lanterns nodding along the walls went cold. And as darkness wreathed the chamber, she spoke her last words: "If you will not enter the fire, then, come the dawn, Kiata will burn in your place. Only your ashes will save us."

With that, the guards were released. A second before their swords sank into her flesh, the priestess fell dead.

CHAPTER FORTY-TWO

"Maybe she was bluffing," said Reiji when I reported what had happened. "It wouldn't be the first time the priestesses tried to deceive you."

"She cast an enchantment," I insisted. "There was power to her words, like when Raikama cursed us. She gave her life for it."

"You think it's a curse?" Benkai asked.

I nodded.

Benkai believed me. "Her order has recruited many followers since Khramelan's sighting yesterday," he said. "They blame any destruction on the demons, so it's likely that whatever malice they have planned will start near the breach. I'll ride out and warn my men. We'll search the area and evacuate the nearby villages."

"Be careful," I warned him. "They still have ashes from the last bloodsakes." Ashes that gave them magic, enough that I worried Janinha's promise to make Kiata burn *would* come true.

"Noted, sister."

Wandei leaned forward, setting down the paper he'd been folding into a fan. "If it really is a curse, then finding the other cultists won't prevent the inevitable. What can we do if Kiata does catch fire like she warned?"

I hesitated, nervous to speak what was on my mind. "Magic is what fuels her curse, so only magic can stop it."

"But how?" asked Wandei.

I turned to Benkai. "When you are at war, who do you seek to be your ally?"

"The enemy of my enemy," he replied easily.

"Exactly," I said. "The priestesses' enemies are the demons. I've . . . I've been thinking I should talk to them."

I expected my brothers to disagree, to argue with me and tell me it was a dangerous idea. My expectations were met. All six of them began talking at once, but I could hardly hear what they were saying. For they weren't the loudest voices in my head. That belonged to my bird.

What are you possibly going to say to them? Kiki trilled. *"I'm sorry, but would you mind slaying all of my enemies for me? As a thank-you I'll bring you cakes for the next thousand years while you remain imprisoned in the mountains. Oh, and please stop making the earth quake whenever you feel angry about being locked up— it's frightening the villagers and waking them up in the middle of the night."*

It did sound ludicrous when she put it that way, but still . . .

"What *will* you say to them?" Hasho echoed Kiki's question.

"Honestly, I don't know," I admitted. "I thought I'd have more time to think about it."

Wandei swatted his fan at a fly buzzing over Yotan. "According to the priestesses, you have one day. If you insist on this course of action, I'd say you better get thinking."

⁓

I went for a walk to clear my mind. Autumn had arrived overnight, yellow crowns staining the trees and frosty dew clinging to the eaves of the Cloud Pavilion. Takkan was supposed to be waiting for me, but I heard him laughing with two children beside the carp pond. Both hung at his sides, pulling his arms and speaking so quickly I could only catch the words *princess* and *story*.

When they saw me, they jolted. Their eyes went first to my hair, loose and unpinned and entirely silvery white, then to Kiki, who sat on my shoulder, her paper wings beating as vivaciously as a real bird's. They waved shyly before remembering to bow.

I waved back, smiling cautiously until they started to giggle. For what reason I couldn't possibly fathom.

"That's Princess Shiori, isn't it?" the girl whispered to Takkan. "Where's the bowl on her head?"

He'd told them about the bowl? No wonder she was staring.

"Will you tell Suli and Sunoo what happened to the bowl?" Takkan asked me.

"It broke," I said bluntly. I wasn't good at stories.

"When she found a way to end the curse," Takkan said, picking up from my words, "the bowl shattered into a hundred pieces, saving Shiori'anma from a horrible, wicked fire."

"I'm glad," said the boy, clapping his hands. "But why's her hair white?"

"From chasing ghosts," I replied. "And battling demons." I bared my teeth and made a monster face. The children laughed. Then they chased gleefully after Kiki—not bothered at all that she was a magical flying paper bird—and I beckoned Takkan to the footbridge.

"Sunoo and Suli," I mused, gesturing at the pair. "Friends of yours?"

"Good friends," replied Takkan. "Their father, Mr. Lyu, is the head messenger."

Takkan had known the gardener's name too. "Do you know everyone in the palace?"

A shrug. "I've become acquainted with some of the staff. They've been kind."

"Unlike your fellow lords and ladies?"

From his silence I could already guess. Gindara's court was full of sycophants and status seekers, and I imagined it hadn't been overly welcoming to my rustic, Northern-bred betrothed. Not even my brothers would have done what Takkan had done for me last winter; he'd opened his home to me when he'd thought me a humble tavern cook and had treated me no differently than a highborn lady. For a lord, even of the third rank, he was hopelessly guileless and unassuming. The court must have devoured him whole.

And spat him out.

"Don't worry," I admitted. "I think they're intolerable too. Why do you suppose my best friend is a paper bird?"

"And all the cooks on Cherhao Street?" Takkan teased.

"Exactly." I leaned over the bridge, watching Suli's braids bounce across her shoulders as she chased Kiki around the pavilion. From the back, she looked like Takkan's younger sister.

"You must miss Megari," I said. "You haven't seen her in over half a year."

"We exchange letters often. That's how I got to know Suli and Sunoo—they take my letters to their father in exchange for stories."

"What kind of stories?" I probed. "I want stories too."

"Most were about you."

Oh.

"I missed you when you were in Ai'long," Takkan said. "Telling stories about you helped."

I swallowed, unable to tamp down the warmth ballooning in my chest. "I'm still angry with myself for losing the sketchbook you gave me," I confessed. "But I'll never lose your letters. I've memorized half of them already. I've been rereading them every night to help me sleep."

"You bruise me, Shiori," said Takkan wryly. "They're that dull?"

Grinning, I mimicked a young Takkan: " 'My sister found a centipede in the granary this morning and—thinking it was a sweet and harmless caterpillar—brought it to lunch. My ears are still ringing from how loudly Mother screeched.' "

Takkan's palm went up to his face. He looked like he wished he could jump into the pond. "Did I write that?"

"You did." My grin turned wicked. I loved seeing him uncomfortable, then chasing that discomfort away in the next breath. I scooted closer until our arms overlapped on the wooden railing. "Your letters are a treasure. When I read them, I feel a little less . . . lost. I feel like I'm where I belong."

I stared into the water, watching orange-and-black-spotted carp nibble the supports of the bridge. "Your heart is your home," I murmured. "Until you understand that, you belong nowhere."

"You said that to the pearl when we were on Lapzur," Takkan remembered.

So I had. I'd been so desperate to get the pearl to listen to me, I'd forgotten that the words came first from Elang. A message from one half dragon to another. I hoped Elang would find his home one day.

"I'm still not sure I understand what it means for me," I confessed.

A shadow came over Takkan's eyes, and I could tell that his thoughts had returned to our present conundrum. He turned to face me. "What can I do to help?"

The simple question, so unbidden and so earnest, made me look up from the water.

"I don't know what to do about the demons," I admitted. "If I keep them trapped, magic stays trapped too. But if I free them . . . I unleash chaos upon Kiata."

"What do you think you should do?" Takkan tipped my

chin up. "I know you, Shiori. You think there's another way. Tell me."

I inhaled a shaky breath and gathered my courage. "I . . . I can't forget the way Khramelan spoke about them. He felt . . . sorry for them. It makes me wonder whether I can reason with them. Maybe even ask for help."

Takkan blinked in surprise. "Well, they can't be any less agreeable than the priestesses."

That got the slightest smile out of me. "True."

I loosened the comb from my hair. I hadn't brought Takkan's gift to Lapzur for fear that I'd lose it, the way I'd lost his sketchbook, and I held it now, admiring the cranes, the rabbit, the moon painted on its spine. "I never asked—did you paint this?"

"Yes," answered Takkan, clearing his throat. "It was Megari's idea to include the rabbit. She said it'd bring luck . . . and the cranes would watch over you." He paused. "She's been folding them like you taught her. She begs for you to come home and enchant them to life. Apparently, Pao has been giving her grief about sneaking out of the fortress, and she could use an army of paper birds on her side."

An army of paper birds on her side. My eyes went round, and I straightened, unable to contain the excitement suddenly bubbling in my chest. "Takkan—I think that's it." I clutched his hands, buzzing now.

"What is?" Takkan asked.

"Can you get me a thousand sheets of paper?" I said. "Send another letter to Megari too. Tell her she's a genius."

434

"We're going to fold paper birds," I announced to the small group that had gathered in my chamber. Takkan, my brothers, and Qinnia sat in a semicircle on the floor, stacks of paper laid out before each of them. "A thousand paper birds, to be precise."

Qinnia peeled a page from her stack. "What are you going to do with all of these birds?" she asked. "Make a wish?"

She was referring to a legend we all knew. To honor Emuri'en and her cranes, the gods were said to grant a wish to anyone who sent a thousand birds to heaven. I'd spent an entire winter folding paper cranes, hoping to gain the gods' ears and break my brothers' curse.

But the gods had been silent for centuries. I no longer trusted them to listen.

"No wish," I replied. "The birds will serve as my army against the priestesses—and the demons, if needed."

From Benkai's and Reiji's frowns, their skepticism was clear: *An army of paper birds?*

Yes, *my* army. I'd need magic to counteract the curse upon Kiata. The Tears of Emuri'en were near the breach—I'd draw upon their power if my own magic wasn't enough, and the birds would help me spread it.

"Trust me," I said before going on to explain the plan.

Over the afternoon, I taught them the proper method for folding paper cranes. Wandei caught on the quickest, and then he started experimenting with the folds and made paper swallows and doves and eagles, even a phoenix. He taught the variations to Yotan and Reiji, who decided they were too complicated and stuck to making cranes. Meanwhile, Benkai, Andahai, and Takkan were furiously competing to see who could fold one hundred birds first.

Qinnia folded the smallest ones I'd ever seen. A dozen fit easily on her palm. "You'll need soldiers of all sizes," she explained.

In the corner, Hasho sat with a spool of black thread, knotting eyes that Qinnia would later sew onto the birds.

"So they might see," he explained when he caught me looking. "Like Kiki."

My paper bird beamed at him. All day she had flitted to and from his side, and it warmed me to see how close they had become.

Together we worked, and by evening we had a thousand birds.

A thousand and one, Kiki reminded me. *Don't forget, I'm the first.*

"How could I forget? You'd never let me."

True enough. She pinched me by my hair, dragging me to the nearest window. *Look at all the stars. See the seven-pointed crane? I've been spreading rumors about it.*

"What sort of rumors?" I said narrowly. "That constellation is Emuri'en's sacred crane."

Not anymore. Now it's you and your brothers. You've one star each.

"That's—"

436

I'm only making sure you're remembered, Kiki interrupted. *If you are, I will be too.*

"Looking after your own interests as always, I see."

I expected Kiki to harrumph, but she took on a serious tone I'd never heard before. *I don't want to be forgotten,* she admitted. *I don't even know what it's like to be a real bird.*

Her earnestness caught me off guard. "I thought you didn't want to be like other birds," I said mildly. "Feathers molting, having to feel hot and cold, eating worms . . ."

A bird can change her mind. Not about the worms, though.

"Kiki . . ."

You should go back inside. Be with your family. Kiki waved her beak toward my family. Andahai opening a wine gourd to celebrate. Yotan playing familiar tunes from our childhood on the flute. Reiji and Benkai loudly complaining how sloppy their cranes looked compared to Takkan's.

Keep a lantern on for me, she said.

Before I could reply, she dove out the window. With a smile perched on my lips, I set a lantern by the window and counted the seven stars of the sacred crane.

Maybe it was my imagination, but tonight they seemed to burn brighter than all the stars in the entire sky.

CHAPTER FORTY-THREE

I smelled the fires at dawn.

The air had gone thick, and I woke up coughing and kicking off my blankets. Seconds later, the palace bells clanged, and the war drums soon followed.

I hurried to the window, and my chest constricted as I searched the horizon. It was the darkest dawn I'd ever seen; the sun was pale enough that I could stare at it without blinking. Clouds splattered the horizon like dark ink. I didn't have a view of the Holy Mountains, but the billowing smoke guided my eyes to a flare of unnatural red light.

The forests were burning. And not with any ordinary fire. The flames were a garish red, as black at their core as a starless night. It was a blaze I knew all too well, one that could not easily be quenched, except by magic. Demonfire.

If you will not enter the fire, then Kiata will burn in your place, the priestess had warned me.

And so it had begun.

If I didn't help, the demonfire would spread. It would destroy everything.

"Tell Takkan to meet me in Raikama's garden," I instructed Kiki, stuffing her beak with a hastily written message. "My brothers, too. Quickly!"

I dressed in record time, lacing the leather armor Hasho had lent me over my chest and pulling on a helmet. Then I scooped up the knapsack filled with paper birds and slid the mirror of truth inside. On my way out, I rapped loudly on my brothers' doors. Miracles of Ashmiyu'en, they all answered, ready to go.

"It's a trap," said Andahai, speaking what was on everyone's mind. "The priestesses want to draw you out."

"One lick of the fire and you'll turn to ashes," Yotan agreed.

"We agreed on this yesterday," I said. "Nothing changes just because it's demonfire. I have to go."

"You waste time by bickering." Qinnia appeared in the hall, one hand protecting her belly, which was just starting to show. "Let her go."

"You should be resting," Andahai said, his voice softening from firm to tender.

"If I weren't with child, I'd come with you," Qinnia said to me, ignoring her husband. One of the tiny paper birds she'd folded had fallen out of my knapsack, and she tucked it back inside. "May you have the luck of the dragons today, my sister. Come back to us safely."

I hugged her, and then off I went before anyone else could argue.

Takkan arrived at Raikama's garden at the same time as me. Like my brothers, he was sheathed in his sentinel's armor, but only the sight of Takkan made my stomach flutter. He'd tied his dark hair back, and I took in everything about his face. The rounded outline of his ears, the sharp slope of his cheekbones, his chiseled jaw. Two of the gold-spun cords knotted over his shoulders were tangled, and I combed them with my fingers, trying not to blush as my gaze fell to the steel plates over his chest. "Good morning."

He gifted me with my favorite smile, a beat before tossing me a rice dumpling. "Breakfast," he said, throwing one to each of my brothers too. "They're from yesterday, so they might be a touch stale, but I figured we'd need our strength. Shiori, especially."

"I don't understand how we'll meet up with Benkai," Reiji said. "We should be gathering our mounts and joining the rest of the soldiers on the way to the mountains."

"You'll be glad you didn't bring your horse," Takkan replied, exchanging a look with me. "The stairs are narrow."

"Stairs?" Wandei's brows knit with confusion. "I don't see stairs."

"I trusted you when you said you had everything planned out," said Andahai, "but—"

"You forget our stepmother was a sorceress," I interrupted. "A very powerful and capable sorceress. Are we ready?"

As Takkan and my brothers murmured their assent, Hasho went to the pond. He had also thought ahead, and he dipped a sheaf of handkerchiefs into the water.

"For the smoke," he said, handing each of us a damp cloth.

He sat again by the pool. A trio of larks had settled on his shoulder, and he let out a low whistle as he stroked their feathers with his wing. He could feel Raikama's magic, just as I could.

I folded the handkerchief into my pocket and took one last bite of my rice dumpling. Then I gestured my brothers to the pool. "Watch."

Holding up Raikama's ball of red thread, I cried, "Take me to the Tears of Emuri'en."

At my command, the pond's water rushed apart, revealing a stairway just wide enough for one person to descend at a time.

Yotan exhaled with amazement. "Raikama had this in her garden the entire time?"

Saves us hours of trotting along the countryside, said Kiki, stretching her beak in a yawn.

Hasho, the only other person who could understand her, laughed. "Benkai's going to be upset he's wasted all these mornings riding back and forth to the mountains."

I led everyone down the passageway, until a light shone through at the end. In fewer than a hundred steps, we had traveled a morning's journey out of the palace.

The instant we emerged into the forest, a wave of heat seared my face. Smoke stung my eyes and entered my lungs, making them pinch painfully. I held the cloth up to my face and tied it in place so I could breathe.

It was impossible to tell where the fires had originated,

but they'd already claimed this part of the forest. What had once been a rich wood of cypress and pine trees was now a smoldering wasteland. Embers sizzled in the dirt beneath my feet as I hurried after Raikama's ball of thread, and it wasn't just the smoke that made my eyes water. It was sorrow too.

Beyond the next hill, a battle raged. Swords clanged, spears clashed. Men and women shouted. Their cries grew louder the closer we came. I only prayed that Benkai was winning. That he could keep the priests and priestesses distracted long enough for me to find the Tears of Emuri'en.

They hadn't seen me yet, but I knew that wouldn't last long. I had to be quick.

Here it is, Shiori! Kiki cried when the red thread came to a halt. *It's here!*

I held in a gasp. All that remained of the Tears of Emuri'en was a shriveled mud pit. A single moon orchid lay upon the cracked earth, its pink petals singed.

A great treasure of Kiata, the last source of magic that outlasted the gods, was gone.

There was still a tickle in the air as I approached the pit, and when I crouched at the rim, its residual power raised goose bumps on my skin. Yet these were only scraps of magic. Threads of a tapestry that had been ripped to shreds. Would it be enough?

Anger throbbed in my temples, or maybe that was the smoke, my panic, my fear. I'd been hoping to draw on the magic from the pool for strength, but now it seemed I had only myself.

I gathered Raikama's thread upon my lap, and my hands

curled into fists as I noticed the heaps of dry wood beside the pit. If the priests and priestesses of the Holy Mountains thought they'd make this sacred place a pyre, they were wrong.

"Keep your guard up," I warned my companions. "They're near."

It was time to work. I ripped open my knapsack to free the paper birds. "Awaken!" I whispered, imbuing my words with power. The birds twitched with life. "Fly!"

That was as far as I got.

An arrow flew past, so close that my ears rang. Takkan pushed me to the ground, and no sooner had we ducked than more arrows flew. One clipped Hasho's wing. Another pierced Yotan's thigh.

With high-pitched cries, our enemies vaulted down from the smoldering trees, and reinforcements charged from behind. Dressed head to toe in white, they wove in and out of the smoke like ghosts.

"Fight!" I ordered my birds.

With a whoosh, they dispersed. Feeding off my own anger and panic, they were vicious. Beaks speared into fleshy white eyeballs, razor-thin wings sliced into cheeks and fingers. Real birds came too, diving down from the sky in a show of solidarity. Kiki let out a cackle every time she drew blood.

Soon Benkai and his soldiers found us. Sweat matted my brother's temples, and every inch of his armor was scorched.

"About time," Andahai greeted our brother. "Why so grim? You could fight these zealots in your sleep."

I couldn't tell whether Andahai was being sarcastic. Neither, apparently, could Benkai.

"It's much more than a few, brother," Benkai replied. Soon I knew what he meant. From behind the mountains poured hundreds of new soldiers, perhaps thousands.

The priests and priestesses had raised their own army—of villagers, fishermen, mercenaries, even nobles and a handful of treacherous sentinels. Their cheeks were smeared with ashes, which allowed them to pass through the waves of demonfire springing from the earth.

"Protect Shiori," Benkai commanded before disappearing into the fray with a primal yell.

The demonfire crackled, racing through the scorched trees toward me. While Takkan and my brothers shielded me from incoming attacks, I focused on the demonfire.

I had to stop it. With a slow exhale, I unraveled my magic, channeling its threads toward the fires. The threads knotted around each fire in turn, squeezing out its life. But for every blaze I extinguished, a new one was born.

I couldn't do this alone.

As if in response, there came a rumble from the mountains. I rocked back on my heels. The demonfire too shuddered, and then it roared back up, higher and fiercer than ever.

I looked up. With the trees gone leafless, I had a clear view of the Holy Mountains.

Shiori, the demons murmured through the wind. *Let us free.*

Could they help me? Would they help me?

The wind whistled against the dagger on my hip. All I

needed to do was offer a taste of my blood, and they would come. One quick gash across my arm would do the trick.

But I couldn't find the courage.

My hesitation cost me. Demonfire sprang in every direction, flames flaring higher than the trees. It came at me without mercy, swelling and roaring like some monstrous beast. No matter where I ran, it followed, destroying everything and everyone in its path.

Andahai had been right. It *was* a trap. The demonfire wouldn't rest until it had me.

With every bit of strength I possessed, I let go of Takkan's hand and shoved him away from me. My betrothed was strong and steady, but I'd caught him by surprise. He stumbled back, out of the demonfire's range.

A wall of flames shot up, separating us. Fire looped around me, trapping me inside and keeping Takkan and my brothers out.

As long as I lived, I would never forget the anguish in Takkan's eyes as he stood on the other side of the fire. His gaze passed over me and ran along the width and height of the flames, as if gauging them for some way through.

There isn't one, I thought. *Takkan, you mad fool—get out of here!*

Priests and priestesses emerged from behind the smoke, charging for the wall of demonfire. For *me*. Takkan's arrows went wild, and my brothers raised their bows to join him.

Bodies fell. Forward, backward, on their sides. Blue-feathered arrows protruding from their backs.

But our enemies were too many. And as soon as the cultists passed the wall, slipping through as if it were made of water, not fire, no knife or arrow could follow.

My birds and I attacked valiantly together as they advanced. I scored a gash across the abdomen of a priest, stabbed a priestess's collarbone, narrowly missed another's heart. But we were only delaying the inevitable.

From behind, someone grabbed my wrist and wrenched my dagger out of my grasp. A priestess swung her spear at my back, and my bones made a horrible cracking sound as I slammed forward onto my stomach. A barrage of kicks came at my ribs, and my chin banged against the hard-packed dirt, my mouth so full of filth I couldn't even squeak in pain.

"Where's your magic now, bloodsake?" they jeered as my concentration broke and the paper birds fell lifeless at my sides.

"This is for Guiya." A kick to my back.

"For Janinha."

"For Kiata."

Pain came in an explosion of white, and my entire world went blank before snapping back into strident color.

I bit down on my lip, tasting blood. They goaded me to scream, to curse or cry out. But I didn't make a sound. These zealots couldn't kill me. Not by beating me to death, anyway. The only acceptable way for me to die was by demonfire so they could collect my precious ashes.

"So full of spirit, Shiori'anma," said a priestess, holding up her spear to catch her breath. "In another life, perhaps you might have joined us."

I wasn't listening. My lips were clamped together, and one of the tiny paper birds Qinnia had folded blew past my cheek.

Awaken, I called out to it. *Help me.*

As its wings fluttered, I called out to the rest of the tiny birds. They were the size of spiders, and Qinnia had been right: I did need soldiers of all sizes. Soldiers small enough to fly unnoticed.

Kiki would say I was out of my mind, and maybe I was. But I was no longer afraid.

I've changed my mind, I told the tiny birds. *Tell the mountains I've changed my mind.*

My paper birds flew over the demonfire, out of my assailants' reach, as small as the sparks spitting forth from the flames. Before anyone noticed they were there, they flew off.

My beating was done, and now two of the cultists were dragging me to the Tears of Emuri'en. Soon twigs snapped against my broken bones, and someone propped me against a sword staked into the pit. I was so weak I immediately slid and toppled onto my side.

No one helped me up.

The priests and priestesses chanted over me. They spoke in Old Kiatan, praying that my ashes would announce the birth of a new era, that the demons would never be free. None of it was novel to me, and I tuned out their sanctimonious words, listening instead to the earth below me.

It was still. Silent.

Hurry, I thought to my birds. *Please.*

Heat scorched my back, and the flames crackled as I pressed my cheek to the dirt. I was in so much pain I couldn't move. But I held on—I couldn't let go of the thread that tied me to the paper birds. Not before they delivered my message.

Finally, the ground trembled. Harder than before. And this time, it didn't stop.

A few of the priestesses stumbled. Their chants faltered. As they regained their balance, they tossed fistfuls of ashes into the air and resumed chanting, faster.

The demonfire grew higher, hotter. It rose from the earth in a tall wall, and as it closed in on me, my sweat simmered. Wood dissolved into ash under my ankles, and the flames crackled against my flesh. I had seconds at best. It took all my willpower not to panic, to hold in my screams and breathe as the demonfire leapt to devour me.

"Shiori!" cried a voice from above. "Shiori!"

I was so delirious that at first I thought it was the demons. I tipped my head back and squinted through the smoke.

Takkan and Hasho! They were in the sky, riding astride the backs of eagles and swans and a whole motley of birds I couldn't see—with Kiki! They hung above me, a gasp above the towering flames.

Takkan's bow was in his hands, aimed downward. I heard the stretch and twang of a string. Three whooshes, one after another. Through the flames I didn't even see the arrows fly.

One by one, the priests and priestesses fell. Knees sank in the mud, and fingers curled into the earth. The ones who lived kept chanting even as they tumbled forward.

The demonfire roared. The window above me closed, the black hearts of the flames writhing around to devour me. But the seconds that Takkan and Hasho bought were enough.

The air turned cold first. Then a dark veil was cast over the sun, choking out its sickly light. Shadows swept over the earth. All around me, the flames shrank into embers, and the forest went dark.

Only the breach glowed. Its fervent red light pulsed brighter and fanned across the forest, searching. When at last it fell upon me, the ground gave a tumultuous shudder.

The demons were here.

CHAPTER FORTY-FOUR

Demons tore through the breach and swarmed the forest. Radiating scarlet light, they were nightmares incarnate, stitched of man, beast, and monster. The more humanlike ones were attired in pale, ghostly armor, while others wore only the hides of beasts: fur, feathers, or scales.

Red-eyed monsters descended upon the priests and priestesses, ending their lives before they even had a chance to scream. A flash of fangs, a hiss of smoke, then, like a flame, they were snuffed out. All that was left was their white robes.

As the wind swept away their remains, Takkan rushed to my side. I could only imagine how I appeared, wilted and broken like that last moon orchid in the Tears of Emuri'en. Ever so tenderly, he lifted me onto his lap.

"You're going to be all right," he said, holding my fingers.

"Don't lie. You're not good at it."

"It really isn't so bad, sister," Hasho chimed in, an even worse liar than Takkan. I wished I could tell him so, but pain spasmed through every point in my body, and I bit down on my lip.

Hasho's smile disappeared, and Takkan gritted his teeth like a man intent on cracking a tooth. He brushed the hair from my eyes, his fingertips gliding over my temples. "Don't let go, Shiori," he said. "Fight."

I *was* fighting—and losing. I could hardly feel the welts on my back or the broken ribs on my side. My body was going cold.

Takkan must have noticed me shivering, for he pressed his body to mine and murmured something to Hasho, who immediately threw me his cloak and started rubbing my fingers.

But it was no use. I could feel the life ebbing out of me. I was dying.

I didn't even notice the demons arrive—until Takkan lifted his head, and Hasho reached for his short sword.

A soft red light bathed them, accentuating their starved and hollow eyes. I prayed that I hadn't made a horrible mistake.

They didn't attack, as they had when Bandur dragged me into the Holy Mountains. They were strangely hesitant.

"Come with us," they said, their voices reverberating in the hollows of my ears. "We have many more waiting to be freed."

"No," Takkan said. "You cannot have her."

The demons ignored him and extended their light to me. I began to float, and Takkan grabbed my hand, refusing to give me up. Hasho came too, blocking us with his body and swinging his short sword.

The demons snarled.

"Stop!" I rasped. "I'll go with you . . . but you aren't to harm them."

One of the demons stepped forward. As his shadow fell over me, my pain became a dull ache. My wounds were still there, but the hurt was gone.

My eyes flew up in confusion.

"There is no need for you to feel pain," the demon said. His voice was neither kind nor cruel. Merely firm. "Come now. We will not harm your company."

"Let me go," I whispered to Takkan, twisting my hand away.

His eyes were glassy with pain. He held on. *No.*

I touched my nose to his cheek, my eyes tracing the peak of his hairline to the dimple in his chin. Then I pressed my forehead to his and, our hands still entwined, reached into my pocket for Raikama's thread.

It was little more than a tangled clump at this point, but there was still magic in it. It shimmered in my hands, warm with light.

I kissed Takkan wordlessly before I pushed the thread into his hands.

The demons seized me. "We have her!" they shouted. "Return. Return!"

We shot up into the clouds, and all I could see was Takkan cutting through the trees, tracking the slip of my form among the fathomless mass of demons. I kept my eyes on him as long as I could. He shouldered his way forward, swift and relentless, his every muscle focused on the singular goal of finding me. Nothing would stop him, not the flying trees up-rooted by the trembling earth, not the violent winds or the sudden fractures in the ground. "Shiori!" he kept shouting. "Shiori!"

"Takkan," I whispered.

An ache rose to my heart, and I pulled my gaze away. Another voice was calling my name. A little voice that my ears picked up immediately.

Kiki.

She led a wave of paper birds toward the breach. *Shiori! You'd better not forget me. I'm coming!*

So she was. With the barest of smiles, I closed my eyes and let the darkness consume me.

CHAPTER FORTY-FIVE

I awoke in the underbelly of the Holy Mountains. Entrapped in cavernous walls, I lay on an unyielding bed of stone not far from the breach.

The breach was rife with magic, and it had grown in the last few days, stretching crookedly across the slope of the mountain in a thick vein. Even from within, it glowed.

With tremendous effort, I propped myself up onto my elbows. Something rustled against the rocks, and I held my breath.

"Kiki!" I cried weakly as dozens of my paper birds surrounded me. "You're here."

Kiki's wing was broken, pierced by an arrow, and she craned her long neck at the paper birds shuffling behind her, hiding behind the rocks. *We couldn't let you come alone.*

I touched her wing, trying to mend it. My thumb brushed against the silvery-gold pattern of feathers, so faint I rarely noticed it. After all these months, I finally understood what it was.

The piece of my soul that connected us.

Don't bother, said my bird, pulling her wing away. *We're not getting out of here.*

"Ever the pessimist, aren't you?"

It was the first time the paper bird's eyes betrayed her. They were soft and wet, the ink smearing. Almost as if she were crying.

It hurt to swallow, and I slowly, wretchedly rose to my knees. "Look," I whispered, "I'm getting better."

Liar.

A liar I was, for I was still dying. Our souls were linked; she would feel it.

"The mountain's quieter than last time," I remarked, tilting my head at our surroundings. No illusions of home or Raikama's garden deceived my eyes, no demons disguised as my brothers beckoned to me. All was still. Empty. Almost . . . peaceful. "Where are the demons?"

My answer came as soon as I asked. Smoke pierced the breach, hissing into every corner. As my paper birds rose into a protective cocoon, the demons materialized.

They cornered me against a wall. Hundreds of red eyes bored through the shadows, watching me with the greatest intent, as curious as they were desperate.

"YOU HAVE ASKED TO RETURN. NOW FULFILL YOUR PROMISE."

Kiki hopped back behind my hair. *You're not really going to free them, are you?* she whispered. *Just give the word, and we'll attack. We can seal the mountains.*

I said nothing, but dread rolled in my gut. I'd told the

demons I'd changed my mind. I'd summoned them to get me—and so they had. Now they were waiting for me, and every second they waited, their anger rose. It heated the mountains, made the earth tremble.

If you have a plan, now would be a good time to implement it, squeaked Kiki.

I scrabbled for a loose rock and pressed its sharp edge into my palm.

"I am going to free them," I said finally.

What? Kiki's inky black eyes bulged. *Have you gone senseless? You can't free the demons!*

"They can't be locked up here forever," I said. "Maybe my ancestors thought so, but it has to end."

They'll kill you, Shiori, Kiki pleaded. *And me.*

"I'll make them promise," I said, more certain than ever. "Immortals are bound to their promises."

That didn't work so well with Bandur.

"It'll work this time." I slashed my hand, holding in a cry as blood welled over the lines of my palm, and I summoned my shield of paper birds close.

"I came here of my own will," I said, my voice hardly more than a whisper. "And I am ready to give you my blood. I will free you, but in return you will do something for me."

The demons stilled, their red eyes aglow against the cave's dark. As my blood trickled down my arm, the droplets landed on my paper birds, painting their heads crimson.

"SPEAK."

"I will give you my blood," I repeated. "In exchange for your oath that you shall not harm any living being in Kiata.

456

Accept my terms, and you will be free once more. Magic will be free once more."

The demons murmured sounds of dissent. "A demon's nature is destruction. We are servants of chaos, and we will not be bound by any oath." They scratched their nails against the walls, and the shrill cacophony set my ears ringing. "Your life is not yours to give, bloodsake. It belongs to us."

"Then we shall see who is faster."

The demons lunged with supernatural speed. In no universe could I have defeated them fairly. But I'd cheated.

I'd known the demons would never accept my bargain. I was helpless, defenseless, with only an army of paper birds. But what they hadn't noticed was that I'd been gathering the strands of my soul and cutting them free.

Lady Solzaya had told me once that she believed that the human soul was made up of countless little strings that tethered it to life. That those strings could be cut one by one. I was counting on her to be right.

Before this moment, I'd always understood that my blood would break the demons' chains and free them from the mountains. But I had never understood the point of my other gift as a bloodsake: why I could lend away fragments of my soul to create new life.

I'd inspirited plenty of things during the last year, yet only once had I given part of myself away for good: when I'd created Kiki.

Of all my enchantments, only she had lasted and stayed by my side and shared my thoughts. I used to think it was because I had smeared my blood on her crown, but I was wrong. It was her wings: the thread of my soul forming a pattern of silver and gold—for all to see.

Such strands burst now from my hair, from my fingertips, from every pinpoint of my being. They hummed like zither strings, and in my mind I swept across the span of them, inspiriting the paper birds at my feet.

Live, I urged them.

My magic worked quickly. Their hearts came alive, beating in sync with mine. With each one that rose, I fell a little, but I didn't stop until I had no more to give.

Only then did I collapse. The demons came upon me, teeth grazing my skin and claws piercing my flesh. I felt no pain. My head and body felt light, as if I were floating. Flying, like my birds as they split away and glided past the breach, laying their wings upon its scarlet maw and sealing it until only one speck of rock was left uncovered.

I smiled and lifted my hand. One last filament of soul dangled from my wrist, and it was the only thread tethering me to life. It would take only a thought for me to send it away and stitch the breach shut once more—but once I did that, I would cease to be.

The demons froze, their gnashing teeth and claws going still as they realized what I had done.

I'd trapped them.

"Accept my offer," I commanded in a feeble voice. "If I die, you won't be free."

"Then die," the demons snarled. "Bloodsakes have always been lured to the mountains. The next will be no different. We will find their weakness and use it against them."

"That strategy has led you to wait for a thousand years," I reminded them. "No bloodsake will be willing to free you, as I am. Without Bandur to lead you, you'll be trapped here at least another thousand years."

"Why?" they demanded. "Why free us?"

I thought of Khramelan, of how he had defended his demon brothers on Lapzur even after they had betrayed him. I thought of the mirror of truth, which had inexplicably shown me a memory of Raikama when I'd asked how to defeat the demons.

And I knew this was the right way.

"Even chaos has its place," I replied. "Without you, Kiata has been out of balance."

Before I lost my courage, I drew a deep breath and went on: "The future I wish for is a Kiata where magic springs once more from the earth and flourishes, a Kiata where demons and gods and mortals live and thrive together.

"You have served your time. Now promise that you shall not harm the spirit, soul, or body of any living being in Kiata. Promise it, and I will give you my blood. I swear it."

The demons said nothing. Their silence stretched an eternity as their hollow eyes bored into mine. I was certain that I'd die before they made up their minds.

Then, finally, they spoke in an eerie chorus that made the mountains tremble. "For a thousand years, we have been confined within these hollow walls. No more," they murmured. "We will swear. We will all swear. We swear it now."

The birds obeyed and flew, carrying my blood to lift the

demons' shackles. As each demon was released, it passed me the barest nod, its face inscrutable.

This was what I'd been born for: to bring magic back to Kiata. To undo what my ancestors had done. It was written into my fate—in the strands of magic in my soul, and in my blood that connected me to the demons. Soon it would be done.

When all the demons had been freed, their chains evaporated in puffs of smoke. But they could not leave yet.

My birds soared above the demons and touched their paper wings to one another in a circle. The strands of my soul wove together in one long beam of silver and gold, and my birds formed a ring around the demons, binding them to their promise.

Finally, it was done. A long shudder shook the earth, and the breach ruptured, its scarlet light flashing. Cracks formed across the mountain wall, fierce gusts of wind punching through. *Go,* the winds seemed to cry. *You are no longer prisoners here.*

The demons needed no invitation. Out into the world they flew, emptying the mountain and taking my paper birds with them. With each one that left, my soul unraveled a thread, and I could feel myself grow lighter. Too light to remain on this earth.

Before long, only Kiki remained, and as the glow of the moon touched her wings, she alit on my shoulder one last time.

Now it's my turn, she said. *I was so wanting to stay with you until the end and see where in the Nine Heavens Lord Sharima'en would put us. That is, if you end up in heaven.*

"No," I whispered. I caught her by the wing, bringing her to my face. "No, you're staying with me."

I can't, said Kiki, the silver-gold patterns on her wings fading.

I started to protest, tears welling in my eyes, but Kiki sounded braver than she ever had. *At least I can say I lived an exciting life, for a paper bird. I wish Radish Boy were here to sing, or your brother with his flute. I'd like to hear some music before I go.*

I brought her close. "Channari was a girl who lived by the sea," I began, my voice hoarse and crackly, "who kept the fire with a spoon and pot. Stir, stir, a soup for lovely skin. Simmer, simmer, a stew for thick black hair. But what did she make for a happy smile? Cakes, cakes—"

Too cruel was the wind. Before I could finish the song, it stole my little paper bird away, ensnaring her in a powerful gale.

"Kiki!"

I pitched after her, but her body had gone stiff and lifeless. A sob tore out of me as the wind carried her out of sight.

"Kiki . . . ," I whispered.

The mountain was still trembling, and I dragged myself to the breach. The last of the demons were departing, each one that passed through the breach making the scarlet light flicker and fade, its edges turning gray like the rest of the wall. The magic of the mountains was returning to Kiata—as was my own magic.

"Eternal Courts," I cursed, noticing how narrow the breach had become. Minutes ago, it had been as high and wide as a tree, and now it was barely a head taller than I. It was closing!

I pressed against the still-glowing rocks, trying to push my way through. In panic, I dug at a fissure between the rocks, dirt and sand spilling between my fingers as the mountain quaked. More wind pierced through, and I could hear birds outside. But I was no demon, and I had no magic left. I could not pass.

"Shiori!" called a voice.

Takkan?

I looked into the fissure and saw a blue tassel swinging from Takkan's belt, then his hand clinging to a narrow ledge on the mountainside. My heart leapt. "Takkan!"

He'd found me. He peered through the crack, his eyes shining with hope. "Shiori. I'm going to get you out."

His face disappeared from view, replaced by the sound of his sword scraping against the crack, trying to make it bigger.

I didn't know whether to curse or cry out in joy. Of all the persistent, stubborn, *stupid* young men . . . "Get out of here, you fool," I croaked, but Takkan still dug, even as the mountain rumbled. "Enough! The breach is closing. You can't save me."

"I am the end of your string," Takkan reminded me. "No matter how long it stretches, so long as you want me, I will never let go."

The knots in my chest tightened, and tears heated the corners of my eyes. I wanted to hear Takkan sing to our children one day, to climb Rabbit Mountain every spring and view the moon at its peak. I wanted to read the book of tales he was writing for Megari, to set lanterns afloat on the Baiyun River with him every year during Iro's Winter Festival, to see our hair turn white with age but our hearts remain young with stories and laughter.

"Move aside!" Takkan shouted as he sent an arrow through the hole, a long thread dangling from its shaft.

Raikama's thread.

My stepmother had used it to pull me out of the Holy Mountains once, and now Takkan meant to do the same. I wasn't sure whether it would work again, but it shimmered with magic as I grasped its end, and that gave me hope. With a shaky breath, I tied it around my wrist.

"Give a tug when you're ready!" Takkan yelled.

I inched as close as I could to the rock. Then, before I lost my chance, I tugged.

There came a strong pull from outside. Rock scraped against my shoulders and dust filled my nose and mouth. I closed my eyes, half thinking that I would slam against the mountain and die. But by my next breath, I was outside.

A pair of strong arms caught me by the waist. The sun was still buried by clouds and smog, but in the reddish after-glow of the breach, I saw the joy on Takkan's face dissolve once he saw me.

Blood soaked my robes, and my body was soft—almost limp. I was practically a ghost, clinging to life by a single strand of my soul. So far gone I could barely feel the pain.

"It's done," I whispered. "The demons are free. Magic is

free." I tucked my head under his chin to savor his heat and to avoid my reflection in his misty eyes. "Now take me home. Please."

His arm still around my waist, Takkan lowered us step by careful step to the mountain's base, and I glanced one last time at the breach. It was but a spark, like a last glimmer of day before evenfall. Then it vanished.

The mountains ceased their trembling; the earth went still once more. And the sun slipped out of a pocket of smoke, gold and radiant as a coin, reminding us that it had been there all along.

CHAPTER FORTY-SIX

Rain loosened from the clouds, dousing the last of the demon-fire. It slid down my cheeks, cool and wet, and washed away the rime of ash on my skin. Beside me, rain filled up the Tears of Emuri'en once more, and as the moon orchid floated to the top of the pool, its soft petals impossibly blooming, I knew that the battles I'd fought had not been in vain.

Magic had returned to Kiata. I could feel it like a song resonating around me. Making the world feel more alive.

"It's back," I whispered to Takkan. "It's in the air, the earth, everywhere. It's wonderful."

As the rain eased, I blinked at the sky. It was a beautiful, blue-as-a-pea-flower day.

"Let's wait here, just for a minute," I said.

With a nod, Takkan stopped. Muscles corded his arms as he painstakingly lay me down, every movement with the greatest care, on a flat rock before the Tears of Emuri'en.

The smoke was gone, and in its place was a soft fog curling

up from the trees as rain tickled the earth. The fog skimmed over Takkan's face, almost hiding the mist in his eyes.

He knew he couldn't save me. My life literally hung on a thread—on one last piece of my soul that I had kept to myself. All we had left was goodbye.

Rain splashed against my face, but I couldn't feel the droplets anymore. I was already drifting, like a kite cut loose, the end of my string only grasping at the earth. Soon it too would float away.

I saw a figure in the far distance, advancing slowly. It was not someone I had met before, yet his very presence cast forth a heavy, inescapable pall, like the weight of the ocean pressing down on my body.

My heart sank in my chest. I had a feeling I knew who it was.

I turned to Takkan, seizing what moments I had left. "Tell me a story."

His dark hair obscured his eyes, and I couldn't tell whether it was rain or tears that tracked down the hard slope of his cheeks. His hands cradled mine. "There once was a girl . . . who'd forgotten how to smile," he said softly. "She was clever and beautiful, so much so that word of her loveliness had spread from village to village and she had many admirers. But when her mother fell ill, all the happiness fled from her eyes, and she became a ghost of her former self.

"Before her mother died, she made the girl promise to wear a wooden bowl over her head and never take it off. It would cover half her face and shield her from unwanted attention. Soon word spread that she was hiding demon eyes beneath the bowl, but she ignored the cruel words that followed her. It made her see who her true friends were, just as her mother had wished. After many months, she met a boy who noticed not the bowl but her sadness. He made it his mission to earn a smile from her. Every day he would walk with her in the garden and tell her stories. Slowly, ever so slowly, the girl warmed to his gentle heart, and the two fell in love."

"He sounds like you," I said, tilting my head back. "A simple, humble lord of the third rank. One who likes to run when it's snowing, and paint storybooks for his sister."

"The boy wished to marry her," Takkan continued, "but the villagers would not permit it. Thinking her a demon, they tried to kill her—only her bowl shattered into a thousand pieces, revealing at last her eyes, which twinkled not with malevolent power but the light of the stars. The boy saw not her beauty but the woman he loved. He married her as soon as she would have him, and their strands were knotted from one life to the next and the next."

I smiled ruefully, almost forgetting the pain. Almost forgetting the strange presence that had been hovering in my periphery, waiting for Takkan to finish his tale.

"I like the ending to your story," I whispered. "I wish it were how ours ended."

Takkan lowered his eyes. They were wet as he pressed his hand into mine, and his voice was husky with emotion. "We are bound, remember? If you have no heart, I will give you half of mine. If you have no spirit, I will bind yours to mine."

"Find the light that makes your lantern shine," I said

softly, quoting Raikama. "Hold on to it, even when the dark surrounds you. Not even the strongest wind will blow out the flame." I tilted my head to look up at him. "You will be the light, Takkan. No matter where I go."

My vision blurred, and my ears rang, robbing me of Takkan's reply. But at last I could see the figure that encroached upon my final moments. He came not cloaked in velvety darkness, as I'd expected, but swathed in a stinging bright light.

Lord Sharima'en himself, the god of death.

"Come, Shiori'anma," he said, his voice cool and detached. "It is time."

I sensed my spirit obeying the god of death and beginning to leave my body. Sleep dusted my eyelids, yet I fought to stay awake. I fought to stay. *No, not yet.*

"You have done well," said the god, his words edged with warning. "Go with dignity."

I don't care. Let me stay. Please. It was useless to plead with Sharima'en the Undertaker. Every Kiatan knew that. But I didn't care how childish I sounded.

"My father, my brothers—they need me. . . ." I swallowed. "And Takkan."

"They'll join you when their time comes," said Lord Sharima'en. "Now it is yours."

"Is it?" chimed a new voice.

The god of death turned, frowning at the shimmering form that had appeared behind him.

Weakly, I lifted my head. Bathed in a crown of moonlight was the lady of the moon. Rabbits with silver-rimmed eyes frolicked at her feet, and she glided to us on a pale cloud.

Imurinya, I thought.

"Look," she spoke, gesturing at me. Her voice was warm and melodious, new to me yet oddly familiar at the same time. "They are bound by Emuri'en's strand."

I glanced down at my wrist and saw that it was looped in a luminous thread, tying me to Takkan. I'd seen it once before, when Raikama lay dying.

"Threads are easily severed," said Lord Sharima'en. "Return home to your rabbits, sister. You have no place here."

"Indeed, it is not my place," Imurinya admitted, "but I also bring word from Ai'long. From the Prince of the Four Supreme Seas, heir to the Dragon King."

My ears perked. *His heir?*

"What do the dragons want?" Lord Sharima'en said testily. "They've never intervened in human dealings before."

"His Eternal Highness Seryu'ginan reminds us that we required the dragons' aid in sealing the demons into the mountains, long ago. They are owed a favor, and they demand a voice in the fate of the bloodsake who has released them." The lady of the moon then paused, and placing weight on each word, she said, "The dragons wish her to live."

Displeasure darkened Lord Sharima'en's expression, and brother and sister said nothing—at least, nothing I could hear. I sensed they *were* speaking. Arguing, to be precise, in the tongue of the gods.

At last, the god of death stepped back, leaving Imurinya to address me. She knelt at my side, stroking my temples. My spirit quavered at her touch, still clinging to my body by just a thread.

"You have demonstrated great fortitude," she said gravely, "and you have pleased the gods with your deeds on this earth. We are not without mercy."

I held my breath, not knowing what "mercy" to expect.

"The lord of death and I have come to an agreement," she said. "We have decided that half is fair. Half is more than most receive."

"Half?" I echoed.

"Yes, half." Imurinya's luminous eyes rested on me. "Shiori'anma, your soul ebbs between life and death—half bound to Bushi'an Takkan, and half to the heavens. Thus, for the remainder of your lifetime, you will spend half of each year on the moon with me."

Kiki fluttered from behind the lady's robes, and if I could have leapt to my feet, I would have.

She'd turned into a real bird, with feathers instead of paper wings, and round, unblinking eyes instead of the inked ones I'd made. Gold trimmed her wings, and a vibrant red crown painted her head.

"She found her way to me," explained Imurinya with a smile.

Will you come? Kiki asked, cheeky as ever. *You look awful. Come—come with us.*

I lingered. I wasn't ready.

"The other half of the year . . . I will spend it on the earth?" I asked. My voice was heady; I couldn't tell whether I'd spoken the words aloud.

"It is a compromise my brother and I have agreed upon," said Imurinya. "So long as Bushi'an Takkan lives, so too will

470

this agreement. When his time comes, you will join him in Lord Sharima'en's realm."

I glanced at the lord of death, who gave an imperceptible nod. Then I looked at Takkan, wondering whether he could hear or see the immortals. He was still at my side, his eyes bleary and raw.

"That sounds fair enough," I agreed quietly. "When may I return?"

"You will return each spring and summer."

"And I'll be normal?" I asked, swallowing. "Human?"

Imurinya chuckled. "Yes, yes. Human enough to bleed and heal, to age and grow in happiness and wisdom. Even to bear children—should you wish."

An intense flush heated my cheeks, but Imurinya must have read my mind, for that was exactly what I wished to know.

"Could I return for the winter and the spring instead?" I asked, knowing it was uncouth to bargain with the gods but unable to help myself. "I should like to celebrate my birthday with my family and see the winter cranes. And Iro," I added. "It's most beautiful in the winter."

Imurinya disarmed me with her bright gaze, so intent that my heart skipped. I felt certain that I had erred, and that she and Lord Sharima'en would take away the compromise altogether.

"Very well," said Imurinya at last. "Winter and spring, it is decided. But for this first cycle, you must wait for spring. Winter approaches, and your body needs to heal."

She lifted one of the rabbits at her feet, and divine light

pooled around us, piercing into the mortal realm. Takkan drew a sharp breath; now he could see her.

"The pledge is made," Imurinya informed him. "Shiori'anma will rejoin the earth every winter and spring, spending half the year with you, and half with me. Come the first moonrise of spring, you will find her on Rabbit Mountain, Bushi'an Takkan."

Takkan blinked, the only sign of surprise he let slip at the sight of the great immortals. He wiped his eyes with his sleeve and bowed his head low. "I understand," he said quietly. "Thank you, Lady Imurinya. I will be there."

"Now say your farewells," said the lady of the moon.

Piece by piece, my spirit reassembled within my body, a tingling sensation flooding every nerve. I lifted my head first, as a test. Then, as the rest of me awoke, I gave Takkan a dimpled grin. That was all it took to erase the sorrow from his face. His eyes went wide with wonder and relief.

"Help me up," I said, and Takkan's hand was there in an instant, pulling me gently to my feet.

I saw now that we were no longer alone. My brothers had come, and they hurried forward.

"At least you won't have to sew when you're on the moon," Yotan teased. "Or will you?"

"I doubt the lady would want me ruining her tapestries," I replied.

"True, true."

I embraced the twins, then moved on to Reiji. Like me, he would be leaving Kiata soon.

We hadn't gotten along particularly well during our childhood, and I thought I'd be at a loss for words. Not today. "I can't believe I'm saying this, but I'll miss you, Reiji."

"You shouldn't," he said mildly. "No one else will put cicada husks under your pillow . . . or dare you to steal snakes from Raikama's garden. You'll find yourself in a lot less trouble."

"So, at last you admit this whole thing was your fault?"

He gave a lopsided grin. "We share equal blame."

I threw my arms around him, wishing I'd hugged him more when we were younger. "This isn't goodbye forever," I said into his ear. "I know you'll find a way to charm your paper princess into a visit when I'm back."

Then came Hasho, his wing folded at his side. "I'm glad you asked for winter. Your birthday wouldn't be the same without you."

I hugged my youngest brother. He had always understood me best.

"We'll have a feast ready for you when you return, sister," said Benkai. "A banquet with all the best dishes, and a sky full of lanterns."

I laughed. "I'm the one who's supposed to cook for you all."

"You will." Andahai winked. Had I ever seen him wink? "We'll make a list of our favorite dishes."

I whirled to him, realizing. "I'll be an aunt when I return."

"And hopefully I'll have a new brother," replied Andahai. He inclined a nod at Takkan. "Don't forget, you still have a wedding to prepare for. Maybe the two of you should wed now, lest you get a notion to stay on the moon for good."

"I won't." I exchanged a shy smile with Takkan. "His heart is my home, and—"

"—where you are is where I belong," he said together with me. He looked down at our wrists, the red strands still visible, their ends knotted. "I'll be waiting for you."

His words were all the music I needed to hear, and I blew a kiss as I followed Kiki and Lady Imurinya on a path of moonlight into the oldest legend I knew.

EPILOGUE

I stood on the brink of the moon, a sea of twilight welling beneath my feet, stars hanging above and below. Though my vantage point was a glorious one, tonight I felt no awe. Only eagerness.

I'd waited six months for this. I wouldn't waste a second.

"I'm ready," I whispered.

A trail of silvery moonlight appeared, unspooling over the star-touched folds of heaven. Down and down it led, among fields of clouds soft as freshly fallen snow.

I moved quickly, unable to match the pace of my racing heart. Or Kiki, whose new wings had made her remarkably swift. As she waited for me to catch up, she made a game of threading between the beams of light that shot after us.

Hurry up, you snail! she cried. *Spring will be over by the time you make it down to earth. I'll never get my cakes.*

I hurried, smiling wistfully. Kiki adored being a real crane, and she never spoke of her papery past anymore. But sometimes, when she was frightened or lonely, she would still try to fly into my sleeve, forgetting that she was too big. That was how I knew she missed her original form, at least a little.

Together we coasted down the moonlit path until a breeze shot forth, cutting through the stillness of the heavens. Imurinya had told us that the sons of the wind guarded the divide between the immortal and mortal realms. This was where Kiki and I would part.

Remember to bring back cakes, she said, making me promise for the hundredth time. *The round rice ones with red bean paste. Mooncakes, too. Imurinya would like that.*

"I'll remember," I said, pressing a kiss on my little bird's head. "Don't cause any mischief for the lady when I'm away."

Kiki disappeared behind a curtain of moonlight, leaving me alone with the sun and clouds. I had come to the end of the path, but Imurinya hadn't told me what to do from here.

I bent down, my fingertips caressing a low cloud as it skimmed my ankles. Below, the sun illuminated the world, and I had the view of the gods. In the South, I spied Gen poring over a trove of books, the mirror of truth glimmering at his side. Then across the Taijin Sea, I caught a glimpse of Seryu racing a pod of whales. His horns had grown into a magnificent silvery crown, and his eyes glowed redder than the sun. *The Dragon King's heir,* I remembered. I wondered how he had managed that.

He must have sensed me watching, for he tipped his head up and looked straight at me—straight at the moon. For the barest moment, our gazes met, and Seryu gave me an enigmatic smile. Then, without missing a beat, he dove back into the sea, roaring past the whales who'd only just caught up with him.

I clapped, letting out a laugh and watching them disappear beyond the horizon. Then, directly below my feet, the clouds shifted to reveal a familiar two-peaked mountain. I almost didn't recognize it without its usual dusting of snow, but suddenly my heart was beating so fast I could hardly breathe. And suddenly I knew what to do.

I leapt.

I don't know if I fell or flew. The clouds obscured my view, and the world rushed up in a whorl of stars and light. But then I landed, my back sinking into the soft contours of earth, and when I felt the sun upon my cheeks, I opened my eyes.

I was lying on grass. Cold, wet grass that pricked my elbows and knees. Shallow pools of mud flanked me, and silvery veins of frost laced the field.

A cloak fell over my shoulders an instant before I was going to shiver.

"Careful of the mud, moon maid," Takkan said softly, kneeling beside me. "It's near frozen. Won't be fun to fall in."

He lifted me safely from where I lay, enveloping me in his warmth, and I touched my forehead to his. My voice came out husky, a mix of joy and disbelief. "Your first words to me are of mud?"

Takkan grinned. "I thought the warning more urgent than a welcoming serenade."

"Consider me warned. Now sing."

"Now? You'll laugh."

"I'd never laugh at you, Bushi'an Takkan."

I said it as solemnly as I could, but my eyes were dancing and Takkan knew me.

"Liar." As punishment, he hiked me higher in his arms. I squealed with surprise and delight as he spun me around and around, his boots sloshing into the mud.

We laughed until our stomachs hurt, the sound of our happiness harmonizing in a song that made my heart feel as full as the pale sun behind the clouds.

When at last he set me down, both of us were so dizzy we stumbled over each other. He caught me by the waist and kissed me.

It was a kiss worth waiting for—whether half a year or half a lifetime—a kiss that made my breath catch and my stomach swoop, and the frost that coated my nose and eyelashes melt with delicious warmth. I ran my fingers through his hair and pulled him close, tickling his nose with mine and watching our breaths steam into the air. I licked my lips, tasting sugar. "Cakes?"

"Chiruan made them for you," confessed Takkan with a sheepish grin. "I tested a few to make sure they were acceptable. Do you want one?"

Cakes over flowers, I'd told him. As my heart squeezed with warmth, the tiniest buds flowered under my feet. Only a thread of magic was left inside me, but Kiata . . . Kiata *bloomed* with it. The way it felt to me was like a layer of love tucked deep inside one's belly. Warmth, even when it was cold. Joy, even when there was sadness. The flowers under my feet blossomed and grew.

"Later," I replied, finally answering Takkan's question. I wrapped his arms around my waist and leaned back against him, feeling his breath stir my hair. "We only have a few minutes till sundown."

I could have stayed in his arms all day, content with my view of the rice fields below, the Baiyun River curving down Rabbit Mountain into the grassy knolls surrounding Iro, the gray-tiled castle in the near distance. But the day was fading, the gilded earth turning silvery with young moon-light.

Not to mention, we weren't actually alone.

A high-pitched giggle gave away the intruder, and I whirled to glance over Takkan's shoulder.

"Megari!" I squealed.

"Takkan told me to give you a song's worth of time alone," said Megari, setting down an unlit lantern. In the year I'd been away, she'd lost some of the youthful roundness to her cheeks, but a familiar glint of mischief sparkled in her eyes. "I chose a short song."

I scooped her into a hug, spinning her once before setting her down. I marveled at her. She was nearly to my shoulder now, and she no longer wore her hair in pigtails but loose against her back.

"Don't comment on how much I've grown, and I won't comment on your hair," Megari warned before I could get a word in. "You're going to get lots of remarks on it. Trust me. Father and Takkan wouldn't stop staring at me when they got home. As if they'd been away for years, not months!"

"My sister is beginning to prefer the company of rabbits to humans," joked Takkan.

A pair of fluffy beasts gamboled over my feet, one brown-spotted rabbit even daring to nibble on my slippers. I knelt to stroke its velvety fur.

"They're usually afraid of strangers," mused Megari. "But not you."

"There are many rabbits on the moon," I replied, letting the creature go. I watched it caper off into the tall grass.

I could feel Megari burning with questions for me, but Takkan touched his sister's shoulder, as if reminding her of some unspoken agreement. With a sigh, she picked up her lantern, swinging it as she sauntered toward the base of the hill, where they had tethered the horses. "Enjoy this time alone. Once you reach home, Mama's not going to give you two a moment's rest."

"Careful riding home!" Takkan called after Megari. "It's getting dark!"

Megari waved to show she'd heard, then once more in farewell. I waved back, watching her recede into Iro. Then my eyes drifted up to the sky, where the fading sun was changing places with a rising moon. A sea of stars glimmered through the gauzy dusk, the seven-pointed crane already brighter than the rest.

"They've renamed it," said Takkan, sensing what had caught my attention, "after a new legend."

"What legend?"

"It's a legend of cranes and demons and dragons—and a princess under a terrible curse. The children are riveted."

He silenced whatever I was going to say by taking my hand and pressing a kiss to my palm. "It's a decent story, but long. I'll tell you later. Tonight, we have guests."

"Guests on the same day as my long-awaited arrival? Who could be so important?"

He knew I was frothing with anticipation. "Did I tell you we have a little demon in the kitchen now? It came a few weeks ago, and it's burrowed itself into the stove. It burns the rice and makes the fire go out when it's in a temper. The cooks are nettled, but Megari likes it. I think it's growing on Chiruan, too."

I put my hands on my hips. Demons could wait. "Who's the guest?"

"*Guests.*" Takkan paused deliberately, enjoying my impatience. "It's your brothers."

My brothers? A huge smile sprang to my face. "They've come?"

"All six of them," Takkan confirmed. "Even Reiji, from A'landi. And . . . your father."

At that, both my eyebrows rose.

Takkan laughed. "That was my reaction too. You can imagine my mother's distress when she got word of his visit. She's spent the last week trying to get the household in perfect order. And she still hasn't quite gotten over the fact that she hosted you an entire winter without knowing your true identity."

"Does that mean she won't let me back in the kitchen?"

"Probably not. For at least a year, I'd say."

"A year?" I lamented. I missed cooking, and from the way my stomach growled right then, I missed eating too. "Well, I have six brothers for a reason. Let's hope she'll be more preoccupied with them than me."

"I doubt it. She does have her son's wedding to prepare for."

I blushed, tongue-tied for once. Then I said, "Megari was

right, wasn't she? It's going to be pandemonium when I get back. Everyone will be staring and asking questions. . . ."

"We can be a little late . . . ," said Takkan.

A *little late?* "Did I hear correctly? My honorable, upstanding betrothed suggests we arrive late to dinner?" I pretended to gasp in horror. "With the emperor, no less."

A smile tugged at Takkan's lips. "For you, I'm willing to bend a few rules."

I couldn't help it. I leapt up—but Takkan was already there. His lips found mine and we locked together, his hands holding me by the small of my back, as I wrapped my arms around his neck and raked my fingers through his hair. We kissed and kissed, staggering until we fell back against a tree, and laughed and shrieked as snow tumbled off the branches onto our heads.

I'd never know how long we spent holding each other against the tree, rabbits watching us curiously. All too soon, the dusk aged and night fell upon us. It was time to go back.

"We should get going," Takkan said, dusting snowflakes from my nose before he led me away from the tree. He didn't let go of my hand as he knelt, retrieving the two lanterns he'd brought. A blue one for himself and a red one for me, tied together by a simple red thread.

"So I don't lose you in the dark," he explained when I traced the thread with my fingers.

"You'll never lose me, Bushi'an Takkan," I replied. "Be it bright or dark, you are the light that makes my lantern shine."

Under the shining moon, we made our way home, our hearts beaming, and the light in our lanterns as radiant as the stars.

ACKNOWLEDGMENTS

Wow—six books in! I'm ever grateful to Gina, my agent, who's had faith in me from the very start. And to Katherine, my editor, for your serious hawk-eye when it comes to making my books the best they can be. And for being the greatest champion of my stories I could ask for.

To Lili, my publicist, for your dedication to ushering my stories into readers' hands and for being amazing to work with. To Gianna, Melanie, Alison, Elizabeth, Kelly, Dominique, John, Artie, Natali, Caitlin, Jake, and the wonderful team at Knopf Books for Young Readers for your support on *The Dragon's Promise*. Thank you for helping me bring my stories to life, and into the hands of my readers.

To Tran, for those dragons! This cover is perfection, and as always, I am obsessed.

To Alix, for making the title sing. It's gorgeous.

To Virginia, for Kiata's breathtaking map, and bringing visual life to my worlds.

To my team in the UK: Molly, Natasha, Kate, and Lydia, thank you for welcoming me to the Hodderscape family, and to Kelly Chong for the prettiest covers in all their pastel glory.

To Anissa, again for your friendship—and for your webtoon and romance recommendations!

To my amazing beta readers—all of whom also happen to be dear friends: Leslie and Doug, Amaris, Diana, and Eva. I treasure you.

To Pasang, I couldn't have written this book without your help. Thank you.

To my grandmother, for inspiring so much of my stories. Readers have you to thank, especially when it comes to the food.

To my parents and Victoria, for your love, endless support, and opinions (and offers to babysit).

To Adrian and my daughters, for being *my* lights. Adrian, I could write a book about what to thank you for, but to keep it short, thank you for the surprise doodles you make on my manuscripts. They always make me laugh. And thank you for the hugs and encouragement I need when things feel down, and for being the first person I want to celebrate with when things are looking up. Love you. Charlotte and Olivia, for being my joys and loves and for being so curious about why I'm always on my computer during the day. Don't grow up too fast.

Lastly, to my readers. Thank you for continuing this journey with me. I hope there will be many more to come!

WANT MORE?

If you enjoyed this and would like to find out about similar books we publish, we'd love you to join our online Sci-Fi, Fantasy and Horror community, Hodderscape.

Visit hodderscape.co.uk for exclusive content from our authors, news, competitions and general musings, and feel free to comment, contribute or just keep an eye on what we are up to.

See you there!

H DDERSCAPE

NEVER AFRAID TO BE OUT OF THIS WORLD

🐦 @@HODDERSCAPE   HODDERSCAPE.CO.UK